D0434780

WES CRAVEN

FOUNTAIN SOCIETY

A NOVEL

SIMON & SCHUSTER

SIMON & SCHUSTER
Rockefeller Center
1230 Avenue of the Americas
New York, NY 10020

Designed by Katy Riegel

Manufactured in the United States of America

1 3 5 7 9 10 8 6 4 2

Library of Congress Cataloging-in-Publication Data
Craven, Wes.
Fountain Society : a novel / Wes Craven
p.   cm.
I. Title.
PS3553.R2776F68   1999
813'.54—dc21   99-23455 CIP

ISBN 0-684-84660-8

ACKNOWLEDGMENTS

As a first-time novelist I needed all the help I could get, and there are many people without whom this book would not have been written. I thank them all from the bottom of my heart: Jeff Fenner, Tom Baum, Richard Marcus, Leslie King, and David Baden, for being there with me in the trenches; Ellen Geiger, who supported this project, and me as a novelist, when the story was a notion and I was untested; Bliss Holland, for introducing me to Ellen; Marianne Maddalena, who endured my absences from our film work and never flagged in the friendship; Laurie Bernstein for all the hard work and support; Dr. Judy Swerling, who kept me reasonably sane; John Power, Larry Angen, Andrea Eastman, Robert Newman, and Sam Fischer, all for being smarter and tougher than I am and with such grace; Michael Korda, for your faith in me; my friends, who didn't laugh; my family and my kids, Jonathan and Jessica, who give me my beginnings and ends. And most of all, Cornelia, for bringing me hot tea and love until I finished.

For Esther Lurie, guide and friend,
who so many years ago urged me to put
this story down on paper.

FOUNTAIN SOCIETY

DETENTION COMPLEX 14—HAIFA

The cell held fifteen men. It was ten by twelve and stank of sweat, filth and fear. The only amenity offered was a hole in the center of the concrete floor which served as a toilet. The cell contained, so far as Rashid al-Assad had been able to gather, three Lebanese commandos who kept to themselves and were dreaded even more than their jailers. One of their number had been beaten badly during capture and was raving with fever and gangrene. This kept the others in a murderous mood.

There were also six nondescript Palestinians, none known to Rashid. From what he surmised they were nothing more than workmen, drivers or ex-army thieves, the usual Shiite dregs. They gave true Palestinian fighters a bad name, screaming under torture, wetting themselves and having nothing of importance to disclose when they quickly broke. He despised them.

The four Syrians were probably spies of one sort or another, more than likely industrial. He ignored them.

There was Rashid himself, proud to be a Shi'ite Muslim and a Hezbollah guerrilla. Not once had he uttered a sound, although they had removed everything on him that could be pulled off with a pair of pliers.

And then there was this tall blond pig of a Russian over in the corner.

This Russian was not to be known, Rashid understood. He was the only other professional there, and he was unapproachable. Someone had tried to fuck him the first night, and the Russian had killed the idiot before he could even open his mouth in protest. The corpse had been removed two days later, when the smell reached the guards two floors above.

In that very guard room Lieutenant Joram Ben Ami, watch commander of the intelligence unit at Haifa, was reading a message from his superior in Jerusalem at that very moment. The call they had both been expecting had been received from Washington at 12:45 P.M. local time, 1:45 A.M. in Washington, which was considered a good sign. It meant that the CIA was transmitting when scrambled telephone messages were least likely to attract attention. The business to which the call referred had been in process long enough to be in danger of random slipups, leaks to the press, unwanted attention from whistle-blowers and bleeding-heart congressmen, but the process had remained secret, and so the Israelis and the Americans were able to continue providing mutual benefit for each other. Ben Ami had been given the order to prepare two more units. That would make a total of ten prisoners shipped to the U.S. over the past six months, in return for which the Israeli air force would receive another five air-to-air Sparrow missiles. An excellent trade, in Ben Ami's opinion.

He chose Rashid al-Assad, the Hezbollah guerrilla, as the first. Rashid was the motherless asshole suspected of bombing a bus of Jewish settlers in downtown Haifa six weeks ago. The only unfortunate thing was that he was to be shipped untouched.

The second unit was stipulated by Ben Ami's commander—it was to be the Russian caught spying for Iraq. He needed to be processed slightly, so Ben Ami relayed the orders to his best team. An ordinary claw hammer was used, both because it was what was on hand, and because they all hated Scud-selling Russians. His teeth came out with surprising difficulty.

Just before dawn, an unmarked American C-120 touched down on the airstrip outside the detention complex. Half a dozen long crates were fork-lifted out of the hold, and the two prisoners, heavily drugged and in handcuffs, were taken aboard by CIA operatives. The plane rose again, and the deal was done.

Twenty hours later, thousands of miles away from this airstrip and from each other, Rashid al-Assad and his Russian companion would be in the hands of an organization so secret not even the CIA spooks who acted as their handlers knew its purpose.

Neither man would survive his arrival for more than a few days.

ST. MAURICE, SWITZERLAND

Nearing orgasm, Elizabeth was having strange thoughts about being caught up in *The Wizard of Oz.*

She was in Dorothy's house, and the twister was sweeping around her, rattling the shutters and roaring in her ears. Wood splintered and she was lifted into the air.

Then at last she wasn't thinking at all.

All week long she had been obsessing about this afternoon, listing in one column all the reasons for showing up, in the other all the reasons for breaking the relationship off. The problem was, the same items kept popping up in both columns.

At least, for the moment, she was free of her most haunting preoccupation—that she would never see Hans Brinkman again.

She arched her back and surrendered to the storm. She heard his cry of release, then despite his best efforts, his heart no longer seemed in it. He fell away, and a moment later he was throwing open the hotel window. He took in several deep breaths of frigid Alpine air.

She tried to catch her own breath.

He turned and smiled that perfect smile, then got back into bed with her, pulled the covers over them both and kissed her.

"That was wonderful," she said.

"But you didn't..." He made a gesture.

"No, but my watch stopped," she said lightly, returning his smile. "Really, Hans, don't worry about it."

He rolled out of bed just as quickly as he had gotten in, and gave a sigh. "I'm a selfish bastard, aren't I?"

"You are, yes, but that's *my* problem."

She tried to make it light, too, but it didn't feel that way inside. She couldn't help asking herself what all these Saturdays had amounted to, when all was said and done. Granted, he was rich and handsome, but she had been with handsome, powerful men before and hadn't felt a tenth of what she felt with Hans, or for him. The others had been devoted to her, had lavished gifts on her—but not Hans. Attention, yes, in unpredictable bursts, but for the most part his days were spent in the world of global finance and his evenings devoted to his marriage, with all of the social life that went with it. Places she did not know and was not invited to. In fact she was, she knew, a complete secret from the rest of his life and the people in it. She did not exist in his world. Only here, in these rooms, for a few hours a month. It was not enough, even though she had allowed it to become everything she really cared about; she knew it had to end, sooner or later. And recently, she reluctantly felt it should be sooner than later.

As Hans dressed she watched him from under the covers, like a biologist studying a baffling animal from a blind. Hans Brinkman was thirty-five, ten years older than she, golden-haired, eyes flecked with green and brown. Like pools in Alpine streams, Elizabeth had thought when she first saw them—cool, and full of hidden life. The afternoon sun glinted off his finely muscled body, his shock of thick blond hair. That last climax had been his third, yet he seemed unaffected. He was an athlete even in bed, she realized, and they were locked in some sort of contest she was probably fated to lose.

She was halfway down a hellish black diamond trail when she had first spotted him—a flash of color shooting by on skis in the brilliant Swiss sunlight.

"On your left!" And then a blur.

This caught her attention in a hurry, since it was usually *her* passing the few who dared this sheer face. But there was something else, too. A feeling that she knew him, or needed to, and it was so strong that it was downright eerie.

Had she glimpsed a boyish grin in that streamlined, racing figure? No, just a wicked grin—she was sure of it!

On full auto, Elizabeth shot out in a breath-stopping arc off an ice shelf she had always wisely avoided before. Half-falling, half-flying fifty yards downslope in the air, she managed to land upright only by a combination of grit, skill and pure luck. But she was ahead of him, and she meant to keep it that way—pointing her skis straight down-hill and tucking into the egg.

But it wasn't that simple. What followed was a race that went from high-end sport to thrill-seeking to giddy terror as the two traded places in a cascade of dare and double dare. They were neck and neck again in the final stretch, a straight, precipitous chute that rejoined the regular slope at its end. And it was at the moment when they had reached that juncture—with the wind tearing at her face and her heart pounding—that a snowboarder on the main slope wiped out directly in her challenger's path. Elizabeth realized in an instant that unless she gave way, the man beside her would choose to slam into this kid like a ton of bricks at ninety miles an hour.

She braked hard, and with a cry of glee the man shot over to her track and was gone without a backward glance.

She should have known then.

Later, at the lodge, he sought her out and offered to buy her a drink. She found herself saying yes, and after they had finished playing jet-set geography, trying in vain to determine where they'd met before, he paid her his first compliment: "We're both crazy, you know," he said.

She laughed and nodded. "You a professional?" she asked, and meant it. He smiled broadly, clearly flattered that she would think so.

"Finance."

She raised her eyebrows, actually amazed.

"You might as well have told me you were a scientist," she laughed.

"I almost was," he said matter-of-factly. Then he seemed lost in thought for a moment, as if he were genuinely fascinated by something he had just glimpsed internally. Then he turned back to her, completely present again.

"When I studied physics I never did *anything* dangerous. Not till I got into high finance. Now *that's* where it's worth putting your neck on the line. Like you do. You in money?"

She blinked. In money? What an odd expression.

"I'm not that smart."

"Yeah, right. What's your IQ, about 140?"

She looked at him, realizing she had no idea.

"Really, I'm good at this," he pursued, intrigued. "Never wrong. SATs what, about 1500?"

"Never took the SATs," she admitted.

"No college? I'm shocked."

"Does that make me a dumb blonde in your book?"

He leaned toward her, frowning. "Elizabeth, you know why men call blondes dumb?" he asked, with a boyish solemnity she found hard to resist.

"No."

"Because beautiful blondes make them feel dumb because they can't express what they feel when they're faced with a beautiful woman."

There was some truth to that, she thought, and it was endearing of him to say so. But it was also completely disingenuous. Looking back now, as she snuggled deeper into the bed and remembered that meeting from a safe distance, she knew beyond a doubt that if Hans Brinkman doubted his abilities in any area, she had never seen the slightest hint. No, the only weakness he had ever displayed since she had known him was an inability to remain close to her long enough for her to take his presence for granted. God, she would love to have that luxury. But instead, there was only the elusive thrill of the unbroken charger—no knight—just the stunning white horse. She had fallen for that mythical energy and had fallen hard to be sure—and now here she was, a year later in the fluorescent glare of reality, blond model in a black book, hotel plaything of an investment banker who barely had time for her.

How predictable was *that?*

She pulled the sheets around her and wondered. Was she afraid to let him go, or just afraid of *him?*

The answer, she suspected ruefully, was both. And that fear, bordering at times on the voluptuous, made Hans all the more intriguing. The fact was that Elizabeth *liked* risk—yearned for the taste and challenge of it. And deep inside she was even convinced that on the other side of such places and situations lay the reality she so desired. From the slopes of Switzerland to the runways of Paris, she had found everything she treasured most by threading passageways of fear to the other side.

Everything she treasured, including Hans.

But this infatuation with her fear had, on one horrendous occasion, nearly cost Elizabeth her looks and her livelihood, not to mention her life, so she also developed a healthy sense of caution. At this moment, with anxiety and hunger and blind anticipation all swirling around her, she found herself watching Hans Brinkman with increasing objectivity.

You can walk away from this, she was thinking. Put it all behind you, girl!

She saw him smile, as though he were reading her thoughts. "What are you brooding about, Elizabeth?" he asked.

She stiffened slightly. The faintly patronizing way he always used her full name—why hadn't that gotten under her skin before? "I was thinking back to when we met," she said.

"Ruing the day," he teased, and before she could agree, "I lied to you, you know."

She looked at him, suddenly afraid. He grinned.

"Well, not an outright lie, a lie of omission. I didn't tell you I'd been stalking you."

By now breathing was difficult. "Stalking me?"

"I'd seen your picture in *Allure*—remember that little reading room at the ski lodge? And when I looked up, there you were in the lobby. It was like magic. As if we were fated to be together. Or as if we'd already met before."

"In another life," she said, trying for flippancy. But it had come out like a statement of fact, and it scared her even more. It sounded so right, even though she had not even thought before saying it. That feeling of déjà vu.

"Something like that, yes. It threw me. I was almost afraid to approach you—I don't know why, it never happened before. So I thought, well, I'll impress her on the slopes, then we'll have something to talk about."

"It worked," she said carefully.

"You impressed me, too," he said almost fondly. He touched her hair. "You aren't starting to regret it, are you?" he asked, and suddenly there was a sadness in his voice that completely unnerved her.

"No!"

He smiled again. Was he happy now? Or was he seeing right through her, amused as only a true cynic can be? She raged at herself in frustration. I *am* regretting it. Come *on*, Lizzy, in the animal king-dom—which is where Hans definitely lives—a smile is just another show of teeth.

"We remind me of that Cole Porter song," he said amiably. "What's it called?"

"I don't know any Cole Porter songs," she lied. She knew exactly the one he was thinking of.

"'Too hot not to cool down,'" he sang off-key. "That what you're afraid of? The Angel's Curse?"

She looked at him. She knew he would say what it was and he did.

"It's a corollary of the Rule of Blondes: men think they're not good enough for you, so they act accordingly. They disappear, or fuck it up, and hurt you. That's what's always happened, right?"

"Whereas you know you're good enough?" she countered, not car-ing to answer that one. What on earth was he leading up to?

"I know," he said, his voice dropping into a gentler register. "We were meant to be together."

She took a deep breath. Whether he had meant to or not, he was giving her an opening she could not ignore. "Then why aren't we?" she heard herself ask. "Are you afraid to upset your home life?"

It was the first time she had alluded to his wife, even indirectly. She felt a spasm of regret as she saw his face cloud over, but she pressed on. "I think we should talk about it," she said, steeling herself for what he might say. And then, when he said nothing, she said, "I'm not really sure I want to go on like this."

He nodded, looking idly toward the window, the distant mountains. "You know, I'm not sure I do either."

Elizabeth's chest constricted. It was bad enough to consider being the dumper. To be the dumpee was terrifying.

"She's gone off me," he said darkly. "She finds me—easily distracted. My mind is too much on my work, she says. Not that I blame her. Lately we travel in our separate ruts—our life seems to work better that way." He shrugged. "Listen, I really don't want to talk about Yvette. Not today." He glanced at his watch.

"Then when?"

He ignored her question. "And yes, I hate hotels, too," he said, reading her mind.

"Then my place. I could use some home-court advantage."

"No. I don't want to endanger you . . ."

She looked at him. "Endanger me?"

"The less Yvette knows . . ." he said, his eyes veiled again. He left the phrase hanging. "Next time we'll talk. We'll have it all out. I promise." Abruptly, he resumed dressing, while Elizabeth tried to sort out her emotions. She watched his body disappear into his charcoal suit until he was just a wealthy, chic businessman again. She tried to control her breathing but couldn't.

With real despair she realized that she was still head over heels in love.

"Saturday, Elizabeth," he said, already at the door and blowing her a gentle kiss. "Same time, okay?"

He was gone before she had answered, softly, irresolutely, with dismay, "Saturday, yes."

She heard him run to the elevator, heard it whir as it descended.

Pulling the sheet around her, suddenly she felt chilled to the bone. She curled into a ball and pulled the duvet over her head until she was hidden in protective darkness.

2

Peter Jance, seventy-six years old and feeling every minute of it, scrambled up the long grade of scrub and hard sand he and his crew had dubbed Mons Venus. His once thick golden hair was a brittle gray mane now, but he was still handsome in a hawk-faced way and, on this project at least, his mind was miles ahead of everyone.

As usual, that put him in a hell of a fix.

Only a few fellow geniuses conceded that what he was working on was feasible. The rest of the scientific community thought he was out of his mind.

And maybe they're right, Peter said to himself, squinting into the distance. It was easy to feel trepidation and self-doubt today, if he had been capable of either. The sun beat down on the sand and mesquite like a blacksmith's hammer, and all around him people were cursing the heat. Instead, Peter found himself glorying in it. Like a penitent celebrating the lash, he mused, though it scarcely diminished his love for the landscape. White Sands Missile Range occupied 3,200 square miles of New Mexico desert, an area as big as Rhode Island, Delaware and the District of Columbia combined, and was now his to play in, a paradise of rolling grasslands, sand dunes and lava flows heaving into foothills and ragged canyons. He loved its life—bighorn sheep, pronghorns, mountain lions. There were golden eagles and horned lizards, rattlesnakes, kangaroo rats and tarantulas. Coyotes, bobcats and foxes hunted here at night; mule deer, roadrunners, giant centipedes and wind scorpions were to be found during the day. Even introduced species like African oryx, a five-hundred-pound antelope from the Kalahari region, flourished here by the thousands. This was one of the little-mentioned perks of working on a super-secret, low-access base: few people got in, and nature thrived.

Except for the part of nature that worked for the U.S. Army. That part inspired less awe, and not a little regret.

The soldiers.

Damn, his gut hurt. Was it his guilt talking or the illness? Or were they now hopelessly intertwined?

You made this bed, he thought, so now you lie in it. So what if the enemy troops hadn't been his idea? When the notion had first come up, three months ago, he had argued against including live subjects, to the point at which Colonel Oscar Henderson, the bean counter in charge of funding this project, pushed the issue to the level of a deal breaker. There were several ways to interpret Henderson's stubbornness: as a sign that he had lost faith in Peter's vision, doubted his abilities, even his loyalty; or merely as a desire to piss on Peter's project so it would have his scent. Power has to be arbitrary, as Peter had come to realize—otherwise it's just sound policy. A lifetime of struggling to maintain his vision while being accused of biting the hand that fed him had driven home that truth.

His wife, Beatrice, on the other hand, leaned toward the theory of the loyalty test to explain Henderson's insistence on live subjects. They had spent a week debating the issue, Peter arguing that it tainted all of them and was unnecessary. Beatrice, of course, called him a pompano—their pet word for a pompous ass—and as usual, she was right. After all, he could turn around and walk back down the hill, couldn't he? Call Henderson's bluff? And was he going to? No. As a matter of fact, the result of his wife's chastisement was to make him more determined than ever to see this project through to the end. All the concerns he had voiced to Beatrice—just so much ritual self-doubt—were merely an attempt to quiet the churning in his gut by flattering his conscience. With the result being, of course, that his symptoms were flaring up more painfully than ever. The pills he was taking put his inner ear on gimbals, and now, plodding skyward through the sand, he had to pee again, despite the fact he'd done so five minutes before leaving the bunker.

"Dr. Jance? Maybe we could slow down a little bit?"

Peter glanced back down the hill. His support team were slogging behind him as best as they could, and one of them, Alex Davies, had apparently decided to take on the job of their spokesman. Peter smiled. Only Alex, in all the world, had the familiarity to suggest he slow down. Peter had known him since he was a kid, and Alex was banking on that. He was a decent kid, despite his pestering. Peter suspected that he might even have a conscience, which was unusual among scientists in this generation. It made Peter like him for it and—come to think of it—for his lack of qualms about speaking up. Despite their constant, collective pissing and moaning, no one else on his team had voiced a serious complaint about any part of this enormously difficult and demanding project on which they labored like indentured servants.

Of course, Peter reflected now, he *had* looked for just such a gung ho, unquestioning quality during the screening process. Wild-card geniuses scrounged from universities all over the United States, this team constituted the best and the brightest scientists working in weapons development today. Wet behind the ears, yes, and in Alex's case somewhat unpredictable, but who else was willing to put in outrageous hours for peanuts just for the opportunity to work with Peter Jance?

Cap Chu, his accelerator specialist, he had shanghaied from MIT. Cap was a second-generation Chinese-American from Oakland, whose unchanging uniform was a Raiders T-shirt and cutoff Levi's, and whose unconscious tendency to mimic his boss's speech patterns often made Peter want to laugh aloud. But in tens years or less, Cap Chu was a shoo-in to write the book on particle weaponry for the next century—and as Beatrice put it, the kid was a steal.

Hank Flannagan, pausing to light a Marlboro, was another diamond in the rough. Flannagan understood the weapons applications of fusion the way angry boys understand a rock's applications to a picture window. His form of relaxation was stretching out on his dirt bike at sixty miles an hour while he sailed through the puckerbush, or jumping ravines so wide fellow riders braked and covered their eyes in horror. Peter, no stranger to physical risk, encouraged him in this hobby. Flannagan returned from these forays not only unscathed, but bristling with solutions to some of the most challenging mathematical problems the team confronted.

The woman among them, just now hooking her arm through Alex Davies's, was Rosemarie Wiener. The fact that Peter was funding a project to achieve an unprecedented kill factor didn't bother her one bit. She was herself a protean thinker in the tactical applications of microwave and ultrasound beams and an avid fan of sophisticated military mayhem. The correlation between raw force and long term survival was not lost on her. She had been raised on a kibbutz and took shit from no one—except maybe Alex Davies, with whom, at this moment, she was flirting hard, the sound of her delighted laughter rising sharply through the shimmering heat.

Peter wondered if it was lust or political instinct. With this generation it was hard to tell. Certainly if there was one among these nascent whiz kids headed for real power, it was Alex Davies, so even if Rosemarie was only networking, she had chosen well. Alex was the grandson of Dr. Frederick Wolfe, a scientist spearheading his own top secret project for the Army, both at other bases and here at White Sands. If Alex himself was something of a catch on his own merits, as a future father-in-law Frederick Wolfe made the kid an all-time trophy. Anyone near Wolfe moved up quickly, and this particular project, code-named Fountain, was legendary on the base, both for the deferment and funding it received and for the cachet it gave to all who were associated with it.

As to what exactly the Fountain Project was, it was a mystery. It was wrapped in secrecy so extreme that even Peter, who warily counted Wolfe among his oldest friends, could only guess at what it might be all about. To make things even more intriguing, Peter's own wife, Beatrice, was employed by Wolfe as a neurobiologist on the Fountain Project. But she, too, was kept on a need-to-know basis—at least judging by what she disclosed to Peter. Her specialty was spinal regeneration, so Peter speculated that maybe it had something to do with trying to cure battle injuries to that stem of stems. But that was only one possibility. Beatrice swore only Wolfe knew the big picture, but Peter found that hard to swallow, considering the ranks of brass coming in and out of Wolfe's compound. Clearly Wolfe and his Fountain Project were the darlings of someone big—perhaps even the Commander in Chief—and that meant its purpose was not only known in detail by some, but considered important. *Hugely* important, judging from the amount of funding Wolfe seemed to enjoy.

Good luck to him. Peter was never one to begrudge a friend's good fortune.

Besides, the fact was the two had known each other since their twenties, and often shared test ranges and personnel—-even, as in this case, family members. Wolfe had given Beatrice a position of power within the Fountain Project, and Peter had agreed to take Alex aboard in return. Peter gave the kid the room he needed to be his own quirky self, while Wolfe had assigned Beatrice to a lab in the Caribbean. On their end, it was an arrangement that permitted the couple to remain close, but not so close they would tear each other's heads off from propinquity, which was what they tended to do when they worked on the same project. This was a great boon to Peter, for he and Beatrice needed each other desperately, and thrived on distant proximity of just the right kind. Too close to each other and they were miserable; too far apart and they were lost.

"Hey, Uncle Peter? Are we there yet?" Saying it with just the right tone of irony and fondness, the kid somehow got away with it. Alex Davies was a wild card, to be sure, but one Peter was glad he'd drawn. Any regrets Peter had personally harbored about having the kid more or less foisted upon him had vanished within a week of the young man's arrival. For one thing, Alex knew the base's labyrinthine cluster of Cray supercomputers like the back of his hand. That knowledge allowed Peter to throw dozens of theorems, algorithms and mathematical models at this project each week, rather than once a year through the usual channels. For that alone, Alex was a godsend. So the fact that Alex got a little cheeky from time to time was of little import. In his own quirky way, Alex Davies was vital to the project's chance for survival and also for its eventual success.

Ignoring the twisting pain in his stomach, Peter kept walking at the same killer pace he had set at the bottom of the hill. Despite his illness, he had more energy than most men half his age. Six feet tall, with no suggestion of a stoop, he had spent his youth and much of his middle age accepting every physical challenge he could find. He had bicycled through Nepal when it was known only to National Geographic photographers, trekked halfway across Borneo surveying for an oil company. He had run marathons all over the East Coast just for the hell of it—and until just recently, he played squash with a ferocity that appalled his opponents.

Not that he'd worked at any of it very hard. His first love, his obsession, in fact, was physics, the source of all the challenges that truly mattered. It just happened that he was gifted with one of those almost freakishly athletic bodies, capable, it seemed for many years, of anything he asked of it. It had given him a lifetime of pleasures and mobility and, most important, had afforded a superb platform for his brain, bathing it in rich, super-oxygenated blood, allowing its undisputed genius to run at full throttle for six decades.

Until the pancreatic cancer.

Yes, too bad about that, wasn't it? In the game of cellular roulette, he had come up double zero.

Not that he'd expected to go to his grave intact—that much of an optimist he wasn't. Still, coming out of nowhere as it had, and in the midst of the most important work of his life, the cancer had felt like an undeserved punishment. It was playing hob with his body at the moment, an infuriating distraction to the workings of his mind. Come on, Jance, he berated himself, clamping his teeth against the pain, stop feeling sorry for yourself.

He struggled to focus on the business at hand, the hundreds of tasks needing completion before he could begin his countdown. He assailed his own disease by reimagining it. If it was some ravening beast tearing him from within, he'd see it as something without imagination or charisma—the pain in his entrails nothing but a dark hamster on a wheel. It almost worked. At least it allowed him to keep walking. And then he was at the target. He stopped before the enemy soldiers, rank upon rank of them, staring as if seeing them for the first time.

And the enemy in turn fixed wide eyes on him. Two hundred sheep bought wholesale from a rancher who knew better than to ask questions. Fifteen cows—dairy beasts past their productive peak and bargain-basement cheap, seventy-five pigs in air-cooled aluminum cages, too smart to be held by collars.

Pigs, for Godsakes.

He averted his gaze, kicking a rock out of his way as he approached the first unhappy creature. He checked its tether, and by the time Alex and the rest of his support team panted up, he was already looking around at the animal's comrades in arms, deployed across the ridge, an enemy frozen where they were tied.

"Well, they look happy, don't they, chief?" said Flannagan, and began to baaa at the nearest ewe.

"Knock it off," said Peter.

"Not having second thoughts, are we?" asked Alex quietly. Peter wheeled around, caught off-guard by the accuracy of the question.

The look in Alex's eye was as playful as it was unreadable, but before Peter could reply, a wind-borne shout reached them from below the crest of the hill. "How the fuck hot is it?" It was the animal wrangler, Peter knew, the local man, what was his name? Something with a P, or was it something with a K—?

God, now the beast was erasing his memory.

Perkins.

Forget the cancer. Just put it out of your mind.

"Forty-eight degrees," someone yelled back.

"*Bullshit*, forty-eight! It's a helluva lot hotter than *that!*"

Peter winced as the sharp hurt intensified.

"Celsius," he said as Perkins ambled up, blue eyes snapping under his Stetson.

"That's over a hundred in Fahrenheit, ain't it?"

"Around a hundred twenty, actually."

The wrangler shot him a look. "Jesus, that's too damn hot."

"Then we'd better get a move on, hadn't we?" said Peter, with a quick glance at the caged pigs, then swinging back around at the sound of Perkins's beeper.

"Sir, it says here to tell you B has arrived," Perkins said, reading the message. "That make any sense to you?"

The pain in Peter's belly instantly eased. For the first time that afternoon, he felt his heart, his gut, his whole body relax.

"It's Beatrice," he said, with a smile, raking his long gray hair back with both hands.

"Beatrice, sir?"

"My wife, the good Dr. Jance. She's coming in with Dr. Wolfe from the Caribbean. She wanted to see the test, actually. Bring her over here, would you, Perkins?"

Perkins frowned in the direction of the animals.

"The faster you get her here," Peter muttered, "the less time these animals will have to suffer." Perkins nodded grimly and started back down the hill. Peter, steeling himself again, returned his attention to the animals.

It wasn't easy. Just the din and smell were appalling; he tried to shut his senses to both. Time was short, and his financial control officer, one Colonel Oscar Henderson, was itching to pull the plug on the whole damn project. Wolfe himself had warned him. The way Wolfe saw it, ever since the fall of the Berlin Wall, there wasn't a politician alive who gave a rat's ass about the advancement of military science unless it got him reelected.

Peter knew he was right. It took a good enemy to keep things going. It didn't matter that there was an increasingly educated lunatic fringe, billionaire terrorists, half a dozen rogue states with nuclear capability to worry about, not to mention a chaotic, paranoid Russia. Peter had used all these arguments. Still, his funding was constantly being threatened. In fact, with the exception of the Fountain Society, which didn't seem to be weapons-oriented, most of the big projects on the base were being cut back.

So Peter knew that every ounce of his waning strength had to be dedicated to the task at hand—to complete his weapon and be able to demonstrate that it could work. Nothing else mattered. Not the lives of a few animals that would have died anyway, not even his own life. It was the work that mattered. And success.

He watched intently, ignoring the black spiral of pain that was working its way through his gut again, as his team fanned out, checking tethers and adjusting telemetry devices. It was zero minus fifty minutes, and time was racing through his fingers like quarks through an accelerometer. His Nobel Prize, his international awards, the laboratory that bore his name at MIT—none of it mattered now, if it ever had. Beyond the acclaim, beyond the misgivings, there was only the *idea,* moved toward reality through painstaking research and development that had gone on seemingly forever until this approaching moment. In just fifty minutes, the instant when everything might come to fruition would arrive. And in that instant, the idea could become substance. If it happened, he knew, the realization of that idea would dominate military thought for the foreseeable future.

But the time factor—the necessity for those hours, months and years of cerebration and calculation and fiddling and trying and trying again—made everything one great race against the very limitation of a man's life span. Stupidly small budgets, arbitrary deadlines, the ignorant carping of the Army brass had all conspired to undermine his work, his dream, his place in the history of science. Experiments that could have worked brilliantly if they had been adequately funded were rushed headlong from the drawing board into the field and discarded forever if they failed just once. The process was nothing short of insane, and it had all come down to this: if this day's trial shot didn't work, he and his research would be worthless and the last decade of his life would be declared an utter waste.

The pain clawed at his belly. Inwardly, he snarled back at it.

You're here, he swore to himself. You're going through with it, and your doubts be damned.

He turned around and pissed against a yucca, ignoring the burn. Somewhere behind him a sheep was bleating as if its throat were cut. Perkins was right. Time to get going or they would all be dead from the heat.

SOUTHERN ACCESS ROAD, WHITE SANDS

Ten miles south of where Peter was working, the desert flattened until it was a griddle spreading as far as the eye could see, bleached sand
blinding and barren to the horizon of the Tularosa Basin. This deso-
late moonscape was bisected by a single two-rut track, and on this a
dust-blasted Range Rover heaved, roiling a plume that stretched a
half-mile behind it into the blistered air.

Inside the Range Rover were Peter's wife, Dr. Beatrice Jance, and
Dr. Frederick Wolfe, who was doing the driving. Wolfe was in his
early seventies, gaunt and pale, with hair like steel wool, thick eyelids
and a mouth turned down darkly with an expression of perpetual disdain. His surgeon's fingers were long and large-knuckled; the huge
dome of his skull was dotted with liver spots the size of quarters. He
had the air of a man who expects the best while he listens for the
worst, and whose slightest disapproval had the force of a curse. Nos-
feratu was the nickname given him by one brash young geneticist who
had been employed by him for just a week. That man soon found himself teaching high school biology in Mexico. Better to be feared than
loved, as Machiavelli, one of Wolfe's few heroes, advised. Better still
to love oneself so completely, so faithfully, that the question never
mattered.

And, in fact, that was the way it worked for Wolfe.

Scientists from all over the world had flocked to the side of this implacable genius, whose experiments in biogenetics were so bold and
far-reaching that no one but he could grasp their complete significance. And with Machiavellian dexterity, Wolfe pitted these scientists
against each other, ego to ambition, in such a way that he got the best
of their work and kept his secrets to himself and his inner circle. Vir-
tually no one he had asked to join him had refused; no one who had
come aboard had quit him voluntarily.

Beatrice Jance was no exception.

As he maneuvered the Range Rover across the desert sands, Wolfe
watched her from the corner of his eye. Beatrice was still magnifi-
cent—her glorious ash-blond hair had long since turned a blazing
white, and there were fresh wrinkles pursing her broad pale mouth,

but her athletic grace was intact, the soft gray eyes still remarkably energetic. But she hadn't returned his smiles, not once in the last thirty minutes. No, of course, her thoughts would all be of Peter. She looked over at Wolfe, catching him looking, and smiled as he looked away. What that smile meant, though, Wolfe was damned if he knew.

"If I swallow much more dust," she shouted over the noise of the wind, "I'll pass a brick."

Wolfe winced faintly. Her offhand coarseness when she wanted to be vulgar was jarring. It was the same with Peter. The problem with these two was, no matter how far apart they were in the course of their work, they were always somehow together. It baffled him, really, and irritated him as well. There was such a thing as being too close. They fed on each other's doubts and anxieties, in his view, especially now with Peter's illness looming over all of them. Touching, how they'd tried to keep Peter's cancer a secret from him, the one man on whom nothing was ever lost, and the one man who could actually do something about it.

"Fortunate for both of us we've arrived," Wolfe said, pulling himself back to the here and now. He produced an ID from his pocket and braked the Range Rover at a weed-choked fence.

A man appeared and scrutinized the credentials. Wolfe eyed him with Olympian impatience.

"Obviously, you're new."

The guard, wiry and humorless, ignored Wolfe's withering glance. From somewhere inside his civilian vest came the crackle of a walkie-talkie. He ignored that, too, until he had finished inspecting Wolfe's ID.

"Six-month rotation," he finally said, and flashed his own ID. Wolfe waved it away. "How was D.C., Dr. Wolfe?"

"Benighted and besotted," Wolfe muttered. "As always."

The guard flicked an uneasy eye toward Wolfe's passenger. "Beatrice," sighed Wolfe, "Mr. Greenhorn wants your credentials, too."

Beatrice dug into her battered leather satchel, pulling out paperbacks, a scientific calculator, a Spinhaler, a tube of sunblock—everything but her papers.

"Dr. Beatrice Jance," she said, as if that explained everything.

The guard stiffened brightly.

"Wife of Dr. Peter Jance?"

She smiled, not threatened. "And he is married to me as well."

"No kidding. Sorry." The guard stepped back, starstruck, and saluted. "You both have a nice day now," he added, pulling out his walkie-talkie to announce them. Wolfe saw Beatrice blink as she glimpsed the automatic weapon slung vertically under his vest. He put the Range Rover in drive, and within moments, guard and shack and razor-wire hurricane fence disappeared in the dust.

"Everyone seems to know Peter," Beatrice declared, still shouting over the wind.

Wolfe looked at her impassively. Was this an instance of simple wifely pride, or was she trying to put a dent in his vanity?

"Any kid admires an adult who likes to blow things up," he said.

"That's probably it," she returned.

Her tone was level, no hint of irony or regret. As faithful to the cause as she is beautiful, concluded Wolfe. Feeling as empty as a used-up pack of cigarettes, he put the pedal to the floor.

Two miles deeper into the desert, Wolfe and Beatrice arrived at the compound of corrals, pens and living quarters Wolfe had called his second home for the past five years. The Fountain Compound, whose low-lying sprawl and air of bland guardedness suggested a prison for white-collar felons, was actually an unlisted unit of the Army's Battle-field Environment Directorate, or BED, one of the many Army research laboratories sprinkled across White Sands.

The Army had begun its residency at White Sands in 1946. In the early years, its Signal Corps had supplied radar and communications support for the American conversion of captured German V-2 rockets at the dawn of the U.S. space program. Now its projects ranged far from rocketry, to weapons systems research and on into biological and chemical means of warfare that were beyond the wildest dreams of even Hitler's architects of death.

Peter Jance's project, code-named Hammer and headquartered fifteen miles away on the same range, was one such undertaking and, here at the Fountain Compound, Wolfe coordinated the most secret of the secret. Fountain was a project sited both at White Sands and at another secret base in the Caribbean, but it was here at White Sands that the latest breakthrough had been accomplished. And Wolfe couldn't wait to show it to Beatrice.

He parked and left the keys, nodding to a man lounging under a cluster of scrawny palms; recognizing the project director, the guard lowered his automatic weapon. Beatrice put on dark glasses against the glare of sun.

"Not exactly the island," Wolfe said.

"It's too damn hot here," Beatrice scowled, spitting out something that had made its way into her mouth. "Even the bugs can't stand being outside."

Wolfe stalked over to a nearby pen. "Maybe that's why the locals don't talk much," he said, and scowled intently at a large pink pig dozing on its side in the straw, its skin shining from the latest application of cooling water. There was a number clipped to one ear, and a hefty bandage plastered across its back.

"Perkins?" he called in irritation.

The instant the pig heard Wolfe's voice it lurched up and began dragging useless back legs toward its nighttime enclosure, squealing all the while. The sight of its discomfort tightened Beatrice's face with concern at the same time that it flushed Wolfe's with rage.

"Perkins!" Wolfe roared, and the pig sprawled in panic, snagging its bandage on the fence. The bandage tore completely off, revealing a frightful scar stitched transversely across its spine.

"Oh, Christ," said Beatrice. "Frederick, where's the control around here?"

"Perkins!"

The pig gave a final shriek and wrenched itself inside the pen. At that moment Perkins pulled up in a dusty red pickup. The truck had an official ATW security clearance sticker in one corner of its windshield—everything else about it was right out of 1956. Perkins swung out with a grin.

"Hey, Dr. Wolfe, you get a look at that pig?"

"What if I did?" barked Wolfe. "You called me here for that? What the devil were you thinking?"

Perkins swallowed, his grin dying. His was a thankless job in the best of circumstances, being in charge of all the animals at White Sands, but with Dr. Wolfe back at this particular compound, he knew his work would be cut out for him. "That pig? No, hey. It's the *other* one I thought you'd wanna see." He swiveled toward a nearby barn and gave a sooo-eeeee! Within moments, a second pig, bandaged like the first, appeared through the open door.

But this animal was different. This animal was trotting. That is until it saw Wolfe. Then it took off like a bat out of hell in the opposite direction.

Wolfe was fascinated by its obvious mobility. Perkins grinned again.

"I was right in telling them to call you, wasn't I?"

"What number animal was that?"

"P365."

Wolfe's voice was hushed. "I'll be damned," he said.

He turned to Beatrice. She was smiling for the first time that afternoon—radiantly.

"Is that one of mine?" she asked.

"It most certainly is," said Wolfe, suddenly taking off after the pig as if he were going to fetch it for her. Perkins shot a quizzical glance at Beatrice, who was staring at it as though the pig were a long-lost lover transformed by a magical spell. Weird people, these eggheads, thought Perkins. He shrugged and cleared his throat.

"They're about ready to go at Delta Range, ma'am. Dr. Jance said you might need a lift."

"You bet," she said. "How's the Gray-Haired Monster?"

"With all due respect, ma'am?"

"Full of piss and vinegar?"

"Yes, ma'am." Perkins grinned and opened the door of his pickup for her. In the distance, Wolfe had cornered P365 for a closer look. The pig was cowering in his shadow.

WHITE SANDS, DELTA RANGE

Fifteen minutes after leaving the animals tethered on the hill, Dr. Peter Jance and his support team were a quarter mile away on a mass of steel, ceramic and exotic materials that cost the U.S. government and its taxpayers more per ounce than gold. Dubbed The Hammer, the whole apparatus weighed one ton, which was about a hundred tons lighter than anything else that had been cooked up during the ill-fated Star Wars period, and that lightness translated into its supreme feasibility as a military weapon. The Hammer, in essence, was the most advanced Directed High-Energy Weapon system ever conceived, and singly the product of Peter Jance's unique vision.

That vision, and the knowledge that informed it, had their roots in the Manhattan Project, where Peter had begun his scientific career, in 1943, as a twenty-one-year-old mathematician; Einstein himself had announced that Peter was the only scientist at Los Alamos who had caught an error in his calculations. They had exploded the first thermonuclear device just thirty miles north on this very testing ground, at a site called Trinity, and a month later had seen two Japanese cities atomized by their device.

Then, after the war, there were the years of building the Tevatron Collider, a behemoth at the Fermi National Accelerator Lab in Illinois. The world's most powerful particle accelerator, the TC shot protons against antiprotons at collision energies of 1.8 trillion electron-volts. Peter had proved that atoms were not merely protons and electrons whirling around a nucleus—he had helped throw open the doors of a "particle zoo" of gluons, mesons and mysterious atomic dust particles called quarks, while the rest of science scrambled to catch up.

But it was during the Reagan administration that Peter had finally come into his own, without the interference that had dogged him after Hiroshima. He proposed and developed everything from rail guns to ultrasound weapons that could melt the eyes and inner ears of any soldier within their range. The problems now were technical, not bureaucratic—questions of size and power requirements. All of the devices were huge, enormously costly, and consumed electricity like Manhattan in July. One shot from these weapons was all you got—it took six to eight hours before they were ready to fire again. None were useful for actual combat.

Until the Hammer.

This weapon prototype promised to be efficient and lethal at the same time. Peter had achieved phenomenal miniaturization by restructuring all of its hardware and algorithms in nanotechnology. There were gears in the weapon that could fit in the gut of a gnat, circuits visible only via electron microscopes, lenses formed from half a dozen atoms. And even more brilliantly, he had arrived at a wonderfully low power consumption by giving it uplink capability to a top secret satellite. It was the satellite that supplied the massive energy stream needed, harvesting it directly from the solar wind by means of huge panels.

If it worked there would be twenty-four such satellites in space within four years, all geostationary, at least two accessible by ground control no matter where in the world it was located. With a thousand of these ground units in place, no rogue state or resurgent tyranny could stand up to the weapon's lethal force and the Army knew it.

If it worked. If he could just stabilize the damn thing. A directed energy weapon like this didn't shoot bullets or shells, it shot particle beams. These were produced by accelerating negative ions to monstrous velocities, then stripping away their extra electron at the last nanosecond—creating a 30-million-watt, 5-million-ampere beam of lithium ions that delivered 100 trillion watts per square centimeter directly to the target.

Because of all that power, the Hammer was a little temperamental. But it had marvelous potential for clean lethality. Until recently Peter had loved it like a proud father.

And if it works, I'll love it again, he thought ruefully, and stifled a reflexive groan—the pain in his belly seemed to be increasing with every tick of the clock.

Peter gave the apparatus one last look, closed the access panel, and turned to Alex Davies, who was eyeing his every move with an un-fathomable gaze. Had Alex caught a whiff of his uncertainty? If so, what in the hell was there to do about it?

"Let's go to the bunker," he said.

Blockhouse A, a full mile from the device and twice as far from the target animals, was a dark concrete pillbox, with firing control room walls ten feet thick. The roof, a full twenty-seven feet of reinforced concrete, had been designed in the 1940s to withstand the impact of a large rocket, such as a V-2, falling from an altitude of one hundred miles at a speed of two thousand miles per hour. The bunker, whose dank air had all the homely assurance of a mausoleum, had been used for the Manhattan Project in 1945. Its flaking concrete was layered with graffiti, most of it written by young physicists who were now household names. *If you're not part of the solution,* Feynman had written in the 1960s, *you're part of the precipitate.* And a favorite of Peter's, from Einstein himself, written by some unknown hand, *Relatively speaking, when does Munich stop at this train?*

A klaxon sounded.

The last observers were crowding in, including Peter's Army shadow, Colonel Henderson—Heartless Henderson to his friends as well as to his enemies, in which latter category Peter found himself almost by default. Henderson was a large-muscled, close-shaven man in his fifties. His teeth were invariably clamped around an unlit H. Upmann Corona Major, and he had humorless dark eyes that were perpetually narrowed, as though scanning a column of figures that didn't add up. Right now, he was gesturing at the monitor that showed the hillside of target animals, spinning out a scenario for a half dozen visiting brass. Peter sat biding his time.

"What we have here," Henderson intoned, "is an assault line of three hundred enemy troops—for argument's sake, Iraqis. They're about to sweep down and engulf an American outpost cut off from all support. Isn't that right, Dr. Jance?"

"It's your movie," said Peter, without enthusiasm. Where the devil was Beatrice?

"And over here," continued Henderson, moving to the next monitor, where the weapon glowed darkly in the blazing desert light. "Here we have the Hammer. Cast of thousands, cost in billions—which oughta buy us a feel-good ending, don't you think, Doctor?"

Peter avoided Henderson's look of baleful skepticism and shot a glance at the door—someone was entering. At the sight of Frederick Wolfe, Peter's heart did a little dance of disappointment. "Glad you could make it, Freddy," he said.

"Wouldn't have missed it for the world," said Wolfe magisterially, lowering his long frame into a chair that had been reserved for him. He nodded toward Alex, who at his grandfather's entrance had shifted casually to a corner of the bunker. "You sure you want Alex here, though? I've seen keyboards blow up at his touch." Wolfe laughed alone, drawing pained looks from the other crew members. His habit of teasing Alex was unsettling to the rest of the crew, who universally liked the kid. Peter watched Wolfe give Alex a pat on the head, and then forgot about them as the door opened again and he saw the face he'd been longing to see—for years, it seemed suddenly, though in fact he and Beatrice had only been apart for a month. He held out his hand, and Beatrice squeezed it, tilting her face up to his for the lightest of kisses.

"Thought I'd have to go without you," he said.

"Never," she said, instantly appraising his anxiety and giving him the look she'd given him so many times before: *You're wonderful no matter what happens.* His heart soared, and the pain in his stomach subsided. "We had a pleasant surprise at the Fountain Compound," she said with a smile. "A little breakthrough."

"And it's good?" he asked politely. Over the last year or so, consumed with his own experiments and occasional misgivings, he had lost track of the direction his wife's research was taking.

"It's not bad. How are you feeling?"

"Better," he lied. "*Much* better."

"Peter?"

"I *am*. Not a spasm all day." He kissed her again. Every good marriage, he was fond of saying, was based on fear. In his case, not the fear of losing Beatrice's love, which was unthinkable, but the fear of causing her worry or pain. "What did you see?" he asked. "One of the sheep?"

"A pig."

"And it was promising?"

"Very. Listen, we'll talk later. I don't want to upstage you," she said. As if I could, was the sweet unstated message in her clear gray eyes. He felt a lump in his throat. If ever the phrase "for better or worse" had concrete representation, it was in Beatrice's unflinching devotion to him and to his work. Fifty years they'd been married. As Peter sometimes quipped, for a couple who were both intensely engaged in scientific research, that alone should have rated them a plaque at the foot of their street. And whereas Peter's achievements had already been granted four pages in the *Britannica*, Beatrice's brilliance in neurobiology was known only to the inner circles of her own specialty. Peter ran his own project; Beatrice worked in anonymity for Frederick Wolfe. Not once—it never ceased to amaze him—had she ever complained. "Break a leg," she said, and kissed him again.

"All right, cut it out, you two," said Wolfe from behind them. He flashed a jagged smile. "Time to save the world for democracy."

Peter gave his crew the once-over. They were ready and focused.

"Uplink with the bird is achieved and locked," said Cap Chu, his Peter-like lilt echoing dully off the concrete. "We are zero minus thirty seconds and counting."

The place fell silent.

Peter scanned the instruments. Everything appeared on track. He wished deeply that he felt the same about his own systems—now the pain was lancing up from his gut and, at ten seconds, he definitely felt the room spinning, saw his hand going out to Beatrice.

Then the weapon fired.

The sound of the pulse was audible even through ten feet of reinforced concrete—a deep, electrical throb that peaked with a thunderous clap of energy. The on-range video screens burned to white.

That's all right, thought Peter, as Beatrice's nails dug into his palm. That's to be expected, he said to himself, and Beatrice relaxed her grip.

What was unexpected was the explosion that followed—a sharp, brutal blow against the bunker that sent all of them reeling. Every red light on the panels flashed, everything that wasn't nailed down toppled, and the blast wave that arrived a heartbeat later slapped clothing against flesh and left ears ringing.

"No one move until we have an all-clear!" shouted Chu, as he clawed his way back up to the control panel.

The monitors were coming back up, and the multi-angled view of the target hillside they offered was the most eerie sight imaginable.

Each station that had been occupied by an animal was now the site of a bonfire of tissue, bone and hair.

There was nothing in sight that resembled life, not anywhere.

Oscar Henderson let out a bellow of delight.

"You *see* that? *God Almighty.*"

Fighting for breath, Peter struggled to his feet. There were ragged cheers and feeble backslaps among a few of the brass, but for the most part an awed hush had descended on the bunker. Nobody had expected a force like that.

"Holy *shit,*" Alex Davies was whispering—over and over, like a mantra. Beatrice, stunned into silence like the others, now stared at her husband, a nameless anxiety rising in her throat. Peter's face was ashen.

"Peter?"

"I'm fine." He walked up to the monitor and surveyed the mayhem at ground zero. Cap Chu peered at him uncertainly, shaking his head.

"What was that audible explosion, Dr. Jance? I thought this was supposed to be a stealth kind of thing, no?"

Peter took a deep, painful breath. He knew without looking. "We had a camera on the weapon, didn't we?"

Chu nodded and punched the switch.

There was nothing but snow on the screen.

"What?" said Colonel Henderson, as Peter bulled past him for the door.

Outside, the temperature had shot up from its normal desert, blast-furnace intensity to something primal and terrifying. On the target hill, the fires were guttering out, hundreds of black plumes drifting into a single dark stratum.

Peter forced himself to look where the weapon had been.

There was a crater of twisted metal and intense flame. Nothing more.

He turned and saw Henderson puffing up toward him.

"Well," Peter muttered gruffly, "we might be able to sell it to the Polish army. Aim it at your enemy and blow your own head off."

"But you're close, dammit!" Henderson said with huge enthusiasm. "I mean, look at the targets."

He stared raptly at a smoking hillside that moments before had been teeming with animals.

"You know what went wrong?"

"The weapon exploded," said Peter.

Henderson was doggedly upbeat. "But you do know why?"

"Yes, I know why," said Peter angrily. "Because we rushed. Because we didn't test adequately. Because if we had pushed forward the deadline as we should have, it would have put us three million over budget. You refused. I thought we might get lucky. I guess not."

Henderson looked at the smoking pit where the weapon had stood.

"We have another one where that came from, don't we?"

"Half-built. Funding was stopped by your office, I believe."

Henderson's thick-featured face twisted into a grin. "That was before you atomized a full division at a kilometer and a half." He threw a large arm around Peter's bony shoulder. "If you think you've got an idea how to fix it, then by God you'll start up again on that second unit tomorrow morning."

"Only one problem with that," said Peter. "We're broke."

"I'll see to it you get your money, don't worry. All it takes is a phone call." Chuckling happily to himself, Henderson strode away, passing Beatrice, who was standing in the bunker doorway. "You oughta be damn proud of your hubby," Henderson told her as he went in.

"Oh, I am," said Beatrice, and gamely held out her arms to her husband, smiling as if Peter had just run a touchdown. She said something, and Peter tried his damnedest to hear what it was, but everything was being sucked into a black vortex deep inside his head, and the rushing sound drowned out every single word.

The next moment he fell as if pole-axed.

3

ST. MAURICE, SWITZERLAND

"Lizzy, I don't like seeing you like this. And I can't believe it's not affecting your work."

"The agency's happy—nobody's complaining," said Elizabeth, staring out over the water as the fall breeze riffled its surface. Winter was in the offing, and the poplars that framed the view of Lake Geneva had wrapped themselves in blood reds and rich gold—parchment-like leaves lofted over the table of the sidewalk café where Elizabeth Parker and Annie Rodino sat having a late lunch.

"I *do* like your hair though," said Annie.

"Do you? It's sort of betwixt." She dabbed at it obligingly. It was longer than it had been in months, and slowly recovering its natural blond color after a Lancôme-mandated foray into piano-key black. Had Hans ever seen her with black hair? She couldn't remember—all she could think of was the fact that she hadn't heard from him in two weeks, but had been having a weird feeling all afternoon that he was going to call and apologize. But he hadn't.

"This guy's bad for you," Annie declared. She was four inches shorter than Elizabeth and ten pounds heavier, with curly auburn hair, freckles and plump little hands that were constantly in motion.

Elizabeth nodded. "I know. Except sometimes I think he's the best thing that ever happened, too."

"You are not thinking straight."

"Granted," said Elizabeth tactfully. She knew Annie, her closest friend, liked to think of her as the vulnerable one and tortured one.

Normally Elizabeth found that ridiculous, but lately it seemed the shoe fit all too well. "I do need looking after, don't I?"

"What else is new," Annie said, sipping her Campari. In truth, the two friends had watched each other's back ever since meeting eight years ago in Paris. Six years before that, Elizabeth had lost her father to a massive coronary. Her mother fell apart, and her own wanderlust took over. She had forgone college for a European adventure. She met Annie in London her first week abroad, and within a week after that the two girls had become inseparable. They both found jobs in the thriving couture business—Elizabeth as a catalogue model, Annie as apprentice to a designer of sports clothing. Both had prospered, professionally and socially. Elizabeth had many suitors with attendant offers to settle down. But it was Annie who had married a droll Swiss investor named Roland, who had come to Milan to investigate what was by then Annie's own line of street-hip clothing.

Annie followed Roland back to Zurich, but the friends had kept in touch religiously, visiting each other as often as possible, especially— as had happened now, in Annie's sober opinion—when Elizabeth appeared to be veering off course.

"Lizzy," Annie said, between bites of her omelet, "the man is a known modelizer. You could be anybody, so long as you were drop-dead gorgeous. Which you are, you rat."

Elizabeth knew she was supposed to laugh, but she couldn't.

"I'm not sure," she said vaguely. "He says we were destined to meet."

Annie shot a look at her and laughed out loud.

"I'd laugh too except that's exactly how I felt," said Elizabeth.

"What you're destined to be is discarded," Annie said, shaking her finger like a mother to a child near a hot stove. "You want to hear my theory on why you're so susceptible? Your dad died when you were little, right?"

Here we go again, thought Elizabeth. "Eleven isn't so little."

"It's prepubescent, that is my point. You were madly in love with your father, and he died before you reached the age of rebellion—no, listen—and now you see men through rose-colored glasses—"

"Not men. *This* man."

"Not only that, but you were the apple of your father's eye. Didn't you once tell me that your mother was jealous of you? Said you'd never make it beyond Sears ads?"

"My mom was a pessimist. Parents worry—she never had any money herself, no career, no education—"

"With the brains you have, she should have made you go to college. Remember, you told me you wanted to be a doctor—that time you gave CPR on the yacht?"

"I wanted to be a doctor when I was six years old. Really, Annie, what's this about?"

"He's married," she said flatly. "Married men go back to their wives."

"He never left her. He's still tied to her. It's a business relationship."

"Lizzy," Annie groaned, "spare me."

Elizabeth sat forward in her chair. "All right, since we're doing Psych 101, try this on: Hans was a math whiz in college, okay? He wanted to be a great scientist—plasma physics, something like that. But he starts messing around in the stock market during graduate school, and soon he's made an absolute killing in technology issues. He quits school and goes into finances and rises like a rocket. But he's not really part of the old-money world he's gotten into. And then he meets this woman Yvette, who's connected and has a father in high finance. He compromises his heart a little and marries her. I mean, I'm not saying there wasn't an attraction there, originally, but—"

She broke off as the memory of their last time together flashed through her head. The lovemaking. The way he had so quickly left the bed afterward, staring scarily out the window as though someone were watching from the street below.

"I mean, Hans is a genius in his own way, just not the way he hoped to be. It's left him a little frustrated."

"Please."

"He wants to do good works. Deep down, I think, he's an environmentalist. He'll leave her, and then I'll be there." She tried a smile. Annie wasn't buying.

"Really, Lizzy—you believe that, I've got a great bridge I want to show you. You're making excuses for him, and you deserve so much more. You're a wonderful, bright, attractive, generous human be-ing—"

"Easy, my bullshit meter is redlining."

"You are. You've got an old soul and you're letting it be corrupted."

Elizabeth made a face. "This New Age streak in you sets my teeth on edge. If I have a choice here, I'll take your psychobabble over this stuff."

"I'll take that as a sign I've touched the truth," Annie said happily. "I think you've lived before—you were born wise. That's why this Hans thing doesn't make any sense, even to you."

Elizabeth threw up her hands in exasperation. "Okay, if you insist on talking gobbledygook, then if I'm an old soul, so is Hans, okay? It's probably why we connected. Great sex and old soulhood—a match made in heaven."

"You're crazy."

Elizabeth grinned, perfectly willing at the moment to accept that appraisal. "Isn't love supposed to be a little crazy?"

"A *little*. Let's say you're on the *Titanic* and you have a gin and tonic in your hand. The ice in the drink is a little. The ice in the iceberg coming at you dead ahead is *not* a little. See the difference?"

Elizabeth said nothing. Then a cell phone rang out at the table. Both women reached for their bags. "It's mine," said Elizabeth, adding hopefully, "it's Hans."

She flipped open her cellular. Right away she could hear he was in his car—and he was apologizing profusely, before she could get a word in. "I've been hellishly busy," he was saying. "Next week, I promise. We'll go up in the Learjet again. You loved that. Or out to the pistol range."

"No," said Elizabeth, with a look at Annie, who was giving her the sternest of looks.

"What do you mean, no?"

"I'm not going to see you again," said Elizabeth. Delighted, Annie pumped her fist in the air.

"What do you mean?"

"I don't know what I mean." It was the truth—she had spoken without thinking, and what had come out had sounded horribly final and wrong.

"You're worried about me. Don't be."

But in saying this, his words had just the opposite effect of what he intended. She immediately found herself worried big-time, wondering what it was *he* was worried about. "It's Yvette," he said, before she could ask aloud.

"What about Yvette?"

"I think maybe she's having me followed. Hey, if you're listening in," he said loudly, "I'm on to you people." And then he added, quickly, "I'm kidding, Elizabeth."

"Are you? It didn't sound like it."

"I didn't mean to burden you with this. It's just stupid paranoia."

She felt a chill sweep through her, and she found herself saying, "Hans, I think *I'm* the burden here. Take care, okay?"

"Elizabeth? I am sorry."

"Goodbye, Hans," she said, and snapped the phone shut.

Annie touched her hand, almost shyly, almost as if she didn't really mean for Elizabeth to have gone through with it.

"You okay?"

Elizabeth nodded. She looked around as her heart sank. The crowd at the café had thinned. It was near dusk and a mist was rising from the lake. Gulls and ducks splashed in for landings near moored boats and the last ferry was tying up at the quay. All at once Elizabeth wanted to be home.

"You did the right thing," said Annie.

"I know," she lied.

"You keep telling yourself that, okay?"

"Okay."

"Promise?"

"I promise," said Elizabeth. For the moment, she meant it and believed it. Fiercely. How long her resolve would last, though—years, months or minutes—she hadn't the faintest idea.

WHITE SANDS—THE FOUNTAIN COMPOUND

Outside the faceless sprawl of government buildings, a layer of snow lay on the mesquite bushes. The guards were zipping up their parkas and hunkering closer to the fires dancing out of the empty fifty-five-gallon drums scattered around the perimeter. There was more security today than the Fountain Compound had ever seen, and more vehicles—Humvees, Avis and Hertz four-wheel-drives, even a mud-encrusted Lincoln Town Car, as well as an Army Cobra helicopter, its plexiglass blister shrouded in protective canvas.

Inside the largest Fountain building, in the largest of the briefing rooms, Frederick Wolfe was holding court in lab whites, his spidery silhouette drifting in the twilight of flickering video images. Before him sat a half-dozen scientists of high rank and even higher clearance, and as many military officers, none of whom, save for Oscar Henderson, was in uniform.

"As we all know," Wolfe was saying, in a voice so calm, so devoid of emotion that it sent a chill through the room, "nothing can be achieved without the ability to reunify a severed spinal column. That's always been the barrier, impenetrable, unscalable. That's square one of what we need to accomplish—reversal of a complete transection of the human spine."

He directed his laser-pointer toward a high-resolution video screen, which showed an anesthetized white rat in clinical close-up. A quick incision laid open its shaved back, revealing the spine from tail to shoulders. Surgical scissors slipped beneath the white thread of nerve and bone, and the spine was unceremoniously snipped in two. Several of the men, including the battle-hardened, flinched audibly. Henderson's deep-set eyes lit up in anticipation.

Nearby, Beatrice Jance watched from the shadows, every muscle frozen. She neither looked away nor winced, despite the pitiful spurt of blood and fluid. In her five decades as a neuroscientist, she had seen far worse. What shone in Beatrice's eyes was different from the visiting officers' revulsion or Henderson's unseemly rapture. It was of such preternatural intensity that under more ordinary circumstances and in a lighted room it would have turned every head. But no one was looking at Beatrice; all eyes were on the screen.

"Admittedly, our methods were crude at first," Wolfe went on. "But the fact is that *any* attempt at reconnection until quite recently was both crude *and* in vain."

He gestured toward his grandson, Alex, seated at a bank of computers and image generators linked to the screen. Alex punched his keyboard and the picture switched to a microscopic shot of the severed spine, the cut end tipped toward the camera.

"Even a small mammal's spine is composed of an immensely delicate and complicated network of bone, fluid, membrane and nerve bundles. Worse, once cut, the spine tends to self-destruct around the breach, compounding the problem. It's as if nature is programmed to finish the job and put the individual down permanently, to save an unnecessary burden on the species."

The observers watched—each according to his own threshold of queasiness—while a series of shots showed increasingly complex attempts to rejoin the severed ends of various lab animals' spines. It was a wretched parade of suture and wire splices that invariably rendered the creatures twitching and incapacitated. Henderson's eyes never left the monitors. Something big was in the air, and he was waiting for it with unabashed attention.

"But then," announced Wolfe, pausing for effect, "we had a breakthrough. Building on work begun in Sweden at the Karolinska Institute, we were able to remove a full quarter inch from the spines of our rats, then use nerve fibers from their chests to bridge the gap."

"Why nerves from the chest?" one of the officers asked, in a voice so faint Henderson had to repeat the question.

"Any place but from the spine, actually, would have worked as well," replied Wolfe. "It's just that the chest fibers were longer. The essential point is, only spinal nerve fibers self-destruct when injured. Those from other parts of the body tend to grow back. For instance, if an arm is cleanly severed, it can be sewn back on and the nerves will regenerate. But until we postulated it," he went on, letting his eyes come to rest on Beatrice, "no one had dreamed of using nonspinal nerve fibers to rebind a severed spine. When we tried it, we found the fibers did indeed bridge the cut in the spine. Not always, and not perfectly, but they definitely did so with a remarkable amount of regularity, and for the first time in medical history we were getting movement from animals in their hindquarters *after* their spines had been severed. Alex?"

Alex punched more keys.

"Subsequently we moved up to rabbits," said Wolfe, "hoping the larger operating areas would make our attempts easier . . ."

A murmur of disappointment rose from the front row. The screen was showing only a procession of dead animals.

"All ended up nonviable," said Wolfe, relishing the emotional effect his chalk-talk, carefully planned and even more carefully rehearsed, was having on these military yahoos. "The increased complexity of their neurology actually worked against us."

Henderson noisily cleared his throat. "If you can't do a bloody rabbit, how can you expect us to fund a project that—"

He broke off, silenced by Wolfe's pointing finger, indicating the screen.

There was something new there now. One rabbit had finally managed to struggle to its feet. The hapless creature wasn't really hopping, but it wasn't dragging itself either. It sort of lumbered, like a little furry Frankenstein.

"Eventually, after much trial and error," Wolfe continued, his voice rising just perceptibly, "we finally were successful in these more complex animals, to the extent that there was not only a lack of mortality but partial recovery as well." He smiled thinly. "We don't usually name our animals, but we called this one Duracell."

From the labcoats, predictably, came a small burst of laughter, but Henderson didn't crack a smile, and the rest of the brass followed his lead.

"Obviously," said Wolfe, somewhat hurriedly, "we had to move on to something even more complex." At this, Alex keyed his control panel and the screen bloomed with the sight of the lively pig Beatrice had witnessed trying to make its escape. There was a lariat around its neck now, held by the grinning wrangler, Perkins.

"We found working on larger animals brought us a certain advantage," Wolfe declared. "Despite the fact that the spinal architecture of pigs is an order of magnitude more complicated—the axons and dendrites are made up of several million interwoven nerve fibers—their increased size makes them easier to see and thus easier to splice."

Henderson was nodding slowly now, as if to indicate to the other honchos his grasp of Wolfe's presentation. What fools these mortals be, thought Wolfe, and lowered his voice dramatically. "But we still were looking at only partial recovery using nerve fibers from other parts of the body. What we needed was a way to fuse the spine back together, original submicroscopic element to original submicroscopic element." And with this he turned to the only woman present—Beatrice. "This is when my colleague, Dr. Beatrice Jance, lent her astonishing discovery—one of truly Nobel Prize caliber."

Henderson heaved a sigh. "Hopefully," he said, "we can cut to the chase and find out what that was?"

Beatrice stood. The men all turned their eyes to her. Wolfe smiled. She was regal; she stopped them in their impatient tracks, she had such presence.

"Beatrice, I'm sure, can explain it much better than I," he said. Beatrice crossed to the screen, with the barest glance at Henderson, who sat up straighter. Inwardly, Wolfe smiled.

"You'll like this news, Colonels," he said. "You might even get a star out of it."

Henderson acted like he didn't hear.

"This is what I've discovered," Beatrice began, in a voice so full of dignity, gravity and downright drama that fully half the onlookers edged forward in their seats. "During postoperative autopsies on higher animals in which spinal breaches had been effected, the subjects were actually mounting attempts at healing the wounds, attempts specific to and emanating from the spinal columns themselves."

"What kind of attempts?" Henderson asked guardedly.

"Secretions," said Beatrice. "Of hitherto unnoticed and unidentified enzymes and trace DNA materials, which at submicroscopic levels had begun a discernible repair process."

"Repair, as in healing?"

"Square one type healing," Wolfe confirmed.

"Are you trying to tell us," asked Henderson, "that if left to its own devices a spine will heal itself?"

"Certainly not," said Beatrice. "This substance deals only with minor spinal perturbations. It's equivalent, say, to a mechanic fixing a scratch, not replacing a smashed fender."

Henderson liked the way she talked. He could understand her. "So, a sprain or something—it might fix that?"

"Exactly," said Beatrice. "Things on the microscopic level. Not of use to us as it is. But what we guessed was that it might be an evolutionary precursor."

"English?"

"An early version, if you will, of something that could be much more powerful if its evolution were to develop."

"What sort of thing?"

"Spinal Krazy Glue?" asked Henderson.

There was nervous laughter, but Beatrice went with it, smiling and treating Henderson like the brightest kid in the class. "That's a wonderful comparison," she said. "A sort of DNA glue. But that makes it very *smart* glue. One that's part and parcel of the spine, has a copy of the spine's unique DNA blueprint within its own composition, and is designed by nature to help the spine return to normal. It's just so relatively weak, so preliminary in evolutionary development, no one's noticed it until now. Probably because no one's thought to look for it."

"Maybe," said Colonel Henderson, "because no one's had the resources you people have had."

"It'll be all worth your while, believe me," Wolfe assured him. "Beatrice's breakthrough has been not only to discover the bonding agent, but to synthesize and amplify it as well."

Henderson blinked. The ramifications of where this was leading were suddenly electric in the air.

"We've been able," said Beatrice, "to take our genetic glue, if you will, paint the ends of severed spinal cords with it, and effect a bond."

"A bond," said Henderson carefully. "As in a total rejoining?"

"It appears so," said Beatrice, nearly inaudible.

A flurry of excited whispers swept through the room. Wolfe stepped back to the podium, standing next to Beatrice. "Our glue is actually a two-function material. First, it's a DNA binding agent, but secondly and vastly more important, it's a neural catalyst."

Beatrice saw the blank looks and jumped in. "It causes severed nerves and synapses to find each other and rejoin themselves—on the submicroscopic level where no surgeon could see, and throughout a network of millions of dendrites—completely beyond any ability on our part to physically accomplish it."

Henderson inched forward in his seat. "This is hot shit," he said. "If it's true."

"It is. And I'm glad you appreciate it, Colonel," said Wolfe dryly. "In effect, we've jump-started a repair process nature might have taken another million years to complete—a natural substance to heal cut neural pathways." To keep Henderson off balance, where he belonged, Wolfe shifted back into silver-tongued mode. "As a matter of fact, Colonel, here's where your clearing away the usual protocol restrictions was particularly helpful."

That was Alex Davies's cue, and in the next instant an extreme close-up of a spinal column appeared on the screen. It was surgically draped, bathed in disinfectant orange, with the skin peeled back on both sides, revealing raw bone and a red and white striation of muscle and rib. As Henderson watched, with a smile of prurient disbelief, the shining beak of a powerful cutting instrument was forced into the tissue next to the spine, then pushed down and under. Hands blotted away the surge of blood, and the upper blade of the instrument came to rest directly over the spine.

"This was the first of the ten subjects the agency supplied," Wolfe said, with a nod at Henderson. "The cut was made at the level of the supraclavicular notch between vertebrae C1 and C2, just below the brain stem itself. Except for the cord and its attendant meninges, the cut involved only the left and right vertebral arteries."

Two pairs of forceps now entered the frame right and left and clamped both arteries top and bottom. In the briefing room, nobody moved a muscle.

"The cut was surgically uncomplicated," said Wolfe, as the instrument's blade hinged down, passing coldly between two vertebrae and cutting through the spinal cord itself. This time the blood and spinal fluids were copious, but Wolfe's voice disclosed not a trace of feeling; he could have been narrating a video about opening a telephone cable. Nearly all the military men shut their eyes, or looked away entirely. Henderson's eyes, however, stayed riveted to the screen, which now was showing, in an even closer shot, the severed stump in cross-section.

"At this evolutionary level," said Wolfe calmly, "we are of course dealing with a system of enormous complexity. Not only do we have a full array of both white and gray matter, but an estimated complex of twenty million nerve fibers. Needless to say, nothing like this had ever been attempted."

And with that, the shot suddenly widened. Now they could see the entire operating theater onscreen, could see Wolfe in full scrubs, along with nearly two dozen other medical personnel, neurosurgeons, anesthesiologists, cardiac-bypass specialists, nurses, as well as several Army officers in uniform. And one other thing was now abundantly clear. The subject of this particular experiment was no lower animal.

It was a human.

Instantly Henderson was on his feet. *"Christ,"* he screamed. "Who the hell authorized photographing faces—what the hell were you *thinking!"*

Just as abruptly the video cut back to extreme close-up. "Colonel Henderson, calm yourself please," said Wolfe. "This is a rough cut and in-house only."

"Wolfe, I want that master tape!"

"The master tape is secure," Wolfe assured him, and the room fell silent again, this time with the ice-cold realization that with that simple statement the center of power had shifted, and it was Wolfe who was the one in control here, not Henderson. God knew where the original tape was, but it put an overwhelmingly powerful trump card in Wolfe's hand. He looked at Henderson without a trace of guile.

"Do you want this to happen or not?"

The question hung in the air.

Quietly, Henderson sat down again. "How far along are you?" he asked quietly.

Alex, watching like a hawk, punched a button and the video footage switched to a new shot, showing an unshaven, gray-faced man on a hospital bed, his torso swathed in bandages. Wolfe and several other labcoats stood beside, urging him to move. The man moved one leg, then the other. The efforts were spastic and weak, but visible.

"That was Subject Five," declared Wolfe.

The video jumped to another subject—this one thinner still, but sitting up on the edge of the bed. Onscreen Wolfe was seen whispering in his ear, and the subject tried to stand. He couldn't, and fell weakly. He was caught by hospital aides, while Wolfe strode away.

"Number Six nearly stood," he said to the room, "but unfortunately he died the next day. But Number Seven was where we started to see real results."

The new segment showed a new man, this one swathed in bandages at the waist, standing successfully, his smile a rictus, his eyes wavering between hope and stark terror. Like all the other experimental subjects, he was Middle Eastern, with a pale, sunken look that hinted at long imprisonment.

Beatrice, who had returned to her seat, studied the screen with a grim, conflicted look. A rank sense of trespass hovered in the room— was she the only one registering it? No, Alex Davies seemed to be affected as well—she noticed his hand was shaking so badly that he miscued a cut between video segments and had to rekey it.

"*Rashid al-Assad,*" Beatrice heard him say under his breath, in an awed, knowledgeable whisper. He knows their names, he knows their histories, Beatrice realized. She was astonished. And chilled.

"By Subject Nine," Wolfe continued, after a silencing glance in Alex's direction, "using material gathered from the spines of previous subjects and combined with synthetic materials, our DNA glue allowed us to achieve our first standee."

Alex punched the right keys this time and the video froze.

"And how's he doing?" asked Henderson.

Wolfe raised one bony shoulder in a half-shrug. "He lasted five days, then unfortunately the splice failed."

"Jesus God," said Henderson.

"Due to scheduling exigencies, we perhaps rushed him onto his feet," said Wolfe. "But it's clear the procedure is workable."

Henderson cut a glance at Beatrice, then turned back to Wolfe.

"Are you one hundred percent sure?"

Wolfe took a cigarette from a pack in his pocket. "What I'm a hundred percent sure of," he said, lighting up as he flicked a look at Beatrice, "is our obligation to try. The fact is," he added, shaking out the match, "I believe we will soon be welcoming our first inductee into the Society."

"*How* soon?"

"Weeks. Maybe less."

"Unfortunately," he added, "we're out of human specimens, not to mention time. That's where we need your help."

Henderson flared. "You think terrorists grow on trees?"

Wolfe stared back at him. "It is too late to care whether they do or do not," he said quietly. "The question you must answer for me now is this: do you think scientists like Peter Jance grow on trees?"

Hans Brinkman was in a foul mood.

To begin with, he was playing hooky, and the fact that he couldn't manage to forget it enraged him. A man of his stature—he ought to be able to take a morning off now and then, go a few rounds at the club without suffering pangs of anxiety about how many people would be screwing up during his absence.

And they *will* screw up, he thought.

He climbed into the ring, ignoring the attention he was attracting. The Sportklub was one of the most expensive in Switzerland, as well as one of the most exclusive—without proper sponsorship (in Hans's case, his father-in-law), you stood a better chance of winning the lottery. The downside to exclusivity, of course, was a certain inbred organic weakness, a tendency toward paunchiness and the early triple bypass—among these tired aging buffalos, Hans Brinkman stood out like a fierce young lion.

A tormented lion, however. He couldn't get Elizabeth out of his head. Or the equally disquieting sense that had been haunting him for the last forty-eight hours, an almost palpable feeling that he had taken a colossal wrong turn, and was destined to pay for this mistake with his life. It was the craziest of thoughts, he knew, but the amount of credibility he was giving it nonetheless infuriated him. Not that he was afraid of death, but he was terrified of losing control.

He didn't like things he couldn't control, including himself. And feeling less than in control of his emotions was entirely unacceptable.

Then there was the sense that people were watching him, not just these bloated idiots in the gym, praying for his sparring partner to cream him with a sucker punch. But people on the street, in cafés, in cars, even outside his chalet this morning. He was convinced someone was *studying* him, and that meant one of two things: either his wife, Yvette, *was* having him shadowed, as he lightly suggested to Elizabeth, or he was now entering the crooked corridors of paranoia, projecting his own self-doubts on randomly chosen strangers.

He tried to put it all out of his mind. He watched the man across the ring, a banking executive five years his junior.

"Set?"

"Sure."

He circled catlike, jabbing and dodging, feinting once, twice, then following up with a wicked left hook that stopped the poor bastard in his tracks. As his opponent staggered sideways, Hans brought up his right and punched the man into the ropes. He danced forward—the man threw up his gloves in terror.

"Okay!" he cried sharply. "You win—Jesus!"

Hans danced away, slashing the air with furious rights and lefts, his feet a blur. He was barely sweating; the other man was drenched and shaking.

"Maybe golf next time?" Hans said casually.

"Maybe not," said the banker. "You'll have a club in your hands then and you'll be twice as dangerous."

Hans shrugged, and then his cell phone began ringing. Vaulting the ropes, he had it on the second ring. Almost immediately he swore in rage, tearing off his gloves and flinging them down.

"What are you, a trainee?" he barked into the phone. "Sell it all. I told you The Hague wouldn't enforce it!" Whoever was on the other end became the recipient of a stream of invective that brought the gym to a standstill.

Then Hans Brinkman was gone, leaving a knowing silence in his wake. The unfortunate caller was going to have a new asshole reamed for him, and Hans Brinkman was so mad he was going to do it in person.

From his Porsche Carrera, en route to the chalet in Monthey, he called the airport and alerted his flight crew to ready the Learjet. But as soon as he hung up, he was swept anew by the feeling of death stalking him. It felt like nonsense when he parsed it sensibly, but it was so overwhelming a feeling, he rationalized that it wouldn't do to fly when he was this angry or this distracted. Having flown his own jet for more than five years he had his share of near-misses when in a mood this black. He called back and canceled the plane.

A good long drive through the mountains, maybe that would flush all this out of his system.

As he pulled into the driveway of the chalet he saw the cream Bentley parked in one of the four garages. Yvette, the last person he wanted to see at the moment, was home from one of her interminable lunches.

At the terrace he paused, still reluctant to encounter her, and gazed over the railing as if for the first time. At 2,500 meters, the view was unobstructed all the way down to Lake Geneva, twenty kilometers to the northwest. The rugged peaks of the Alps, sprinkled with hamlets, spires and cascading streams, cut sharply into the sky. Hans realized that usually he witnessed this immense beauty while he was fuming into a cell phone; he could have been in a lead cubicle for all the view was worth.

Now he realized its majesty. He realized, too, he'd miss it if he didn't have it.

He crossed past the Olympic-sized pool and into the bedroom, tossing an order out to a maid who was cleaning the mirrors. She scurried to the closet, hauled down a suitcase and began to pack for him. He pulled off his sport clothes and threw on a suit and tie, selecting a dove-gray Schiaparelli double-breasted suit he'd had custom-made in Paris, and matching it with hand-crafted loafers from Cleverly in Royal Arcade, London.

Give all this up? Who was he kidding?

By the time he was dressed, the maid had shut the suitcase. He was turning to leave when Yvette rushed into the room and stopped dead in her tracks.

"Pas encore?" she said, with gentle irritation. She had lustrous dark collagened lips, and wore enough gold jewelry to finance a revolution. "Who screwed up this time, darling?"

"The Zurich branch. I'm going to fire the lot of them."

"What about the Taverniers' party?"

"You'll be fine," he said. "They're more your friends than mine."

She gave a tight laugh. "Small wonder—you're never here. When can we expect you back?"

I loved her once, he thought. And now she's got private detectives. "Sunday, late."

And then he thought, Sunday, oh Jesus. Elizabeth.

He had planned to call her back, apologize for standing her up, even reshuffle his schedule if need be. Her last goodbye had been so abrupt, so final. I'll call her from the road, Hans thought, avoiding Yvette, who scrutinized him sadly from the other side of the bed.

"Lose something?" she asked.

My goddamn sanity, Hans thought, visions of Elizabeth racing through his brain—every particular precious detail—her body in all its mystery, her sweet face and silky hair, the heartbreaking sound she gave each time he entered her, her secret gravity, the soft pale down on her belly, her flashes of sardonic humor, her clear gray eyes—

He forced himself to stop thinking about her. Thought about the details of getting the hell out of there. Okay, so where was his wallet— in his other pants, where else would it be? Now came the question of the car. He debated taking his '37 Lagonda Rapide, an automotive jewel he had recently purchased from Coys, in Kensington, but took the keys to the BMW 750il instead—he needed speed and reliability for this run. Besides, in his agitated state, if the Rapide broke down during this particular trip, as it was wont to do, he just might torch it on the spot, which would be a shame, since it had cost $500,000.

Face it, he thought, as the BMW took the first curve outside the chalet gate and Yvette's face vanished from the bedroom window above, you *need* Elizabeth. You crave her like a junkie craves his fix. You've been trying to kick her for months, but you know in your heart you're scared shitless of losing her. Call her from Zurich, in the middle of a board meeting, and if you have to, tell her some goddamn lie she might appreciate.

Or tell her the truth, he thought abruptly. Tell her you've decided to change your life.

BETHESDA NAVAL HOSPITAL, MARYLAND

Something deep inside Peter shook him, a white-hot rage and fear and urgency. Waking with a start, he found his wife leaning over him. Next he became aware of the tubes in his arms, the monitoring sensors pasted to his chest. And the terrible ache in his belly.

"Peter?" said Beatrice.

He struggled to sit up, and found he had no strength at all. He fell back and stared at her.

"Where the hell am I?"

"Bethesda," Beatrice said, scowling at him as if she had caught him smoking in bed.

"What?" he croaked. "What's the matter?"

"We've got to talk."

Peter looked slowly around, as though expecting to see the walls of the bunker, everyone walking out after the blast. "Is the team all right?"

"Everyone's fine," she said, in a small voice.

"But what? We lose our funding? Henderson say 'I told you so'?"

She shook her head, fighting back tears, and took his hand. For a moment she seemed unable to speak.

"Tell me," he said. "I can take it."

"Peter, it's not looking good right now for us."

"You're leaving me?" he asked, noting the hospital room was rotating slowly without actually moving. What a neat trick, he thought, and one that might serve as an atomic paradigm of some sort.

"Peter," said Beatrice sharply. "Be serious."

"I am being serious," he said. "Actually, I was thinking of spin momentum—"

"You're dying," she said.

Peter said nothing. Was that all she had to tell him?

"Did you hear what I said?"

"I'm dying. Yes, I know. Aren't we all?"

"But you're dying a hell of a lot faster, you stubborn old fart. Stop playing games with me."

"All right," said Peter. The pain in his gut was making it difficult to speak. He tried to smile. "I gather," he said, with forced mischief, "you've been talking to those quacks again."

Beatrice closed her eyes briefly, then opened them. "Even a first-year medical student could figure this one out. It's metastatic. It's in your liver and your marrow."

"And God knows where else."

She gripped his hand.

"Peter, there's a *chance*. There's a possible solution."

He fixed his eyes on the slowly moving ceiling, counting the rows of perforations in the acoustical tile. "And just what might that be?"

Beatrice looked in her lap. "Frederick thinks we're ready at our end."

"*Ready?* Ready for what?"

He could see she was steeling herself, choosing her words, fending off confusion and conflict. In a crisis, this was her way. "Henderson likes what he saw on the testing range. So do the other brass."

"Yes, I know what Henderson likes."

"They're more excited than ever."

"About the weapon."

He heard her teeth click together.

"About *you*. Your longevity."

"I'm delighted for them. And what miracle has Wolfe got up his sleeve?"

"So you do know. You know it's Freddy."

"It's always Freddy. Tell me, Beatrice, stop beating around the bush."

And so she began to talk. For a while he couldn't be sure he hadn't slipped into a nightmare. The difference was that when a dream became too stressful, he had developed long ago the knack of waking himself from it. But there was waking up from this one. Beatrice was going on and on, in a pseudo-confident drone that reminded him of nothing so much as Frederick Wolfe himself. And the fact was, Wolfe *had* told her exactly what to say, prepped her so thoroughly that she scarcely had to think. The more she said, the calmer she forced her voice to become. The problem was, the horror of what she was saying juxtaposed with this bogus calm made Peter's head feel like it would explode.

"God in heaven," he heard himself say. How long had she been sitting there beside him? The light outside the window was now a dismal gray.

"Peter, you must have guessed what was going on."

"Never," he insisted wanly.

"My research? I know you've lost interest in the past year, but come on—you knew the implications. What did you think was going on here? And in the Caribbean? The fertility clinic Freddy used to run. Did you think he was involved in it out of the goodness of his heart?"

"Why not."

"Don't tell me it never crossed your mind. What this was all about?"

"Of course it crossed my mind. There's nothing I'd put past Freddy. I just didn't think—"

"*What?* What didn't you think?"

"That the technology was there," he said hopelessly. "That it would ever be."

"Well, it's there. It's here. And here *we* are."

He felt the little strength he had left trickling away. "You're right," he admitted. "I turned a blind eye."

Beatrice folded her hands patiently. "Whether you like it or not," she said, with the barest edge of regret, "you're a charter member."

"Charter member! What is this, Cooperstown? Does Wolfe think he's running a country club? Charter member of what?"

"The Society."

"Typical of Wolfe—tricking it up with euphemistic bullshit—"

She took his hand—her own was shaking. "They had to call the subjects something. The Fountain Society, you know, for the Fountain of—"

"Beatrice, please, I'm ill, not stupid."

"I'm sorry. Don't get testy. Please."

"God, Beatrice, doesn't this appall you?"

"Of course it appalls me. I never thought it would come to this, but it has. And we did discuss it, you just don't remember."

"We did *not* discuss it."

"When I had that blood dyscrasia scare? The thrombocytosis? And the hydroxyurea wasn't working?"

"That was a thought experiment," said Peter.

She was a marvel of persistence. "And what did we conclude?"

He knew, but he couldn't bring himself to face it. "This is different," he said. "This is monstrous."

"Why? *Why* is it different? You agreed—a necessary evil. A wretched Hobson's choice. That's the best life offers sometimes. And this is one of those times."

Peter gazed toward the darkening window. Now he thought he saw smoke drifting. Maybe it was his dreams. Burning. Maybe it was his life turning into ashes.

"Peter, please! There isn't any time. There's even less than you know."

"That's hardly the point."

"It is *precisely* the point."

"And what about my work, come to think of it? What the hell was that all about? Building something to vaporize whoever displeased people like Henderson? God help us. This disease, Beatrice—maybe it was meant to happen—"

"Oh, for God's sakes, Peter, listen to yourself—"

"Maybe I did it to myself. Maybe it's a punishment."

"From where? On high? For what? For doing what you were born to do? A Thousand Year Peace, Peter, that's what the Army's talking about, that's what they think the Hammer can bring—"

"Oh, really? They're ready to put themselves out of business? Now who's turning a blind eye?"

She flared. "Then for me, all right? If not for yourself. You bastard!" she cried, and suddenly she was weeping, the tears welling up through her rage. Peter gazed at her and saw the terror, and the stark, wholesale love. He shut his eyes—her emotion was too intense, too evocative. If he was about to die—and there was no doubt about that, no doubt whatsoever—his entire life should be flashing before him. But it wasn't. What came surging up in his vision was *their* life together. The love, the houses, the beds, the laboratories, the gritty determination to make it work, the very length of it. Scarred and sinewy and *there*. All this was about to vanish.

But it couldn't be salvaged at a cost like this.

"No," he heard himself say. "Not even for you."

After he said it, he thought that at least he might feel better. He rolled over and waited for something. Deliverance, perhaps. Instead, he found that he merely rolled over into more pain.

By the next night, he felt himself sliding, driven down a slick decline by a cold wind. He became increasingly aware of something huge and black gaping before him, sucking him toward an oblivion that was terrifying in its completeness. The pain was now incredibly intense—beyond anything they could give him to quiet it.

It had been less than twenty-four hours since he had declared his adamant refusal to Beatrice, and yet it seemed like ages. The pain was time's elasticizer and reagent. It stretched seconds to centuries and stoked his fear. Suddenly he felt everything he had believed with all his heart slipping away, leaving him with only a raw desire to be delivered from his torment at any cost. Everything else was revealed in the white-hot light of this impulse as idiocy, or, worse, as hateful threat. He tried to rise back to the level of his own humanity, but it was like trying to crawl naked up a frigid, mossy waterfall. To his utter surprise, he only wanted to live.

When he opened his eyes, there was Beatrice, sitting by his bed. He reached out his hand, felt her take it, and for the moment he felt anchored. She had read his thoughts, and she was there to answer his prayers. The warmth of her flesh made him feel the cold of his own even more keenly. He shut his eyes as a sudden, even more brutal pain swept over him and the breath stopped in his throat. He felt his heart racing like a horse trapped in a burning barn, and he heard himself sealing his own fate.

"God save us all, Beatrice. I'll do whatever you say."

She took in her breath in a sudden expression of relief. He in turn was filled now with a sense of panic; he was already afraid it was too late. And the pain had become unbearable.

"I need a morphine drip," he said hoarsely.

"Peter. Thank you."

Her eyes were already tearing up as she turned toward the corridor: Frederick Wolfe was already there, a spectral shadow in the doorway. How long had he been hovering, so near he knew the instant Peter had relented? Beatrice gave him a nod and Wolfe clattered off down the hall, shouting names. Almost immediately there were running feet and muffled voices, then myriad shapes hovering over him like so many angels of death, and with a sense of incredible excitement and relief he felt the needle enter his arm. The last things he saw were these: Beatrice with her hand clutched to her face, shaking with sobs, and Wolfe's pale form beside her, long fingers tented as in prayer, black eyes gleaming over a triumphant smile.

Then the world went out like a light.

JURA MOUNTAINS, SWITZERLAND

A hundred kilometers outside Bern, on his way to Zurich, Hans was still obsessing about Elizabeth. To ease the ache, or at least to give it a more pleasing shape, he put on a CD of *Kind of Blue,* the Miles Davis session from the late 1950s, with Coltrane and Bill Evans and a handful of other players who got it so right it never failed to improve his mood. Elizabeth had introduced him to the album, sweetly asking his permission one Saturday to play it while they were making love. At the time, he had rudely assumed that she was trying to take charge of their lovemaking. Only now was he coming to realize that she was searching, perhaps unconsciously, for some way to distract him from his own selfish pleasure and thereby prolong hers. God, he thought, she's put up with so much crap from me.

And she's good for you. Wasn't that what this music was telling him? Every riff brought back sensations of touch and smell and texture, small shimmering reminders of their afternoon delights. He turned it up loud and rolled back the sunroof.

It occurred to him that perhaps he'd fallen in love.

Instantly a part of him railed against the thought. Let's not get carried away.

Then think of a better word, he countered to that voice. And there was silence.

No way am I going to ditch this woman, he thought fiercely. On the contrary, we're going to see more of each other. Nights as well as days, weekdays as well as weekends, and Yvette's suspicions be damned. We're meant to tough this out—fated to, and they both knew it. He had a sudden impulse to simply find Elizabeth and keep driving, change his name, grow a beard and disappear with her to Bora Bora.

He pressed down on the accelerator. The big twelve-cylinder engine responded effortlessly and the car shot up into one of the winding passes of the Juras. He was filled with love even for these mountains. He realized that as far back as grade school, geology had been one of his passions, and he'd found no place better to indulge that love than in these dark namesakes of the Jurassic, an awesome labyrinth of stone, firs and cascades seldom driven at this early hour. Roaring now through the ancient cuts, he drifted back in time to the shallow seas and emerging life-forms that had lent their remains to these heights.

I should have become a paleontologist, he thought. Anything but what I did. He looked out through the window, and once again felt calm, suspended in a prehistoric vastness that dwarfed his petty concerns. He could feel the ancient oceans roiling as tectonic upthrusts buckled them skyward into the peaks now soaring about him.

I should drive this road sometime with Elizabeth, he mused. She probably loves these mountains, too. Those times I took her flying—those were some of the best moments we ever spent together—banking over snow-capped peaks, wondering at the majesty. Jesus, were there any bad moments? Right now he couldn't recall a single one.

Call her, you coldhearted idiot. Tell her how you feel before you *forget* how to feel.

He racked his brain for her number. As soon as he'd had the sense he was being followed—that Yvette had hired PIs—he'd taken Elizabeth's number off all his speed dials. He called two wrong numbers before remembering the right one, and then the mountains bedeviled the connection. Static, dead line. He kept trying, time after time. He was about to give up when he heard her voice, faint and forlorn and hopeful.

"Hello? *Hello?*"

"Elizabeth? It's me."

"*Hans?* You're breaking up. Where are you?"

"On my way to Zurich. It's the mountains, I keep losing you, I'm going to talk fast, okay? I want us to be together. Did you hear that?"

Static. Then, "Yes. Yes, I heard it."

"You don't believe it. I know. It's true. I want to find a way to make it work, and the hell with Yvette and everything else, okay? Elizabeth?"

"I don't know what to say."

"Say yes. Say you want to be with me, and then we're unstoppable. *Do* you? Please."

An agonizing pause. "Yes. Yes, I do."

"I know I've been a complete asshole—"

"Nobody's perfect. Hans, I've been so afraid—"

"Of what?"

"Of what? Of what you told me—people listening in—what if someone's listening in right now—they could be—"

Hans didn't hear the rest. He'd just topped a curving rise and a huge black van loomed in his windshield, stopped sideways across the bulk of the narrow road, its hood raised.

"Christ!"

"*Hans?*"

He braked hard and the BMW dug in, but he was too late. He was going to ram right in front of it for good measure. The man, who'd been peering into the motor, jerked up in horror as Hans swore and wrenched the wheel toward the precipice—an act he never would have considered before—but Jesus, it was the only way to avoid killing the poor bastard. The 750 hit the galvanized steel of the guardrail hard, careening off and across the roadway in a shrieking spin. Going downhill now, it struck the mountain face like a thunderbolt, glass shattering and chrome flying in crazy arcs. All his airbags deployed in a blast of rubber, gunpowder and cornstarch desiccant. Temporarily deafened, he thought he was safe now. Then a split second later the wind tore the bag away and the car was heading straight back for the rail.

This time he struck dead-on and the guardrail ruptured, leaving only the yawning chasm below. But it had taken the last of his momentum, and it was there that Hans's battered BMW came to rest, teetering on the brink of the road's cut with fifteen hundred feet of thin Alpine air falling away beneath him. Only a shift in weight stood between him and two and a half kilometers of Jurassic stone two thousand feet below.

He was too dazed, too shaken to understand his peril, and he moved, feeling his head to see if it was still there. Then he heard the shout.

"Don't move! Christ!"

The cry cleared his mind just enough for him to realize he was literally on a vehicular seesaw. The man from the van was running toward him. Hans leaned back in the seat and felt the rear wheels of the car settle back onto the road. He tried to open his door, but it was jammed solid.

"What the hell were you doing across the road like that?" he roared, furious. The man from the van raised his hands in a calming gesture.

"Just take it easy, buddy—easy!"

He realized that the car was tipping back toward the abyss.

Hans froze, staring through the windshield as the view tilted chillingly down. Then there was a thump and the car settled back, horizontal once more. Hans glanced over his shoulder and saw that a second man had leapt onto the trunk of his car, and a third was racing to join him. The van driver was at his window, urging him out.

"Just come right out the window—it's all right now, fellah!"

American accent. He should have known—the bloody tourists and

their goddamn van. He practically dove through the window—with
the van driver helping to pull him out and onto his feet. Hans swiveled
to confront him and felt a sharp sting in his arm.

He jerked back in confusion, thinking for a moment he had caught
his arm on a jagged piece of steel. But he was clear of the car. It had
come from something the man was holding in his hand—a small dark
device with a trigger and a needle.

"What the hell you think you're doing?" cried Hans, intending to
scream at them but hearing his voice come out as a slurred grunt instead.

Then everything went black.

The three men moved swiftly, an experienced, well-rehearsed
team.

"Close one," the van driver grunted as he lifted Hans's feet, eyeing
the car at the edge of the abyss. One of the others nodded as he
grabbed Hans's shoulders.

"Who knew he'd be going so fucking *fast*? Jesus!"

Within a minute they had him in the back of the van, stripped of
his clothes, while a fourth man, naked and handcuffed, watched in
stark terror. He was roughly Hans's age, the same height and sandy
hair, though his pallor suggested he had done considerable time in
prison. He was praying to himself in Russian.

The other men freed him from the cuffs, ordering him at gunpoint·
to put on Hans's clothes. The Russian was shaking, obviously not
knowing what the hell was going on but smart enough to know it was
not good. Like Hans, his body was in fine youthful shape. But his face,
with its absence of teeth that had been knocked out by an Israeli hammer, looked oddly senile.

As soon as the men had dressed him in Hans's clothing, matters became simple. They bludgeoned him to the ground, carried him to the
car and threw him through the side window into the driver's seat. One
of the men emptied five gallons of high-octane gasoline over the unconscious Russian and the car's interior, then threw a match.

There was a guttural orange explosion, and the two other men
jumped off the rear bumper.

Gravity did the rest. The car tipped forward, then slid off the brink and fell, turning slowly for nearly five seconds before it struck an out-cropping. At the impact, the gas tank exploded, and the vehicle be-came a comet of fire and twisted steel. By the time it came to rest far, far below, the van had vanished from the road above.

Within two hours, Hans Brinkman, now on an IV drip to induce coma, was aboard a specially outfitted gray C-20, the military version of the Gulfstream III executive jet. With a maximum speed of 576 miles per hour and a range of over four thousand nautical miles, the craft was ideally suited to this mission. It was registered to Air West, a front corporation owned by the National Security Agency. The req-uisition came through such a filter of organizations within the secret hierarchy of American intelligence that the flight was rendered effec-tively nonexistent.

Hans was monitored by Dr. Emilio Barrola, sixty-five, a specialist in neurosurgery handpicked by Frederick Wolfe. Barrola was six foot two, with green eyes and flaring nostrils, dark flowing hair and the powerful hands and long graceful fingers of a concert pianist. He wore thin, wire-rimmed glasses, a tailored pin-striped shirt, and was as ambitious as he was accomplished. He was perfectly aware that his participation in this project could easily land him in prison if it were ever brought to public light. He also knew he could be vaulted into the upper reaches of scientific achievement if he and his colleagues pulled off what he was convinced they were about to, and his heart pounded against his ribs despite his outward calm.

As aide and muscle for Barrola, there was thirty-two-year-old Lieu-tenant Lance Russell, also handpicked, in this instance by Colonel Oscar Henderson. Russell was over six feet of muscle and bone with a mind as simple and honed as a trench knife. His hair was buzz-cut, the scalp beneath revealing a deep indentation across his left tempo-ral lobe, a remnant of shrapnel from a Baghdad search-and-kill mis-sion. His eyes were a startling pale blue, almost white. Russell's instructions were to guard Hans's body with his life and to kill anyone who threatened its well-being. As a multiple black belt, expert in un-conventional warfare and unhampered by anything resembling a con-science, Russell was superbly equipped for the assignment.

The flight was passed namelessly, by NATO air traffic controllers, from one military sector to another, until it was well out over the North Atlantic. One hundred miles off Long Island it was met and refueled by a New Jersey Air National Guard Boeing KC-135R Stratotanker, operating on sealed orders and flown by senior officers only. From there the Gulfstream jet was acquired by the NORAD radar net in Colorado Springs. It slipped down the East Coast of the United States, monitored by watchful eyes three thousand feet beneath a granite mountain, a tiny blip among tens of thousands representing not only every aircraft in the air, but each satellite and piece of space junk larger than a basketball. It was designated FS2308, priority one. Other than that, it was absolutely anonymous.

Over the Florida peninsula it turned ten degrees ESE, passing over Grand Bahama Island, Nassau and a string of lesser islands and cays strewn across a turquoise sea, until Cuba was visible. The aircraft avoided Cuban airspace, but came close enough to pass its flight control over the Marine air traffic crew at Guantánamo. It flew on past Haiti and the Dominican Republic, then began dropping flaps over Puerto Rico, dumping altitude. The fortress in San Juan harbor slipped by just at sunset, so low that the flight crew could see the tourists below. Then a tiny dot hove into view, just off the eastern end of Puerto Rico.

Vieques Island.

The twin jet touched down on auxiliary fuel and came to a stop at the far end of the tiny runway. The airport was completely still. Usually host to VFR, or visual flight reference, air traffic, it was typically quiet after sunset. Tonight that stillness was ensured by six Marine Humvees stationed around its perimeter with orders to keep all civilians out.

A single vehicle, a black Chevrolet Suburban, moved out to meet the plane. Behind its deeply smoked windows was a virtual hospital. Colonel Henderson met the plane, shook hands with Lieutenant Russell, then saw to it that Hans was transferred into the vehicle with a minimum of fuss.

Even as the car pulled away, the C-20 gunned its engine into a take-off roll. Despite its low tanks, it would not be allowed to tarry here; it had been routed back to Guantánamo for refueling and reassignment.

By the following evening, both plane and pilot would be in Indonesia removing an operative who had successfully assassinated an errant banker for the IMF. As with the assignment just completed, the pilot would know nothing of these details, and would care less. The plane and its echo were gone almost as quickly as the Suburban.

The Humvees fell in before and behind as the whole caravan vanished into the night. Within minutes, the only sound was the vibrant chorus of crickets and tree frogs signaling the beginning of another night's struggle for food and procreation.

5

ST. MAURICE, SWITZERLAND

Elizabeth had not slept for thirty-six hours.

The day before, on a Calvin Klein shoot, she had been gripped by a sudden lethargy. It was nearly the unshakable sort that Annie had described experiencing the year she had come down with Epstein-Barr—dozing in her chair between setups and reacting so slowly to the photographer's directions that he had ended up screaming at her. Then came the dreaded huddle: the account exec, the art director and the client debating whether or not to scrap the day's work and hire a new model. That's when Elizabeth finally got herself together and forced herself to focus, so that by the end of the day they were all love-you-let's-work-together-soon again, thank God.

But it was mortifying. She was a pro—no one had ever said less, not from her very first days as a catalogue model. She dragged herself back to her apartment and checked her messages. Nothing from Hans. She threw herself in bed, hoping for a deep, cleansing sleep, but instantly her mind switched into high gear. Sometime after midnight she got up and read, racing through most of *Sense and Sensibility*. It only left her heartsick for Hans, still worried stiff, and not one blink nearer to sleep. She had tossed aside Jane Austen, switching to a well-thumbed paperback edition of *Alice in Wonderland*, which at least felt closer to life as it really was.

Then she did something she swore she would never do: she phoned Hans in his BMW, the only number she was allowed to call.

There was no answer. The party she was trying to reach was, according to the digitized voice, out of the calling area. Out of the calling area? Where was that? Had he taken off for Rome for a bowl of pasta?

Why hadn't he called her back?

She was making herself tea in the predawn light, trying to think positively, when the phone rang. It was Annie and she was choking back tears.

Either the world was contracting or Elizabeth was expanding like Alice, because she felt as if her head were pinned against the ceiling.

"Annie, what *is* it?" she asked fearfully.

"Lizzy, I have awful news."

Elizabeth almost asked if it was Annie's husband, Roland. But she knew it wasn't. Then she seemed to go deaf. Annie was rattling on and on and she couldn't make sense of the words.

"You thought something like this might happen. You had a premonition, you said so that day at lunch, didn't you?"

"A premonition?"

"I remember when he called you, you said to him—'I'm not going to see you again.' And then after that, you said, 'I don't know what I mean.' I thought you meant because you were breaking it off, but—"

Elizabeth's whole body went numb. "You're talking about Hans."

"Oh, God. Oh, Lizzy. You're in shock. I'm sorry."

"No." She struggled to breathe. "Tell me again. I'm here."

Then Annie was laying it all out in a broken rush of words. Motorists had noted the damaged guardrail the next morning. The first man to stop thought he had seen a charred wreck, far down below. Authorities had been called and climbers were sent down.

"No," said Elizabeth ferociously. "No."

The phone fell from her hand onto the bed, and then she picked it up again.

"It was his BMW, baby. He was in there. There were tire marks, Lizzy—the car skidded over two hundred feet. They say he was going way too fast. His wife told reporters he was angry when he left the house. Somebody had screwed up at a bank or something, and he was going to give them hell. Either that, or he fell asleep at the wheel. I'm so sorry."

"He didn't fall asleep," said Elizabeth.

"Well, but how do you know that—"

"What about the other car?"

"What other car? There was no other car. He lost control—"

"Annie, I was talking to him!"

"You were *talking* to him?"

"Yes! He yelled out—swore—as if something had gone wrong—it had to be another car. Then the phone went dead—"

"Baby, there was no other driver involved. Lizzy?"

"It's okay," said Elizabeth, sinking to the floor and sliding into a corner. Her mouth had gone dry and she felt like she was looking at everything through a darkening glass.

"Do you have to work today?" Annie asked gently.

"We finished yesterday." And then she was crying, cold and terrified like a child lost in an ice storm.

"Lizzy? Lizzy, sweetheart, are you still there? I'm on my way over. Hang tight, okay?"

Hans Brinkman's death sent shock waves through the entire European Economic Community. His circle of friends was considerable, and the roster of his connections, sycophants and admirers larger still. Those who were allowed past the cemetery gates into the invitation-only funeral numbered over four hundred. They filled the chapel of Zurich's Fluntern Cemetery and spilled out onto the surrounding lawns where they listened beneath the two-hundred-year-old trees to the eulogy, broadcast over loudspeakers.

Annie, who had insisted on driving Elizabeth to the funeral, was late picking her up. By the time they both arrived at the cemetery, Elizabeth was dismayed to find they were limited to listening with the crowd outside.

"It's a closed coffin anyway, I think," Annie said lamely.

"Then I need to see the coffin."

"Lizzy, I'm sorry, I needed to stop for gas. They wouldn't have let you in anyway."

"No, they wouldn't, would they?" She was suddenly conscious of all the casual onlookers, the funeral geeks, the not-quite-important-enoughs, fanning out on every side.

That's what I was to Hans, she thought. Not quite in his life. But no, she realized, with sudden ferocity—they had connected that night on the phone. She had sensed a deep and intuitive oneness with him then, a secret intimacy neither had dared to describe. *I want us to be together,* she thought—wondering at the intensity, the virtual bodily hunger to be close to him now in death. Was it a feeble, selfish concept, the need for closure? No, no way. She needed to be *there,* in the midst of the real mourners, the ones who had cared for him. If she had her way she would throw herself on the coffin and cry out his name.

Behind her, two men in blue pin-striped suits were eyeing her, talking in whispers. Yvette's PIs, assigned to keep her from causing a scandal?

There was another car—she was sure of it!

Annie had said there wasn't, damn it! She wrenched her attention back to the voices coming over the PA.

A minister was concluding his remarks, speaking of the transience of life and of God's surrounding arms in a place untouched by earth's sorrows and the ravages of time. Next up were colleagues and old schoolmates, all of whom spoke eloquently of Hans's attributes as a visionary banker, Olympic skier, pilot and sportsman. For a full hour she listened intently to the tributes to Hans's tenacity, vigor, intelligence, ambition and cunning.

She kept waiting to hear just one person talk about how Hans had touched his heart, but no one did. Not a soul.

It sent a chill through her body.

When they were about to bring the casket out for burial, the guests were invited to the grave site. Elizabeth and Annie walked together down a broad avenue of elms that sang with cicadas. She felt briefly heartened—at least now she was going to see him laid to rest. Her pulse returned to normal. But when they arrived at the designated sector, they found it cordoned off, with men checking names against a list. People not on the list were politely turned away and invited to

sign the guest book in the chapel. There was no way Elizabeth was going to be on that list.

"It's the wife," Annie growled. "If she's not excluding people, it's
not a real event." She gave a worried frown: Elizabeth's face had gone
pale with an emotion she couldn't identify. "Come on," Annie tried.
"You're just torturing yourself. Why don't we go get drunk."

Elizabeth sadly shook her head. "Annie, don't be offended, but I
think I need to be alone. You go on and see him buried. You can tell
me about it after, that'll help."

Annie thought about that for a moment, and then rejected it. "I'll
drop you off at home."

"No, I can grab a cab," said Elizabeth. The wheels were starting to
turn. "I'll just write something in the book at the chapel, and maybe
take a walk."

"Lizzy, are you sure? You look a little unsteady."

"A little, I guess. But, Annie, I'm fine," Elizabeth assured her, and
kissed her on both cheeks. She waited until Annie headed off, past the
two men in pin-striped suits, one of whom had a camera slung over
his shoulder. She waited until Annie was out of their sight. Then she
turned and went the other way.

She didn't go to the chapel—what could she possibly write? Instead, she went out onto the avenue and walked up Zürichberg-
strasse, along the cemetery's outer wall. An unseasonable thaw had
melted the snow; water was streaming in the gutters and the sky was
far too bright for her mood, which was moving toward black. A couple walked by, laughing, arms around each other, the girl's hand joining the boy's in his coat pocket. Elizabeth put her head down and
walked faster. Across the street was the north end of the Zurich Zoo,
marked by another tall, ivy-covered wall. She could hear some sort of
animal baying—a deep, repetitive *ugh-ugh-ugh* that filled her with
dread. She felt trapped between the unknowable realm of death on
one side and the unfathomable wildness of instinct on the other. A
hundred yards down the length of the cemetery's southern wall she
stopped and looked around carefully.

There was a tree that had grown between the sidewalk and the
eight-foot-high wall. It had rough bark and was straight as a pole.

Without another thought, she put her back to the rough gray brick of the wall, braced her feet on the trunk of the tree and went up it like a rock climber scaling a facade. Moments later she dropped down the other side of the wall inside the cemetery, finding herself in a stand of birches with no sign of a live human being anywhere in sight.

She felt better already.

Making her way through the trees into a deserted utility yard, she crept past sheds full of machinery, rolls of Astroturf and heaps of dead flowers until she entered the grounds of the cemetery itself.

Here she stopped and listened again. A slight wind stirred the birch leaves, and a dove was cooing somewhere, offering a plaintive counterpoint to the distant sound of the minister reciting the Lord's Prayer. She headed for the sound until she caught sight of the sun glinting off the chromed winch that held Hans's casket. She crept closer.

She was close enough to see a tall woman with full pale lips approaching the grave. Once there, she dropped a rose on the casket, then stepped away, pulling a black veil across her face.

Yvette, thought Elizabeth, ducking discreetly out of sight behind one of the larger crypts. It occurred to her suddenly that Hans had never shown her a picture of his wife, nor had she ever asked to see one. She was almost sorry she had seen her now. The woman looked so strangely blank, so bitter, so distracted, as if—the thought came to her suddenly—Hans had somehow left the woman he had married penniless.

Or was that her own desolation talking?

She tried to feel the loss, the reality of it, but the tears refused to flow. Was everyone else feeling empty at this moment? Was that Hans's legacy? To leave behind nothing but blankness and bafflement?

Then Elizabeth caught sight of another woman, this one standing slightly off from the rest, sobbing so deeply her shoulders shook. No one seemed to know what to make of her, or who she was, and several people moved a step or two away, embarrassed.

For Elizabeth, suddenly the floodgates opened. She found herself crying so hard she was wracked by a physical pain that hit her in the gut and twisted her throat so badly that she thought she might choke.

With that, she lost all hope of remaining hidden. She, too, was sobbing out of control, causing several of the mourners to turn in her direction. The grief-stricken woman also turned, and her eyes locked on
to Elizabeth's like a traveler lost in an infinite desert catching a
glimpse of another human being. Elizabeth felt a flash of recognition.
She struggled through her grief to think who this woman might be.
Hans's mother? No. It couldn't be. She was tiny, this woman, sinewy
and dark, almost Mediterranean, with a closed-off, deferential air,
even in her grief, like a forgotten aunt or a beloved old family servant.
Hans's nanny, maybe? Did he ever have a nanny? And if this wasn't
his mother, where *was* she? Or his father? Were his parents even
alive? What did she or anyone, for that matter, really know about this
man? What did *anybody* know, apart from the realities of his financial
success and sports trophies?

The woman was approaching her.

Elizabeth started to back away, then held her ground. What she
had mistaken for a Mediterranean complexion, she now saw as the
woman drew closer, was a leathery suntan. The woman came right up
to her, reached out a tiny hand and gripped Elizabeth by the wrist.

"Elizabeth," she said, her eyes intensely meeting Elizabeth's as if
over some invisible abyss. Startled, Elizabeth shot a glance toward the
woman with the black veil. They were out of earshot of the other
mourners, but the small, tanned woman's hand was still on her arm.
Elizabeth felt an icy chill. "How do you know my name?" she asked.

The woman's lips tightened. "I'm—I was—his mother."

"Oh. I'm so sorry." So Hans had actually spoken of Elizabeth to another human being, to his mother no less. Her heart was beating so
hard she was having a hard time breathing. She stood there in a
daze, listening to the woman breathe, feeling, for a brief moment at
least, strangely calm. It was the first time she had ever been with anyone who knew Hans, someone who had loved him. That fact alone
seemed to give her strength.

"I was hoping to talk with you," the woman said, her eyes red and
her voice husky from tears.

"You were?"

"Yes, I was," the woman said matter-of-factly, and her deep-set brown eyes studied Elizabeth. She had a Southern accent—Texas, Elizabeth guessed.

"I think I could use talking to someone about now," Elizabeth admitted quietly.

"I can imagine." The woman stuck out her hand. "I'm Rose-Anne."

With a covert glance in Yvette's direction, Elizabeth shook it, then dropped her voice. "You knew about me?"

"Oh, yes."

She gathered her courage. "Then there's something you should know. I was talking to Hans moments before he died. Before the . . . accident."

She realized as she said this how frightened she was. She looked back toward the widow. Yvette was now staring right back at her, and in the next moment the two men in pin-striped suits she had noticed outside the chapel turned slowly around to face her way as well.

"Maybe you shouldn't be here," Rose-Anne said abruptly.

Elizabeth looked back at her, feeling suddenly that time was running out. "Something doesn't make sense," she said hurriedly. "About his death. About the way he died."

Rose-Anne nodded gravely. "You know the restaurant Kronenhalle?" she asked.

Elizabeth blinked in confusion. "What, in Zurich? By the river?"

"On Ramistrasse, yes. Meet me at the bar, next Tuesday. Three o'clock. Is that good for you?"

"Three o'clock. Yes. That's fine. I'll be there."

"I'll look forward to it," said Rose-Anne, and releasing her grip on Elizabeth's arm, she turned back toward the knot of mourners. Elizabeth saw one of the men whisper in the other's ear. The second one nodded, and Elizabeth felt a stab of anxiety so acute she ducked out of sight behind the monument and started running back into the birch grove.

My God, she thought wildly. *Yvette had him killed!*

No, but that's insane, she decided.

But why are they watching me?

If they are watching, *if* I'm not going crazy. She forced herself to stop and look back. Through the trees she could see that nobody was looking at her now—all eyes were on the grave—Yvette, Rose-Anne and the others were turned again to the ceremony as Hans Brinkman's casket was lowered into the ground. She could not see the two men in suits, however. Elizabeth turned and ran back to the sheds, her heart pounding. She found a ladder tall enough and slammed it to the wall, scaled it and jumped to the sidewalk. From there she ran for a long time, as if her life depended on it. And for all she knew, it did.

VIEQUES ISLAND, COMMONWEALTH OF PUERTO RICO

Vieques Island was unique in the Caribbean.

To begin with, it was half-civilian, half-military, and known to very few off-island civilians. A scant six miles from the east end of Puerto Rico and officially Puerto Rican territory, Vieques was an island torn between contrasting eras. Cattle and egrets dotted its heavily wooded hillsides, and its fifty-one square miles held only eight thousand year-round residents, most of whom earned their living from raising livestock, fishing or farming sugarcane much in the way of their sixteenth-century ancestors. The other Vieques, very much of the twentieth or even the twenty-first century, was host to a vast United States naval installation that dominated both its eastern and western extremities. This base, a two-island monstrosity ordered by President Franklin Roosevelt in 1940, was called Roosevelt Roads. It was composed of 31,000 acres, 8,600 on Puerto Rico, and some 22,000 acres on Vieques itself. In addition to seventeen naval station departments, Roosevelt Roads contained sub-bases or facilities for the Army, Marines and United States Coast Guard. It was a virtual hive of military activity, and much of that activity was classified.

The eastern end of Vieques was a gunnery and bombing range, and had for three decades been the center of fierce controversy. Both the local community and various environmental groups had fought its existence since the 1960s, angrily claiming that it had more craters than the moon. To add insult to injury, the Navy had recently returned to practicing with live napalm as well. Colonel Oscar Henderson knew some tree-hugging sonofabitch would forever be surveilling it through binoculars, and that was why, as far back as 1958, he had vetoed Frederick Wolfe's idea of building his lab on the eastern shore, no matter how many feet down it could be buried.

Instead, he had funded a state-of-the-art facility at the far end of the western compound. Since the island spanned 33,000 acres, the bulk of it owned by the Navy, there was plenty of spare room to build the necessary buffer zone. And so, beginning in the early 1960s, Wolfe had been authorized to conduct his experiments in genetics here, operating under a blanket of secrecy that had allowed him unprecedented freedom as a government scientist.

A close friend of a string of secretaries of the navy, Wolfe had promised results that would pass down great benefits to humanity, beginning with the personnel of the Navy itself. But more important, politically speaking, he promised the Navy brass he would monitor any changes in civilian DNA that might be occurring—as was feared by certain bleeding hearts—as a consequence of the range's lesser known activities. It was known in-house that the munitions being tested on the bombing range released an increasingly exotic mixture of particulates and gases into the air each time they exploded. On a typical day of bombing practice, perhaps three hundred tons of munitions—TNT, NO_3, NO_2, RDX and Tetryl—loosed their smoke and debris downwind. The Navy was nervous, but since it was nine times cheaper to fly in their fighter-bombers from their base at Cherry Point, North Carolina, than it would have been to send them to its alternative, Nellis Air Force Bomb Range in Nevada, no one wanted to close the range. Besides, who wanted to wait for the goddamn Air Force to find room in their schedule when the Navy had its own class-A bombing range right here?

So Wolfe had monitored and advised, keeping everyone placated with his genetic experiments, none of which the Navy really understood, or wanted to.

And to further ingratiate himself, Wolfe volunteered to open and run a first-rate OB-GYN clinic on the base, one that would make it the envy not only of the rest of the Navy but of the entire armed forces.

It was an instant hit, and one of the most popular and successful services Wolfe offered was fertility counseling.

The small white clapboard clinic on an obscure naval base on an even more obscure island soon became a mecca for Navy families frustrated in their attempt to have children. The word quickly spread that Dr. Frederick Wolfe had the golden touch when it came to ensuring pregnancies, and couples young and old flocked to his door.

Over the course of fifteen years, before the clinic was absorbed by Bethesda Hospital in Maryland, over fifteen hundred children were born in Vieques, and of these, nearly two hundred were the result of in vitro fertilization, donor sperm and, later, fertility drugs.

Frederick Wolfe was a hero on the base. Absolutely no one questioned a single thing he did.

His prestige soared even higher when he was awarded a top secret contract by an agency so classified that even the Navy was not copied on its intent or progress. The Navy did, however, benefit from a healthy increase in Wolfe's funding, gladly adding a ring of iron-clad security around his outermost facilities, and, once again, asking no further questions.

It was into these facilities that the body of Hans Brinkman was delivered.

"So, bottom line, what are the chances?"

Emilio Barrola, the neurosurgeon, peered over his wire-framed glasses. The question had come from the observation gallery, at the tail end of a surgical briefing. Ordinarily he would have ignored it, but these people, the Colonel Hendersons of this world, were paying for this procedure, so he owed them a reply. His mentor, Wolfe, would have known exactly what to say, but at the moment Wolfe was nowhere to be found in the operating theater. Wolfe was in his own private green room, entering an alpha state so profound that legend had it a contingent of Buddhist monks had once been dispatched by the Dalai Lama himself to observe its effects. The monks had come away scratching their heads. The story was apocryphal, of course, but the trance was real and, as far as Wolfe was concerned, absolutely crucial to peak performance. So Barrola, for a while at least, was on his own.

"The chances? One in a thousand, perhaps. Perhaps one in a million. It is foolish—" He retracted the word hastily. "Rather I should say difficult, to put a number on it. One has to think in terms of expectation—the probability times the reward. Failure costs us nothing except what you gentlemen have so generously allotted to this experiment." That was good, he thought, he wished Wolfe had been here to hear it. "Whereas, success," he added, pointing in the direction of the subject in a papal gesture, "brings us all incalculable benefits. To put it another way—"

Behind Barrola, standing next to the operating table trying not to let this blather get to her, Beatrice Jance gripped her husband's hand. Pomposity had always had this effect on each of them. Whether they were exposed to it in a lecture hall, a committee meeting, a party or a movie theater, they always reached silently for each other, holding tight until the embarrassing moment had passed. It was just one of their many rituals of marital telepathy that had evolved over the years, unknown to anyone but themselves, and impervious to circumstance.

Peter, desperately weak, couldn't squeeze back. But that didn't prevent Beatrice from holding on to his hand as she gazed up at the OR lights. Get on with it, she thought—we have nothing to lose but our souls.

Then she heard the commotion of an arriving gurney, and though her view of the other man was blocked by a wall of surgical sheeting, she knew *he* was there, not five feet away. Hearing the muffled scurry of the man being shifted to the table and positioned, she clutched Peter's limp hand all the harder, and forced herself to look.

"Can you see him?" Peter asked, his voice barely audible.

She looked back at Peter's face, the eyes incredibly intense.

"Does he look like me?"

She was trying to keep her face from twitching.

"Peter, it is you."

A terrifying image flashed into her mind—a painting she had once seen of a huge man, a misshapen giant, clutching a much smaller helpless human figure in his fist, about to cram it into his mouth. Goya, she remembered. One of his works. What was it called? Oh, yes. *Saturn Devouring His Son.*

She heard herself take a sharp breath, as a team of nurses approached the table. They were waiting for her to let go of her husband's hand.

She knelt and kissed him unashamedly, then walked away. Peter's mouth opened, but whether to speak or cry out it was impossible to say.

The draping of the body began immediately. Within seconds Peter had vanished from view under a sea of green surgical cloth. The nurses moved quickly, and in a matter of minutes, only his head and upper legs remained exposed.

Barrola gave the signal and the anesthesiologist inserted a tube down Peter's windpipe.

Through this, he administered an exquisitely delicate cocktail of barbiturates that sent Peter into a profound sleep—in fact the same low-grade coma Hans Brinkman had been plunged into ten hours before. The barbiturates radically lowered Peter's cerebral O_2 uptake, and thus his requirement of blood. After twenty minutes of adjusting and readjusting various gas mixtures, the anesthesiologist turned both Peter and Hans over to their respective cardiac teams.

Swiftly, two incisions were made in each man, one into the large femoral artery just beneath the surface on the inside of each man's thigh, another into the femoral vein. Into these openings large-bore catheters were inserted and sealed. With both Peter and Hans the next step was the same: the blood was pumped from the artery into the huge masses of tubing, chromed pump cylinders and coolant chambers that comprised one of two multimillion-dollar artificial heart machines. Just as powerfully, it was pumped back into each man's veins. In effect, their hearts had been bypassed and rendered superfluous.

At this point, the observers in the gallery—those who had listened attentively to Barrola's briefing—edged forward in their seats. Something different, something new, was about to be added to the process. The pump technicians spun dials and flipped switches, the machines hummed and thumped, and the core temperature of each man began to drop dramatically, along with the temperature of the operating room. Personnel not working the artificial hearts took the opportunity to slip into sterile down vests, their breath becoming visible as the brains of the two men on the tables reached hypothermic arrest.

This procedure, as Barrola had just explained, had been perfected both in civilian and government operating theaters and was key to the success of heart bypass operations and transplantation. But it was extraordinarily tricky. Now they were at the critical juncture. With the body temperatures of each men at 23 degrees Centigrade, 7 degrees below normal, Barrola ordered that each man be injected with a strong solution of potassium chloride.

Their hearts stopped as if a switch had been thrown. The flatline alarm split the air suddenly, and droned on, unbearably, until someone thought to turn it off.

Barrola took a deep breath.

In heart transplants, the usual procedure was to pump blood to every part of the body *except* the heart. This much had been accomplished countless times in ORs around the civilized world. But Frederick Wolfe had taken the procedure in a whole new direction, and Barrola had been his eager, if now slightly nervous, protégé. The hearts of Hans and Peter had been stopped as a first step only. Once a sufficiently low brain temperature was achieved, the blood was entirely drained from both bodies. There was a name for it, and Alex Davies, watching from the front row of the gallery, supplied it to Colonel Oscar Henderson, who, from the look of alarm on his wide, weathered face, was slowly losing his hopes of seeing a star on his epaulets any time soon.

"It's called desanguination," said Alex grimly.

"What the hell's that?" Henderson demanded under his breath.

"It's what vampires do in the movies," Alex said. "Or coroners do in morgues," he went on, seeing Henderson blanch. He gave a faint smile and Henderson didn't ask another question.

The shunt back into the bodies was shut down, and within ten minutes the lifeblood of both men was in the machines and nowhere else.

Without blood in their bodies, no oxygen was reaching any cell in either brain, or any other organ for that matter. There was a technical term for this condition as well, and Alex Davies, watching with rapt attention, mouthed it for the benefit of the surrounding brass.

It was called death.

There was no trick, really, to bringing patients back from this state. Wolfe had done it many times before and, in fact, this technique too was used in leading medical centers throughout the Western world. But what was about to follow was not. What was next was simply un-thinkable, and there was only one neurosurgeon in the world with the technical wherewithal, the absolute sanction and the unfettered hubris to pull it off.

Barrola personally made the call to Frederick Wolfe.

His mentor generally took fifteen minutes to emerge from his deep alpha state, even for operations vastly more simple than the one he was about to perform—just enough time for the final prep.

The heads of both Peter and Hans had been shaved clean. With Barrola working on Hans and his best assistant working on Peter, lines were drawn around the circumference of each head, beginning at the occiput, running around the temporal surfaces—just above the ears on Hans, just below on Peter. On both, the line passed across the face, transecting the orbit of the eyes dead-center and continuing across the bridge of the nose. Mirror lines met from the other side. Then, employing state-of-the-art laser cutting tools, Barrola and his assis-tant made the cutaneous cuts. Since the bodies were essentially drained, there was only the barest trace of blood. The work went quickly.

For Barrola, the most delicate and rewarding cut was around the eyes, and it was no accident that he, who counted among his many skills plastic surgery, had been assigned to work on Hans. This was the host body, and it was vital that it function perfectly afterward, includ-ing the tear ducts, which he delicately skirted now. The eyes them-selves didn't matter. Eyes were anatomically nothing more than extensions of the brain, and the brain of Hans Brinkman was now ir-relevant.

Barrola completed his cuts and stepped away. Nurses would do the busywork of peeling back the scalp to expose the bone beneath. He moved to Peter, supervising the final step of this preparation, fitting twin titanium disks over the dying scientist's eyes. It was critical that no accident of saw or splinter of bone compromise their structure. Peter's eyes and brain were what mattered here.

The moment Barrola finished, the gallery fell silent.

Frederick Wolfe was entering the operating room.

He was walking tall, as though the Zen state had added inches to his long-boned frame. Gone were the looks of adoration he had usually bestowed on Beatrice, the irascible disdain with which he intimidated the military, the nonchalant imperiousness with which he treated his grandson, Alex. Nearly all traces of maliciousness or mischief had been stripped away by meditation and the unique urgency of this moment. He was in total control, of himself and of this operating theater.

Assistants slapped up X rays, while others started the CD player that would play, at full volume, his favorite recording of Richard Strauss's *Vier letzte Lieder* throughout the rest of this night. The melancholy masterpiece, completed just months before the composer's death, never failed to fill Wolfe's heart with a deliciously painful poignancy, especially when Jessye Norman sang it. Military men squirmed, and Beatrice wished she could squeeze Peter's hand, but Wolfe himself was blissfully and properly indifferent to their opinions. This was *his* time, *his* place, *his* operation. For now—and, if there was any justice in the universe, from now on—he was indisputably the most important scientist in the world.

He turned away from the X rays. He had memorized them the night before and there were no changes.

"Let's not waste time," he said.

"I'm ready if you are," said Barrola, more meekly than he had intended.

"More than ready. Let's go."

Wolfe moved to Peter, Barrola to Hans. Each man was surrounded by his own surgical team. Each knew that if he failed he would never again rise to another such opportunity for power and fame, at least not within the labyrinth of secret projects that comprised the cutting edge of military-medical technology. On the other hand, both knew as well that if they succeeded, their prestige would rise beyond their wildest dreams. And Wolfe himself was aware that as progenitor and genius of this project, his would be the credit for a discovery comparable to that of DNA, the key element in a passage from one level of human evolution to the next.

His hand had never felt steadier.

He personally did the fitting and adjustment of the Mayfield clamp, a gangly apparatus of jointed steel that terminated with four prongs, looking like nothing so much as an elaborate set of ice tongs. The Mayfield clamp was designed to hold its subject's head immobile in the ideal position so that no jiggle, no slip of placement, could ruin the control of the surgeon's hands and blades themselves. The clamp had to be set perfectly to Peter's skull, and to this end a small horde of technical specialists moved in around Wolfe, as did a second around Barrola.

Wolfe fussed and chided as bolts were tightened and loosened, joints flexed and readjusted. When the clamp was in the shape he thought best, he had them affix the entire apparatus to Peter's table. Then the tongs were brought to the skull at the four points of the compass and tightened down. The tiny runnels of vestigial blood were quickly blotted away by nurses, while the technicians began to raise the upper half of the operating table itself.

Up in the observation gallery, Alex Davies watched Beatrice Jance turn away for the first time. Peter's body, half supported by the rising back of the table, half-hung like a slab of meat from the clamp, was propped up like a derelict on a park bench.

I wonder what she's feeling, Alex thought, his bright eyes fixed on Beatrice. His own emotions he couldn't have named, and wouldn't have bothered to. They were an unholy mixture of revulsion, amusement and exquisite sympathy for the dying man on the operating table, a man whose genius he revered. There was something else, too, deep and perverse. It was a secret wish to see the entire operation end in a chaos of spurting blood and exploding equipment, while that abominable Nazi music rang out. It was the same lame highbrow bullshit his grandfather had tried to ram down his throat ever since he was three years old.

His head sank onto his chest. My God, thought Beatrice, glancing over, Alex Davies had fallen asleep. Then she forced herself to look below again.

The technicians stepped away from the tables.

Wolfe glanced over at Barrola. He was ready as well. Wolfe took a careful, deep breath, bringing himself to his center until he could feel his breath in his *ki*. Then he quietly asked for his Midas Rex to be brought in.

Barrola did the same.

In came the brass-headed bone saw, big and powerful and utterly without glamour—pure 1960s technology. The Midas Rexes were air-powered, and the fat green hose that ran from the compressed-air tanks made them look like something more suitable to a garage. But their power minimized the danger of splintering bone, so cleanly did they cut. Control was supplied by the surgeon, and Wolfe and Barrola were the best.

After fifteen minutes of careful sawing, the OR looked like a smoke-filled back room and Alex Davies had perked up again. The fine dust from both men's skulls twisted in delicate whorls under the intense lights, mixing with the raw breath of the two dozen technicians and doctors laboring in the frigid room. It was impossible not to watch.

At last the machines fell silent. They were handed off to technicians and stowed; they would not be needed again. Wolfe paused over Peter's body and looked up at the gallery, meeting Beatrice's eyes for the first time. He could sense her anxiety, but also her gratitude, and this filled him with pleasure. He knew that she knew what came next, and loved the fact that she was to witness it—witness to his genius at work. But to his dismay she was looking too pale, shaking her head, obviously unwell. A moment later she rose and made her way shakily up the gallery steps to the exit door.

He realized that he wouldn't see her again, not until the operation was over. He turned back to Peter, lifted the top of his skull off, and dropped it into a stainless steel basin.

There, gleaming grayish pink in the argon light, was what Wolfe had been born to preserve, the brain of what so many people, unacquainted with his own prodigious achievements, regarded as the greatest living genius of the twentieth century.

It was Wolfe's task now to ensure that this instrument would continue functioning into the twenty-first century as well. It was a task he had begun to prepare for thirty-five years ago, just two buildings away in his OB-GYN clinic, with the birth of Hans Brinkman himself.

Within six months of their first meeting, Frederick Wolfe and Peter Jance had become colleagues and, in the openly competitive fashion of scientific prodigies, close friends.

In their prime, they had shared this base with dozens of the top scientists working for the U.S. government, each developing something that the Pentagon hoped would ensure its hegemony in those postwar years. Peter was busy blowing things up on the eastern range of Vieques, working at that time on rail guns, huge cumbersome devices that shot super-charged particles via what seemed now like medieval technology. He could never get them small enough to be practical, not even for battleships, and his failures were the source of much merriment to Wolfe and Beatrice, as well as to himself. Nevertheless, the feds loved Peter because the guns, big as they were, blew hell out of half an acre of island every time they fired. They had great hopes for his future. They knew it was only a matter of time.

Wolfe was already far advanced in genetics, and as part of his quest he would call upon friends to serve as sources for material. Nothing drastic—just a pint of blood here, a skin scraping there; in return Wolfe would give them framed DNA printouts to hang over their desks. In the case of Peter and Beatrice, he also tried to help them through a difficult pregnancy, even though Beatrice had a raft of uterine fibroids that stacked the odds against bringing a fetus to term. Beatrice had miscarried, and she and Peter had never tried again.

Wolfe sometimes thought Beatrice blamed him for the failure, believing, as she had once hinted in an unguarded moment, that his resentment of their potential happiness had somehow doomed her pregnancy. Nothing, as far as Wolfe was concerned, could have been more absurd. A married philosopher, as Nietzsche once observed, belongs to comedy—and so, in Wolfe's view, did a married scientist. Jealousy was beneath him, and therefore out of the question. True, Peter's greater fame sometimes made Wolfe chafe, but it was a feeling he quickly dispelled by reflecting on how much more far-reaching and profound his own achievements were destined to be.

During those years, he had to work in secret, in virtual anonymity, hiding his brilliance. And indeed, the project that would some day place him in the scientific pantheon, far above Peter and everyone else, had begun almost casually.

It was by then common knowledge how to clone not only plants but animals at the level of tadpoles, and in Wolfe's mind it made no sense whatsoever that it shouldn't be possible to do the same with humans as well. It didn't call for mad-scientist apparatus and blasts of lightning—all it required was a certain amount of daring, and the gift of insight and an understanding of genetic structure which no other researcher could match.

And a healthy egg or two.

Which were almost laughably simple to secure, inasmuch as Wolfe ran a clinic that regularly drew worried couples from all branches of the service to his door. Eggs were his stock-in-trade. And if his experiments went awry, well, a miscarriage was nothing out of the ordinary for parents already used to disappointment. On the positive side, each time a pregnancy continued on into another trimester, he was an absolute hero.

And so it was child's play, really, once he had perfected the nanotechnology to remove the DNA from his friends' skin scrapings intact. Extracting it from the eggs of the women who came to him for help was no problem. As long as he got it all, it didn't matter how scrambled the DNA was. The real trick was inventing a glass pipette small enough and sharp enough to puncture a single human egg without destroying it. Once he had perfected this tool, he was home free, and using the Wolfe pipette, he both removed the DNA that was there, and injected the DNA of his fellow scientists.

He was successful nine times.

Including the time he inserted the DNA of Peter Jance.

The pregnancies were achieved through various guises—sometimes as a result of purported in vitro fertilization, sometimes through supposed insertion of donor sperm. It was done hundreds of times, most ending in failure.

But nine times it worked.

And the beauty of it was, only he knew. Only Frederick Wolfe knew the names of the DNA donors, only he had access to the dossiers the feds kept for him on the recipients, so great was their faith in his scientific genius.

Wolfe realized that he was on the brink of incredible new breakthroughs. But he became aware as well of a certain suspicion around the lab, so he stopped. He had what he wanted, the secret knowledge that he was now, at the very least, a genius on a par with Peter Jance or anyone else in the world of science. *He and he alone had created nine healthy human clones!*

He hung back and watched. For years.

Each child, each clone, was born to a couple who suspected nothing. Those who thought donor sperm had been the source of fertilization were of course the easiest: there was no suspicion when the child resembled neither parent. But even those parents who looked to find some resemblance were seldom disappointed. Whenever possible, Wolfe had taken pains to use DNA from friends who in one way or another resembled one or the other of these parents. With a few exceptions, the delighted couples assumed they were the full biological parents.

The parents and their children, of course, were transients. Service people, they were soon discharged or transferred, and it wasn't long before Wolfe had living miracles on five continents. He read the reports of their lives with a devotion so avid in its intensity that it registered on the parents as avuncular delight, winning their fierce and unquestioned loyalty. They were sure he had the best interests of their children at heart.

But it wasn't too long after his initial achievements that something far more interesting had occurred to Frederick Wolfe. Since each of these children was an exact cellular match to someone he knew, there would be, when time and circumstance demanded, absolutely no rejection of any part of one body grafted into the other.

None.

Almost instantly, it hit him: what it really meant in its fullest realization. And that final, stunning vision was the seed of what Wolfe knew would place him in the history books forever. All he had to do was go to the right people in the military and tell them what he could do for military research, unbelievable as it might sound.

At first the reception was guarded. They literally could not believe it. But he went over the whole proposal so carefully, in such detail, and with such attention to its potential that they finally believed. They were not only convinced; they were thunderstruck.

Then the money came, and the name—the Fountain Society.

In theory, he had explained, there was no reason on earth why any man or woman of genius—certainly his friends whom he had already duplicated—couldn't be projected indefinitely into the future, riding piggyback on the bodies of their clones. And since nearly all of these clones were representative of major weapons scientists who were, despite their achievements, moving inexorably into their senior years, time was of the essence. The military got the message more quickly than he had ever hoped. His project was enshrouded in secrecy and funded with a generosity so extreme Wolfe could only surmise that they hoped he might start cloning *them.* He was overjoyed, and felt that he was at the brink of the greatness he always knew should be his. The truth was that if all the procedures were perfected—and he was certain they would be—then Frederick Wolfe would be forever enshrined as the genius of geniuses, the man who wrote and orchestrated the defeat of death itself.

Twenty hours after removing the lid of Peter Jance's skull, Wolfe continued to work with an intensity that galvanized the entire operating theater. Twenty hours was the absolute limit that the brain could survive without oxygen, no matter how cold. Wolfe was racing against the clock, and the clock was held by the Grim Reaper himself.

The procedure had been elegantly ruthless. Since Peter's body was no longer needed, Wolfe had cut into it deeply, approaching the priceless gray matter from below the brainpan. He had isolated the twelve ancillary nerves, as well as the four branches of the carotid arteries, cutting away and removing all the surrounding tissue. By doing so he was able to leave the neural and arterial connections conveniently long before severing them from Peter's body.

The brain's ultimate tether was the spinal column itself. This was cut between the first and second vertebrae with the same precision laser Wolfe had used on the other nerves. The low-heat ray was so discriminating that it could pass between two carbon molecules without damaging either. Appropriately enough, the laser was a product spun off from early weapons work by Peter Jance himself, though at the moment neither Peter nor Beatrice, who had not returned to the operating theater, was there to savor this pleasant irony. The stub of brain stem was capped temporarily to keep the cerebrospinal fluid from draining. Without this fluid, which provided energy for cell function in both the brain and spinal cord, as well as proteins and lymphocytes that helped guard against infection, Peter, or more precisely his brain, wouldn't last a day.

With the cut made and the capping accomplished, there was nothing anchoring this brain to Peter's body. Wolfe gingerly lifted it out. With a gently sucking sound, the brain and its satellite eyes and optic nerves rose out of the massive exit portal Wolfe had opened in the top of Peter's skull and face. This precious assembly he lowered carefully into a solution of dilute saline water, where it floated glimmering like some exotic creature pulled from the deepest reaches of the sea.

With Hans, the procedure was more crude. Cutting the skull above the ears, the team simply scooped his brain out, needing only to expose the roots of the ancillary nerves passing though the bottom of his brainpan from his body itself. These connective elements, twelve nerves and four arteries, were what was needed to be preserved. That this came at the cost of Hans Brinkman's brain itself—normally a catastrophic loss—was in this case inconsequential. As dazzling as it might have been, Hans Brinkman's brain had never been more than a shadow of Peter Jance's, lacking the indefinable God-given something that had elevated Peter's genetically twin brain to genius from the day he was born. Hans Brinkman's brain, now a heap of pinkish–gray slush resembling the contents of a dropped Jell-O mold, was taken away in a stainless steel pan.

Now began the final and most harrowing procedure: the marriage of old brain to young body.

How to accomplish this had proved devilishly tricky for Wolfe, and the procedures had been perfected at the cost of whole herds of pigs, calves and primates. The problem was the ancillary nerves, the twelve vital sets of neural cabling at the base of the brain. They controlled a host of functions, including facial movement and feeling, movement of the shoulders and head, balance and sound and smell. One trunk line, the vagus, ranged all the way down into the body cavity to affect the sensory, motor and autonomic functions of glands, digestion and heartbeat. Even though Beatrice's genetic glue worked on these fibers much more quickly than on the more complex spinal column, their anatomical location presented the most delicate of challenges. Just behind the throat and at the very base of the brain, they were hell to access.

The equipment and procedures Wolfe brought to bear on this problem wouldn't show up in civilian labs for decades, if ever. There were micro-laser scalpels, bonding sheaths grown from fetal pig tissue, an exquisitely small and powerful CAT scan apparatus that allowed them to operate entirely by virtual/video facial screens, and robotic grasping devices small enough to fit between spine and trachea without causing so much as a hiccup. They made it feasible. But the procedure itself called for a virtuoso performance on a level never seen before. Even those watching in the gallery knew Wolfe was pushing the very edge of the envelope. Right now, the brain of Peter Jance was nothing more than three pounds of frigid protoplasm, and the body of Hans Brinkman was as cold as death, bloodless, and with a heart that had not beaten in eight hours. Until the connections were made, no one in the operating theater could say anything at all had been accomplished, beyond a massive expenditure of the U.S. government's time and money.

They completed the first splices, racing against time.

Early impedance checks by the neurological monitoring team re-vealed brain-body communication. Though the activity was far from normal, information was passing from one realm to the other—which electrified the room and caused Oscar Henderson's lips to start mov-ing in something resembling prayer.

Even Alex Davies craned forward, gnawing on a thumbnail. That the connections were functioning at all meant it was possible, just possible, that this operation, this leap in evolution itself, could suc-ceed.

The two men worked on for hours while the assistants ticked off, for the benefit of the gallery, the completed joins, brain-side to body-side. Wolfe and Barrola worked like men possessed, hands in robot servo-controls, feet controlling focus and pan by floor pedals, making tiny puffs into servo-control tubes that translated the intensity of their breath into attitudinal positioning of robot fingers.

There were readings of one sort or another across every splice. Whether they would normalize was anyone's guess. But now, some-thing far more difficult had to be attempted. No one in medical his-tory had ever accomplished what was to happen next, not even Wolfe.

The reconnection of brain stem and spine was resistant to success by an order of magnitude that made all of what had gone before seem rudimentary. There was, Wolfe desperately reminded himself, some reason for hope. The cuts on both sides, Hans's spine and Peter's brain stem, were flawless—no ragged ends of injured spines to con-tend with here as there would have been in a disastrous fall, for in-stance. And the contact planes between Peter's brain stem and Hans's spine were unique in an even more important way: because Hans was a clone of Peter, each severed end was part and parcel of the other, perfectly matched, cell to cell, fiber to fiber, DNA to DNA.

They began the procedure to reconnect.

A rich coating of Beatrice's DNA bonding agent was spread over each end and allowed to percolate into the surface of each cut for sev-eral minutes. It allowed time for the DNA elements of the adhesive to replicate the neurological fingerprints of each stump so that there was no difference between each surface of adhesive and the original spinal portion over which it had been painted.

Then, at the precise moment when the two planes of adhesive were neither too fluid nor too solidified, the two sides were joined. Using laser technology developed for the alignment of submicroscopic hard-disk computer assemblies, Wolfe and his team aligned old brain stem and young spine so precisely that the identical matrixes of their fibers were butted together, bridged by Beatrice's bonding material. Instantly, the replicated surfaces of the DNA glue began flowing together at the subatomic level, following the original DNA roadmaps first drawn when Peter's maternal and paternal DNA had sundered themselves and fused their halves together into the blueprint for a new and unique human being.

The splice was reinforced with a thin but powerful stainless steel collar no bigger than a napkin ring. All that was left to do now was to splice the twin arteries that ran down each side of the spinal column.

"We are reading cross-bridge neurological activity," a voice blurted out. The man, a member of the neurological monitoring team, almost stammered, struggling to remain at least outwardly calm.

Wolfe looked up carefully.

"Volume?"

For a moment, the technician's jaw was slack, his voice stilled. As a target volume of electrical impulses between the rejoined halves, Wolfe was hoping for twenty, perhaps even thirty percent. That would allow the body to live, and perhaps provide for some movement in the lower limbs. Under these conditions, Peter could survive in a wheelchair. Steven Hawking had done just fine with that.

"Eighty percent," the technician gulped out. "No, eighty-four!"

Wolfe stared at the man, who returned a wild-eyed grin.

"It's improving by the second, sir."

Wolfe swallowed. "And the cranial bundle?" he asked quietly.

"All connections reading across the splices," reported another specialist, buried behind banks of monitors. "Improving in clarity. All others holding even. No degeneration."

A hush fell over the room.

Wolfe nodded cautiously. "Beatrice's Super Glue seems to be performing beautifully," he said. He bent over Peter's new body. "Let's finish him up. We might get lucky."

With exquisite care they laid the eyes into the lower half of their sockets—the lateral cut across the eye orbits made that simple enough—then fit the upper half of the cranium. After applying Beatrice's glue again, along the skull, along the edge of the sinus and eyelid, along the scalp, they wrapped the bandages. The only remaining step was to graft Hans's superior corneas onto Peter's seventy-six-year-old eyes, giving him clean windows through which to gaze upon his brave new world.

Then the main work was done.

Wolfe sank back, put on Mozart, and drank a cup of latte *macchiato,* prepared by a specially trained mess sergeant. The man knew exactly what Wolfe preferred to drink and when, including a jeroboam of Cristal champagne that had been left to chill in the green room. Time for that soon, when the last instrument was laid down. While Wolfe rested, Barrola and his team reconnected the carotids. As soon as they were finished, Wolfe was on his feet again.

This was crunch time; everyone in the theater knew it. Now was the hour of triumph or defeat, for bringing this man on the table back from the anterooms of death, or pulling the sheet over his face forever.

"Call Beatrice," Wolfe said quietly. "She should be here."

A nurse hurried off.

"Start the pump," he ordered.

Technicians scrambled. The chrome cylinders of the remaining artificial heart throbbed, the tubing between machine and Peter turned scarlet, and the return of blood into body and brain began. Peter's bluish flesh began to flush pink

"What are we going to call him?" Barrola wondered aloud.

Wolfe shot him a look. "I mean," Barrola said, hoping he hadn't offended, "he's not quite Peter and he's not quite the other one either."

Wolfe smiled, suddenly affable. "He was Peter before, he'll be Peter after, and he's Peter now. Period."

"But then, who is that?" asked Barrola, gesturing toward Peter Jance's corpse. It lay now abandoned like a car with its engine pulled.

"A metaphysical question," Wolfe allowed. "Not really ours to meddle with. People are who they are when they're alive. What dies

ceases to exist. What never was never is, what's transferred is transformed, what's borrowed or stolen becomes the property of the new
owner. We're just moving atoms from one container to the other.
They're still the same atoms, and their energy is eternal and without
name."

"But to people outside—"

"Outside what?"

"Here."

"We'll announce his death, of course."

"Then who do we say this is?"

Barrola looked warily down at the body of Hans Brinkman, now
planted with the brain of Peter Jance.

This is the trouble with modern science, Wolfe thought. Ulti-
mately, no matter how unique your vision, you need collaborators.

"Why would we want him outside, anyway?" Wolfe said in exasperation. Barrola frowned as though searching for a reply, but Wolfe
cut him off with a curt gesture. Beatrice was entering the operating
theater.

She approached the gallery railing, pale and tentative, almost fragile, staring down at her husband. The entire room froze in silence—
she looked around at the gallery, at Wolfe, then back down at Peter.

It wasn't Peter, she was thinking. No wrinkles, no appendectomy
scar, no veins on the back of his hands. And yet by God it *was* him—
as she barely remembered him, back when they had first been together, joined by passion and the deepest possible love. Except now
he looked somehow . . . clearer. Cleaner. Not an ounce of fat, with
sculpted muscles, a gym-trained body, a perfect machine—at once
normal and strange, known and alien.

"Fully resanguinated," the pump crew reported.

Beatrice looked at Wolfe, her heart filled with terror. Whatever,
whoever—that was her Peter—and he wasn't moving. Not at all.

Wolfe gave her a firm nod of reassurance—then bent again to his
task.

"Paddles! Quickly!"

Beatrice watched them wheel over the CV resuscitation machine.
For the past several hours—was it three or eight, she had finally lost

count—she had been in hell. What in God's name had she been thinking, letting Wolfe talk her into giving Peter the injection, thereby taking all the moral responsibility onto herself, and even allowing herself to hold out such unreasonable hopes? He might have survived the cancer, despite his flagging resistance and his doubts—miracles did happen, after all. But not on this scale, not—

"Clear!" shouted Barrola as he clamped the paddles to Peter's exposed chest.

The body gave a fierce jump and fell still. Everyone waited for the machine to recharge. Beatrice gripped the railing of the observation balcony, knuckles turning white.

"Clear!"

The body convulsed again and once again it fell back. Lifeless.

Barrola looked hopelessly at Wolfe. Wolfe glared back. Barrola thrust the paddles down again.

"Clear!"

The body flopped, spine arching. Wolfe clenched his teeth, fighting back despair. How could the splice hold against this torque? The body fell back once more. There it lay, like so much cold meat on the table.

Then someone gave a shout.

"I've got a pulse!"

It was the anesthesiologist as he jumped and stared at his instruments in disbelief. Then they all heard it—the unmistakable beep of the heart monitor, picking up the beat of life within the sleeping body.

Peter Jance was alive.

"EEG," Wolfe yelled, his voice tight.

"Full alpha and delta neural activity," came the cry. "Functional at coma level. All neural pathways reading strongly. Marked improvement from last survey!"

They all stared at each other, stunned. A peculiar silence fell over the gleaming room, over the scores of exhausted technicians, surgeons and specialists. The silence held for what seemed like an eternity, until it was punctured by the sharp pop of the cork shooting out of the neck of the jeroboam of Cristal. Everyone turned to see the grinning mess sergeant rushing into the room with the foaming bottle, followed by an assistant with a tray of champagne glasses. Cheers and shouts filled the air. The cardiovascular team was doing a touchdown dance, and nurses were crying and embracing. In the gallery, the military brass slapped each other's backs, crowding around Henderson to offer their congratulations.

Only Alex Davies did something different. He slipped out the gallery door so quietly that no one noticed. Below, Barrola was holding his hand out to Wolfe, who stared at it a moment with an expression of regal indifference, then shook it. In the gallery Beatrice had her hands cupped over her mouth. Barrola handed Wolfe a glass of champagne—Wolfe raised it to everyone in the room, smiling as he raised his eyes to Beatrice, now sobbing happily behind her hands. He drank deeply, stripped off his latex gloves, let them drop to the floor and left the room.

They met on the upper floor. Wolfe put his arms around her frail shoulders, held her tightly and walked her down to the parking lot.

"What can I expect?" she asked, her voice thickened by emotion. "Will it hold?"

"There's no precedent," he said, blotting his damp forehead on his bony wrist.

"I know that."

"So we'll just have to see. In a few days Barrola will do the plastic surgery. That's a no-brainer. "

"Freddy—"

"Sorry, bad choice of words. Your bonding agent, it worked wonderfully. Now it's just a matter of time doing its job."

She stared at him without appearing to breathe. "And will it?"

Wolfe took a deep breath, drinking in the look of need and gratitude in Beatrice's glistening gray eyes.

"Beatrice, we'll have to see. But between the two of us? I think we have an excellent chance of seeing our Peter smiling back at us in a relatively short while."

He gave her a gentle hug. Outside the building he ushered her into a waiting Town Car that swiftly bore her away. Then he collapsed into his own, his driver shutting him into the cocoon of air-conditioning and Mahler's Ninth. He helped himself to an Armagnac from a flask he kept next to his seat, and wondered if he should have offered to spend the night ministering to Beatrice's state of mind.

It's what she really wanted, he thought. Yes, he sighed, surrendering to the sense of triumph percolating through his system—but all in good time.

After the champagne had been drunk and the brighter lights had been dimmed, the seventy-six-year-old body of Peter Jance, a victim of cancer and age, was bagged along with the ravaged remains of Hans Brinkman's brain. The bag was sealed and transported to an incineration unit; within minutes, its contents were reduced to gases and ash. The former wafted up into the pale azure of the Caribbean sky, the latter were collected and, as ordered, were delivered to Frederick Wolfe personally. The next morning he would deposit them into the first of nine empty stainless steel urns he kept in a locked cabinet in his private quarters.

Five miles away, in Vieques's cafés and bars, nobody was the wiser. The tourists ordered their mai-tais and Heinekens, untroubled by questions of scientific hubris or medical ethics. The economy was healthy. The military was unchallenged. Life was good.

What quickly became thought of by the cognoscenti of Wolfe's inner circle as the rejuvenated Peter was transported to a heavily guarded post-op unit, where the next morning, still sleeping, he was joined by his wife.

Once alone with him, Beatrice lay her head on her husband's chest. Some part of her knew quite well indeed that it was in fact her husband's host's chest, but she kept those thoughts as shut away as Wolfe did his stainless steel urns.

She kept herself steady—for him, she told herself. Peter doesn't need your doubts. He needs you to be strong, to project heartfelt encouragement into the mind and spirit now held within that container—as she'd always tried to do in the past. If she had violated some natural law, or had doomed herself and Peter to some retribution she couldn't yet dream of—well, it was too late for regrets. Although she had been silently praying for the past twenty-four hours, she hadn't the least confidence that there was a God or, if God did exist, that there was any logical reason why she had offended Him or Her or It irrevocably. Nature was full of an implacable desire for survival, and even more filled with eons of experimentation of unfathomable complexity and even more bizarre combinations. And it all seemed without reason. At least she had a reason. She wanted survival for herself and for the man she loved.

All the rest could go to bloody hell.

6

On her way to the restaurant Kronenhalle, Elizabeth found herself crossing the Limmat River on the Quaibrücke, a gently arching stone bridge where she and Hans had once dared to rendezvous, before Yvette's suspicions had driven them indoors. In the weeks prior to his death, she had lingered here on several occasions, reliving the delicious moment when he had kissed her in front of God and a busload of tourists, several of whom had snapped their picture. Today, as then, swans and ducks plied the clear water, boats bobbed in the marinas of the Zürichsee and, with high gray clouds capping a pale post-rain sky, the air was clear all the way to the snow-peaked mountains. But now her heart was in her throat—the icy wind blowing off the water pierced her to the core. Worse, she knew it wasn't the cold that was plaguing her: it was a bone-deep fear that was making her shiver so hard her teeth chattered.

Spooked, she jogged across the rest of the bridge, turned left and followed Rämistrasse to the address of number 4. Inside, the Kronenhalle was an Art Deco extravagance of carved wood, etched glass and early-twentieth-century art. Rose-Anne Brinkman was waiting at a back banquette, wearing a floral print dress and a gold turban. The bartender, a pale Italian, was lighting her cigarette. Rose-Anne patted the seat beside her and Elizabeth slipped cautiously into the red booth.

"How are you feeling?" the woman asked straight off, looking deeply into Elizabeth's eyes with her quick blue gaze.

"I've been better," said Elizabeth warily.

"Me, too. Marco," she called to the bartender, who was watching them in the bar mirror. "Bring the young lady something to warm the pipes—make that two Courvoisiers." She turned back and got down to business. "Where you from, Elizabeth?"

If she hadn't seen this woman sobbing at the cemetery, she might have thought her incapable of mourning. In the artificial light, she seemed hard as nails. It might be the alcohol or the form her grief was taking—but whatever the cause, Elizabeth reflected, it would make it easier to share her suspicions, which had grown alarmingly since the funeral. Last Sunday, unable to get Hans's voice or the sound of the broken connection out of her head, she had driven into the Juras to the accident site, and had seen something she couldn't shake. "Originally? Lansing, Michigan. You?"

"Waxahachie, Texas. Married into the Navy, so Pensacola, Guam, Switzerland and Cherry Point, North Carolina came into the picture, too. Oh, and Vieques."

"Vieques?" said Elizabeth. The name rang a faint, haunting bell. "Where's that?"

"Oh, just a little nothing island in the Caribbean. So," she said, reaching out and tapping Elizabeth on the wrist, "you knew my son."

At the sudden gentleness in the woman's voice, Elizabeth felt her heart lighten, and in the same moment warned herself to be careful.

"Through a mutual friend," she fibbed.

"You were lovers," Rose-Anne corrected sharply.

Elizabeth flushed. "Did Hans say that?" she asked in the calmest voice she could summon, putting her hands in her lap so the woman couldn't see them trembling.

"Didn't have to," she declared. "Plain as the nose on your face. Leave the bottle," she added to the bartender as he set down their drinks. "But yes, he did talk about you."

It was music to Elizabeth's ears. "Often?" she ventured.

The woman smiled slightly. "Often enough. Never said boo about the others. And you know what I say? Good for you."

She lifted her drink, inviting Elizabeth to touch glasses. "He had lots of other women?" Elizabeth asked, putting glass to glass.

"Does the Pope wear funny white shoes? Come on, you must've known that just from how smooth he was. Drink up."

Elizabeth did as she was told. The liquid burned as it traveled down her throat and expanded into a pleasant fireball. Rose-Anne nodded approval.

"Myself, I'm drinking more these days," she said, and swallowed her own in several fast gulps. "Brandy and Patsy Cline, they get me through these nights." She refilled Elizabeth's glass.

"If it helps you," Rose-Anne said, "the others meant nothing to him."

"How do you know that?" asked Elizabeth, at once frightened and heartened by the woman's frankness. She was afraid by how much she wanted to believe her—and yet terrified not to.

"Because I asked him." Rose-Anne laughed. "I'm not shy. Fact is," she said more carefully, "I was worried about him."

Elizabeth went on alert. "Worried?"

"He must have told you about Yvette."

"A little," Elizabeth allowed.

"Not that I'm any big fan of affairs," Rose-Anne said. "I'm from Texas—we shoot women who mess with our men. But they had already bled each other dry. Hans lacked a certain clarity, let's say, about what was really important in life. Always did run just a little ahead of his headlights."

Elizabeth found herself smiling. "If you mean what I think you mean, he did, didn't he?"

"And his dad and me, we couldn't help him. He was his own kid always. Well, except for flying, but that came later, after Dave died. After Hans gave up physics."

The woman's voice was matter-of-fact; Elizabeth felt a chill. "His father isn't alive?"

"You see how close-mouthed he was? Don't know where he got that trait—didn't come by it honestly. No, hon, my husband's dead almost thirty years. SAM missile got him over Hanoi in 1972. No man could've done it. Dave could fly circles around a sparrow hawk."

Elizabeth nodded. "Hans loves to fly, too."

"It was the one thing he probably remembered his father talking about. The rest, well, Dave just knew flying. Hans seemed interested in everything, and a lot of it more complicated than either of us could get our brains around."

Elizabeth thought a moment. "Vieques."

Rose-Anne looked up.

"What about it?"

Elizabeth shrugged. "I don't know. Ever since you mentioned it, the name has been echoing in my head, like Oz or Tara, you know?"

"Nope."

Elizabeth laughed. "I don't either, except it's got a kind of children's-tale feeling to me, like a place you know about but not in real life."

Rose-Anne blinked. "It's not make-believe. In fact, it's where Hans was born. Little island off Puerto Rico. Big Navy base. Dave used to fly bombing practice there with his squadron." She hesitated a moment, then continued. "They had a fertility clinic, too."

For no reason she could name, Elizabeth felt her heart speed up. "A fertility clinic?"

"Dave and I had gone five years trying. God bless Dr. Wolfe, we used to say."

"Dr. Wolfe?"

"Doctor who ran the clinic. Hans owed his life to him—we owed him our happiness. All that time we had waited—it seemed to make us love the boy all the more. Though sometimes," she added sadly, "it did seem like a one-way street. When Dave died? It didn't seem to rattle Hans at all. Kept it all inside, I guess." She smiled a bittersweet smile and looked off. "How'd you deal with your dad's death?"

Elizabeth gave a wary frown. She had only mentioned this once to Hans, in the middle of the night after lovemaking had left them exhausted but too happy to sleep. "Hans told you?"

Rose-Anne nodded. "In a funny way you were like the glue between us—talking about you brought us together. You were a service brat, too, weren't you?"

"A service brat? No. I mean, my dad was in the Navy, yes, for a while. I kind of blotted out most of my childhood."

"A parent's death can do that. And then you had your own brush with mortality, isn't that true? You were quite a skier, Hans told me. And then, what, you had an accident?"

He had talked about her so much it astonished her. She felt exposed, briefly, but then warmed, as she realized exactly what that implied. She kept her face oblique. "Yeah, an accident," she said.

"See, now *you're* clamming up. Racing on skis, wasn't it?"

Did it make it worse, knowing how much he had cared about her? "Bit of bad luck. A rut in an icy track at the wrong split second—I went through the snow fence at about seventy, I guess."

"Went into the trees, Hans said. Smashed your face. Horrible."

"Well," said Elizabeth, "I was never quite Olympic caliber."

"Didn't spook you?"

"Actually, it had the opposite effect."

Rose-Anne laughed, and there was affection in it. "So Hans said. You like to ride things out—get to the bottom of things. And it sure didn't ruin your looks."

"In fact," Elizabeth admitted, "it improved them. They did a better job on my face than they did on my knee."

"Well, they must have had something good to work with. I can't get my hair done without seeing your face in some magazine or other. She took a drink, then smiled conspiratorially. "Want to see some pictures of Hans?"

Without waiting for an answer, Rose-Anne opened her purse and pulled out a sheaf of snapshots. Old pictures, mostly, in funny formats, small, long, trimmed—even a few yearbook photos.

"Hans in junior high, star pitcher of the baseball team."

Elizabeth studied the picture avidly. Hans at fourteen was already Hans.

"And here he is on the high school diving team. All-state two years running. A natural athlete—whatever he took up. Straight As, too—like you," she said fondly.

Elizabeth leafed through the snapshots, absently running her finger over Hans's face, feeling again that odd sense of kinship that had haunted her from their very first meeting. She found a snapshot of him in his early twenties, standing next to a Cessna two-seater, shoulder to shoulder with a grinning, spade-bearded man twice his age.

"That's the day he soloed," said Rose-Anne.

"This his father?"

"His flight instructor. Said Hans was a natural. But then Hans seemed to do everything easily—except make real connections with people. You, I think, got closer than anybody."

Elizabeth fought back the lump in her throat and went to the next snapshot, Hans as a tiny boy. All smiles, standing on a beach holding a big red ball about his head. Without asking, she knew this was Vieques. "He looks so happy."

Rose-Anne squinted. "Hans loved Vieques. Always wanted to go back, never got around to it. He was so busy, he never had time to take a rest. Maybe he'll rest now," she added quietly. Her voice sounded bitter for the first time, almost angry. "So," she changed subjects, "what's this thing that doesn't make sense?"

Elizabeth took a deep breath, her heart taking off at a gallop. "I was talking to him," she said, "just before the accident. Somebody did something stupid—another driver, it must've been—he was about to crash into him when he was cut off."

Rose-Anne blinked. "You sure about that?" she asked soberly.

"That's what it sounded like to me."

"The police didn't mention another car. There was only one set of tire marks."

"It's not just that," said Elizabeth. "I drove up there, where it happened? I found his tire tracks. He braked hard. You could see that very clearly. Then he must've swerved. There was a big dent in the guardrail with the same color paint on it as his car."

"He went through the rail."

"Not there, he didn't. He went back across the road, hit the rocks, and bounced back to the rail a second time."

Rose-Anne took another sip of her drink. Elizabeth realized how hard it must be for her to hear this.

"So," the woman said, "he went through there, right?"

Elizabeth checked the bartender. He was watching them in the mirror again until he noticed her looking back. Then he busied himself polishing a glass. Elizabeth leaned in closer to Rose-Anne and lowered her voice.

"The tracks stopped at the edge of the cliff. The car didn't have enough momentum to go over. You could see where the frame rested on the edge, and where the tires had sunk in after it stopped. He stopped, and *then* he went over the edge."

Rose-Anne looked away and finished her drink.

"So, what're you saying . . . ?"

Elizabeth frowned. "I don't know." She finished her drink as well but they didn't reorder. Rose-Anne looked back at her, and Elizabeth asked, "Rose-Anne, tell me, did Hans ever mention being followed?"

Rose-Anne straightened. "You really *are* turning into a sleuth, aren't you?"

"If that's what it takes."

Rose-Anne smiled as if she understood, reached out and patted Elizabeth's hand. "Matter of fact, he talked about it all the time. Last week I visited him, he was having his house swept for bugs."

"What do you make of that?"

Rose-Anne looked at her and then laughed. "I think it shows how little Hans knew people, thinking Yvette was having him tailed. She didn't give a damn about his affairs. He was her meal ticket, hon. Period."

Elizabeth looked at her. "Meal ticket? I thought her father—"

"Was rich? Nope. Connected, sure. Used to be rich, maybe. But when it came to actual plunk-down-on-the-barrelhead cash, the family was damn near hand-to-mouth. The reason they *looked* rich was because their capacity for denial was as overblown as their lifestyle." She shook her head. "Yvette was completely dependent on Hans."

"Maybe she did it for the money?"

"Maybe Hans's estate will keep her afloat for a while, but no, Yvette will go through that faster than a cow can crap. She was dumb, but not dumb enough to kill the goose that laid the golden eggs for her every quarter."

Elizabeth sighed. "But he was so sure something was going on."

"One word for that. Paranoia."

Elizabeth stared at the photo, Hans with the beach ball held aloft, a palm tree rising behind him, the turquoise ocean. It was as though she were expecting the picture to move, the palm to start waving in the breeze, and Hans to call out to her in a little-boy voice.

She felt Rose-Anne's hand on her arm again.

"Really, Elizabeth, don't beat up on yourself. You've got to take the hit and go on. That's what I'm doing."

But she couldn't. Somebody had made Hans crash, she felt it in her soul.

But if not Yvette, who?

VIEQUES ISLAND

That Peter had survived at all was a miracle, and it brought other miracles in its wake. With the exception of a few easily repaired bleeds, his body was alive and his condition stable. Even more encouraging, early CAT scans revealed no lesions or anomalies in his brain. His autonomic functions were normal, and the reflexes in his extremities were at full strength. This implied strongly that the brain stem had survived undamaged. So far as Wolfe and his assistants could tell, all the major splices had not only held but were now transmitting neural messages bilaterally as fluently as they would in a pristine body. The brain had survived the transfer, and the body had survived the implantation. The outcome, Wolfe declared, with a bow toward Mary Shelley, was "electrifying." Henderson continued to send flowers and champagne every day.

Wolfe had ordered the chemicals keeping Peter in his protective coma be withdrawn at the end of the first week. Within two days Peter's higher brain waves were sending the needles of the EEG trembling into tentative bursts of activity. Barrola had recommended a Valium drip, in case there was some kind of psychic trauma hidden in the marriage between body and brain that would overwhelm Peter's psyche once he awoke. Wolfe, however, saw no evidence of anxiety in Peter's brain scans, and had discontinued the IV. All Peter's cortical readings, in fact, were approaching normal.

With the exception of an auxiliary oxygen tube, Peter was taken off life support.

The body kept breathing on its own.

The cardiac redcart team was taken off alert, as was the emergency surgery unit. Except for security patrols, by degree and echelon the remainder of the Fountain Compound stood down, catching their first rest in weeks.

Meanwhile Wolfe and Beatrice and Emilio Barrola waited to see what would happen next, watching at Peter's bedside in overlapping shifts, never daring to expect more miracles than they had already been granted, and always prepared for the worst.

But the miracles kept coming. Every day.

Indeed, Peter's brain appeared to be thriving in its new environment. The waves grew in vigor until they approximated normal human deep-sleep consciousness. Electrodes taped to his eyelids gave evidence of REM, a strong indication that he was seeing images in something approximating a dream state. He was alive and sleeping well, in fact.

But there was a difference, a crucial difference.

When morning came, he didn't open his eyes.

Morning after morning.

After five days of this, Wolfe began to show impatience.

"He should be waking by now," he grumbled. Seeing the blood drain from Beatrice's face, he instantly regretted having said anything at all. Like Peter, whose deputy he had become, he abhorred causing her pain.

They tried mild injections of stimulants, without results. They tried loud noises: nothing. They touched him, they slapped him. Nothing. Beatrice read to him from Lewis Carroll, her favorite author, and from Thomas Pynchon, who was Peter's. Nothing. She described every hotel they'd stayed in on vacation, and, when Wolfe was out of the room, highlights of their erotic life together. Nothing. They tried playing Haydn, for whom Peter had cultivated a preference over Mozart and consequently adored. They tried Ornette Coleman, whom Peter particularly detested.

Nothing.

"How long are you going to wait?" Beatrice asked, as one week turned into three, and worry moved into despair.

"I don't consider it my decision," Wolfe answered prudently. He knew she was testing his loyalty, as if sensing, beyond her single-minded focus on Peter's welfare, that he as head of the entire project had other fish to fry. But the fact was he had at the moment no other experimental subjects on whom to practice, and no wish to think of anything else but the survival of this key organism lying before him.

"You're thinking of pulling the plug on this, aren't you?" she asked, eyeing him as would a creature with its back to the wall.

He looked at her with as much kindness as he could.

"Beatrice. To begin with, there's no plug to pull. To withhold nourishment, at this point, given the vitality of his brain waves, could be construed as actionable—"

"Freddy," said Beatrice, wincing as she turned away from Peter's body, from the humming, blinking monitors, "*You're* the heartless one, not Henderson."

"I'm agreeing with you," Wolfe protested. "He's completely viable and we're not going to abandon him in any way!"

"Although," a voice piped up behind them. It was Alex Davies, who had taken Barrola's shift while the surgeon was off doing big-ticket surgery on the mainland. "Who'd bring the malpractice suit, when you think about it?"

"Alex," said Wolfe gently, "that will do."

Alex looked at Peter and rubbed his chin.

"Maybe he's afraid to wake up," Alex said, ignoring the rush of blood to his grandfather's face.

"What do you mean, afraid?" said Beatrice tightly.

"Don't encourage him," said Wolfe.

"Afraid of what?" Beatrice persisted.

Alex passed a knuckle under his nose. "Afraid of facing the finer implications, you know what I'm saying? I would be. He was supposed to die, he was ready to die, and then you guys made him an offer he couldn't refuse." He looked at them and grinned, guileless.

"Maybe he's afraid to rejoin you two. God knows what you'll ask in return."

They glared at him.

He threw up his hands. "Just being whimsical. Sorry."

There was a vein bulging on Wolfe's forehead by now as he fixed Alex with a laser eye.

"Alex," said Wolfe, "you're free to go. Now."

"Just a thought," said Alex and shrugged. He gave a friendly wave and walked out the door. "Anyone want coffee?" He stopped and looked back, then shrugged again and disappeared.

Beatrice turned back to Wolfe.

"Maybe Alex has a point," she said.

"I'm not sure I heard any point," Wolfe grumbled.

"Then what's the answer? Why isn't Peter coming out of his coma?"

"I don't have an answer," he declared, acknowledging to himself that this woman was getting on his nerves.

"That's not the right answer!" Beatrice shouted back at him. "I want my husband back!"

Wolfe blanched. Was it possible, what he suddenly found himself suspecting—that in some perverse and jealous chamber of his soul, he didn't *want* Peter to wake up? Absurd, he thought. If Peter dies, I've failed. The rest is childish nonsense. "There's no right or wrong here," he pleaded with her, feeling off-balance and impotent. "Obviously we'll do everything we can. Considering all we've got invested, to do less would be madness."

"Oh, I see," said Beatrice coldly. "Now it's a money issue—"

"Of course that's not what I meant," he protested. "What we've *all* got invested—emotionally, spiritually—Peter especially—Peter's life is of paramount importance here—that goes without saying."

"No, Freddy. That *never* goes without saying. Ever."

It was said in cold fury, and then she was out the door.

Wolfe listened to her footsteps echo down the hall, and in a rare spasm of self-reproach cursed himself for his tactlessness. All that hard-earned gratitude and affection—were they going up in smoke? Don't be an idiot, he told himself. He turned again to Peter, and vowed inwardly that he would win it all back as soon as Peter came around. Then we'll see who owes what to whom. "Right, Peter?" he said aloud.

On the monitor, the EEG seemed to surge for an instant, as if in reply. Good Lord, thought Wolfe to himself, you're getting as flaky as your grandson. And, thinking of Alex, he hurried out of the room to tell the little bastard never to embarrass him in front of Beatrice again.

7

VIEQUES ISLAND

Beatrice had moved into Peter's room; she no longer trusted anyone else to keep watch. Wolfe's cavalier attitude still rankled, and Alex Davies seemed to be avoiding her.

She caught up with him finally at a table in the base cafeteria. He made some polite inquiries about Peter's condition, although she suspected he already knew. She decided to be blunt.

"What's going on between you two?" she asked him.

"What do you mean?" said Alex disingenuously.

"You know what I mean. You and your grandfather."

Alex shrugged. "The usual."

"He dotes on you," Beatrice declared gently.

Alex let out a laugh. "Yeah, maybe. Like the way Lear dotes on the Fool."

"You're anything but a fool, Alex."

"Protective coloration," agreed Alex with a smile, and poked at his food.

"Do you think Frederick still believes in the project?"

"You mean in Peter Jance?"

This kid was always a step or two ahead of where she expected him to be. "All right," she said. "Do you think he's in it for the long haul with Peter? Has he confided in you?"

"As far as he can, I suppose," Alex said. "He'll stick in there with Dr. Jance. It's a matter of pride, if nothing else. Besides, science must go on, right?"

"Perhaps everyone deserves to live a little longer. Maybe it would help advance the acquisition of wisdom." She felt cold inside. Not even she believed that. Alex smiled thinly.

"Scientists first—that was always how he sold it. And with the implication, of course, that military leaders came in a close second. That was because he needed them for funding, by the way, not because he respects them."

She looked at the kid, and saw in his eyes all the hidden doubts she had about the project herself. Just for an instant. It was far too threatening to the necessary survival of her husband to question it that way.

"I'm surprised," she chided. "You don't think it's the government wanting the president to live in perpetuity?"

Alex shook his head, taking her jest as a straight comment. "No, the military's more powerful than any president—they're around far longer, and they've got better security." He grinned impishly. Was he serious, or putting her on? She didn't know. "But eventually he'll dump the military and look for private-sector funding—that's where the real money is now. Corporations. They'll pay through the nose for immortality, and they've got the deepest pockets." She watched him. She still didn't know.

"What about artists? Philosophers?"

He just laughed. Then he leaned forward and said in a surprisingly earnest voice, "Peter's the ticket. If he survives, the sky's the limit. Grandpa will never give up on him, he can't afford to."

Why wasn't she comforted? Then she remembered the word.

"If?" she asked. "Do you know something I don't?"

"When," said Alex. "*When* Peter survives. Listen," he went on, as though reading her mind, "I don't know anything you don't. It's just—" He let it drop.

"What?"

He looked at her with a strange expression, then shrugged and said, "Problem is, there's not much you know that *I* don't."

He looked at her as if to let that sink in. And it did.

"Like . . . like what?" she asked, and was almost sorry she did.

Alex looked off for a moment with a smile, like a little kid that's far too smart to be patronized might if he were being talked down to.

Then he looked back and said matter-of-factly, "He took skin scrapings from all you guys, right? Back in the days of the fertility clinic?"

Beatrice put down her fork; suddenly she lost her appetite. "Frederick told you that?"

Alex laughed again. "Well, sorta. He keeps it in an encrypted computer file, but that just made it more intriguing." He looked at her like one friend to another. "You ever read *Peanuts*?" he asked.

"You mean the comic strip?"

He nodded. "You know Snoopy, the beagle, how he says 'Anything on the floor is mine'? Well, my feeling is, anything on a computer is mine." He smiled. "There isn't an encryption logarithm I can't break. He took DNA from all of you guys."

She was only able to nod her head slightly, astonished to have something so hidden in the past spoken of so offhandedly, especially by someone young enough to be her own grandson. But he wasn't through surprising her.

"Yours included. Right?"

She felt her blood run cold. She heard her voice as if from another room. "Yes, I suppose he did."

"Well, there you go," said Alex.

"And you know who the clones are," Beatrice managed after several deep breaths.

"What makes you think that?" he said, trying to smile but twitching just noticeably.

"That day at the briefing," said Beatrice. "You knew the man whose spinal nerves had been joined. I heard you say his name."

"Rashid al-Assad," said Alex after a moment. "He was a guinea pig, not a clone. No, my grandfather's got all the clone data kept somewhere else—maybe in his head, maybe buried in the backyard—who knows?" He said this last a little too brightly, and immediately stood. "Look, I'm sorry to blurt and run, but I've got some differential equations to solve. Second-order suckers. Want to be up to speed when your husband comes around—which he *will*," Alex assured her softly, giving a thumbs-up as he went out the cafeteria door.

Beatrice watched him go and wondered whether everything he'd said about his own knowledge was true. It occurred to her he might know everything, whether it had been planned that way or not. It also occurred to her that if that were true, it might be the reason he was included so intimately in Wolfe's program. He might know—literally—where the bodies were buried.

She made a mental note to keep a closer eye on Alex, and to try to talk to him again soon. But somehow it never happened. In the following days, both Wolfe and his quirky grandson vanished off her radar screen, along with her own research. Her only thoughts were of Peter. She brought a cot into his room, forsaking sleep in order to monitor his progress. His vital signs hadn't changed, he refused to wake, but she knew in her heart he was *in* there; and she suspected—hoped to God—that he was in there intact. "Locked-in syndrome" was the term Wolfe had used to describe it, hinting (even as he attempted to console her) that if Peter didn't come out of it soon, he might indeed die after all.

Beatrice, refusing to be handled, retorted that Wolfe didn't know Peter. Peter was a fighter. Peter never gave up.

She prayed Peter still knew that as well.

Two more weeks went by. She spent countless hours simply sitting by his bed—studying him, this man who was at once her husband and a stranger.

But such a familiar stranger.

He was Peter at age thirty-five, and it took her back to their earliest days, and her own youth. Peter had been forty when his DNA was harvested, but his clone was even younger, his skin ruddy and resilient, nails smooth, hair glossy, abundant and blond, lips soft and full.

She marveled at it all, even as it made her shudder.

After three weeks, there was hardly a trace of scar tissue left on his body. Beatrice's genetic bonding material had fused the skin back together almost seamlessly. In a darker moment, it crossed her mind that she could make a fortune in cosmetics if she were working in the civilian sector. That would be someone else's good fortune, she mused, years into the future, when all this knowledge was declassified and accepted as routine. For now, if they only knew, governments would kill for the secret she had discovered, and for what it had allowed Peter to become.

"You look exactly the way you did in 1958," she told him, caressing his strong, graceful hands. "Remember 1958?"

She stopped. Something was different in the room. What?

"*Explorer I*, when it made it into orbit? How many times did we make love that night—three? Four? It was your math that made that flight possible. God, I was so proud of you."

What was that new sound?

She glanced over at the screens. Was it wishful thinking, or was the heart monitor showing a slight increase in pulse?

She gripped his hand more tightly. "Remember Von Braun? We hated his pomposity, we thought he'd grab all the credit, and then he thanked you publicly? And you were imitating him, and we started to laugh—remember that four-poster bed? And the champagne he sent us—the cheap stuff?"

No question about it. Peter's heart was beating faster.

"Yes," she said, her own heart in her throat now, "you remember. What else about 1958—come on, you used to love this game. Elvis went in the Army, what else? Van Cliburn won the Tchaikovsky Competition, Pasternak won the Nobel, what was that Miles Davis album you used to make me listen to, until I finally broke down and learned to enjoy it?" Peter's chest was heaving and her eyes were tearing. She leaned into his ear, trembling. "*Kind of Blue*, that's right—and what about the new Pope? One of the ten best years of the century, 1958, what were some of our other favorites?"

His breath was coming in rasps and she reached to adjust the intertrachial catheter. She had barely touched it when his hand came up and pushed hers away.

"Hurts," he croaked.

The word was barely audible, but Beatrice gave a shout that brought the nurses running and, behind them, Frederick Wolfe. The light in Wolfe's eyes, though it signaled less than total optimism, made her heart beat even faster. She hugged him, and he held her, as they waited for Peter to say more. He had sunk back into sleep, but—God willing—if the signs were as they seemed, the worst might be over.

Peter not only was alive, but was fighting his way back.

Sometimes he could see the room he was in.

For three more days, he fought to reach the light, each time losing it just as it seemed within his grasp. Then reality would waver like a station dialed in and out on a gigantic radio, eventually swinging him over into endless striations of static, alien DJs and cosmic noise.

Heroically he struggled to remain awake, to retain his awareness of Beatrice at his side, holding his hand, stroking his forehead, desperately sensing, even as he was slipping in and out of it, how much he craved that homeland of rational consciousness.

And then he would find himself drowning again. The liquid was pleasure, and he was looking up at Beatrice. Her lively gray eyes were full of grateful tears; her mouth was moving, but no words were coming out. Her face grew smaller and the touch of her hand was so light he couldn't feel it, and then he was somewhere in perfect darkness again, without pain or stress or thought, swathed in a womb of primal being. Helpless and pure.

But even there he was wrapped in the warmth of his terrible, wonderful secret: I'm alive, he kept telling himself. I've been reborn. The pain is gone, the cancer is gone, as if it had never been there at all.

"Beatrice?"

Was that the first time he'd managed her name? He could see her eyes, two gray suns in an ocean of darkness.

"I'm here. Peter? Can you hear me?"

He struggled to make his thoughts clear. "Not here," he said.

"Yes, you are. You're here."

"Not me. I'm not me."

Her silence told him everything. She forced herself to speak.

"I said yes, didn't I?"

"Yes. And thank God you did."

It was his turn to be silent. His mind seemed to be hovering high above the bed, as though fighting to escape the body where it didn't belong. He was terrified.

"Peter, are you cogent?"

His tongue was thick. "'M I hungry? Yes, hungry."

She was laughing. The sound of it dispelled the horror for a moment, filling his heart with something like delight.

"I felt you did it for me," she said.

"Didn't," he managed.

She didn't say anything. She knew what he meant. She felt his anguish, even his guilt. And his nascent hope as well. Her maternal instinct to comfort him was enormous; she wanted to protect him in his newness. She leaned close to him and whispered in his ear.

"Peter, remember what you said? About how things were meant to happen? Well, this was meant to be."

"S'a miracle," he said with difficulty, and his eyes misted.

"Yes, a miracle."

Suddenly he was crying like a baby. In the next moment he wanted all the tubes yanked out of his body. Nurses were called to restrain him. After a few minutes he calmed down. He asked for solid food.

"Peter, not yet."

"I'll walk out," he said, his voice ragged but stronger than before. He was unsure whether he meant it or was trying to make her laugh, but it had that effect. Beatrice laughed, and nurses ran to confer with Wolfe about food.

Wolfe was cautious, but Peter was given the equivalent of baby food, a mash of nutrients that he apparently found delicious. He ate with the fierce pleasure of a child at his mother's breast.

Whenever he asked for something, people jumped as never before. His thoughts grew more complex once he was satisfied. He wondered if he now had some terrible leverage, now that he was the pioneer craft in their exploration of this brave new world. So fragile and singular upon such an uncharted sea. And there was no denying that was true—it was the first thing Beatrice had described to him, once they were able to carry on a sustained conversation. He couldn't find it in his heart to tell her how frightened he was himself. He told her how normal he felt, although every time he glimpsed his new body, he was terrified by its otherness. He dissembled, and did it well. He didn't have to lie about everything, to be sure. He told her of his overwhelming love and gratitude to her for staying by him, for all she must have suffered during the hellish procedure and its uncertain aftermath. Thanks to Beatrice, even thanks to Wolfe and his shadowy organization, he was alive.

But when he was alone, he was accompanied by a leaden fear. He was himself and he wasn't. He would never be purely himself again. He was a third thing. The eeriness of his situation haunted him, never so much as when he was about to fall asleep. Worse was when he was hurled groggy from his frequent nightmares, long arduous affairs in which he reexperienced the pain of his cancer, as if whatever remained of his soul was telling him to be thankful, to forget guilt and savor life.

A week after he had regained consciousness, Peter suddenly began spewing out theorems, postulates, formulae—all manner of random shards of textbook physics—as if his brain was up and doing calisthenics after a long, long sleep. And soon he had to stop and think before he could ask where his doubts had gone. At week six, he stood on his own for the first time. In isolated bursts, he now found himself speaking cogently about the Hammer, pouring out ideas that were fresh and original and sent Wolfe scrambling for stenographers.

The next day, he asked for a full-length mirror.

Beatrice watched him as they wheeled it in. He stood in front of it a full five minutes before speaking. The sight of his body, its evoking familiarity, seemed to mock him. It's me, he told himself. Then why did it look and feel so foreign? Until the age of sixty or so, he had felt a seamless continuity between his past and his present, as if he'd never really been different, in mind or body, from what he was at age twenty, almost as if he'd never been a child at all. And here he was again, age thirty-five, and the effect was every bit as startling as standing in front of a funhouse mirror, or seeing himself from an entirely new angle in a clothing store mirror. That can't be me, he said silently to his reflection. And it isn't, his reflection answered back.

"S'been a while," he said thickly. His speech control, though improving, was still uncertain, especially when he was talking about things that frightened him; the science had come forward easily, almost unbidden.

"Since you looked like that?" said Beatrice gently. "About forty years."

"N'even while shaving."

She understood without his having to elaborate—that over the years he'd fallen into the habit of not really looking at his reflection at all, for fear of noticing some new collapse or blemish; his dermatologist had, in effect, become his mirror. Beatrice knew the feeling all too well.

"Body's better'n mine was."

"Well, different," she said.

"He took good care," he said. That, of course, was at the root of it. Somebody else had owned this body. He, an aged man in a process nature had mandated for all time and all species, had gone against that law and stolen this body for himself. He wondered if in the process he had forfeited some precious part of his own identity. A part of him was sure he had. But another part, a growing part, stirred in restless rebellion against such doubts. This part, and he suspected it was the body itself, wanted only to live. In that sense, the body was his now, no matter how dark that truth might be. You can't very well give it back, anyway, *can* you? he told himself.

"Thank God he took care of it," Beatrice was saying.

He swung around slowly to stare at her. He saw her flinch, and then realized that she was suddenly self-conscious of her own body compared to his. He took her, somewhat clumsily, into his arms.

It felt good to hold her. The familiar smells of her hair and skin thrilled his senses, and he loved her with all his heart. Perhaps that was all that mattered.

Over the next few days, she showered him with attention of every sort, and he reveled in it. He complained about the bad food at the Fountain Compound and they sent out for seafood from local restaurants. He found his speech improving every day, and he began to eat ravenously, including items he had learned to avoid, like cream sauces and rich cheeses. He discovered he could read a newspaper at ten feet, and smell night-blooming jasmine when the nearest bush was apparently a quarter mile away.

And he began to have erotic dreams. They were vague enough to report to Beatrice. Whoever his partner had been, she had vaporized instantly upon waking.

"I don't suppose it was me," said Beatrice.

Peter laughed. "Of course it was you," he said. "Who else would it be?"

She accepted his statement, and so did he. Although he actually had no idea if that were so or not.

In a much shorter time than anybody had ever dared hope to expect, the key members of Peter's team were flown in from White Sands. Hank Flannagan, Cap Chu and Rosemarie Wiener got off at Vieques Airport knowing only that they were in for an exciting surprise, and that they should be prepared to stay. Beatrice hunted down Alex Davies, who had been avoiding her. She found him in his tiny cubicle, the cinder-block walls utterly bare except for an enormous velvet clown painting. He was so engrossed in his computer screen he didn't look up as she entered. She caught a glimpse of a file name, H. BRINKMAN 1963-? Alex was scrolling through it furiously. As Beatrice took a step closer, he spun around with a yelp.

"Sorry to startle you," said Beatrice. What was he up to? The screen was layered with windows, but when she tried to read further, Alex swiftly clicked back to his screensaver.

"Just catching up on some e-mail," said Alex. "What's up?"

He was acting awfully furtive, but Beatrice had her priorities. "We're having a briefing on Peter. His team is arriving and we need to discuss the cover story."

"Yeah? How's the old man feeling about this? Excuse me, the *new* man."

"I think he feels two ways," said Beatrice.

"Appropriate," said Alex. "So, you think he's going to be able to handle it? Old cowboy, new horse?"

"I'm sure he'll do just fine," said Beatrice, somewhat stiffly. "His brain's functioning better than ever."

"Old arteries and all."

She was blindsided by that one. Why the hell hadn't *that* occurred to her? The veins and arteries in his brain would be as old as he was; they'd have to be even more careful. "You've seen what he's come up with already," she reminded him, trying not to show the effect of his maddeningly casual comment. "He says it's only the beginning. He's ready to get back to work, full-time."

"That's terrific. That's great." Alex raked a hand though his hair. "So yeah, do we have a cover story?"

"We want to say that Peter's son is taking over. Peter Jance, Jr."

"Whoa, great name," said Alex, spinning in his swivel chair. "How long did it take Grandpa to think *that* one up? You think they're gonna buy it?"

"Why wouldn't they?"

"Well, for one thing," Alex said, "you're childless."

"And why would anybody know that?" said Beatrice. This was what she was here to talk about. "Unless it was part of your pillow talk with Rosemarie Wiener."

He barked out a laugh, caught off-guard as she had hoped. "Pillow talk? I don't remember any pillow talk. Pillow fights, sure. I'm just being an alarmist. Peter Jance, Jr., fine. And what has this guy been doing all his life?" He thought, then snapped his fingers.

"He's been working on a project of his own."

"What project?" Beatrice asked.

"Classified. So top secret its very existence couldn't be acknowledged."

"Kind of like the Fountain Project. Or the Hammer."

"Exactly," Alex smiled. "Like father, like son."

Beatrice nodded. "I suppose it could fly."

"It will," Alex said.

And it did.

The only other explanation, that Peter Jance, Jr., was actually Peter Jance's clone housing Peter Jance's brain, could hardly have occurred spontaneously to Flannagan, Chu or Wiener.

Peter had never shared personal matters with his staff, preferring always to focus on the work. The sudden appearance of his son was therefore more intriguing than surprising. Besides, Flannagan, Chu and Wiener had spent most of their professional lives on classified government projects, away from family and friends, so they had a deep respect for secrecy. As far as they were concerned, it was the way of the world. The worrisome moment came when Rosemarie began to flirt with her handsome new superior—pumping out the pheromones, as Alex observed to the others. Beatrice studied Peter's face, despite herself, watching for signs that he was responding, but saw nothing there but professional enthusiasm; and when the briefing was over, Peter hugged her tenderly.

"I'm back," he said, and gave her a kiss on the cheek.

To everyone around him, Peter's newfound enthusiasm was contagious, erasing the aura of strangeness that made the first few days a little awkward. As far as Wolfe and his cohorts were concerned, this man, who a few weeks before had been at death's door, had simply had his body pushed backward in time, like a watch rewound and reset. With the exception of the toned physique, he was the same man, with all his memories and genius intact. He simply had his youth back again. In a way, as Wolfe commented, it seemed absolutely normal.

"As natural," Peter observed, "as a new pair of sneakers."

"Exactly," said Wolfe. "Ponce de León, eat your heart out!" There was a flurry of obedient laughter from the military types in the room. Ordinarily, Wolfe was not given to this sort of merriment. Alex cleared his throat.

"Unfortunately, Ponce de León ended up getting murdered by the natives."

"Alex, go work if you can't enjoy this."

"I'm enjoying, I'm enjoying." Alex pasted a bright smile on his face and walked away. The celebration resumed. Beatrice passed around paper cups, and the inner core helped themselves to Henderson's champagne.

The next day, Peter couldn't remember who he was.

It happened subtly, and at first they thought he was joking. Then his left side went numb and he lost use of his extremities. They rushed him back to bed and administered anticoagulants, along with cholesterol-reducing drugs designed to help reverse the sclerotic changes in his seventy-six-year-old cerebral blood vessels. He responded within a few hours and they gave him a CAT scan. There was a cloudy area in his left hemisphere, but it cleared even as they shot the scans.

"Could have been anything," Wolfe said quietly, his expression grave. "One tiny fleck of clotted material from any of a dozen sutures. We're lucky it hasn't happened before."

By the next day, Peter was joking about it, but the general mood had grown somber. He was placed under twenty-four-hour watch, and a strict protocol was established to monitor and test his physiological parameters three times a day.

Meanwhile he harassed the clinic's nurses, in a wheelchair.

"Where's Hawking? I'll race him to the chow line," he shouted, but nobody joined in the laughter. Beatrice retreated to their room, trying to keep herself from flying apart. Flannagan and Chu wondered what had become of their new boss and why their lab sessions had been put on hold, and Rosemarie Wiener was in a lovesick funk. Oscar Henderson phoned Wolfe every hour, demanding progress reports and asking when in hell they could expect work to resume on the weapon.

But it would be a while. Peter had only partial use of his left arm and leg, and his recollection of the previous day was poor, including the astonishing ideas that he had presented.

With heavy hearts, they began the process of teaching him what he had taught them only twenty-four hours earlier.

ZURICH

Elizabeth hadn't slept for three days.

Last night she had managed no more than a two-hour doze, plagued by nightmares. She saw Hans's hands snaking out from beneath wet, heavy soil, his hands caked with mud. She heard him in her kitchen, making them breakfast. She saw him lying in a web of pain, writhing in agony as the net bucked and some hideous arachnid with steel mandibles rushed to enfold him. She had never dreamt anything so frightening, and after a certain point, sleep was no longer an option.

To ease the anguish, Annie suggested meditating. Meditation had worked for Elizabeth in the hospital, after her skiing accident, while she was recovering from the blown knee and the spiral fracture in her leg and, later, from the pain of massive plastic surgery. She constructed a huge white room in her mind, then went around throwing open all the doors and windows. She put herself in the center and waited. Presently she saw the gossamer drapes heave inward as if an unfelt wind had entered the room.

"That was Hans," Annie told her later. "You're helping him find peace."

But Elizabeth doubted if the exercise was helping. That night, as she tried to take a nap, she could feel his hands groping at the edges of her fatigue, fingernails scraping at the seam between waking and sleeping.

She had to get out of the house.

She went to the police again to report the marks at the brink of the canyon, as if a car had rested there. They told her the case had been closed, refusing even to take a statement.

She spent a couple of afternoons with Annie, but Annie's New Age prescriptions were starting to grate on her nerves, and Elizabeth was reluctant to burden her with further doubts. Besides, in her own mind Annie had already accounted for Elizabeth's problems.

"You're reliving your dad's death," she declared. "His heart attack was senseless, and so was Hans's accident. That's why you're inventing these theories. You're trying to control things after the fact."

"The car didn't go over the edge fast enough to make a clear tire print," Elizabeth insisted. "He could have gotten out. The car must have been pushed or tipped."

"By his wife's detectives?"

"No. I don't think that anymore."

"No, because his mom showed you how that couldn't be true. Lizzy, you're like those people who predict the end of the world. And when the world doesn't end, they have to find some reason it didn't.

Like their prayers kept it from happening. It's called cognitive disso-
nance. I'll give you a book to read . . ."

On one day, the worst so far, Elizabeth had driven to Fluntern
Cemetery with a pocketbook full of cash and offered the operators of
the cemetery's grave-digging backhoe a healthy bribe to dig Hans up.
They were North Africans, and thought she was joking at their ex-
pense. When she had convinced them that she was not, they took the
money and instructed her to come back at midnight. She'd done as
she was told, terrified, but determined to see Hans face-to-face.

But the gravediggers didn't show up. Worse, the police did.

She was humiliated when Annie and Roland had to bail her out,
and further mortified when she had to hire a lawyer to have the crim-
inal charges dismissed. She escaped with a stern warning, but meanwhile her modeling agency had heard about the case. The head of the
Helvetica office told her that if she ever tried a stunt like that again,
her career as a model was finished.

She had been so long without sleep by then, though, it hardly mattered. Photographers were starting to comment on her haggard look,
and the calls for her services were thinning to a trickle.

Annie started leaving the names of psychotherapists on her answering machine.

Elizabeth ignored the messages. As for the dwindling job offers,
she found she didn't much care. She was glad for the free time. She
needed to do more investigating.

She found the drivers of the ambulance that had responded to the
crash, and questioned them closely. One was particularly helpful in
describing the clothing of the victim—the few scraps that hadn't been
charred to ashes, including the Schiaparelli tag inside the jacket.

Hans had a Schiaparelli suit that he favored for meetings. Dove-
gray flannel, as she recalled, as soft as a bird's plumage.

She asked about the general build of the body, and anything unusual the driver had observed.

"There is one thing," the driver recalled. He was a Frenchman with
prominent pink gums and a postage-stamp mustache.

"What?"

"I don't like to talk about it, mademoiselle. Maybe somebody at the morgue could help you out. They have pictures, you know. They keep them under lock and key, but I have a friend who could show them to you."

"What's your friend's name?"

"That depends on you."

Elizabeth started to take out her wallet, but the man shook his head.

"Not that," he said simply, and gave an oily smile.

Elizabeth felt her throat tighten. "You *did* see something unusual?"

"On my mother's life, I swear it."

I should have built a shrine to Hans, thought Elizabeth, and let it go at that. Paste his picture to the wall, the one from Vieques, surround it with candles.

Hans, I'm doing this for you, she thought shakily, as she unbuttoned her skirt.

She left the driver's apartment without showering. But before she did she truned and looked at the creep with such intensity he flinched. "If this is bogus," she said coldly, holding up the piece of paper with the morgue attendant's name, "I promise I will come back and this time you will feel nothing but pain."

At the morgue she found the attendant who had taken in the body. He was wary of her, as if she were a clochard who had wandered in from skid row. When she glanced in the dissection room mirror, she was shocked by the wildness of her hair and eyes. She gave him ten thousand francs and he pulled the records.

The photographs appalled her.

There was little more to the body than a burned torso, arms ending in charred stumps, a head that was more bone than face. She had intended to photocopy or steal the dental records, but her first glance at the close-up of the skull told her that was hopeless. There was nothing approaching teeth left, only a dark hole where the mouth should be.

She threw up in a wastebasket, and when she looked again the attendant was sealing the records away.

"Just a second, I'm not finished," she said, and grabbed the close-up of the skull out of his hand. "Where are his teeth?"

"*Comment?*"

"His teeth. He doesn't have any teeth. I want to see his dental records."

"*Pas de dents.*"

"Exactly. That's what I'm saying. There should *be* teeth, there should be dental records—*où sont-ils? Comprenez?*"

"*Non. Je ne comprends rien. Allez. Vite.*"

As the attendant turned away, she slipped the skull photo under her coat and sprinted for her car. In her rearview mirror she saw the attendant bolting out the door after her—she accelerated wildly, running two red lights on the way back to her apartment.

She double-locked the door, jerked open a drawer and took out the photo Rose-Anne had given her, *Hans Age 7* inked on the back. *Vieques 1970.* Hans's face smiled out at her, the small plump lips vaguely parted—

She took the skull photo out of her coat, staring at the dark, toothless, empty hole.

The phone rang. The police again, thought Elizabeth, and let the machine pick up.

"Lizzy, it's Annie," said the voice. "I've got a new name for you, this one you *have* to check out: Dr. Bender—he's Swiss, he's a Jungian, he's got a waiting list a mile long, but he's willing to see you right away—"

Elizabeth snatched up the phone.

"He didn't have any teeth."

"Who didn't? Lizzy, what are you talking about?"

"Hans. His teeth were gone. Teeth don't burn up in a car fire. Not if the bones don't, and his skull was intact."

"Poor baby, what have you been up to now—"

"Annie, did I ever mention Vieques to you? Does that ring any sort of bell? Because that's making me crazy, too—I keep thinking I've been there."

"Vieques? No. What is it?"

"It's an island. Never mind, I'm going to look it up on the Net, I should have done that long ago—"

"But what's this about teeth? Lizzy?"

"Unless it wasn't . . ." She was thinking aloud now, hardly conscious of Annie on the other end.

"Wasn't what?"

"Unless the body wasn't Hans. And that's why there weren't any teeth to compare against his dental records." The thought struck her with such force she had to sit down on the bed.

"Oh, wow—" said Annie.

"Exactly," said Elizabeth.

"—you're still in the denial stage, aren't you? You should be way past denial and into anger. That does it, Lizzy, I'm calling Bender."

Elizabeth snapped to. "No. Annie? It's okay. Forget I said anything. Really, I'm all right. I *am* angry."

"You sit tight, you don't go anywhere. I'll be right over."

Annie clicked off and Elizabeth hung up the phone. She picked up the two photos, one in each hand. Hideous as the skull was, the contrast was even more hideous: innocent boy and—what? Innocent victim?

Could it be? Was Hans alive? It was no more than a hope, a desperate supposition, but suddenly Elizabeth felt calmer than she had in weeks. She rolled over on her futon and pulled her coat over her body and immediately was drawn into a fathomless sleep.

When she awoke, it was the evening of the next day, a worried note from Annie was under her door, and she had the too-much-sleep hangover from hell. Her head ached, her clothes clung to her and smelled of stale sweat. She staggered up, then went into the bathroom and relieved herself. When she looked in the mirror she saw the deep creases from the futon on her face, the rat's nest of her hair.

It didn't matter now. I'm not crazy after all, she thought.

She stripped off her clothes and showered with water that was so hot it enveloped her in a steamy cloud. She let the water and heat and soap carry it all away, the fatigue and dirt and shame and memories of what she had done and how she had been during the past few weeks.

She made a project of it: shampoo and conditioner; hair tied back; teeth brushed and flossed; sweats and tennis shoes. A big pot of coffee, a steaming cup in her hand as she turned on the computer, hot liquid coursing down her throat as Microsoft Windows came up with its oddly comforting orchestral flair. She hit "Start," then "CompuServe 4.0 for Windows 97," then punched in her password. She was about to click on "World Wide Web" when she heard the cheerful digitized voice saying, *"You've got mail."*

She clicked it on, and every hair on the back of her neck stood up.

```
Subj:   Lucky You
Date:   99-02-28
From:   IslandMan@AOL.com
To:     SwissMs@Int'lAccessCompuServe.com


CONGRATULATIONS. YOU HAVE JUST WON A COMPLIMENTARY
STAY AT THE INN ON THE AZURE HORIZON, VIEQUES IS-
LAND, PUERTO RICO, IN CELEBRATION OF OUR 20TH AN-
NIVERSARY. CONFIRMATION TO FOLLOW BY FAX. IN OTHER
WORDS, ELIZABETH, WISH YOU WERE HERE!!
```

ROOSEVELT ROADS NAVAL STATION, VIEQUES ISLAND

The effects of Peter's stroke—though no one was prepared to say, unequivocally, that it *had* been a stroke—proved transient. By the end of the week he had made what appeared to be a complete recovery. His work on the weapon was going well, his team was back in the loop, his outlook appeared to have brightened. Though he sometimes stopped in mid-sentence to stare into the middle distance, on the whole he was less removed from others and from himself. To Beatrice he confided that his brain still felt as though it were hovering outside his body, unworthy to take possession of its new home or, worse, searching for the phantom body from which it had been amputated. When these spells came upon him, a spark of terror would light in his eyes. Beatrice was learning how to spot the signs and was able to get him through the difficult times.

"You're a pioneer," she reminded him, hoping to flatter him past his fears. "No one's ever been through this before."

"No research to consult."

"Exactly. But do you know what it reminds me of?" she asked. "The car."

He laughed out loud.

In 1961, when Peter had won the Nobel Prize in Physics for his work on the properties of plasma in vacuums, he had used some of the prize money to buy a BMW. He'd taken a lot of ribbing for showing up with it at the lab, but owning that car had taught him something about himself.

As first he'd been overwhelmed with buyer's remorse, feeling embarrassed by the BMW's enormous cost. Next he felt undeserving of its luxurious appointments and, oddly, incompetent to drive something so damn fast. Beatrice had talked him down from his guilt—after all, he was hardly the first Nobelist to treat himself to an expensive car. As for being intimidated by its speed and size, within a week he found he could put the pedal to the floor on the highway, and park it just as easily as he could his old Volvo. Its power and agility began to awe him—as Peter phrased it, to represent him. He loved the way he could zoom away from everyone else at stoplights, accelerate to one hundred miles an hour within seconds, or tear around a curve without any sway.

One day on one of those arrow-straight, two-lane blacktops out to Los Alamos, when he could see ten miles of empty road stretched out before him, he had opened it up full throttle and watched in fascination as the speedometer passed 100, then 120, then 140, until sage and scrub and yucca became a blur. There was only road and distant mountains, suspended in time and velocity. He was thinking back to his boyhood and the day he had first grasped Einstein's relativity equations, when the car lifted off an invisible rise in the road and landed not on macadam but on hard sand. The rest was a funnel of dust and spidering windshield, bits of broken cacti, wheels of blue sky and a screech of barbed wire twanging like a gigantic guitar string as he ripped out two hundred feet of turf and flew on.

When the car finally succumbed to friction and the resistance of many otherwise immovable objects, he sat silent and elated behind the wheel. A huge dust cloud surrounded the car. From inside, there was only a faint brown light, well suited to the contemplation of his mortality.

"And how did you feel?" Beatrice said. "Do you remember?"

"I felt happy."

The car, amazingly, had landed upright. He was alive, unhurt. He had gone faster than he had ever imagined he could. He would never have to own a car like this again because in that moment he had experienced it more intensely than most people would during a lifetime of careful ownership.

Best of all, he no longer felt old.

"You remember when you came home that night?" asked Beatrice.

"You were ready to kill me."

"I thought you had lost your mind."

"'Those wrecked by success.' You showed me the passage from Freud."

"And the next day we bought a VW bug with the insurance money."

"But I did feel reborn. At age forty."

"Maybe," said Beatrice, "you can have that feeling again. Once you get past *this* buyer's remorse."

In the weeks following the incident with the BMW in the desert, Peter began some of his most audacious work. One breakthrough followed after another. And the feeling had lasted for years.

But nothing lasts forever.

Slowly, so subtly that he was hardly aware of it, he had begun to slow down. He stopped taking physical risks, he gave up exercising regularly.

"And you were drinking more," Beatrice recalled.

"I don't want that to happen again."

Unless he was just saying it to please her, it was good to hear—a sign that he was starting to regard his new body as a challenge rather than as a forbidding mystery.

"Why *should* it happen again?" she challenged.

He had the body of a thirty-five-year-old now. His muscle tone was amazing; his sense of awareness was astonishing. He had a blood supply that sent his brain into overdrive with the promise of dissolving whatever plaque had built up in his cerebral arteries. But despite not having any more relapses in the last two weeks, he couldn't shake the thought that all this stunning progress could vanish in an instant.

"That's only the guilt talking," said Beatrice. "You let me worry about that, all right?"

Alone and usually in the bathroom (the only place he was afforded privacy), he would study this body he had been given, running the back of his fingers lightly over the taut skin of his neck, dabbing under his eyes where he had been accustomed to seeing satchels of flesh. He practiced telling himself that this was not some alien staring back at him in disbelief, but his own birthright, a fact that still seemed a dangerous lie. No matter how you rationalized it, this was still someone else's body. He was like a father looking at his son.

"What does Freud have to say about infanticide?" he asked Beatrice one morning.

"Peter, you can't keep dwelling on this."

"I'm not dwelling, I'm just asking."

"It's *not* your son."

"Yes, I know," he said, as though reciting his catechism: "It's merely a part of my body arbitrarily split off and allowed to grow independently. Cell for cell, gene for gene. My own personal property. Me. Just forty years younger. I say it's spinach, and I say the hell with it . . ."

He was venting, she knew, demanding that she make her case over and over again, which she was willing to do. In the end, he always felt better for it, the way he had felt in that BMW. Aware of its strength and perfection, he had at first been uneasy, then comfortable, and then ecstatic to be inside that shining, flawless machine. Finally, it wasn't a matter of being *in* it at all but rather of simply *being* it. Fit. Filled with energy. *Young!*

Then there was the question of sex, she reminded herself.

Starting in his fifties, sex for Peter had become less and less a priority or pleasure. Eventually, as he moved into his sixties, after exhausting tension-filled hours in the lab and on the test range, he simply couldn't be bothered. But even though the sight of Beatrice naked still had the ability to stir him, he couldn't bear to look at himself unclothed. The only mercy was that his eyes were so bad by then that without glasses he could barely see his flaccidity and wrinkles.

Now things were different. Sex, finally, was proving to be the most effective solvent for guilt. He was constantly aroused now, routinely rolling out of bed in the mornings tumescent and ready. One morning, he woke wet and sticky, and this time the images from his last dream were still vivid.

He had been floating in a sea of stars with a woman he could only describe—and only to himself—as the Angel of Eros. She was blond, this woman, in her mid-twenties, lithe and athletic and infinitely caring about his pleasure, responsive to his every thought and movement. It was the most luxurious and satisfying sex he could recall.

Before he could strip off his shorts, Beatrice saw the stain.

"Oops," he said sheepishly.

She tilted her head, trying to smile. "Congratulations. You must tell me about it."

In the past, they had made a point of sharing their dreams, unless any of them might prove hurtful, which was almost never. Now he demurred; the Angel's face was still etched in his consciousness. "Hey, you know what I've noticed? I'm sleeping on my left side again. Remember when my left shoulder stiffened up, and I had to sleep on my right? And I started to have insomnia, and when I did fall asleep I had these left-brain dreams. Now suddenly it's no problem, which is deeply strange—"

"Is that what you call it, a left-brain dream?" She looked at him, only slightly amused.

"Another thing. When I put my clothes on in the morning—didn't I used to put my socks on first?"

"Why? Are you putting them over your shoes now? We'd better have you tested again."

"No, I mean before I put on my undershirt. Now the socks come last. It's a small thing, nothing to worry about, just interesting. In the shower, too, I seem to do things in a different order. Soap my chest before my arms. Didn't you once do some work on cellular memory?"

"In graduate school. It didn't amount to anything."

"Circulating peptides, messenger RNA—wasn't that the theory?"

"What has this got to do with your nocturnal emissions?"

"Did I say that's what it was?"

"Either that or you're masturbating again."

"Well, you remember what Oliver Wendell Holmes once said."

"Please, let's stick to the sub—"

"A law student approached him—he was in his eighties—and asked him, 'Justice Holmes, you're the wisest man in America, can you tell me when a man stops masturbating?' And Holmes said—"

"'—You'll have to ask someone older than I.' Peter, stop babbling. You're not eighty-five, you're thirty-five, and I'm not in the least embarrassed—"

"Okay, of course it was a wet dream. Haven't had one of those since I was peeing straight up in the air."

"Was she attractive?"

"Was who?"

"The girl in your dream. Anyone we know? I assume you didn't have an orgasm dreaming of Madame Curie."

The hell of it was, he felt like he *did* know her. As if he had a dream about her before many times, but had forgotten everything when he woke up. And now suddenly she had surfaced again. But this time he was remembering her during his waking hours. In fact, he felt he couldn't have forgotten her if he tried. Some fragmented image of her emerged either in the front or the back of his mind for most of the day.

"You ought to be careful," Beatrice said wryly. "You don't want to have another stroke."

"No, I think this is good for the circulation," replied Peter with a smile.

Afterward, with Peter in the shower, Beatrice placed a call to Wolfe.

"How's our patient doing?" Wolfe asked.

"Horny as a toad," Beatrice said. "What are you putting in his orange juice?"

Wolfe's answering laugh had, as always, a touch of the grotesque. "Not a damn thing. His glands are pumping away, his vascular system's unclogged. He's a stellar example of the male body in its prime! It means he's healthy, which is terrific news for us. And for you specifically," he went on hastily. "It's time to count your blessings. You would have been devastated by his loss. Instead you have a new husband, a stunning breakthrough in genetics and a man functioning to his full capacity, happy once more in his work."

"Off and on."

"He's bound to have his doubts. He's got an enormous adjustment to make. He'll be just fine."

"From your lips to God's ears," she said, but secretly she didn't think God was listening anymore. If He was, she was beginning to feel, there might well be hell to pay some time soon.

An hour later Peter was on the treadmill in the medical lab, wired to heart and lung monitors by Emilio Barrola. Gradually Barrola increased the machine's incline, adding more and more stress to Peter's system. The problem was that Peter wouldn't limit himself to rapid walking. Despite Barrola's protests, he soon broke into a trot.

His heart seemed to handle the added stress without any trouble—no arrhythmia, no extra systoles, and nothing that could be traced to clogged cerebral vessels. Barrola was tempted to throw caution to the winds and simply marvel; the prior day's test, an ultrasound Doppler of the carotid arteries, had indicated that the flow of blood to Peter's brain had vastly improved. But there was no reason to tempt fate—Peter had been saved from certain death to perform mental, not physical, miracles. And so over his patient's objections, Barrola switched off the treadmill. Nevertheless, Peter's excitement remained high. Buoyed by the day's results, he dressed hurriedly and reported to the lab, where his team awaited him eagerly—especially Rosemarie Wiener. Braless, brushing his arm with her breasts as they all crowded around him at the blackboard, she clearly was offering herself. Peter wondered whether Rosemarie was the Angel of Eros, transformed by his dream into a vision of perfect happiness.

Not a chance, he decided. As a matter of fact, the notion had clung to him all day that his dream woman and her attributes were real. He knew she was a fantasy, but it gave him a thrill just to think of her as real, a thrill that seemed only to accelerate his genius.

"My father was employing the Purcey Protocol for this procedure," he told them, as the chalk flew and Rosemarie's eyes sparkled. "That was the foundation of his work until his death, so we'll continue that way. However," he said, luxuriating in the flood of ideas coursing through his brain, "let's experiment with gamma rays doing the switching of the core generator. And let's reverse the circuitry polarity of the epsilon switches. According to my calculations that should greatly enhance transmission rates at the same time it cools core temperature. If this proves to be true, the overheating problem will be solved and we'll have nearly twice the power in the strike beam."

Day after day, he continued with a string of plans, theories and instructions for the realization of the new version of the hammer. By week's end, it was clear to the team that Peter Jr.'s proposals were not only as stunningly original as his father's, but practical as well. The brainwork for the new weapon, now code-named Grand Slam, moved toward completion at a pace that elated Oscar Henderson. Peter Jance had become his own brilliant successor. It was time to begin the first stages of actual construction. Even Wolfe was dazzled.

Later that night, as Peter and Beatrice moved toward their separate beds, Peter, for the first time, felt how heavy a burden this newness must be for her. He noticed she took pains to change into nightclothes out of his sight, and had slipped into bed while he was brushing his teeth.

"I've been an idiot, haven't I?" he said.

"Oh, I don't know."

"That's a yes. I'm sorry. I've been so wrapped up in myself. And in getting back to work."

"Can't blame you for that."

She had been sleeping on a small folding cot. Peter went over and sat on its edge. Beatrice looked up at him with a wan smile.

"It's still me, Beatrice."

She nodded. "It's just going to take some getting used to."

"I still love you."

She didn't answer, but her eyes welled up with tears—not at his words, but at his obvious need to say them. She could count on the fingers of one hand the times they had actually reassured each other of their devotion, and the word "still" had never come into it. Love went without saying. To speak was to lie. "I know you do," she said.

He caressed her hair. He could smell her breath. It was a bit stale, but even so he eased in beside her.

"I don't know if this is right," she said.

"How could it not be?" he asked.

He took her in his arms and kissed her. Beatrice felt the warmth of his lips, the remarkable fullness, the warm hardness of his belly and the ever-warmer prod from further down. She giggled nervously.

"How about it?" he whispered. "You game?"

"I'm not *that* old," she said quietly.

"You'll never be old to me."

"Won't I?"

"No," he said firmly. "You're wonderful, B. The loveliest woman in the world. An angel."

"In that case . . ." she said, looking up at him from a well of sadness and love and understanding. Gently he lowered himself toward her, and she turned out the light.

PUERTO RICO

Within three hours of getting the fax confirming IslandMan's e-mail message, Elizabeth left Zurich. She was able to book a seat on the 10:20 A.M. Swissair flight to Boston and arrived at almost the same hour, local time, as when she had left. Despite her American passport, she was detained and searched by customs, evidently because she had no luggage except for her shoulder bag. The search revealed a change of underwear, a T-shirt from the Brussels Film Festival and a pair of jeans.

"Traveling kind of light," remarked the customs officer.

"Just a spur-of-the-moment trip, I guess."

They took her to a curtained-off booth where she was subjected to a full-body search by a bright-eyed female agent with big hair.

"Back in the U.S.A.," Elizabeth said sourly.

The woman's head came up.

"We could X-ray you. Make you take laxatives."

"Why would you want to do that?" Elizabeth demanded. She was ready to throttle this woman.

"We've found as many as thirty condoms full of heroin in people's intestines. How long have you been in Switzerland?"

"I've lived there five years."

"Nature of your business?"

"I'm a model. Helvetica International Agency." If customs checked, she knew, they'd be told she had been fired for trying to have a corpse exhumed. They'd probably lock her in a room and throw away the key.

Instead the agent took a step back. Apparently being a model carried some peculiar weight with her.

"My daughter's tried to get into modeling," she said. "Maybe you could help her."

"I could try," said Elizabeth, sensing an easy out.

"She's got the three Bs. Beauty, brains and business sense. I've read that's what it takes now."

"How old is she?"

"She'll be fifteen next July."

Elizabeth scribbled her name down on a pad, along with Helvetica's U.S. number. The agent waved Elizabeth through with her rubber-gloved hand.

"It was just procedure. No offense."

"None taken. Gook luck with your daughter's career," said Elizabeth, buttoning her jeans. She had to run to make her connection—American Airlines was as far from International Arrivals as you could possibly get and still be in the same airport. She barely made the plane.

American Flight 97 took her into Puerto Rico's San Juan International, the airline's Caribbean hub, east of the city, touching down at 8:30 P.M. With no luggage to retrieve, she was in a cab by a quarter to nine and in the lobby of the local Hyatt by 9:15. The flight to Vieques didn't leave until the following afternoon, so there was time to kill. She immediately placed a call to the Puerto Rico tourist bureau on the off chance that they hadn't closed for the day. By dumb luck it was not only open for another fifteen minutes, it was also located on the second floor of her hotel.

Elizabeth told the clerk, who had a round, smiling face marked by acne, that she had come to collect her complimentary voucher. To which the woman responded by saying she didn't know what Elizabeth was talking about. Elizabeth showed her the faxed confirmation.

"Vieques Island? I don't think so. What hotel again?" She squinted at the paper.

"Inn on the Azure Horizon."

"I'm sorry, miss. I don't think they offer things like that."

Elizabeth could feel her heart accelerate.

"First off, this isn't one of our faxes, see? Ours would have our own letterhead." She produced one of their fax forms with a letterhead displaying palm trees and gulls against a beach. "This one, see, is blank." She reread the letter. "'. . . won a complimentary stay at the Inn on the Azure Horizon . . . in celebration of our 20th anniversary . . .' No see," she said, "even that. Azure Horizon's been out there, oh, maybe ten years tops. So that part's wrong. I'm not even sure they're still in business—"

Elizabeth was already out the door.

At the Hyatt front desk she found there was a 10:30 P.M. ferry to Vieques from a town called Fajardo. Fajardo was nearly forty miles by the coastal road—a fifty-dollar cab ride with no guarantee she would even make the ferry. Upstairs was a room with a shower, room service and a soft bed. Couldn't it wait till morning?

Of course it couldn't. What were the odds of getting a fax from *any-body* from Vieques Island? The place was a microdot on the map, known, among the people she knew, only to the mother of Hans Brinkman, or—

Could it possibly have been . . .

From the moment she had laid eyes on the e-mail, she hadn't dared to complete the thought for fear of jinxing it. No, the thing to do was to get to the island as soon as possible, then investigate carefully, methodically, keeping her wits about her. She would refuse to think that she was rushing headlong toward a fate she had been avoiding all her life. Or that someone or something who knew her more completely than she even did herself was giving her an opportunity to use all those talents Hans had once accused her of squandering, just to reach this fate. This destiny. This man.

Sure, she would.

Beauty, brains and business sense . . .

She went outside, booked the most roadworthy cab and the youngest driver she could find and told him there was a hundred dollars in it for him if he could get her to Fajardo in time to make the 10:30 ferry. The cabdriver got rid of his cigarette and opened the back door of his '85 Cougar.

For the next hour she hung on for dear life as the cab careened down the coastline of Puerto Rico. To distract herself from what she felt would be her sure demise, she turned on the flickering dome light and read what little she had been able to pull off the Internet about Vieques.

Vieques is a small volcanic island lying just off the east coast of Puerto Rico. About three thousand years ago, the first humans reached the place by moving up the island chain. Dating from about 200 B.C. there are records that remarkable Indian cultures lived there. Finally a Frenchman, Le Guillou, clamped a Western colonial hand over it, converting the place to the cultivation of sugar in the name of Spain. Within a short time the trees were gone and the island was planted with cane from coast to coast. It then was traded and raided from hand to hand between imperial powers. In 1898, control of the island passed from Spain to the United States. Conditions remained unchanged on the island until the Second World War.

In 1941, the U.S. Navy took over three quarters of Vieques Island for training and the testing of ordnance. Much of the native population was summarily displaced, and instead the island rocked to the sound of shouted orders and the thunder of bombs, rockets and artillery shells from both aircraft and ships. It was listed as an adjunct to the massive Roosevelt Roads Naval Station on the main island, and hosted Camp Garcia for the Marine Corps, as well as seventeen NAVSTAR departments and twenty-four tenant commands for the Navy, Army and Marines.

A military base, thought Elizabeth. Of course, Rose-Anne Brinkman had told her that.

So why was she suddenly feeling so uneasy?

In the years following the Cold War things had calmed down, according to the article, and a certain amount of tourism had spilled over from Puerto Rico to help replace the vanished sugar industry. But mostly the island was quiet, best known for its mangrove swamps, deserted beaches and wildlife.

So what had happened to the military? What had they been up to for the last ten years?

When the bulb in the dome light blinked out and refused to come back on, Elizabeth resigned herself to watching the foliage flash by and counting the number of gigantic bugs that smashed against the windshield.

She just made the ferry, bought a two-dollar ticket and went aboard. Built to accommodate four hundred, the craft was carrying only a few dozen party animals returning to their inns from San Juan's casinos. Elizabeth left them to their revelry around the Formica bar and went out on deck.

The sky was ablaze with stars, the sea smooth as glass. She stayed on deck until the ferry pulled into its terminal in Isabel Segunda. Ahead were the seven-story ruins of a lighthouse and, high on the hill across from the dock, the dark silhouette of a Spanish fortress. The air was warm, nearly 80 degrees, and alive with a high, sweet chirping sound. In her heightened awareness, the sound assaulted her senses.

She could still hear it from the terminal rest room, where she had hastened upon docking—the facilities on the ferry had been completely out of the question.

"Tree frogs," said a voice from the next sink.

"*Coquís*," nodded Elizabeth, a little startled by her own knowledge.

"You've been down here before," the woman said. She had metallic red hair, an open, friendly face and severely plucked eyebrows.

"No, I haven't."

"Let me guess. You work for a zoo? Or you just watch a lot of *Animal Planet.*"

"I don't know how I knew," said Elizabeth uneasily, drying her hands. The word *coquís* had come out of her mouth as though she had heard it a hundred times. "I must have read it on the Internet or something," she said without conviction; suddenly she realized she had left the Web printouts in the cab. "You work for American?" she asked, noting the airline insignia on the woman's lapel.

"Uh-huh. Puerto Rico's our hub, and Vieques is my favorite place to escape to. Why?"

"Ever heard of the Inn on the Azure Horizon?"

The woman frowned. "Doesn't ring a bell. Is that where you're staying?"

"I thought I was," said Elizabeth, holding open the door as they left the rest room together. "There seems to be some doubt whether it even exists. You think I'll be able to get a room tonight somewhere else?"

"Here in Isabel? You didn't make a reservation?"

"I kind of took a flyer."

The woman grinned. "He must be gorgeous."

Elizabeth managed a tight smile. "He is," she said. He is, he was, he is.

"I'm sorry," said the flight attendant, noting the unease in Elizabeth's expression. "Really none of my beeswax. It's just that, you know, it's usually why women come to the island." She stuck out her hand. "Mary Blanchard."

Elizabeth hesitated for a fraction of a second, then shook it. "Elizabeth Parker."

Five minutes later, she was sharing a cab with Mary Blanchard and two of her colleagues, one of whom was dead certain she had seen Elizabeth in an in-flight movie just the other week. She wouldn't take no for an answer.

"I *know* I know your face," she kept insisting. The three flight attendants amiably rattled on about men and craps tables and asshole passengers, and Mary Blanchard offered to let Elizabeth sleep on the couch in her room at their hotel, a revamped turn-of-the-century French sugar plantation called Casa del Francés. It proved to be a pleasant enough place overlooking the ocean and the town of Esperanza. The owner, Ivor Greeley, a crusty New Englander with a fondness for antediluvian slang, realized there was now an extra member in their party and took twenty dollars for his trouble.

"I'll have a unit free tomorrow," he told Elizabeth. His eyes were lively and brown and he had graying blond hair brushed over a shining bald patch. "You can pay in advance or you can take it on the arches." Then, in welcoming his new guest, he sent them a complimentary bottle of rum.

For the first time in weeks she slept straight through the night. Toward morning, she dreamed she was floating in a sea of stars. It was heaven, she realized, liquid, oceanic and salty, and then Hans was there with her. The gently rolling water glowed with a million pin-pricks of light as he entered. Then he was gone and she was chasing him up a flight of ancient stone stairs, to the heights of El Fortín, where he managed to disappear into a sudden crowd of angry farm animals. Goats were bleating outside her window, a rooster was crowing and she realized she was awake.

El Fortín?

She picked up a guidebook that was on the television, leafing through it until she found the illustration she was looking for. El Fortín was the fortress she had seen from the ferry, the last Spanish stronghold, according to the picture's caption, in the New World.

I must have glanced throught this last night, she thought, tossing the guidebook aside. Unless—

Unless what?

Unless Hans had talked about Vieques. No, but he never did. Never spoke of his childhood, never mentioned it once. And Rose-Anne had given her no such details.

Then how did I know?

She knew Annie would say she was channeling Hans. The thought was ridiculous, but then why think it? Did it mean that in her heart she believed he was dead? No, she said to herself—he's alive. That wasn't his body in the coffin, that's why you're down here, that's why you're putting yourself through this craziness.

Fine, okay, just keep telling yourself that. But then how *did* you know? Her father, the Navy man, had done more than his share of traveling, uprooting his family from one base to another. Could he possibly have been stationed here? I would have remembered, she thought, or I would have been told.

She had no answer. Absolutely none.

Outside the window, the light was clear, the air fresh and filtered through an abundance of greenery. She left a note for Mary Blanchard and slipped outside. Shore birds flashed against an azure sky, their cries exotic. The air was warm against her skin, too warm for the clothes she was wearing.

Ivor Greeley was on the terrace drinking coffee and working a crossword puzzle as she walked past.

"Java?" he asked, and when she nodded, fetched it himself.

"I need to buy some clothes," she told him.

"Absolutely. You're going to roast in those. Don't you got any shorts?"

She shook her head. "I left kind of suddenly."

His eyes narrowed. "You on the lam? Got the heat on your tail, in trouble with John Law, price on your head?"

Not yet, she thought wildly. "No," she said.

"Too bad. Nothing exciting ever happens around here. How's the coffee?"

"It's wonderful," she said politely. She had only had a sip of it.

"Cuban," he said with pride. "It isn't legit, that's why it tastes so good. I hate someone telling me I can't buy somebody else's coffee just because they don't have the same politics as Uncle Sam. Back where I'm from we tossed a whole lot of British tea into the harbor for the same reason."

"You're from Boston."

"Very good. I have a niece goes to Emerson, she thinks World War II and Vietnam were the same war. So how come a bright girl like you travels with no luggage?"

She was saved from having to answer the same question again by a deep rumble rolling over the trees beyond the terrace.

"Sounds like it might rain," she said.

He nodded. "We get rain sometimes, in the mornings. But that's not rain."

"Just thunder?"

"Not thunder neither. The Navy's bombing this morning. Five-hundred-pounders, I'd say from the sound of it. Got to keep those land crabs in their place, you know."

There it was again—the Navy. What had all this to do with the Navy?

The bombing lasted for another hour, through breakfast, which she ate at a nearby restaurant, fried snapper over rice and *arepas,* a delicious fried dough that brought back more vague, untraceable memories. Clearly she was overamping, perhaps compensating for her anxieties about who had invited her to this unnerving paradise by pretending everything was oddly familiar. The food soothed her nerves, and when the shops opened she bought shorts, T-shirts and a well-worn work shirt at a secondhand shop patronized by locals. In another store, she found sunglasses and a small nylon backpack that would hold it all. Her old tennis shoes would do just fine.

Next stop was the tourist bureau. The woman at the desk, a sunny octogenarian with snow-white hair, was also skeptical about the fax. But she confirmed that the Inn on the Azure Horizon was real enough, and suggested that Elizabeth head over there.

When she finally located the place, she was surprised by its elegance and charm. It was an old country inn right on the beach, its lobby filled with wicker and bamboo. She checked with the desk clerk, a handsome woman with a paper rose in her hair who was entering bar receipts into an adding machine. Indeed, there was a reservation in the name of Elizabeth Parker, but she was there a day early.

"I caught the ferry," said Elizabeth. "So did I win a free stay here?"

The woman cocked her head. "Free?"

"I mean, well, look at this." And once again Elizabeth pulled out the fax.

The woman read it and grinned. "You must have a boyfriend on one of the bases, huh?"

Elizabeth tightened. "Why do you say that?"

Delving into a frayed ledger book, the clerk ran her finger down some handwritten notations until she came to one that included Elizabeth's name.

"See here? The room was booked from Roosevelt Roads. That includes both bases and goodness knows what-all branches of service. But it came from the base, no question about it. Paid by credit card and open-ended. Must want to see you pretty bad, huh?"

Elizabeth felt a sharp twist of fear.

"What's the name on the credit card?" she asked.

The woman peered into the ledger and shook her head. "Just an account. Some kind of letter and a code number. We get a lot of that. Military tricks for security, you know. Lots of secret stuff going on over there on those bases. Local kooks think they're breaking down an alien spacecraft, what's that called again?"

"Reverse engineering," said Elizabeth, trying to maintain a semblance of calm while she shoved the fax in her backpack.

"Nobody from there will ever talk about what goes on. It's two worlds, really. *Us* who live here, and *they* who do whatever the hell they want to, do it whenever the hell they want to. Want to see the room?"

Elizabeth shook her head. "No."

"You're checking in, though, right?"

She turned on her heels. "No. I'm afraid I'm not."

"It's a beautiful room!" the woman called after her.

Elizabeth was out the door, halfway down the walk, when she heard the door fly open behind her and the woman cry out again. Elizabeth wheeled, as if bracing for an attack.

"Ma'am, I found a telephone message. I'm sorry I didn't see it, it was in the back of your box."

Elizabeth stopped, frozen in her tracks. "What kind of message?"

"You won't be able to read it, the night girl took the message." The woman squinted at the pink square of paper in the sunlight. "It says he'll meet you at the airport."

"Who?"

"I don't think there's a name." The woman studied the note again. "I'd assume the guy who sent for you, no? So do you want the room now?"

"No, I don't, not right now." Elizabeth grabbed the message. It was, in fact, illegible. "But you can tell me something."

"Anything. You came all this way, I'd hate to lose your business."

Elizabeth unfolded her tourist map. "Where will the plane be coming in?"

The Vieques civilian airport was a sun-drenched asphalt strip not far from Isabel Segunda, where the ferry docked. Elizabeth had rented a Honda Civic and was hunkered down in the front seat drinking a Coke and listening to the radio. There was informal chat about the weather, which came from Roosevelt Roads Naval Station on the main island. Temperature 78 degrees, humidity 68 percent, dewpoint 68, wind from the east at eight miles per hour, conditions slightly overcast, visibility ten miles.

She glanced at her watch: 6:45.

The news about the weather was suddenly drowned out by an aircraft roaring overhead.

She turned the radio off. The plane was already banking out of its downwind leg and making its final approach.

It was a Cessna Navajo twin, flown by Caribair. Elizabeth watched as it stopped at the end of the runway, then picked up the binoculars she had borrowed from Ivor back at the hotel. "For bird-watching," she had told him. She was a safe hundred yards from the parking area, where a half-dozen cabs and rental cars waited.

She watched the plane taxi to the small terminal with its pilot's door open for ventilation against the heat. In the parking lot, people started getting out of their air-conditioned cars.

Everyone except for one. Like her, he was sitting low in his seat in a Range Rover with a license plate unlike any of the others.

U.S. government, she bet.

Wisps of cigarette smoke were wafting from a crack in the window. As the passengers disembarked from the Cessna, she watched the person behind the wheel crush out his cigarette and sit up tall.

Not Hans.

He was at least ten years younger, maybe no more than twenty, with messy hair and a sharp face. Kind of scary, and really intense. And not Hans.

Come on, Lizzy, she thought, did you really expect it to be him?

And if you didn't, why is your heart sinking?

The Range Rover didn't move. Elizabeth swung the binoculars back to the Cessna. The pilot and co-pilot were coming out of the plane; there were no more passengers. She watched as the young man punched the dashboard in frustration, then pulled out of the parking lot. He drove slowly at first, then veered past her so quickly that she had to duck down in her seat.

IslandMan, she thought.

She waited until it was a dozen car lengths away, then followed.

He drove straight to Esperanza, following the line of cars and cabs that had picked up the tourists at the airport. Elizabeth put a truck carrying diving gear between her and the Range Rover and hoped to God the kid at the wheel was looking forward. Halfway down the main drag of Esperanza, he pulled to the curb. Elizabeth did the same a block back and waited. The kid got out and crossed the street.

She followed him with the binoculars. He was heading for the beach and the Inn on the Azure Horizon.

Her heart in her mouth, Elizabeth eased the Honda out of park and rolled by, stealing a glance. She could see the guy in the lobby, talking to the same woman she had spoken to earlier, the one with the paper rose in her hair. She was shaking her head at him and shrugging, and then Elizabeth couldn't see either one of them. After circling the block, she stopped where she had paused before. The kid came out of the hotel, plucking irritably at his Scooby-Doo T-shirt, got back into the Range Rover and roared away.

Again she followed, taking care to keep at least two cars between them, although he was driving much faster this time and threatened to disappear.

He drove back to the airport on a different road, then headed north. Fifteen minutes later, as they passed El Fortín, he hung a sharp right. Elizabeth had a sudden notion that the kid knew he was being followed. She glanced in the rearview, as if to gauge how far back she had to stay to remain unobtrusive, and caught sight of a second SUV, hanging back, slowing as she slowed. Its windshield was catching the sun, so she couldn't make out the driver's face, but she was now convinced *she* was being followed, so she hung back even further. No, now the second SUV was turning off onto another road and she could glimpse a family through the side windows. She looked back for the Range Rover: it had disappeared from sight. Cursing herself for getting spooked and losing her quarry, she floored the Honda. Coming over a rise, she could see the road ahead for a quarter mile, but the Range Rover was gone. There were dirt tracks running off into the scrub everywhere. Which one the weird kid had gone down was impossible to tell.

Well, Lizzy, she thought, you blew that, didn't you?

She took a deep breath and realized she had been holding the steering wheel so hard that her hands ached. She was scared, wet with perspiration and definitely shaky.

Pulling over to the side of the road, she lit a cigarette. Probably you're damn well better off, she told herself, inhaling deeply and forcing herself to calm down. The fact was that having lost the scent, she was now feeling something like sweet relief. She could go back to the hotel and shower, have a margarita, maybe look up the flight attendants.

She started her engine and drove into a pullout to turn around. But as soon as she did, she found herself staring at a fortified gate and an armed U.S. Marine who was watching her, very carefully indeed.

Her blood ran cold. Above his head was a simple sign in a concrete gate: CAMP GARCIA—U.S. MARINE CORPS. The Marine was walking toward her. When she tried to pull away, she stalled the car.

Shit. He was at her window.

"Help you, ma'am?"

"No, thank you, just turning around."

He nodded and offered her a little salute. He looked all of fifteen but she guessed he was probably eighteen. When he had leaned over to talk to her she couldn't help noticing that the muzzle of his rifle swung right past her face. She felt her hands shaking again as she restarted the car and drove away, checking the rearview mirror. No, he hadn't jumped on the phone, and no, when she returned to Esperanza and her room at the Casa del Francés, there were no messages, no jittery kid waiting in the lobby, no soldier hiding in her closet, no monsters under her bed.

Yes, Lizzy, she thought, you are the most paranoid idiot on this island.

Either that or this time by sheer dumb luck you have picked the door without the tiger behind it.

For two days, Peter Jr. had been working his staff fiendishly. Now they were as elated as they were exhausted. This genius son of someone they had worshipped and then had mourned had in forty-eight blazing, astonishing hours completely reconceived the weapon.

"Where have you been all our lives?" Rosemarie Wiener wanted to know. "You Jances are all such bundles of secrets." She stared at Peter so shamelessly he had to laugh. His refusal of her advances hadn't dimmed her fires, but it *had* fueled her curiosity. When he left the room for a moment, she turned to Alex.

"He looks so much like his father."

"Yeah, so what's the problem?" Alex said. "Sons have a habit of doing that."

"Almost too much. His dad's picture in the *Britannica*? It's practically identical."

"Maybe he's a clone?"

"All I know is," Rosemarie said, not even dignifying the comment, "he's definitely hung-up on his mother. Every time I see Beatrice, they're always together. I mean, I know they just lost the old man, but they're *inseparable*."

"Yeah," Alex agreed, rubbing his head as he punched numbers into a handheld computer. "Wouldn't be surprised if he was sleeping with her."

"Yuck! You are *so* not-funny, Alex."

"What *I* want to know," said Flannagan, who had been on the Internet that morning, "is why when the old man won the Nobel, the articles mention him thanking a wife, but he never mentioned a thing about the kid."

"Because, duh," said Alex, "the kid was minus two years old. Do the math. I'm tired of doing all the heavy lifting around here."

Alex walked away, and the others looked at each other.

"What's eating him?"

"Not me," said Rosemarie, and went back to work closer to Peter Jr.

No one else paid too much attention to the issues of Sr. and Jr. Jances. There were other things far more exciting to talk about. The fact was, the math *was* coming together. The new weapon was turning out to be twice as small and three times as lethal on paper and on Alex's computer models. The next move was from theory to hardware.

It was evident that this next stage was coming soon because Heartless Henderson had been in and out of the lab a half-dozen times in the past three days.

"We'll be moving back to White Sands next week," the colonel told Peter in private. "You feeling up to it?"

"Fit as a fiddle," said Peter, scribbling the words HOT DO NOT ERASE on the day's blackboard. "And ready for love." He stowed his notebooks and grabbed a pair of running shoes out of the same desk drawer.

Henderson was not amused. Peter's workout obsession had become a subject of daily concern to Barrola and the rest of the medical staff, except for Wolfe, who to Henderson's mind had become way too laissez-faire.

"You going back on the treadmill again?" said the colonel. "Are we sure we're not overstressing our brain arteries?"

"I can't speak for yours, but mine are fine. Besides, Freddy gave his okay," Peter lied. Ever since the operation he had been chafed at having to answer to Henderson, instead of enjoying the more collegiate handling he received from Wolfe.

"You sure?"

"*Mens sana in corpore sano.* Or didn't they teach Latin at West Point?"

"Fuck you, too," said Henderson sharply. Really, Jance was getting too ballsy for his taste. All this GHIP—Genius Has Its Privileges— was starting to put his teeth on edge. "Barrola says it's a needless risk."

"Barrola wouldn't run if his ass was on fire," Peter said with a cool smile. "I need the release. You wouldn't want me to go psycho on you, would you?" He jogged past Henderson, and was gone.

That afternoon he ran for half an hour and barely broke a sweat. He was monitored by one of Barrola's worker bees who had been instructed to notify her boss at the first sign of a blip. She found a benign irregularity in the AV bundles, but a quick comparison of Peter's and Peter Jr.'s EKGs proved it was congenital. As punishment for her vigilance, the techie had to sit there another forty-five minutes while Peter jogged up the equivalent of Machu Picchu.

Back in his own quarters, he showered and changed into fresh clothes. The bare, tawny walls and low ceiling made him feel claus-trophobic. Their suite had all the charm of a Motel 6, and while Beatrice had tried to perk up the place with a spray of dried chrysan-themums in a giant Erlenmeyer flask, the three rooms now felt alien and confining, old and small—too small to contain his newfound en-ergy. He went out onto the balcony, the only real perk they had been granted. Beatrice found him there when she came in from dinner, staring off into space.

"Peter? You all right?"

He nodded without turning to her.

"Not feeling light-headed again, are you?"

He stiffened. "I'm fine, I'm just listening."

"To?"

"The ocean."

"You can't hear the ocean from here."

"Yes I can," he said matter-of-factly. "I can smell it, too."

She came over and sniffed the air. "I can't smell a thing."

"It's really amazing. You see that bird beyond that tree?"

He pointed. "Where?" she asked.

He pointed again. She saw a slight blur. "You sure that's not a leaf?"

"It's a sandhill crane," he said. He took her hand and squeezed it. "Remember you taught me how to spot those? A month ago I wouldn't have seen it at all, let alone the red on its forehead. Or am I confusing two different species? You were always better than I was at this."

She squeezed back. "You're trying to be nice. I appreciate it."

"B., I'm not trying to be nice."

"But I do wish you'd put your own laundry in the hamper from now on."

"Okay. I will."

"I'm sorry to be so squeamish. The sheets as well?"

"*Okay*. Mom."

The moment it was out of his mouth he regretted it. Maybe they were right, Henderson and the others. Maybe he *was* turning into a wise-ass.

"You know I didn't mean that," he instantly said. "I'm sorry, B."

Beatrice was pursing her mouth, a sure sign that she was shutting down. Her hand in his was a deadweight and he let it go.

"If you want to yell, yell at my autonomic nervous system."

"Am I yelling? *You're* the one who's yelling."

He hadn't raised his voice at all. Or had he? A fight was coming on, a bad one, and he knew he should leave until the storm blew over. But for some reason he couldn't move.

"I am *not* your mother," she said through her teeth.

"We could try sleeping in separate beds again," he said lightly, "if it really bothers you."

"All right," she said.

"You don't mean that. I was joking. Come on, B."

"In fact," she said, turning away sharply, "it might be a good idea if we slept in separate suites."

"Beatrice, stop."

"Your team is starting to talk."

"Let them talk. They don't know we're sleeping in the same room—this whole wing is off-limits."

"Maids talk."

"Come on, you're really being impossible. Come here."

He tried to take her in his arms, but she pushed him away. Tears sprang to her eyes.

"It's an ugliness," she said.

"Shh. Take it easy . . ."

"I'm old. You're young. That's the end of it."

"The end of what? Please. B.? Stop doing this to yourself. I'm no different. I'm me."

She sat down on the terrace and lit a cigarette. Peter recognized the blue pack—Gauloises, Wolfe's brand. "You're turning into a jerk. Everybody says so."

"Turning?" he said, trying to smile. "Well, I suppose I should be grateful for that. Since when did you take up smoking, by the way?"

"Since I felt like it." She angrily blew out a stream of smoke. "Was it her again?"

"Was it *who* again?"

"The one you've been dreaming about all week. Miss Autonomic Nervous System. The blonde with the big breasts."

"I never said she had big breasts."

"Okay. You were dreaming about her."

"Beatrice," he lied, "I was joking." He started to touch her hair where it curled over her ears, but then he drew his hand back. "You're the only blonde I dream about," he said, but he couldn't bring himself to look at her. "Look, if you want to talk about my sexuality—"

"Oh, right. That's really what I'm dying to discuss. You know what? You're insufferable," she said as she crushed out her cigarette, stood up and went back into the bedroom.

Fine, turn your back on me, he thought, letting a wave of self-justifying anger wash over him. What have I done that I couldn't help doing? Nothing. It's not as if I never had wet dreams before.

Yes, you did when you were fifteen. And it was never the same woman night after night.

Okay, B., so you guessed it, he thought, gazing out past the palm trees toward the sound of surf. So what are we going to do about it? It's a mad affair locked in dreams. It's nonsense. It's meaningless.

The woman's face swam up inside his eyes.

Damn, he thought.

The dream was coming back. He could feel her hair moving through his fingers, a silken cascade that kept changing color, from blond to black to orange and back again. He traced her firm, receptive flesh, felt the easy weight of her, the supple lines, the perfection of how it all fit together, all of it utterly familiar. Though he fought it, he remembered with breathtaking clarity the ecstatic meltdown that had crowned last night's appearance. For the first time since she had found him in his dreamworld, she showed her face clearly. It was at once maddeningly familiar and utterly unknown, with a high forehead, full lips, huge gray eyes with the faintest hint of scar tissue at the supraorbital ridge. Amazing how the mind could do that—invent features, geographies, buildings, landscapes, in minute details, continuously, moment to moment, *ab nihilo*.

Sure, why don't you turn this into a science project? he thought. Keep forensic notes on her! That's sure to keep your hormones at bay.

But it really had to stop. She was starting to get in the way of his work, appearing even in his creative moments like a spirit who could not bear separation. B., if I had a choice, I'd pluck her out of my consciousness like a weed, he told himself. He walked away from the terrace's railing.

"And since when, by the way, does Wolfe give you his cigarettes?" he called into the apartment.

A door slammed somewhere inside.

"Beatrice?" he called.

Almost in denial he walked through the few rooms, thinking he might find her doing something normal, something like brushing her hair or making herself tea.

She was gone.

He made no effort to follow. Instead, he sat down and poured himself a vodka from the bottle Beatrice kept in the freezer. He hadn't had a drink since the operation, but after a Beatrice fight, he deserved one.

He tossed it back.

The liquor burned like acid and made him double over as he rushed to the sink to spit it out.

My God, he thought, catching his breath, *this body has never tasted hard liquor before!*

Jesus, there was a ton of things he had to teach himself. The only problem was he was no longer sure which part of him would be doing the teaching and which the learning. Then the girl's face swam up before him once more. This time it filled the sky.

9

It was impossible for Peter to sleep.

It wasn't simply the absence of Beatrice. Dozens of times in their marriage she had spent whole nights at her lab, on occasion because her work demanded it. Sometimes it was out of pique, but she always returned the next morning.

He was used to her storming out on him—he had often stormed out on her himself and spent the night in *his* lab. In their courting days, whenever they got into one of their wilder arguments, he would drive her home, declare they were through, then drive around the block until she reemerged. Then they would sit silently in the car, sometimes for hours, until one of them surrendered and apologized.

She had her father's stubbornness and pride, and she wasn't about to yield to any boyish pretender to the throne of modern physics. Her father had been one of those linchpins of the revolution, a colleague of de Broglie and Bohr, a cranky, imperious man who despite his immense charm and influence on funding committees and politicians had little time or patience for his only child. Beatrice had, without quite realizing it, struggled to escape his gravitational field and establish herself as a scientist in her own right. Peter liked to think he had given her the confidence to break away, even though Beatrice, who continued to worship her father, would have denied there was ever a need to rebel. In her eyes her father was a demigod, and Peter was obliged to agree.

Her father was Beatrice's sole blind spot; about Peter she had no such illusions. She simply loved him. His desires were hers, her dreams his, and there wasn't anything one of them needed the other couldn't supply, happily and completely. Unless, of course, they were fighting. The arguments happened often enough to keep them on their toes and to keep the marriage from turning stale. From roughly their twenty-fifth anniversary on, the brouhahas never lasted for more than a few hours.

But this felt different.

This time, Beatrice had gone and stayed away for two days. She was still on base, of course, sleeping in one of the rooms reserved for visiting brass. But she hadn't blinked. And neither had he. His mind was telling him to go to her, say whatever was necessary to get them back on track again.

But his body was saying something else.

What exactly it was trying to tell him he hadn't worked out yet. His legs, for one thing, had been twitching for two nights, like a frog in a biology lab or a dog dreaming of a rabbit. Lack of potassium or zinc was the usual diagnosis, but never in a body this young. And the muscle relaxant Wolfe had prescribed had done nothing but make him drowsy and indifferent to the fact that his team had now fallen two days behind schedule.

And when the Valium wore off, he was still indifferent.

In fact, he'd been playing hooky for the past forty-eight hours.

What in hell was *that* about?

He couldn't sort it out. A good part of the time he had spent browsing various databases, searching for information on cellular memory. Most of it was pseudoscience, strange speculation about the storage of memories in RNA phase angles, tricked out with late-1980s experiments on bacteria which, in some mysterious fashion and without actually mutating, remembered how to metabolize what their ancestral cells had been fed. Some of the material was outright Lamarckian nonsense, some of it assumed more molecular biology than he had ever mastered, none of it dealt with higher animals. With the exception of one particularly gruesome experiment in which decorticate cats had supposedly learned how to navigate a maze after having digested their mommy's and daddy's RNA.

Ridiculous stuff, grisly, unbelievable. But still he found himself thinking who was *he* to talk about gruesome experiments? Or things unbelievable?

As though to punish himself, he read through the cat protocol three times. No, the methodology was all wrong. The experiments proved nothing. All this browsing was getting him nowhere.

Besides, he had a better laboratory close at hand.

His own body.

He started with the obvious differences. Not only were the muscles more highly developed, but the reflexes were quicker, too. He had noticed this one morning when he had accidentally dropped one of his anticholesterol tablets. At the same split second he realized the pill was rolling off the counter, his hand was there to catch it. Lightning fast. Instantaneous. Much faster than his old body had ever been at any time.

The man must have been some athlete, thought Peter. He might even have done some boxing. That first morning when Beatrice failed to return, Peter had been standing in front of the mirror in a coiled, choleric mood. Suddenly he found himself throwing left and right jabs at his reflection.

Hard to imagine, though, that a man with his endowments would risk getting his brains scrambled in the boxing ring. Unless, of course, he hadn't valued his intellect, or was so good that he didn't have to worry about being pulverized.

What the hell are you doing? he thought, feeling another spasm of guilt. You don't really want to know all about that, do you? You've been through it with Beatrice, ad nauseam.

But you're a scientist, he thought. You're only doing what you were born to do: trying to get to the bottom of things.

For example, trying to account for the fact that he could juggle.

He had discovered this hidden talent that very morning. Nothing fancy, just three oranges, but it was something he had never done before, although he had tried to get the hang of it when he was younger. He had seen the oranges in the kitchen and casually picked them up, and while his mind was distracted trying to work out the formula for a new pulse beam, suddenly the oranges were in the air. And as soon as he noticed what he was doing, the oranges went flying.

It was too interesting to let go; he couldn't wait to tell Beatrice. And for Wolfe, of course, the molecular biology would be right up his alley. Late that afternoon he gathered up his printouts and walked through the long hot breezeway to Freddy's office.

Wolfe was with Alex, he could hear them behind the closed door. The older man was speaking sharply to his grandson; no doubt Alex's absences from the lab had come to his attention. After a moment, Alex emerged, gave Peter a quick hello, and sauntered off down the corridor. Wolfe was at his desk, a hand over his spotted, furrowed brow.

"I was going to come see you," Wolfe said. "Glad you saved me the trouble. I hear we're falling behind. Is that true?"

"Nothing we can't make up," Peter said casually. He eased over to the terrace doors. Wolfe's office had a verandah twice the size of anyone else's on the base, with the possible exception of Henderson's. "You hear those?" he said, staring out into the gathering darkness.

"Hear what?" said Wolfe.

"The *coquís.* The tree frogs."

Wolfe cocked an ear, then shook his head. "Obviously, my hearing isn't as good as yours."

"Some species, you can estimate the temperature. Count the chirps in fifteen seconds, add forty."

"Fascinating," said Wolfe dryly. "Is this what you wanted to talk to me about?"

"I'd forgotten what a nature buff I was."

"Beatrice was the bird-watcher, I believe."

"Yes," said Peter with sudden emphasis, "but I was, too. And now—" He left the sentence unfinished.

"Now what?"

"Now," said Peter, gazing out the window again, "I use nature to test instruments of mass destruction by incinerating innocent animals."

Mistaking Peter's dreamy tone for misguided sarcasm, Wolfe let out one of his barklike laughs. "Not to put too fine a point on it." In the next moment he saw that Peter was deadly serious and the smile left his face. "Is that why you've come, to be talked out of your doubts? Hasn't that always been Beatrice's job?"

Something disingenuous in Wolfe's tone made Peter take notice. "You know we've been fighting?"

"No, I didn't know that," Wolfe said, much too quickly.

"Couple of nights ago. Just one of our rows. We're both black belts in marital argument, so it's nothing to worry about." Now *he* was dissembling. "Actually," he said, "I've come to talk about this body." And he slapped the side of his thigh.

Wolfe frowned. "Is that how you think of it, as 'this body'?"

Peter nodded. "At first I was terrified of it. Now I'm just deeply curious. For instance, I know it had knee surgery—I discovered four quarter-inch scars two days ago. I'm not bulked up enough for football, and the circumferences of the forearms are identical, so he probably wasn't a tennis player. I thought perhaps a skier—perhaps a pro skier? The knee feels flawless, which probably means a world-class surgeon. Was the guy well-heeled?"

Wolfe stared at Peter as if he'd cursed in church. "Why are you asking me these questions?"

Outside the window, the *coquís* sang. "Because I can juggle."

"I'm sorry?"

"I shadow-box. I have dreams about people I must have known. There's something really strange at work here—I've been doing some research into cellular memory—"

"Oh, Peter, spare me—"

"I know, it's mostly crackpot stuff, but listen, okay, and don't laugh. I read about this case—a woman who had a heart transplant. As soon as she got out of the hospital she stopped in for a beer and pizza. Now the peculiar thing was, she hated pizza and had never taken a drink in her life. And this kept happening to her and now she had to find out who her donor had been. She lived in a small city, so it wasn't hard— there had only been one death within twenty-four hours of her transplant that would have left an intact heart. A twenty-five-year-old guy killed in a motorcycle accident."

Wolfe nodded wanly. "He was on his way to get pizza and beer. It was his favorite meal and he did it once a week, like clockwork."

"You've heard the story before."

"It's complete and utter bullshit," said Wolfe, lighting up a Gauloise.

"How do you know? Did you ask the woman? Freddy, I swear, these dreams I've been having—and the juggling, how do you account for that? There's something here, but the biology is beyond my competence. We could work on it together," he offered, adding, as he saw Wolfe's black eyes begin to flash, "in my off hours."

"*What* off hours?" asked Wolfe. "You're two days behind as it is. I'm sorry, Peter, it doesn't even interest my little finger."

"But it interests me. Did he like to box? Was he married? What did he do for a living?"

"And was he an animal rights activist? And does that account for your crisis of conscience?"

"Well, no, I wasn't thinking that exactly—"

Reddening, Wolfe shot out of his chair. "Peter, have you completely lost your mind? I'm just glad Henderson isn't here to hear this. My God, you know the rules."

"I *don't* know the rules. I know precious little at all about this project."

"I meant the rules of secrecy. I'm sure you're perfectly familiar with *that* kind of protocol. It's not as if you've just fallen off the back of a turnip truck in the world of classified projects."

"I want to know the rules of *this* project—they were made in my absence. I'm the first subject, I have a right to know things." Then he took a breath, and said lower, "I have the right to know who my donor is, as well."

Wolfe looked truly distraught. "What do you think, this is an adoption story on *Oprah* or something? That is absolutely classified information."

"I could ask Alex."

"Alex? Why on earth would you do that?"

"He's in the loop, isn't he? Beatrice caught him browsing in the Fountain files."

Wolfe's face went pale.

"I know what she thinks she saw. She didn't and he wasn't. She didn't know what she was seeing."

"Or maybe I should talk to Henderson?"

"And do what?" said Wolfe, flaring up again. "Threaten to abandon the project? You feeling suicidal these days? I know Henderson, Peter, better than you do and this is one dragon whose tail you don't want to jerk. He has a violent temper, and once he's mad, he stays mad. You have your life back, don't jeopardize it."

"Gee, that sounds an awful lot like a threat, Freddy. Is that what we've got here?"

"That's your overheated imagination talking, Peter. I've never found it necessary to threaten anyone. I'm telling you, just get back to work and don't rock the boat. People are jumpy enough already. As for this business of telling Beatrice your sex dreams about beautiful young women, I'd advise you to stop. In fact, I'd go further: I'd advise you to put all that crap out of your mind. I'm counting on you to be professional and honor the commitment we've made to each other." He sighed. "I don't want to see all this fall apart, and, Peter, I don't want to see you get hurt like some teenager going off the road because he's getting head for the first time."

"I see," said Peter, getting up. Wolfe was smiling again, faintly, and sucking on his Gauloise.

"I love you like a son, Peter. Now get out of here."

Peter blinked. Like a *son?* It was altogether too much. He got the hell out of there.

Instead of heading for his lab, Peter went back across the breezeway to the restricted wing and into his room. Beatrice wasn't there. The walls were closing in on him again and his legs had begun to twitch with a vengeance. He wondered if he should go over to the gym and hit the treadmill. Then, gazing up at the darkening sky from his terrace, it struck him that he was sick to death of the goddamn treadmill. You ran and got nowhere.

He took a Valium and lay on his bed. But he was unable to quiet his mind. Before long something else struck him: this woman he had been dreaming about? How did Wolfe know it was a woman? The only way was if the old bastard had talked to Beatrice. What the hell was going on here?

Another question occurred to him. What the devil had Wolfe meant when he said people were jumpy enough as it is?

Who besides him was jumpy?

Elizabeth lay in her bed at the Casa del Francés and wondered about the tree frogs. She had read somewhere they were no bigger than silver dollars, but that they sounded much larger. Why she should dwell on these creatures disturbed her. She had never seen a *coquí,* and yet the image of one, with its dark bulbous eyes and prehensile toes, kept drifting through her head, staring out at her from inside a mason jar. According to Ivor, the owner of her hotel and her new best friend, kids in the South used to go hunting for tree frogs after dark. Her dad had been stationed in Mississippi—Hattiesburg, some place like that—so maybe that would explain it. They needn't have come to Vieques at all.

If I *have* been to Vieques, she found herself thinking, something traumatic or unmentionable must have happened here. Or was it simply that her insomnia was turning her mind into a sieve?

Since the day she had followed the guy with the messy hair to the Inn on the Azure Horizon, she had only managed to sleep for a couple of hours at a time, waking with a start at the slightest noise. By day, she had driven several times past the inn, but never did she see any sign of the kid or of his Range Rover. Yes, the woman at the desk had told her, a young fellow had stopped in and asked after her once since they had last spoken. She asked if Elizabeth wanted her to let him know where she was staying in case he came back.

She did not, thank you very much.

She thought of calling Hans's mother and telling her where she was, just in case.

But just in case of what?

She had twice gone back to the civilian airport, too, once to check out the Caribair arrivals and once to check out departing flights. But no one she knew arrived or left, and she herself wasn't going anywhere until she understood something about what had brought her here. That mysterious voice from the Internet haunted her: *IN OTHER WORDS, ELIZABETH, WISH YOU WERE HERE—*

Whether or not she had been on Vieques before, she felt deeply that she belonged here now and that to leave would be cowardice. But what she could actually do to feel in any way proactive rather than just hanging out passively at the hotel she did not know, and that drove her crazy. She wasn't used to living her life like this, and the only way she was able to live with it at all was to convince herself that, in some mysterious way, she was being asked to wait. Wait as a monk might wait for enlightenment by surrendering to something completely beyond his reckoning, something personal, something all-consuming.

So she waited. And thought.

Who knew she was staying at the Casa del Francés besides her three flight attendant friends and Ivor Greeley? No one she was aware of.

She knew she had to do something, even if it meant wandering the streets. *Anything* to shatter this paralysis, she thought, grabbing her car keys.

She padded through the darkened hotel and into the parking lot, where an old man was asleep on a chair. He had flowing white hair, enormous blue-veined eyelids and a three-inch scar along his jawbone. He was supposed to be the guard, so one night Elizabeth had asked him, in halting Spanish, if he had seen anybody resembling the young man with wild hair hanging around during his watch. He said he absolutely had not, but now, as she watched him snoring away in his chair, she knew why. Still, she didn't have the heart to wake him.

There was no need to worry: he didn't move even when her headlights swept him on her way out to the street.

She drove into Esperanza and walked aimlessly for an hour along bright avenues and quiet alleys until she found a bar called Bananas. Mary Blanchard had mentioned that it was one of her hangouts. The place was noisy and full of Americans, including Mary and her two buddies.

"Hey, Lizzer, pull up a stool!"

She did, and they shared a plastic bucket of fried onions and a round of Coronas. After regaling Elizabeth with stories of drunken celebrities and live births at thirty-five thousand feet, Mary slid her chair closer.

"So what happened to this hunk you were supposed to meet down here?" she asked. "Don't tell me he stood you up?"

Elizabeth sipped her beer. "Afraid so."

"Unbelievable. Fine. So what we have to do now, I think, so it's not a total loss, is get you laid, all right?"

Elizabeth begged off. "I think maybe it's time to go home."

"You mean, home home?"

"I think maybe it is," said Elizabeth, with sudden conviction. "Thank you all for everything. Really. You've been great. I don't know what I would have done if I hadn't run into you." She gave Mary an impulsive hug, almost like a sister she had met and now was leaving again, and left the bar. Something about the loud music, the smell of beer, the notion of people looking for one-night stands saddened her terribly. He felt so near, somehow, she felt she should leave immediately.

But by the time she was back in her car, the conviction had vanished and instead of returning to the Casa del Francés to pack, she drove up the coast. If he feels near, she thought, it's stupid to leave. Leave when he feels very, very far away. He didn't feel that way right now, not by a long shot.

There was a full moon painting the sea. She passed Sun Bay and Half Moon Bay, and then stopped the car about five miles beyond when something odd caught her eye just past the trees. A soft pale glow rising from the beach below, too weirdly green and too diffuse to be from house lights.

Maybe someone was shooting a movie. Mary had said several had been shot here—*Heartbreak Ridge* and *Lord of the Flies*. But she couldn't see any of the usual trucks or signs of crews and all she could hear were the *coquís*. She got out of the car.

Have I been to this beach, was I here as a child? Or did I drive past it the day I tailed the strange kid? She closed her eyes, trying to block out the sound of the tree frogs. The air and the surf reminded her of Cannes. She locked the car, then stood there, undecided.

Maybe I should just drive back to the hotel and take a hot bath, she thought, an altogether pleasant and sensible notion.

Instead, she started walking toward the sound of the ocean.

Peter stared down from his terrace. It's not that big a drop, he thought.

There were guards at the front of the building, but only an hourly patrol around back. As for the motion sensors, they only pointed outward into the trees, not toward the residence wing. The power panel was located at the end of the corridor in a utility room he had scoped out after dinner. If he had to, he could disable the sensors.

And he *had* to. He had had it with the rules and regimen and he was sick and tired of being treated like a freak.

I'm not a prisoner, he thought. I'm voluntary.

Jesus, now he was thinking like a mental patient. In fact, the meeting with Wolfe had left him feeling like a lunatic, his mind buzzing with crazy questions and his body in high agitation, like a newly captured animal before it submits to its cage.

It's not as though I'm going AWOL. All I want to do is run barefoot on the beach. Is that too much to ask? He pictured himself jogging through the water, feeling the sand against the soles of his feet, smelling the salt air, seeing the moon on the bay. Hell, everybody else has celebrated my rebirth—now it's *my* turn.

He changed into running clothes and climbed over the balcony. For a moment he hung from the railing, feeling the ease of his muscles, knowing that this would have been impossible for him to do just a short time ago. He smiled, then let go, dropping easily to the ground, silent as a cat. A loping run brought him soundlessly to the end of the building. Slipping into the doorway, he opened the panel, found the circuit breaker and tripped it.

He listened.

No alarm. No stirring of feet. Hell, the place was in the middle of a Marine base on a tourist island owned by the U.S. military. How worried could they be?

He started off through the woods.

Once he was far enough away from the compound, he broke into a run, feeling the muscles in his legs propel him powerfully, effortlessly through the trees. With a growing sense of freedom he watched the moon appear and disappear through the palm fronds, felt the air rush in and out of his lungs, heard the sounds of the night yield to the gentle lapping of the sea. Within ten minutes he was on sand and in another five, he broke out onto the beach.

It was a restricted beach, earmarked for the practice of amphibious landings in time of war. The last time it had seen any soldiers was before Desert Storm. Now it was deserted: back to nature, thought Peter.

He took off his shoes and started running barefoot: it felt even better than he had imagined.

Elizabeth had almost turned back a dozen times, but each time she stopped she felt some wordless gravity pulling her on and began to walk again, beating her way through dark grasses, palms and mangrove, often losing the glow she had seen earlier and finding her way only by moonlight or by feeling her way like a blind person. She figured she would give it five more minutes, or another hundred yards, all the while thinking, *You're being really stupid, you know that? What if you run into some drunks or dope smugglers or wild animals?* She realized she was sounding like her own mother and forced herself to continue on. Then, when it was simply too dark to see anything, she stopped and caught her breath.

What the hell was she doing, traipsing around in the middle of nowhere like this? Were there poisonous snakes on this island? Quicksand? *Lions and tigers and bears. Oh my!*, she thought, and turned back. She had taken no more than three steps when a sudden dip in the terrain sent her pitching forward, a bush caught her foot, and she sprawled forward into pitch-black air.

She hit, none too gracefully, and rolled ass over teakettle through a thick stand of brush, then clunked against a dune. Unhurt, breathless and glad she was in one piece. She even laughed at herself. It had been a long time since she had done something like this, just on impulse. Because of the pale green light everywhere around her, she realized she could see perfectly well.

Then she saw the bay.

It was hidden from the road and ocean by way of a narrow passage between two steep, jasmine-scented hills, but from here it was spread out before her like a magic carpet of emerald stars. It glowed as though lit from beneath, a dreamy, drifting greenish blue like a million galaxies had been caught and steeped in water. It took her breath away.

It looked absolutely familiar.

I know this place, she thought. *But why?*

She dimly recalled Ivor Greeley, back at the Casa del Francés, telling Mary Blanchard and her friends about something called Phosphorescent Bay. This must be it, she realized, and she had found it as though from memory. Standing up, she brushed herself off, feeling wonderfully at home.

As she approached the bay, the moon disappeared behind some clouds, but there was no diminution of light—the surface of the water was its own light and it shimmered and shifted in hue as she reached the pale strip of beach. Once there, she could see that the glow was radiating not from one central source but from millions of tiny points. Light-emitting organisms, she guessed, without knowing why it didn't feel like a guess at all.

And then she remembered her dream, the one in which Hans was a sea of stars. It was *this place*—she was certain of it—as certain as she was of her own name. How could she come upon—by some deep and hidden instinct—a place she had seen only in a dream? Fear came rushing back, almost as if she were in the presence of a ghost, and she turned to get the hell out of there.

But she never moved beyond that. Someone was running down the beach toward her.

As he came closer and closer, it was harder and harder for her to breathe. *No, it couldn't be.* In town, in the bars, every third man had looked like him for a nanosecond, until it wasn't, of course. She waited for her heart to quiet down. But this time it went right on pounding.

The man slowed to a trot and then stopped, raking both hands back through his pale blond hair in a gesture she had seen a hundred times. He was staring at her and she was staring at him, neither moving an inch until the moon came out from behind a cloud. And then they actually saw each other: and there was not a shadow of a doubt in either one's mind any more.

Elizabeth saw Hans.

And Peter saw the woman he had been dreaming about since the moment he had occupied this body—the Angel of his dreams, right down to the eyelash, and it scared the living hell out of him. He had never seen her before in the flesh, and yet he knew in the depths of his soul that this was the woman he had loved in his dreams without reservation or boundary night after blissful night.

For a moment, neither of them could move or speak. Then Peter saw her take a step closer, and another. Then he moved toward her, hearing her call out.

"Hans?"

Hans! His name was Hans! He found himself running toward her. As soon as he did, the woman streaked toward him, laughing. Crashing together, they flung their arms around each other.

"It's you. It's really you. But how—"

He silenced her with a kiss. "It's me," he heard himself say.

"I'm so frightened—"

"Don't be frightened. Shh," he said, seeing tears spring to her eyes. Without another word they held each other. The night fell away and they sank down together, fumbling at each other's clothes, breathless with joy. The only thought in Peter's mind was the complete and terrifying certainty that this woman, with her pale hair and clear gray eyes and exotic cheekbones, this strong, loving creature, this passionate Angel, was the lover of his clone. Then all thought vanished as his physical need for her, a thing so unabashed and physical he barely felt it coming, hit him, canceling all doubt and fear. Waves of light flowed over them; he entered her so swiftly he couldn't believe it was happening. For the first time in his life, his body had seized utter control of his mind, taking whatever it could find to give love to this woman.

She seemed so hungry for him, too, such a miracle of warmth and energy that he climaxed almost immediately. Instead of being disappointed, she seemed delighted, letting out a little yelp of surprise and gratitude, then burrowing into his arms, kissing his neck and crying softly. They lay together until their breathing smoothed and their hearts went from gallop to walk.

"Oh God," was all she could say.

"Amen," said Peter, utterly tongue-tied.

"Hans, tell me what's happening."

Peter searched desperately for something logical to say, then spoke the only truth he dared.

"I can't speak yet . . ."

He pulled her out into the warm water, feeling her breasts soft against his chest.

"That wasn't your corpse in the car. I knew it. But whose *was* it?"

Corpse? He shook his head helplessly. "I don't know."

"Jesus, you're in some kind of trouble, aren't you?"

He laughed, soundlessly, without meaning to. Was there some kind of trouble he *wasn't* in now?

"I have a knack for the obvious," she said, with girlish embarrassment. And then, "Does this mean I'm in trouble, too?"

Good Lord, I hope not, Peter thought, and lied. "No," he said. "Of course not."

"Was it you who sent that e-mail? Are you IslandMan?"

E-mail? IslandMan? He felt a shiver go through him and tried to adopt a neutral expression. Tell her to go home, he thought desperately. Tell her to get the hell out, tell her to forget about you, tell her that you're never going to see her again.

"I missed you so much," he said, feeling tears burn his eyes.

Was that his body speaking for him or was he now speaking for his body? Or was there no longer any difference? This last thought simultaneously frightened and liberated him. He watched, mesmerized by her beauty as she gazed out over the luminescent bay.

"I dreamed about this place," she said.

"Did you? I did, too, I think."

She looked back at him and smiled a lovely smile. So much warmth in it, such affection. "You used to come here, didn't you, when you were a little boy."

He frowned. "Did I mention that?" he guessed.

"Not really." She darkened. "You never told me anything. Was that fax from you? Who was that kid in the car?"

His head spun as he pulled her closer. He could feel her trembling and realized that he was as well. "I don't want you to worry," he said. "But I want you to be careful. We can't stay too long together here. Not now."

She stared at him in alarm. "I can't leave you after just finding you!"

His heart spoke again. "I don't want you to leave," he said. "But . . ."

"I should be scared, shouldn't I? I *am* scared."

He nodded gently. "What car did you see?"

"A Range Rover, driven by a young guy, maybe mid-twenties. He was waiting for me at the airport when my flight landed and then he came to the hotel."

"You spoke to him?"

She shook her head, feeling suddenly so sane for doing what had seemed so crazy. "I didn't take the plane. I snuck over on the ferry and watched the plane come in. I saw him, he didn't see me."

He felt a burst of admiration. She was smart and brave and intuitive. And lucky, he began to think, too. Who *was* that?

"Did he look military?"

"I think his car was. He just looked—kind of *intense.*"

His mind was racing. He kissed her softly, hoping his pounding heart wouldn't betray his own growing fear. "Change hotels."

"No need. I'm at the Casa del Francés."

"Good. That's good."

"Hans, your mother . . ."

She left the sentence hanging. All he could do was nod, torn between his desire to know more about his past—everything possible, as a matter of fact. And about this marvelous woman. But also by a terrible fear of betraying himself as an imposter—or worse. "She okay?" he asked lamely.

"She's okay. She was devastated, as you can imagine. But she's tough. We talked. A lot. About you."

He squeezed her hand. "The less she knows . . ."

"Yes. I understand. I don't suppose you can tell me either."

"No. Not yet." Peter thought: I'm in hell and I'm in heaven and I can't tell the difference. "Can you live with that for now?" Christ, he thought, I don't even know her name.

"Yes," she said. "So long as I don't lose you again."

"You won't lose me," he said with utter conviction, taking her face in his hands. Their lips met again and then they were making love, more slowly this time, a thing that was tidal and profound and full of mystery. There was a point when both of them were crying, and then they passed beyond even that. He felt her tremble on the edge and hold back, and then give in, coming over and over. And then it was his turn—and still later *their* turn—until everything just fell away, the sea and the moon and the stars, and there was only the two of them together, suspended in a miracle of light against the primordial darkness. How much time had passed? He had lost all track, and it was a long while before the uneasiness crept back in.

But creep back in it did. He had no idea how long he had been gone from the base.

"I have to go," he said.

He felt her tighten. "Where?"

He shook his head, and to his relief, she answered for him.

"Not yet. Okay. When do I see you again?"

"Tomorrow night," he heard himself say.

"Should I believe you?"

"Yes," he insisted, meaning it.

"Will you tell me what's going on then?"

"I'll explain what I can," he said carefully, as though he were testifying in a court of law. "The Casa del Francés?"

"Yes."

"Wait there. Don't go out. I'll try to be there by six. Can you wait that long?"

"Of course I can."

He looked in her eyes. Everything was as he had dreamed it, down to the barely discernable scar tissue along the eye sockets, the strangeness of her face and its amazing, unaccountable familiarity. "What name did you register under?"

She frowned, puzzled. "My own name. Oh, you mean because of the kid. No, I had to give the hotel my credit card."

"Yes, of course." All right, he thought, I can find out her name when I get there. "Good-bye," he said.

He kissed her deeply and disappeared.

Elizabeth watched him go.

She waited until he had vanished around an outcropping of rock, then put her clothes back on and started back for her car. She felt as if she could almost have been dreaming, or had, perhaps, gone mad. But for the first time in weeks, she felt crystalline and strong. She had Hans back again, one way or the other, and nothing else mattered.

And not only was he back, but he was back as a Hans tempered by an experience she hardly dared guess at, informed by a depth she had never felt before. There had been a sensitivity in his lovemaking that for the first time put her pleasure ahead of his own, and a gentleness, a sadness and, in the midst of their passion, a sobriety and tact that were light-years away from the Hans she had known. As if he had matured overnight, turning from being a brash and cynical boy into a tender, caring man wise beyond his years.

What in God's name had he been through?

Almost giddy, she realized that she knew less than ever who her lover Hans Brinkman really was—and was more compelled than ever to find out.

10

Peter went back through the trees in a daze.

What the hell is going on and how am I going to find out about it? Worse, what did I do tonight, what was *that? How could I do that to Beatrice?* And the most frightening question of all: who the hell *am* I? He knew the answer to none of these questions. All he knew for sure was that something disastrous had happened and if he didn't pull himself together, worse was to come.

That he had betrayed Beatrice for the first time in their marriage had begun to torment him the instant he left Phosphorescent Bay.

There had never been anyone but Beatrice, not even during those first difficult years, when they had fought every day, when neither knew from month to month whether the marriage would actually last. And there *is* still no one, he tried to tell himself, as he ran back down the beach, watching his pale shadow before him on the barren sand. He thought wildly that perhaps he had just experienced a fugue episode. Maybe something had gotten miswired between his brain and his body during the transplant and now he was locked in a dream and couldn't escape. He could see that therein lay madness, but it also made perfect sense. Whatever the reason, he was terrified of three things: that somehow the membrane between fantasy and reality had been ruptured irreparably, that his conscience had been dealt a mortal blow and that he would never again enjoy the safety and order of the rational world he had to this moment so much taken for granted.

What am I going to tell Beatrice?

The wise thing, the soul-sparing thing, would be to keep everything to himself. Still, he couldn't get rid of the feeling that he had de-

stroyed the covenant between them, and that he was in danger of ex-
pulsion from the haven of stability and warmth he had known with
her for so many years.

Worse, he wasn't in this alone. There was this woman, this amazing
nameless woman to whom he was in no way entitled, whose very existence threatened his sanity and, more to the point, whose own safety
was now imperiled by events he had set in motion. Don't fool yourself, he admonished himself, *you're* responsible for what happened,
however it happened, and you owe it to her to see that she gets out of
this safely. You're going to keep your promise: you have to see her
again.

Or was that only his lust talking . . .

No. It was much more than lust, he knew that. Have you ever
known anything with Beatrice like what you've just experienced? he
asked himself, point-blank. The question terrified him. In the early
years, perhaps her passion was at its height. But had his own passion
and sensitivity been equal to hers? Not until tonight, with another
woman, *this* woman, with years of experience behind him and a new
body allowing him to use that experience, had he felt such bliss. And
it was no dream. It was real, as real as his betrayal of everything decent and principled. You selfish bastard, he raged, first you sell your
soul, and now you've sold out your marriage. At least have the de-
cency to deliver them both to the devil without excuses.

And for God's sake, use your brain and figure out how in hell she
had come here in the first place!

More specifically, who on earth had e-mailed her?

There was only one person he could think of: Alex Davies.

Alex must have been nosing around in the Fountain files, just as
Beatrice had claimed and Wolfe had subsequently denied. The track-
ing of the clones might well have included wives or lovers, so Alex
could know the name of Hans's lover. And if Alex Davies knows about
the girl, who else does? And how do I confront them?

He stopped running, ragged and spent, facing the answer to that
question.

He couldn't—not without putting the young woman from the
beach even more at risk than she was now. Jesus, he thought, as he

made his way quietly through the palm grove toward the compound, you really have fucked up this time! Nearing the condominiums, he slowed, trying to make as little sound as possible. Then he became aware of a high-pitched whine in his ear, like the wire-thin hum of an ancient television. He stopped, listened, then realized what it was: someone had turned the infrared sensors back on.

Just then something big and fast slammed into him from behind and knocked him flying.

"Freeze. Do not move! Get your fucking hands over your head!"

More shapes—heavily armed men in dark uniforms tearing in on him. In a daze he realized he had been tackled by Special Forces guards and that he now had a half-dozen high-powered weapons pointed at his head, off-safety and ready to fire.

"I'm Dr. Peter Jance!" he screamed. And then, remembering: "Junior!" Somebody kicked him hard in the ribs—once, twice. Next he heard new shouts and a woman screaming, Beatrice's and Wolfe's voices.

"What the hell you think you're doing, you idiots!" Wolfe raged.

The guards fell back. Beatrice ran to Peter, helping him to his feet. Out of the darkness Oscar Henderson emerged, barking out orders. The guards stood to attention. Peter rose slowly, holding his ribs, watching as more men came running from every direction, securing the perimeter. Against what he hadn't a clue.

Henderson took in the scene with a glance, his mouth twisted in contempt.

"My, my, is it Spring Break already?"

Peter wheeled on him. "I was just taking a jog on the beach. What are you running here, Henderson, a goddamn prison camp?"

Henderson surveyed him coldly, his voice low and tight. "No, a military base, Dr. Jance. Home to three thousand fighting men, fourteen commands and an undisclosed number of highly sensitive and secret projects, of which you are one."

He bellied up to Peter as though Peter's being a young man now gave Henderson the right to deck him if he so chose. "And sensitive, secret projects do not go jogging on the beach at night without an escort. Not on my watch." He spun on Wolfe. "I suggest a leash."

He stalked away with his men, leaving Peter to face Beatrice.

She looked at his wet, rumpled clothes, his unruly hair and his evasive eyes, then walked away without a word.

There was a moment of awful silence. Then Peter felt Wolfe's hand at the small of his back, guiding him toward the restricted wing.

"Nice job, Peter," Wolfe said. "Really first-rate. How far did you get?"

Bite your tongue, thought Peter. Whatever you say to Wolfe tonight, Beatrice will hear it tomorrow. "Look," he said, trying to take the edge out of his voice, "I'm not a lab rat on a running wheel. If I want to run on the beach at night instead of using your goddamn treadmill, I will."

"And the risk to your cerebral arteries be damned."

"They're *my* cerebral arteries. Unless, of course, you don't want any more work out of me."

"Now who's making threats?" Wolfe said through his teeth and then pulled back. "I'll arrange for bodyguards who can keep up with you."

"Alone," said Peter.

"Can't allow it."

"I run alone. That's a deal-breaker."

Now Wolfe was scrutinizing him. "If I could be sure that's all you were doing."

Say nothing, thought Peter. "All I'm doing," said Peter, "is clearing out the cobwebs."

Wolfe cocked an eyebrow with suspicion. "And they're cleared out? You're back with the program?"

Wolfe's eyes were bright, daring Peter to say no.

"Back with the program," said Peter as he watched Wolfe's expression stiffen.

"That's good to hear. You can run on any beach on the base at any time."

Wolfe stuck out his hand. Peter shook it, feeling Wolfe's long bony fingers tighten around his knuckles. He gave me life, now he thinks he owns me, thought Peter.

"How're your ribs?" Wolfe asked.

"They hurt like hell, thank you."

"You're welcome," Wolfe said. "Now let's get you into the clinic."

The two old friends walked off together, side by side. That way, Peter knew, neither had to turn his back on the other.

By the time Elizabeth got back to the Casa del Francés, it was four in the morning. On the return trip from the beach she had been jumpy and paranoid, circling two blocks in a figure-eight before parking her car outside the gate. She, too, was unable to pass through security, in this case the white-haired guard in the folding chair. He had locked the gate, forcing her to ring the bell. But he didn't respond. She could see him in his tiny booth next to the driveway, propped against the wall, his pearly-white scar visible in the moonlight. She leaned on the bell until a light came on in a downstairs room, and then Ivor Greeley appeared in the door in an old terry cloth bathrobe, carrying a set of keys on a big ring.

"We usually don't have guests coming back this late," he grumbled.

"Ivor, I'm sorry. I tried to wake the guard, but he's not even moving."

Greeley threw a look at the old man, then called, "*Toro!*"

The old man lurched forward, his blue-veined lids popping open. Greeley patted Elizabeth's shoulder, noting her soggy clothes.

"You just have to know the trick. He used to be a matador in Mexico City. Got himself all busted up when he overstayed his welcome. Somebody had to give him a job."

"Not much in the way of security, though, do you think?" said Elizabeth, with a backward glance at the street.

Ivor shrugged. "You didn't get in, did you?" He walked back into the hotel while the ex-matador made an elaborate show of relocking the gate.

Elizabeth went straight to her room, double-locked the door, lay back on her bed and tried to piece together the night's events.

First, why was Hans here? And why had his death been faked? Who was that in the morgue photographs? Who was that in his coffin?

No answers made sense. Drugs? A Colombian cartel working through the islands toward Miami? Or had he embezzled some huge amount of money that now had its rightful owners putting out a hit on him? No, she decided, it's something even more bizarre than that. The thunder on the island, the military bases—it must be CIA. Or black ops. The career in finance, the high-profile marriage, were they part of a cover story or was that really Hans? He hadn't known about the e-mail, though he had tried to pretend otherwise—she had seen that in his eyes. The kid in the Range Rover, that was news to him as well. *Bad* news.

Who had summoned her down here if not Hans? And why? Her unshakable feeling of having been to Vieques before, almost as if she had lived here as a child, what did *that* have to do with anything?

She thought of Rose-Anne—how devastated she had been at Hans's death, how gamely she had tried to rebound from her grief. Would Hans put his own mother through such agony with no warning?

Only if he were a completely different man from the one she had known.

But wasn't he?

Never in all their months together had Hans made love to her the way he had tonight. What had happened down here to liberate him? Was it simply being back in *his* childhood home? Or was it that he no longer was leading a double life?

And if he *was* CIA, why, when she happened upon him at what might well be his base of operations, had he been so tender, so loving, so spontaneous? Or was that all part of the act, a result of his training?

Impossible. If that was an act then the world makes no sense at all.

She thought of calling Annie, but dismissed it immediately. The fewer innocent people involved the better. Rose-Anne? That was a more difficult question. No, not yet, she thought, popping up from bed for the third time to check to see if anyone was watching from the street. Until she assessed how much danger she was actually in, it was possible that Rose-Anne might even be in on it. Hadn't the woman encouraged her to come down here by mentioning it so often? And by telling her how much Hans had cared for both her and this island?

Mother and son in the CIA together?

At this point, thought Elizabeth, nothing was too peculiar.

With visions of Rose-Anne and Hans, clad head to toe in black and mowing down hordes of drug-runners with their AK-47s, she fell headlong into a deep and uneasy sleep.

In the core lab of the Fountain Compound, Peter Jance, Jr. was dreaming.

His team buzzed around him, brimming with ideas. He had planted those ideas in their heads, and over the last week they had blossomed brilliantly. Cap Chu and Rosemarie Wiener had finally worked out the ancillary equations for the enhanced propulsion beam, and Hank Flannagan had completely redesigned the fusion circuitry to fit in half the space and handle three times the power of possible voltage surges. Alex Davies had run a dozen alternate models of the completed weapon through a Kray and was reporting, in a low robotic voice, on his success.

Meanwhile Peter stared at his shoes. The think tank smelled of the sea and chalk dust and Rosemarie Wiener's new perfume, the latest personal secret weapon in her arsenal.

"—fully destructive to living tissue. The enemy, in effect, will melt in the beam. Buck Rogers to the nth plus one," said Alex dryly.

"Yeah, but will it blow up again?" said Cap Chu.

"I've been running continuous trials and we're already into the millions. Not one failure. Money-back guarantee."

Peter raised his eyes from the pale green linoleum. He felt miles away—back in Phosphorescent Bay, in that warm, glowing water, melting into the embrace of a nameless Angel. "And the ramifications?" Peter heard himself say.

They all turned around.

"We win," Flannagan said.

"What about the people who are going to be vaporized by this thing?"

A silence fell over the room. Only a civilian would bring this up, or perhaps a college sophomore, and Peter was neither.

"They'll go quick," said Flannagan, "and they'll probably deserve it."

Peter felt the soles of his feet begin to twitch. "Like the Nazis, you mean."

There were nervous glances all around. "Yeah, okay," said Cap Chu. "Isn't that why your dad helped build the A-bomb? To beat the Germans to the punch?"

"In the beginning," said Peter, "that was the rationale. Then we—" he began, and then corrected himself, "—my dad and others realized the Nazis had gone down a blind alley. Their idea of a nuke was loading an atomic pile aboard a ship and sneaking it into an enemy harbor. But we—" he continued, glancing at Alex Davies, who was chewing thoughtfully on his lower lip, "—they went ahead anyway. Because it was there. Once they knew they could make it, they didn't want to stop."

"Yeah, but still," said Rosemarie, "what if the Nazis rise again? And this time around they know what they're doing?"

"When the Nazis come back," Alex Davies assured her, "they won't be wearing swastikas. They'll be wearing business suits and talking about living in peace and harmony." His eyes shone with mischief. "Kind of like us."

"Who says?" said Cap Chu.

"Charles Manson—his very words. I'm sorry, dude," Alex Davies turned back to Peter, "you were saying?"

Peter rose and looked out the window. "What if," he said, "this technology we're perfecting is further miniaturized to suitcase size, which it will be sooner or later, and it's stolen or given away via some rider to some bill nobody really gives a shit about and ends up in what we laughingly call the wrong hands. Then we're looking at New York *really* sizzling in the summer."

They all looked at him for a long moment, then Cap Chu burst into laughter.

"God, you're good."

"I'm sorry?" said Peter.

"I thought your dad was a put-on artist, but you're way better." The others laughed, all except Alex, whose eyes had been following Peter like a hawk.

"In any case," Alex said, "if the computer trials continue to pan out, we'll be going back to White Sands soon."

At this, they all went on alert, Peter included. "No shit?" said Flannagan.

"So," said Alex, fixing Peter in his sights, "it's a little late for liberal angst."

Peter met his eyes until Alex turned back to the chalkboard.

"Damn," said Rosemarie, "I was about to get accredited in scuba."

"Maybe you can take up sand diving at Los Alamos," said Flannagan.

Their conversation bubbled on, excited or disappointed by the prospect of moving back to the desert depending on each person's proximity to girlfriends, family or favorite bars. Peter heard none of it. All he heard was his inner voice, urging him to think fast and to find a way to get that woman to New Mexico.

Studying the bank of video monitors in Henderson's office, Wolfe turned to the colonel.

"He's in dreamland again," Henderson agreed.

They could see Peter from two angles, wide and close. While his team scurried about the lab, arguing, scrawling on the chalkboard, Peter sat staring at the concrete wall as though it were a picture window.

"No doubt about it," said Henderson. "He got his pencil shaved in town. There's a big singles scene there, you know."

"Really?" Wolfe asked deadpan. Beneath his own concern for the project's future, he detected a faint echo of perverse satisfaction. If Peter was cheating on Beatrice, there might be a chance it would spell the end of their marriage. Had it ever been tested before? Not to his knowledge, although over the years he had often secretly prayed for something to go wrong between his two old friends, something that might leave the field clear for himself and Beatrice. But priorities were priorities: by straying off the base, Peter had put himself and the entire project at risk, and the heedlessness had filled both Wolfe and Henderson with alarm. The difference between the two men was that Henderson was much more ready to act.

"If I had my way," said Henderson, "I'd take him down with a tranquilizer gun and perform a partial castration."

"I wonder what Beatrice would say to that," Wolfe responded.

"I think she'd be the one to hold his nuts. Let's get his ass in here." Henderson pushed the button that hid the video screens and called for his aide.

Five minutes later the door opened and Peter walked in wearing a look of distracted irritation. Henderson opened and closed the subject in one breath.

"Jance, you've got to stop screwing around."

Peter eyed him. "No more Coltrane in the think tank."

"That too." Henderson came around his desk, his manner heavily paternal. "Look," he said, placing a giant hand on Peter's shoulder, "I know it must be a hoot. Suddenly you're in a young body, with all that testosterone running around in your brain, but—"

Peter shrugged Henderson's hand away. "It's much more than that," he said.

"Then why don't you tell me about it? And wipe that damn smirk off your face."

On his old friend's behalf, Wolfe felt his gut tighten up. "Oscar," he said, "there's no reason to be hostile."

"It's all right, Freddy," said Peter, drawing himself up. "You want to hear about it, Colonel? Fine. It's not just hormones. It's a liver that actually cleans my blood. It's a heart that floods my brain with the richest, most oxygenated blood I've enjoyed in forty years. Another example—my knee joints. Instead of calcified, bone-on-bone hinges, they're finely tuned machines—ligaments, cartilage and muscles perfectly toned and intact, cushioned by fully functional menisci. It's a pleasure to climb stairs again. And I have lungs that don't grow congested when I run. I can smell, taste, feel, see and hear a million things I'd either learned to despise in their ruined form or forgotten existed at all. You know the overtones I can hear now on a violin string playing a Bach partita? I'd forgotten there *were* such things."

"I'm talking more about your dick," Henderson said. Peter's icy eloquence, Wolfe knew, only served to increase Henderson's anger.

"As in, the dick that's leading you around."

Peter returned his gaze. "I don't know what you mean."

"That's bullshit and you know it's bullshit."

Peter gave a defiant laugh. "Go fuck yourself, Colonel. I don't have to dance for you."

Henderson came at him in one fluid move, slamming him against the wall, hand crushing his throat before Peter could even throw up an arm in self-defense. Henderson pushed his face into Peter's, his free hand waving Wolfe away.

"Jance," he said, "I know more ways to kill someone with my bare hands than you do from behind a machine a safe mile away, so don't get smart with me. I don't mind looking in the face of the people *I* do." He inhaled deeply, then said very quietly, "You better watch your ass, Peter, or you and your love toy will *both* end up on the scrap heap."

Peter's eyes flinched with real fear. Enough was enough, thought Wolfe. "Henderson," he said, as calmly as he could, "if you continue in this vein I'm going to have to report it to Washington."

"If you don't, I will," Henderson said quietly. He held Peter's eyes for another long second, then let go. Peter stayed on his feet, but Wolfe could see that his eyes had teared up from the assault to his windpipe and his breath was hoarse and desperate. Henderson confronted both of them. "I know you two are the geniuses and your names will be in all the books when mine's just a numbered stone in Arlington. But, by God, I've been *ordered* to see that this project does not get derailed by *anybody* and I include *everybody* in the word 'anybody.' No exceptions."

"You kill me, you won't have much of a project," Peter rasped out.

"That's your trump card, is it?" said Henderson. He stepped closer to Peter. "You think your friend Wolfe put all his eggs in one basket? There's plenty more where you came from."

Wolfe saw Peter stiffen with suspicion. "Meaning what?"

"What makes you think you're the only one?" Henderson shot back.

Peter couldn't speak. He looked at Wolfe, and Wolfe said as discreetly as he could, "Oscar, I'd like to be alone with Peter for a moment?"

Henderson wavered, then shrugged. "It's time our boy learned the facts of life. Office is yours."

He went out, slamming the door behind him. The damn fool, thought Wolfe. This was a conversation he had been hoping to avoid, and now that it was forced upon him, it would have to be handled with perfect delicacy. The sight of his old friend with Henderson at his throat had stirred complicated emotions, most of them unwanted.

"What was that supposed to mean?"

Wolfe looked at him cautiously. "I think you know."

"I don't. I'm sorry." Wolfe saw Peter's eyes dart away, as if he were about to tell a lie. "What was that threat he made? Who does he think I saw?"

Wolfe continued to eye him. "You tell me. Did you see someone? Have you been with anyone?"

Peter stared back, too fixedly. "No," he said.

Wolfe let it go. "I believe you."

"And what's this about 'others'?"

"Naturally," said Wolfe, beginning to rummage through Henderson's desk, "if it works out with you, there will be further attempts. That was always the Society's plan."

"But that's not quite what he said, is it? Are there others in the works?"

Careful, thought Wolfe. This man's senses are at their peak, and even before he could always smell an outright lie. "In the works? No. You're the only one, Peter, I swear." Under a pile of *Soldier of Fortunes* in Henderson's drawer he found a fifth of Jim Beam. "Eureka," Wolfe said. He took a brief swig, then offered it to Peter, who shook his head.

"This body didn't drink."

"But your brain does. Come on, I miss my old pub-crawling pal."

Relenting, Peter took the bottle, drank, and winced. "Christiaan Barnard or Mengele?"

"I'm sorry?"

"Which doctor are we, Freddy? How will we be remembered?"

"Oh," said Wolfe, savoring the bourbon rush, "I thought it was something like that."

"And I know what you're going to say. If we stopped every time we got cold feet, we'd still be living on a flat earth without penicillin." The liquor burned in his gut, but his head felt a nudge of relief.

"Praying to the savage gods," said Wolfe, "atop bloody ziggurats. Actually, I wasn't going to take that tack—"

"You ever read *Gulliver's Travels?*"

"Not since I was ten years old."

"You remember the Studbugs? Or the Struldbruggs, or some damn thing?" He accepted the bottle one more time, what the hell. He had his own fond memories of drinking with Wolfe in the old days. "Anyway, Swift had Gulliver find this place where people were born every so often who wouldn't die. The only difference between them and everyone else was that they had a red dot on their foreheads and they lived forever. And what happened was that everybody who had a normal life span grew to despise the Studbugs. Everybody got born, lived and died, but the damned red-dot ones stayed around forever."

"As I recall," said Wolfe, "they made them their leaders."

"You're thinking of some other book," said Peter. "Everybody hated them because they hogged everything. They never died or left their land or money to anybody; they never gave up the business to the son, or disappeared so that the daughter could assume the full mantle of adulthood. Oh, and they stank after a while, too. You see what I'm saying?"

"Actually, I don't."

Peter looked at him. Could he be this out of touch with what now seemed to be an obvious truth? "Species need to refresh themselves, Freddy, not be thrown into artificial stasis! We're trying to do an end run around two billion years of evolution."

Wolfe emitted a sharp laugh. He leaned across the desk. "*We're* two billion years of evolution, you sap! It's the Entropic Principle,

Peter—the laws of nature exist because our brains can imagine them. And improve upon them. *We're* evolution's quantum leap. We labored through trial and error for millions of years until we invented *ourselves!* We go from biplanes to lunar-landing craft in a single lifetime now, and if it can be thought of, it can be done. And *will* be done. Period."

Peter took that in for a moment, then countered, aiming for the sole weak spot he thought Wolfe might have. "What's Alex up to?"

"What?" said Wolfe.

"Why is he sending out e-mails?"

"E-mails? I don't know what you mean," he said. "My impression is that Alex is back on board. Is there something I should know?" he asked, watching Peter carefully. The frightened look had come back into Peter's eyes—the same look as when Henderson had threatened his so-called love toy—and it occurred to Wolfe that maybe there *was* someone. Well, if there was, she shouldn't be that difficult to find. "I'm sorry, Peter, I'm not following," he said.

"I think you follow more than you want me to know," Peter said. "And why, by the way, have you been seeing so much of Beatrice?"

Somebody has to, thought Wolfe, realizing with a start that he had almost said it out loud. "You've behaved badly to Beatrice," he said stiffly, putting the bottle down. "If I try to console her, I consider I'm doing three people a favor."

This seemed to chasten Peter. He took a long pull from the whiskey; this time it felt good. "In any case, thank you for calling off your dog," he said.

"Henderson isn't my dog," said Wolfe, "so there's no way I can call him off. If you get my drift."

"I do," said Peter.

"It's serious business, Peter. Many lives are at stake."

"Including mine."

"I'm afraid so, yes. This is not something you opt out of. You've signed on for life."

"And beyond."

"Exactly."

"I appreciate your candor," said Peter. "And you're right about evolution."

"Am I? I'm glad to hear that."

"And actually," Peter added, rising unsteadily, "that little bit of freedom you've given me? I swear it's increased my brain's output. I think we're almost home."

"Really, Peter?"

"Really. We're on the verge of actually assembling the weapon."

"Lethality equal to what we saw on the range? I want to pass this on to Henderson."

"More. No residuum at all. Adversaries will simply vanish by the battalion," said Peter, sweeping an arm through the air. "The trick will be limiting the killing, not trying to heighten it."

"So we're home?" said Wolfe, watching Peter carefully.

"I'd say so."

"Remarkable," said Wolfe. They were home, so Peter was expendable. Henderson had been more right than he knew.

"It's strong enough to wipe out every living thing within five miles, plus break down the atomic structure of the larger molecules. Carbon molecules, for instance, might just fly apart. That might make rocks turn into miniature nuclear grenades, for all we know. And Freddy, the best part? This will confirm everything you told them the Fountain Society could deliver. You're going to be able to write your own ticket after this. You can tell Henderson to take a hike, have the funding to do whatever kind of experiments you want to do. Take us all into the twenty-first century."

"And no more doubts?"

"No more doubts. Except now I have to pee."

"Well," said Wolfe, "I'm glad these little talks are helping."

They both laughed, gripping hands in a firm handshake. At the door they even embraced. Wolfe watched Peter walk down the hall toward the rest room, then closed Henderson's door. He really thought he was giving a performance, Wolfe thought. Charming the pants off me. And all for what, to buy a little time with your inamorata? Peter, dear deluded fool, I could always talk rings around you, couldn't I? And now I know that I can drink you under the table as well.

He recapped the Jim Beam, stowed it back in the drawer and pushed the button that reexposed the surveillance monitors. A video screen picked up Peter leaving the rest room, dabbing at his mouth with a paper towel. Wolfe grinned, realizing that Peter had gotten sick from the liquor. And then the most pleasant realization he had had in a long while struck him: one day very soon he, Frederick Wolfe, would truly have it all.

Later that afternoon, Peter lay on his bed staring at the ceiling's acoustical tile. His head ached from the bourbon and his senses felt minutely dulled, but he could still feel the woman as if she were lying beside him, the texture of her hair, the touch of her hand, the taste of her mouth. For several days he had practiced fending off the memory of their night on the beach, not always with success, but now, with Henderson's threats ringing in his ears, he found he could think of nothing but the woman.

End up on the scrap heap. You and your love toy.

Did that mean Henderson was already aware of her existence on the island? Had Alex Davies somehow tipped him off? Not willingly, no, he couldn't imagine that being the case. Of all the people on the base, Wolfe included, Alex was least adept at concealing his contempt for the military. But with Alex, anything was possible. Whose side, for instance, was he on, if anybody's? He couldn't ask Alex directly without further implicating himself and the woman as well.

Then what was he supposed to do? Warn her—tell her to take the next plane back to wherever she had come from.

No. The threat was real and his duty to the woman was clear, whatever his emotions. He had promised to see her again, and now there was every reason in the world to go. For another few minutes he lay on the bed, trying to calculate how he could slip away and return without inviting any more suspicion.

A key turned in the lock.

Peter bolted upright, half-expecting to see Henderson, but instead it was Beatrice. He saw the anguish in her face and it made him instantly heartsick.

"I'm sorry," she said. "I assumed you'd still be at the lab."

He gave a half-shrug, feeling utterly sheepish. "The thoughts weren't flowing," he said.

"I'll only be a moment," she said. "I left some things behind."

He watched her cross the room, brushing past the Erlenmeyer flask of dried flowers to open the drawer of a scarred blond bureau. Watching her graceful movements, seeing the pain in her eyes, he felt a sudden urge to confess, to share his own pain and confusion. Beatrice, I'm in trouble, I need your advice.

"What have you been working on?" he said gently.

She shot him a look: how quickly they forget. "Use of genetically altered blood," she said tonelessly. "In combat trauma."

"Yes, of course, I'm sorry."

She nodded, just barely, but it was enough for him to feel encouraged.

"I feel terrible," he said.

"Yes? About what?"

If Henderson knows, she surely suspects, he thought.

"About the way," he said, experimentally, "we've grown apart."

"Only six inches or so, I'd say. But it does make a difference."

At this flash of wit—which seemed to imply ignorance of any third party to their difficulties—Peter took heart, rising from the bed and going to his wife. She moved away, but not toward the door, which further gave him hope.

"I was told we're going back to White Sands soon," he said.

No, he was wrong, she was angrier than he had assumed—she was starting to empty her drawers, packing a small suitcase. "You really feel you're ready to travel?"

"Of course I am," he said.

She turned and looked at him, moving a strand of hair from her eyes. "Or would you rather stay here?"

He tightened. "Why would I want to do that?"

She hesitated a moment, keeping her back to him. "For the sake of your recovery," she said. Her voice sounded hollow—as though she were trying to convince herself there was nothing more than his health at stake. As she dropped some toiletries into her bag, Peter moved closer and touched her hair.

She pushed his hand away. "Please, don't condescend."

"To want to touch you, B., is not condescension."

"And don't call me B. That's what my husband used to call me. Beatrice will do just fine, thank you."

Peter sank.

"Beatrice, please? Don't abandon me because I'm different now. I need you."

"Do you, Peter?"

"Yes," he said. His voice, echoing back to him from the blank walls, sounded choked and puzzled. He felt like a child watching an adult weep at a funeral, knowing he couldn't possibly understand the pain around him, yet the tears were welling up in spite of his confusion. Turning, she saw that he was about to cry, and he felt her break inside. If I can still feel that, he thought, there's hope. "I'm still me. You're still you. We knew there would be adjustments—a few changes—"

"*A few changes!*" she said. "Jekyll and Hyde are slouches compared to you!"

He had to laugh. And then so did she, though with less ease. But she let him take her in his arms, and as soon as he did, she began to cry. Silently he stroked her hair. "It's been hellish," he said.

"Has it? I'm glad." She wiped a tear from her cheek. "Would you care to be more specific?"

He didn't know how to begin. "Wondering who's in control."

"You or your body?"

"It's driving me crazy. It's frightening. And the doubts are coming back. In spades."

"Tell me." She folded her hands in her lap as though trying to hide the wrinkles.

"I'm not old anymore. I don't have an old man's thoughts. Old men are much more comfortable making weapons of mass destruction," he said, relieved for the moment to be taking the high road.

"But you *were* young, Peter, when you went into weaponry."

"Maybe so. But why does it feel so different now?"

"And why is the sky blue? And why is there something rather than nothing? You tell me, Peter, because I don't know anymore. You bought this body with your career, so there we are."

"Yes, here we are." He held her tighter. "I've missed you so much."

"Have you really?" She was near breaking again.

"Yes," he said, kissing her. Her hands trembled as they moved to his chest, then slid down his shirt, over his trousers and to his crotch.

He felt no passion. None whatsoever.

He looked away guiltily. She took her hand away.

"Beatrice, I'm exhausted, that's all it is."

She pursed her lips. "In spite of your youth."

"Don't turn your back. Give me a chance."

"Peter, *is* there someone else?" She was looking at him from the corner of her eye. This is it, he thought. "Because really, I don't care if it's just your body jumping over the fence like an alley cat. Under the circumstances, I could forgive that. But if it's you doing the jumping . . . if there's someone that *means* something to you . . . That's what I'm asking."

He lifted her chin, turning her face toward him. "Beatrice, there never was anyone but you."

Her gray eyes froze. *"Was?"*

"And never will be."

"You swear?"

No, there was a wall beyond which he could not pass. He couldn't lie to Beatrice, the way he had lied to Wolfe. He was aware in full measure that if he did, his soul would indeed be lost forever.

And then he lied anyway.

"I swear," he said, wanting with all his heart to believe it was true.

"You're lying," she said.

God help me, thought Peter.

"And you're a wretched liar, too, you shit."

Helpless, he watched her snatch up her handbag, walk briskly to the door and out of the apartment. Then, even before he could move, she was back, tears in her eyes. But now there was a terrible fury as well.

"What the hell am I doing? she asked no one in particular, and threw down her bag. "*You* get out!"

She threw open the door and stepped back. The power of her rage was overwhelming. There was a primal force in her eyes, more devastating than any weapon he could dream of devising. It smashed into his very being and exposing his selfishness in all its squalor.

He walked out, and heard the door slam behind him.

Outside in the corridor, his feet seemed glued to the tile. Voices were drifting in from the breezeway, one of them Henderson's. Prying himself loose and muffling his footsteps, he hurried in the opposite direction, out the side exit and across the stretch of weed-choked sand toward the palm grove, barely acknowledging the guard who was posted on the path to the beach. Within minutes he reached the water's edge and started running toward the lights on the horizon. A half-hour later he was at the base boundary, about to cross over to Phosphorescent Bay. From there he could walk or hitch a ride to Esperanza and the woman who was waiting for him at the Casa del Francés, unaware of the dangers swirling around them both.

Except there was a naval guard, a Seal at the fence between the two beaches.

"Dr. Jance?"

"Yes, that's right."

"This is as far as we're authorized to let you run, sir."

Peter held on to his composure. "I know that. Just thought I'd say hello before turning back. Pretty bay over there, isn't it?"

The Seal glanced back over his shoulder at the luminous blue water and shrugged.

"Yeah, I guess. God knows what kinda shit's in there to make it glow like that. Probably radioactive runoff from the base."

Peter nodded, then turned back the way he had come. He ran, panic rising as he put more and more distance between himself and his goal. At the far end of the beach he stopped. Another guard, a quarter mile ahead.

He looked left, he looked right, and then he looked out to sea.

You can do this, he thought.

Removing his shoes, he slung them around his neck and waded into the water. He'd been a strong swimmer in his youth, but then he instantly realized this body hadn't learned the same skills. It struggled through the surf, having to focus with all his strength, literally teaching his muscles and limbs how to navigate the water. It took a good fifteen minutes to find any semblance of the crawl stroke he had won swimming meets with in college.

A hundred yards out into the open sea he turned right and swam parallel to shore, fighting a considerable crosscurrent. For an hour he churned on in this manner, each exhausted pause sending him drifting backward, cursing his clumsiness and plunging forward in renewed desperation. In the second hour, he experienced severe cramping and, despite the warmth of the water, his extremities began to grow numb.

And then something bumped him, something big. Peter swore and kicked out in panic, flashing on all the varieties of shark that were endemic to these waters. When his foot hit metal, he realized he had collided with the buoy that marked the channel into the marina in Sun Bay. He clung to it until he regained his breath, then struck out for shore.

In another twenty minutes he was washed up on the beach. He had lost his shoes, and was chilled to the bone, shaking so hard he could barely see straight. Stumbling to the road, he flagged down a car of astonished German tourists and told them his sailboat had sprung a leak. They bought his story and kindly drove him to Casa del Francés, even giving him a pair of tennis shoes that, unbelievably, fit.

Thanking them profusely, he staggered toward the inn. Despite his exhaustion, he had never felt so purely in the moment—like Byron swimming the Hellespont. Or—and his mood darkened at the thought—like a salmon fighting its way upstream to spawn and die.

You hypocrite, he fumed, you didn't have to go to all this life-threatening trouble. You could have found some other way to warn her. A phone call would have sufficed.

No, they must be monitoring all my calls by now, he thought. You would have put her life in even greater danger. You're doing the right thing.

He rang the bell at the hotel's gate. Inside the guard's shack, a white-haired old man with a scarred, sunken face sat dozing on a folding chair; steadying himself, Peter beaned him with a well-aimed pebble from the driveway. The man snapped awake, shuffled over and let Peter through. Peter tipped him a soggy ten-spot and, fighting for breath, asked for the American woman with blond hair. The old man beamed and pointed at the lighted window.

"*Olé,*" he said, waving this strange gringo whose body shook like a leaf in a hurricane inside the hotel.

Elizabeth heard the tap on her window twice before she realized it was him trying to get her attention. Her heart leapt as she raced down the tiled stairway to the lobby. There she found Peter, disoriented, soaked and shivering, face pale as paper, eyes glazed. And he had also lost the power of speech. It was all she could do to get him up to her room and strip off his soggy clothes. She dried him with a towel and rubbed some color back into his hands, then helped him into her bed, pulling the covers over him. She sat beside him, finally having the time to be astonished at his condition.

"What happened, Hans? Sweetheart, you can tell me. What's going on?"

At the sound of the endearment, Peter's whole body started shaking again and he held on to her for dear life. He was terrified—and not just of losing his mind. As a result of his exertions, his entire left side had gone numb, just as it had blanked out after the operation. Both his hearing and eyesight were blinking on and off like Christmas lights. The strain of the swim, following Henderson's stranglehold, might well have dislodged one of the sensitive splices of nerve at the back of his throat. His heart was pumping harder than it ever had before, as though desperately trying to force enough blood through the still-brittle, seventy-six-year-old vessels in his brain. He was an accident waiting to happen, an old man riding a fiery stallion and he couldn't let go of his fear.

When he could finally form a sentence, he found he was afraid to speak.

"That kid you saw. At the Azure Horizon. Did he have wild blond hair? Looked rather strange?"

"Yes."

Okay, it was Alex. "Was there anyone with him?"

"Not that I saw."

"No military man? A colonel? Ham-faced, big jaw, bulging temples? Brutal-looking guy? Doesn't ring a bell?"

She stared at him, a terror in her warm gray eyes. The same color as Beatrice's, he realized, the irises bright, the white clear, the way his wife's eyes used to be. Her voice, too, was a throaty alto. And then he thought: God help you, Jance, that's the oldest dodge known to man. *Beatrice, I just couldn't help myself, she reminded me so much of you.* No, you weasel, that's your hard-on talking. In that respect, his circulation was working perfectly.

"This colonel, does he know I'm here? At this hotel?"

"If he doesn't," said Peter, "he'll figure it out pretty quick."

"How? Why? Hans, what is this all about?"

He couldn't tell her, but he could prepare her. "You would hate me if you knew. And I don't want you to hate me."

"Why not?"

It was out before he could censor himself. "You mean too much to me."

You bastard, he thought. Tell her she's got to leave—that's what you came to do, not lead her on.

He was starting to shake again, and she was squeezing his hand.

She looked at him, took a breath, then asked "Hans, are you CIA?"

All right, he thought, you can buy some time here. "If you think I'm CIA," he said, attempting a smile, "then the Agency has a bigger image than they think."

"Those photos of your corpse, those were faked, weren't they? The accident?"

"More or less," he said, feeling his soul slipping through the fingers of this half-assed lie.

"And your mother? She doesn't know, does she? Or was she lying to me?"

"She doesn't know." God, he thought, how many other people are at risk here?

"Hans, she's suffering."

"I know," said Peter doggedly. "I couldn't tell her. It would have put her in jeopardy." And that's why you have to go, he thought, but still couldn't bring himself to say it.

"Do you want to get out? Is that why you're in trouble?"

"Yes," he said. This finally was the truth, even if it was one he had been afraid to fully admit to himself. And why this fear? Because Beatrice was still loyal to the cause? Perhaps, he thought, it would be noble to think this was the only reason. But at that very moment, he heard himself blurt out another. "I've fallen in love with you," he said.

She kissed him on the forehead. "I know, Hans," she said with a wonderful tenderness. "Your mom told me."

He pieced that together as best he could. But a subtle shift was taking place. He no longer wanted to know more about Hans. Now he wanted to know more about this woman. "Won't they start to miss you at home?"

"Yes, sure, the career, I guess. And Annie."

"I would think so," he said. "You really should go back."

She shrugged, as if it were already too late. "My agency, they've lost interest. After you 'died' I went to pieces. Lost some bookings."

An actress? A singer? A model? She was studying him gravely. "I even slept with somebody else," she said.

He felt a stab of jealousy and it thrilled him. "Listen, I understand, I disappeared on you—"

"I did it to find you. Because," she said, "I love you, too. Incidentally."

His heart swelled. "You took an awful chance."

"Story of my life. Hans, did you mean what you said just now? About getting out?" She was in front of him, cross-legged, excited, sweeping back her hair.

"Yes."

"Then why don't we? I can't stand it any more if you're not there. I think about you nonstop. Back in St. Maurice I wasn't sure about us.

I was starting to think I was some sort of masochist for staying with you. But everything feels so different now—"

"The danger," he said.

She gave him a peculiar look. "No. It's not just the danger. It's you. I feel so close to you now. Before, you were so impossible."

"Maybe I still am," said Peter. Tell her. Now.

"No. You've changed. I can feel that we'll make it work now. I don't care who you are or what you've done, if you really want to be with me, that's all that matters." Her brow furrowed. "Do you have your passport with you?"

Passport. "Not on me."

"Where is it? Are you in a hotel? I could go get it if you're still feeling woozy."

"You can't. It's on the base."

She remembered that razor-wired gate, the armed guard, and felt a chill. "Is it safe to go back there? Maybe you shouldn't."

"I have to. My traveler's checks, my passport, everything's back there." Come on, he thought, you owe her this much: "This isn't going to be easy. There's someone else on the base."

She stopped. He could feel her defenses come up. "A woman?" she asked.

"Well, yes."

"Is Yvette here with you?" she asked, as if it all might be one vast conspiracy now, involving even his wife.

"No," he said. "It's not that. Not Yvette . . ." He paused. He was getting in way over his head. "You don't know her, believe me. But I can't just abandon this person, there's too much danger."

"Someone involved in this thing with you?" she asked almost shyly.

"Yes. Extremely involved. Very much at risk. And you, you're already in danger—"

She nodded slightly, trying to make sense of it. "The man you mentioned? This colonel?"

Peter took her hand. Looked in her eyes. About this he could speak the truth. "He wields a lot of power—I can't begin to describe it," he said, seized in the instant with a sense of his own mortality and with a frightening realization that his coming to her that night was completely rash. The project was all that Henderson or any of them cared about. No one was indispensable, including him, especially with his half-drunk boast to Freddy Wolfe that the success of the new weapon was a fait accompli. In doing that, he now realized, he had put himself fatally at risk. Inside, he laughed bitterly at himself. The irony was that he had been trying to convince Wolfe of his loyalty, as if his words might speak louder than his actions. "How much money do you have? Enough to rent a boat?"

"Sure, with my faithful Visa."

"Do you know how to handle one?"

"I'm sure I could figure it out, but why—"

"Because they may be watching the airport. Do you understand how serious this is?"

She nodded, undaunted, even excited. "And you're coming with me?"

He steeled himself. "That remains to be seen."

"I understand," she said, eyes dimming with disappointment. "You're keeping your options open."

"I'm thinking about your safety," he said firmly. "As well as mine. Tomorrow, midnight, four hundred yards off the coast, halfway down the southern stretch of the military zone, just past that bioluminescent bay where we met."

Where we met *again*, he thought, wincing to himself. But she hadn't picked up on it. Her gray eyes were bright. "Midnight. I'll be there."

"The boat has to be big enough to get us to Puerto Rico."

"Then what?"

"Then we catch a plane."

"Together?"

She was gazing at him hopefully, lips slightly parted. Suddenly, instead of answering, he was kissing her and she was straddling him, pulling her T-shirt over her head. He ran his fingertips gently over her breasts, the lightest possible touch, and she smiled and closed her eyes as if to say, you know me, you know me perfectly. Within seconds, they were moving together in a light of their own making. It passed beyond understanding, his love and desire for this woman, beyond cellular memory or anything his science could conceive, and it alarmed him deeply. The effortless way he picked up on her every mood shift, every subtle alteration in her need, their easy rapture and total unity, all this terrified and electrified him to the core.

Midnight came. He waited while she dressed and dried his clothes in the hotel's laundry room, briefly waking the proprietor. Then she led him downstairs to her car. She woke the sleeping guard with the word, "*Toro,*" and he jolted awake and opened the gate.

Elizabeth drove them to within a mile of the base. For a quarter of an hour they sat in her rented car saying nothing, unable to part. At last he opened the door, got out, and at the instant he turned around she was climbing out from behind the wheel. They kissed again under the canopy of stars, this time for so long he lost all sense of danger. He watched her make a U-turn and drive back in the direction of the Casa del Francés. For the last two hours, neither one had spoken a word.

I know her, he thought with a shudder. I know her so well.

Everything but her name.

And Beatrice?

At the moment, he couldn't even picture his wife's face without seeing this woman's. It was as though they were the same face. That was the most terrifying thing of all.

Back in her room in the middle of packing, Elizabeth stopped and picked up the phone. If, as it seemed, she was going to vanish for a while, there were people she should call. Annie, of course, and maybe her landlord, and the people at Helvetica.

And Rose-Anne, Hans's mother.

It was now one o'clock in the morning, and eight hours later in Zurich. She dialed Zurich information using her calling card and asked for Rose-Anne Brinkman. She was given two numbers, one for an R. Brinkman, one for a Rose-Anne Brinkman.

At the first number, a young girl answered in German. When Elizabeth asked if Rose-Anne was there, the girl said she *was* Rose-Anne.

Elizabeth apologized, dialed the second number and waited through four rings.

"Yes?"

"Rose-Anne? It's Elizabeth."

Silence.

"Rose-Anne, hello?"

"Elizabeth, where are you, you sound so far away."

Lizzy, she thought, don't say anything that isn't necessary.

"Rose-Anne, I've got some shocking news."

"Oh, Lord, should I be sitting down?"

"Yes." Elizabeth took a deep breath. "It's about Hans."

"God, what now?"

"No, it's good news. Hans is alive."

There was complete silence.

"Rose-Anne, did you hear me? Are you okay?"

There was a sharp crack on the line, then utter silence.

"Rose-Anne?" She listened hard. *"Hello?"*

She looked at the phone as if the instrument itself held an explanation for its silence. She pressed the receiver button, looked for the redial button. There was none.

And no dial tone.

It took her a long moment to realize that the line had gone dead. A serpent of fear coiled into the room. It wrapped around her and stifled her breathing until she became dizzy.

She went to the window and looked out, and listened for any sounds that shouldn't be there. Outside was a cluster of date palms, an oblong of asphalt, and a lead-blue sky with a few cirrus clouds. Somewhere, a twin-engine plane was circling. She rechecked the street, then crossed the room and opened her closet. She was packed and closing her bag when she heard a tiny creak outside her door.

Then a knock.

Then a long pause.

Someone was listening on the other side.

She put her ear to the door, then jumped back, scared silly by a second, sharper knock.

She held her breath until her lungs ached.

"Miss Parker? Are you in there? I can see your light's on."

Ivor Greeley. She exhaled, tried to sound normal.

"Yes, Ivor, what is it?"

"We gotta talk."

"Why?"

"Can you open the door?"

She looked around for a heavy object. "Can't it wait till morning?"

"You have to leave in the morning. I just thought I should tell you that tonight, since you're up."

She stared at the door, the hotel regulations, the exit diagram, as though they were instructions from God. Why was Ivor awake at this hour?

"Leave? Why?"

"I think you know why."

"I'm sorry, but I don't."

"Because, Miss Parker, your credit card's no good."

She regrouped. It was a simple misunderstanding of some kind and Greeley didn't sound threatening at all. A little put out, but entirely businesslike. She undid the chain and pulled open the door. He stood there sad-eyed, shrugging.

"Sorry, I didn't mean to spook you. But you're gonna have to leave first thing tomorrow. You can spend the rest of tonight here, of course."

"Listen, I've got another card, let me get it for you."

"No, that won't do any good either."

She stopped halfway to her purse. "Why not?"

"Because," he said sternly, "when I called Visa they said the card was stolen and that probably any other card you gave me would be, too. Really, I don't have time for these kinds of shenanigans in my hotel. That's why I got out of Boston in the first place."

He turned on his heel and walked back down the hall. In the garden beyond, a parrot began to shriek. Elizabeth closed her door, then reopened it.

"Ivor?" she called. His head reappeared, eyes narrowing. "Did you turn off my phone, too?"

He looked bewildered. "No. Your phone? No, I wouldn't even know how to do that."

He started off again.

"One other thing, if you wouldn't mind telling me?" He swung around with a look of impatience. "The person at Visa who told you that? Did you happen to get her name?"

"Now why would I do that? Anyway, it was a man, very polite. Said maybe you were just a runaway wife and I shouldn't be too hard on you."

He turned and disappeared for good. Elizabeth shut the door and relocked it. No way that had been Visa, she realized with a sinking feeling. She paid her bill in full every month. Hans had warned that they would trace her here, but now that they had, now what? Without a credit card she wouldn't have enough money to rent a kayak, let alone a boat that could make it to Puerto Rico. She sat down on the bed and thought hard. Call Annie, have her wire money. But could she get it here in time? Or would it get to her at all?

She picked up the phone. Still dead.

Get out, she thought. Get off this goddamn Vieques as fast as you can.

No. Not without Hans.

But what if he's not coming? He had hinted as much and had lied to her so many times in the past. He had kept an entire identity hidden, so how could she trust him now? The look in his eyes, when she had mentioned the photos of the body. So strange, almost startled. And why hadn't he asked more questions about his mother? And the way he had told her he was married, as though it would be news to her, as if they had never once talked about Yvette. Had the CIA messed with his head, selectively erasing his memories? And who was this person on the base to whom he was so loyal?

Obviously, I don't want to know, she thought. Otherwise I would have asked.

He loved her, that was all she cared about. Of that, crazily, she hadn't the slightest doubt. But the question was, did that make her an even bigger fool? His love had drawn her into danger, and now she was even less certain about him.

What she really knew was that she didn't want to spend another second in this hotel room. It was totally unprotected, accessible from the street by a sturdy trellis. She was being evicted, she couldn't talk to anyone, and her phone had probably been bugged. *Go!*

She grabbed the car keys. Somewhere public, that's where she had to go. Maybe to an all-night bar or to any place where there were other people. She would have to hold on until morning and, one way or the other, get the boat Hans had asked her to rent and make their rendezvous.

How? She didn't have a clue.

Approaching the front gate of the base on foot, Peter was an immediate target of suspicion. The guard, a jug-eared kid with a Texas accent, unslung his M-16 and asked Peter to stop right where he was and present identification. Peter handed over his wallet, still waterlogged, which didn't help matters. The guard clicked his weapon off safety onto fire, then read the driver's license.

"This yours?"

"Yes, I'm Peter Jance. I work on the base. Is there a problem?"

"Yeah, there's a problem. You look pretty young for someone born in 1924, that's the problem."

Jesus, Peter thought, they never even bothered to give me false identification papers. Where there's stupidity there's hope.

"That's a misprint," he fumbled. "I was born in 1964. I've just never had the time to have it corrected."

"And this photo is you?"

"Yes," said Peter, toughing it out.

"I heard of bad driver's license pictures, but not this bad." The guard handed it back. "Why don't you go back to town, dude? You ain't funny."

"I'm Dr. Peter Jance. Check your personnel directory."

The guard yanked on a large red earlobe and gave him a look of mounting impatience.

"Stay there." He went to the guard shack, made a call, listened, and hung up, returning looking downright pissed off. "No one by that name listed. You'd do well to get moving."

He adjusted his weapon so that it pointed in the general direction of Peter and leaned against the doorway.

"All right," said Peter. "It's a classified project, so I'm probably *not* listed. Call Dr. Frederick Wolfe."

"Yeah, right."

"Beatrice Jance. She's my wi . . . mother."

"I ain't calling nobody. And you need to get out of my face unless you want to be in a whole world of trouble. Sir."

"Call Colonel Henderson, then. He'd be delighted to see me, I'm sure."

At the mention of Henderson's name, the guard blinked for the first time.

"Colonel Henderson knows me," Peter assured him.

The kid picked up the phone again. He dialed someone—an aide, Peter prayed, not Henderson himself. After talking for a moment, and then listening intently for a few more, the guard slammed down the phone, turned and trained his weapon on Peter.

"Get down on the ground spread-eagle, you sorry motherfucker! Now!" The kid was jumping out of his skin and Peter did as he was told, lying abjectly on the asphalt while the guard fidgeted and made sounds with his weapon that Peter didn't want to think about. Finally a vehicle roared up and several men approached swiftly.

He was just about to look up when two pairs of hands picked him up bodily—tonight's guard and the guard he had encountered the night before. They opened the door to the Humvee and shoved him inside. He hit the floor hard. Someone new jumped in beside him, holding a gun to his face and telling him to hold still if he fucking knew what was good for him. The vehicle fired up and hung a sharp U-turn, roaring back onto the base.

At the entrance to the restricted wing, the driver stopped and the other guard threw open the door, instructing Peter to go wait in his room until further notice. Peter watched as the new guard—a small, quick Italian with a New York air—waved his 9-millimeter at Peter's suite of rooms. Peter took out his keycard, tried not to shake as he swept the card through the magnetic slot, and entered through the side door.

Walking down the hall, he felt like a bug under a poised heel. If ever there was a doubt that all his charisma and privilege could be taken away in an instant, it was gone now. There was everything in the way he had just been treated that spoke of his own physical disposability. He could almost hear the orders that must have been given, something to the effect that if Jance gives you any problems, waste the bastard.

His suite was dark and deserted, with no sign of Beatrice or her belongings—just bare beige walls, two forlorn botanical prints in the bedroom and the well-worn Motel 6 furniture. Even the Erlenmeyer flask, Beatrice's one personal touch, was gone, its spray of dried chrysanthemums scattered on the floor like so much refuse.

"Beatrice?" he called into the dark.

No answer. He was alone. Free and abandoned at the same time.

With rising panic, he yanked open drawers, gathering loose cash, traveler's checks, his passport and as much clothing as he could cram into an old duffel bag. Then he looked at the door. They had told him to go to his room and wait. They'd not said he couldn't go elsewhere, but they sure as hell hadn't included that in his options. In fact, there were no options.

Go to your room. Wait.

Fuck them. He needed to get out of there. And before he did, he desperately needed to see Beatrice. To make amends, to say goodbye, to plead for her forgiveness. He thought that perhaps all he could do, really, was to say that he had become, or was becoming, someone or something other than what he had been. It was a possibility they all should have thought of, each of them. Only now there was no more time for thinking. Based on the sorry reality of what they had created, now there was time only for action. He had to be with this woman, this nameless magnet of life force and longing that was drawing him with an attraction he could never have resisted, even if he wanted to.

And he didn't want to.

He went back to the corridor, closing the door quietly behind him. The hallway lights, tissue-sized moths banging soundlessly off their globes, shone yellow and dim all the way to where the breezeway branched off. Strange moth shadows chased over the asphalt-block walls. How was he going to find his wife? He had no way of knowing if Beatrice was in her lab, or in her new room, wherever that might be. Maybe she was in some dark cabal with Wolfe and Henderson. He would have to find somebody who knew where she was.

Maybe Rosemarie Wiener or Cap Chu or Flannagan? One of them must know her whereabouts.

Reaching the entrance door, he peered outside. Immediately he jerked back. Just outside, two guards had been positioned, armed and equipped with walkie-talkies.

He was imprisoned, he realized, and his jailers were armed to the teeth and pissed off at him.

Had he been stupid to come back?

No, he told himself, without his passport there was no way to disappear. And to disappear was the only course open to him now. Even if he had never encountered the woman on the beach, he had by means of his protean work completed his weapons design without completing any escape plan, rendering himself superfluous. And by openly questioning what they were up to, he had actually pushed himself into the dangerous classification of major irritant. His wife couldn't stand to be in the same apartment with him. His old friend and competitor, Frederick Wolfe, would now probably just as soon see him dead. Henderson would forget him in a day and be glad the bottom line was more secure. And beyond Wolfe and Henderson?

Above them was just a dark presence, a Kafkaesque world of shadowy agencies and faceless powers to whom he was only a pawn. He had a glimpse, then, of the whole apparatus of power, vast and multidimensional, ranging from the violence of the quark-riddled atoms to the parry and thrust of nations, empires and DNA. In this maelstrom, he was nothing. And in this there was no way to escape oblivion if that's what they wanted. His entire chain of genetic material, fragile but vital and stretching back to the beginnings of the species, now hinged on the brink of utter and irrevocable extinction, and he was powerless to fight it.

He stood in that cold wind for a long, dark moment.

Fuck it. Death was the ultimate emperor without clothes. If they blasted him to atoms today, his atoms would merge with those of other poor bastards, roaches, lost species, burned rain forests and the endless compost heap of passing humanity and reassemble in a millennium or two into the stuff of stars and brave new worlds somewhere else. There was no death.

Fuck it all.

He had to find Beatrice now, but *could* he? He had no idea. Worse, he felt the notion rising that if he could not see her, he didn't want to leave. Should he just fling himself out the door and scream her name? He had a notion of Brando in *Streetcar* and realized how ridiculous that was. But then *what?*

At that supreme moment of doubt and pain, two male voices rang out from the end of the hallway. A swath of light swept across the wall, and a lean, disheveled figure emerged from a door.

Alex Davies. Hunched and cursing. Expecting Wolfe to come barging out after his grandson, Peter prudently backed toward his room, turning the knob behind him and tossing in the old duffel bag.

But the door at the end of the hall slammed shut and Wolfe didn't appear. There was only Alex, charging down the corridor in a blue rage.

When he saw Peter, half in, half out of his room, Alex stopped dead, then approached at a slower pace.

"Motherfuckers," he muttered, turning one way and then the other, as if some pointed rejoinder had just occurred to him, making him want to go back and restart the battle with his grandfather. But he didn't have the stomach for that. He sagged against the wall and ran his hands through his hair, looking near tears.

"He's out of his fucking mind," he said to Peter, as though Peter had been privy to every word.

"Alex, do you know where Beatrice is?"

The kid looked at him strangely, then laughed shakily and shook his head. "Man, I don't know. She's gottta be pissed at you, though."

"But you have no idea where she is?"

"Not a clue. Grandpa put her up someplace, I don't know where. You want me to give her a message if I see her?"

"Yes. Tell her that I apologize, that I'm sorry for everything. Tell her I'll be in touch."

"Why, where are you going? Peter?" Alex peeled himself off the wall and stepped closer. "Hey, don't be stupid, if you're thinking of being as stupid as I think you are. These guys aren't just playing with you, you understand that, don't you?"

"Yes, I do understand."

Alex took that in, realizing from the look of devastation and surrender in Peter's face that he indeed *did* understand. "Wow. So what *are* you gonna do?" he asked.

"Watch my ass," said Peter, a phrase he had heard over and over on the base. He knew he had already said far too much. Inching back toward his door, he began to make goodbye gestures.

Alex Davies glanced over his shoulder, then approached Peter and socked him lightly on the arm.

"I'm with you, man," he said conspiratorially. Then, with a cautionary arch of his brows, he raced off down the corridor. The instant the kid was out of sight, Peter ducked back into his room, grabbed the duffel bag and went out onto the balcony, moving quietly as a cat. Looking down, he saw the sentry, still on guard, and on a cellphone talking to someone who sounded like a girlfriend.

Luck, thought Peter. Bastard's breaking regulations and giving me a break all at once.

In one smooth move, he vaulted over the railing—feeling in that split second of falling utter release and commitment. And then he slammed into the kid and took him to the ground.

The kid didn't have time to yell before Peter had him up against the wall, nailing him with a left hook and a right cross that drove his head back into the stucco, dropping him like a sack of lead shot.

He looked at the guy's weapons. In his heart a blind fury was growing, fed by lack of information, a tsunami of guilt and the overwhelming sense that his life would never be peaceful again. This was beyond life or death. This all had to do, he realized with a blinding insight, with the survival of this woman who had loved him so completely that his entire being had been altered. He suddenly wanted nothing more than to protect and defend her and make a place for themselves outside the madness his life had become.

So be it. Removing the guard's service pistol, he then unloaded the rifle and threw the clip of ammunition into the trees. Then he turned and ran. Beyond the breezeway, he veered past the core labs through a field of waist-high grass toward the motor pool. The Humvee that had brought him from the gate was in its berth; the keys were in it. It was the simplest of matters to slip inside. He did not have so much as a second thought, nor any thought at all when he came to the front gate doing nearly sixty and saw that the guard had already been alerted. The muzzle flashes registered no more than heat lightning on a distant horizon; he felt no fear whatsoever. He slammed the accelerator to the floorboard and crashed through the gate, sending the guard diving for his life. Peter was vaguely impressed by his driving skills. After the BMW episode he hadn't cared much for speed, but now his right foot had a mind of its own, and even his hands seemed to know what to do. Without a moment's hesitation he put the Humvee into an effortless J-turn that snapped it ninety degrees onto the two-lane blacktop and out of sight before another base vehicle could follow.

He followed the road over the hill, then slowed and cut stealthily into the bush, taking care to leave no signs of egress. Then he struck off cross-country, sometimes on farm roads, sometimes on cattle lanes, once even following a stream, as he had seen Hopalong Cassidy do once in a film he had loved as a kid. He smiled grimly. This was fun, really it was. Perfect for the job, the Humvee flew over the varied terrain with all the competency its engineers had designed and the taxpayers had paid for. Something to be said for the military after all, thought Peter bitterly. Even better, this would save him from traveling on five miles of twisting highway and keep him away from roadblocks. The bay. All he could concentrate on was reaching the bay.

Elizabeth had decided to drive into town and get lost among the tourists. But when she arrived at her Honda, she found it up on the hoist of an Island Towing truck. The driver, a native with long hair and lots of attitude, looked up with a don't-fuck-up-my-day look.

"What the hell you doing?" she demanded.

He didn't bother to take the cigarette out of his mouth, or to stop lifting the Honda. "Confiscating this car."

"At three in the morning?"

"Best time to find it home."

"But that's *my* car."

"I think it's Hertz's car."

He locked off the hoist and walked back to his truck's cab, pursued by Elizabeth.

"But they have my American Express imprint!"

"Card's no good," the driver said. "No credit, no car." He slammed the truck's door and fired up the engine.

Elizabeth raced back to her car and squinted through the windows to see if she had left anything inside. The tourist map and the rental agreement were jammed between the front seats, but before she could open the door the truck was gone, taking her Honda with it.

"Fucker!" Her shout was lost in the night, and with the truck's unmuffled roar, she knew the driver hadn't even heard her. Not that he would give a rat's ass, she thought.

She stood for a moment, furious and wondering what the hell to do next. Then another kind of thought came to her: the *coquís* were silent.

Looking around her, she realized it was completely dark and utterly quiet. She was alone and so very small against the stars.

She walked back through the gate. For some reason it was open. As usual, the ex-matador was tipped back in his folding chair, and the thought came foolishly to her that she ought to report him. Maybe that would put Greeley enough on the defensive that she could enlist his aid in renting another car. But she didn't have the heart. She called to the old man.

"Toro! Toro!"

He didn't stir.

Then she noticed something under his chair, a glint of moonlight in a widening pool. Stepping closer, she saw that his pants were also dark with it.

It was too thick, too red to be anything but blood.

For some reason she couldn't scream, though terror shrieked inside her head. She crept closer, hoping she could somehow help him, the hair on her arms rising like insects crawling on her skin. Despite the darkness, she now could see that his throat had been slashed from ear to ear.

She was running before she knew it.

She tore across the parking lot and into the hotel, taking in with a desperate animal awareness just how *open* tropical places were: open verandas, open terraces, strips of thin bamboo where doors should be. In the darkened lobby, she stopped.

She could hear music from the owner's apartment.

"Ivor! Call the police!"

No answer.

She wondered if he had decided to have nothing more to do with her. *"Ivor?"*

His door was half-open.

She went to it and tried to ease it open a little further, but it wouldn't budge. Something was up against it on the other side. From the way the flimsy door gave at the top but not at the bottom, she knew that whatever it was, it was on the floor.

Putting her shoulder to the door, she got it open far enough to poke her head through the opening.

What she saw sickened and terrified her. There was Ivor, an ashen mask of horrified surprise on his face. Next she noticed the blood. A moment later she realized she was standing in it.

Turning on her bloody heels she ran back to her room, slamming the door and bolting it. The lock was old and worn and the whole door so flimsy it could be penetrated with a fist. Grabbing a heavy wooden chair, she tried to wedge it under the doorknob, but it wouldn't hold. She looked around for something even heavier to drag in front of the door, but the largest thing in the room was the bed and it was so light she could move it with her knees.

Quickly, she snatched up the phone. There was still no dial tone, but now there was some noise on the line and, after a pause, a man's whisper.

"Russell? You get her?"

She dropped the phone before she realized it was slipping from her grasp. As it clattered to the desk, she knew that whoever was on the other end would be instantly alerted. The first wave of panic flooded through her body.

She stumbled into the bathroom and pulled the bolt across. Two barriers now stood between her and whoever was out there, she told herself, which might give her enough time to escape through the window over the bathtub. Throwing open the shower curtain, she very nearly climbed into the arms of a bearish man wearing Bermuda shorts and a Budweiser T-shirt.

"Hey," he said, lurching toward her.

But she had already leaped back, screaming at last, until she slammed against the locked door that knocked her into a sudden state of hyper-alertness. It was as if some primal self were saying—*This is life or death!* Fortunately the huge man with the beard had caught his foot on the edge of the tub as he made his move, falling flat on his face on the floor behind her. It gave her the instant she needed to fumble the lock open, but a split second later the man grabbed her ankle.

Now thinking with absolute clarity, she brought her free foot backward as hard as she could and caught him flush in the face. She heard something crack and hoped she had broken his nose, her panic lessening with the realization that she could hurt him. As she spun in the open doorway she saw him rise up, clutching his face with both hands. Blood was pouring through his fingers and his eyes were blind with tears, but he was holding a fillet knife and stumbling toward her. Everything was coming at her with a kind of slow-motion intensity, like a series of slalom poles on a downhill run. Finally making it to the hall door, she flung it open and ran, only to collide immediately with someone standing in the outside hallway.

This man was in his mid-thirties, with bone-white skin, clear blue eyes and close-cropped hair. She caught a glimpse of his creased trousers and fitted shirt, realizing that he had to be military. She saw him bring a leg up, reach under the cuff and pull out a knife. He was a Seal, she knew, and the knife was standard-issue. How she knew this she had no idea, but she did and there it was. She staggered back into the room and the man with the bloody nose stood up behind her.

"Jesus H. Christ," the Seal said, "why don't you just make a mess of it, pal?"

"She's tough," the other man said, grabbing Elizabeth by the hair. He had his hand on her blouse and murder was in his eyes when the Seal spun him around and put the knife to his chin.

"Right now your nose is bloody. You want to dispense with it altogether?"

"Hey, fuck you, Russell," said the bearded man, his eyes twisted down toward the knife touching his left carotid artery. He softened his voice a little. "You said this gig would be easy."

"I also said," the Seal responded calmly, "that you were not personally authorized to harm her."

The bearish man blinked slowly, as though trying to locate some plug that had just been pulled in his cortex. The effort at reconnection apparently failed: despite the Seal's warning he hauled Elizabeth against his crotch and tried to force his tongue into her mouth. The Seal reversed his knife and drove down with the pointed steel end of its handle, punching through the bearded man's skull and penetrating a full inch into his brain. Jerking upright with an incredulous look on his face, the man pitched backward over a coffee table and crashed to the floor. In seizure, he thrashed, his arms twitching while a thin thread of foam trailed from the corner of his mouth. Then he was still.

Elizabeth, suspended in that icy space between terror and nausea, stared at a spot on the wall.

"Amateur Night," said the man named Russell. He turned to Elizabeth. "Come here," he ordered, taking a length of rope from his back pocket. He's going to hang me, Elizabeth thought wildly. Grabbing her wrist, he twisted it behind her. He was incredibly strong, slamming her into a wall until she could not move. She felt her head pulled back by the hair, she saw the knife arc toward her throat, and then it stopped.

"If I wanted to," he said very quietly, "I could have already killed you. But I follow orders." As he began to twist the rope around her wrists, someone crashed into him from behind.

The attack was so sudden and fierce Elizabeth thought for an erratic moment that it might be some sort of wild animal. In horror, she watched as the Seal flew away from her, another man on his back as the two crashed over the couch and onto the floor. In the next second she saw that it was Peter, lurching up, seeing the Seal diving for the knife. Peter fell on him, grabbing his wrist the split second before Russell caught him with an elbow under the chin. Peter reeled back and Russell leapt on him, planting a knee on his chest and stabbing down. Peter jerked his head sideways as the blade sliced just past his ear, burying itself in the floor. Russell swore and struggled to pull the knife free. Before he could, Elizabeth grabbed the chair she had tried to wedge under the doorknob and smashed it down on the back of Russell's head.

The Seal fell forward hard, the blade of his knife disappearing beneath his body. Whether it had entered him or not was impossible to tell, but one thing was clear: he wasn't moving.

They ran for their lives.

They raced through the lobby and into the parking lot. There they braked hard as they found themselves in the gun sights of the Navy Seal's only remaining backup.

It was the tow truck driver, still clearly civilian, but this time he was armed.

"Where's Russell?" he asked. His voice was unsteady and he looked off-balance upon seeing another man with the girl.

"Upstairs," said Peter, trying to keep his voice from shaking. Then, winging it, he said, "It's been called off. She's not the one." Putting a guiding hand on Elizabeth's shoulder, he walked her past the kid. He had seen enough of her to realize that her eyes looked remarkably calm now, although her ability to speak seemed to have deserted her for the moment.

The tow truck driver followed at an uncertain distance. He was ten years younger than the guy upstairs, eighteen at most, and certainly no Seal. A bootleg operation, Peter thought. Henderson, clearly the mastermind of this mission, probably didn't want it on the books.

What would his bosses say if they knew he had ordered the ending of a life they had paid so much to extend?

"Hey!" the kid abruptly yelled. Peter and Elizabeth turned to find him pointing his pistol directly at their heads. "Let's go up and see if that's what that Army guy says," he stuttered.

"He won't be especially happy about that," Peter said ominously. "He's taking a nap. Sueño. He's not at all pleased when someone wakes him while he's sleeping. He gets really very angry."

The kid flicked a glance up at the windows and licked his lips. "No, you'd better come upstairs with me."

Peter feigned an attitude of disgust. Beside him, Elizabeth let out an exaggerated sigh.

"Look," she said, "you want to keep your tow truck or not? If you don't get out of my way, I swear to God I'll have the police on you faster than a duck on a June bug."

The guy looked at her, unsure of himself.

Peter moved forward, putting the gun to his own forehead and making sure the driver could see how unafraid he was.

"If you're going to do something, do it here. But first be aware that you'll be killing Dr. Peter Jance of the Advanced Weapons Testing Program, U.S Army, Department of Defense, and you will be hunted down and killed like a dog for doing that."

The boy finally blinked.

Peter stole another look at Elizabeth, realizing what he had just said. *Jesus.* Maybe she'd assume it was a cover identity. Maybe he'd never have to tell her because this kid will shoot them both. But the kid didn't. Lowering his gun, he cleared his throat.

"You stay here. I'm gonna go talk to him."

He turned and went into the hotel.

Peter gave a sign and he and Elizabeth tore off.

"Down here!" he hissed, running toward the Humvee hidden behind a screen of sweet olive.

"How did you know?" she asked as they ran.

"When you didn't show up at the bay, I figured I'd better check up on you."

"Thank God. You saved my life. You were wonderful."

"I didn't really have time to think," he said truthfully then stopped, seeing the weird look on her face. And then he heard the safety clicking off.

He turned to see the kid with the pistol: this time he was shaking and furious.

"You're crazy, man, killing that guy. Now you're fucking dead 'cause you saw my face and I ain't gonna—" His voice was drowned out by a horn blaring in the road behind him. Swinging around, the kid dropped the gun in panic and dove out of the way as a Range Rover with government plates, lights flashing, bore down on him. It missed him by inches and jammed to a stop near Peter and Elizabeth. The back door swung open. Peter caught a glimpse of wild blond hair and knew it was Alex. He reached for the woman's hand but she was backing away. She had seen Alex, too, and all she knew was that he was the mysterious guy who had stalked her when she had first arrived on the island.

"It's all right," Peter assured her. "Come on."

Still she didn't move, which gave the kid with the gun time enough to retrieve his weapon and wheel on them. Peter and Elizabeth dove into the Range Rover as it lurched off down the road. Peter thought he heard the 9mm go off, but Alex had his foot to the floor and nothing much could be heard over the engine's roar and the wind whistling through the windows.

"Welcome to Vieques. Finally," Alex said to Elizabeth. Then he shot Peter a funny look in the rearview mirror. "You all right, Doc?"

"I'm fine," said Peter. But as the adrenaline began to ebb, he felt a twinge of pain at the top of his ear and dabbed at it. There was a division now in the top rim of his ear and it hurt like hell. But the blood was already scabbing over and Peter counted himself lucky to be alive. Almost put an end to this wonderful body, he thought, and realized how proprietary he felt now toward it.

"That guy in your room, did you get his name?" Alex asked. Peter was watching Elizabeth. She was looking out the back window. Turning, he saw a line of three vehicles speeding toward them, headlights blazing from around a curve.

"Get down!" Alex yelled, and they hit the floor. As the government cars streaked past without slowing, the three in the Land Rover nearly stopped breathing. Alex gave a cheerful wave to their taillights, and then gave the all-clear signal.

Peter and the woman sat back up. "Russell," she answered, shaking now.

"Henderson's guy," Peter said in recognition. "Where are we headed?"

"Airport," said Alex, swinging around to meet Elizabeth's gaze. He seemed about to say something, then Peter ordered him to watch the road and Alex changed his mind. Eyes now forward, he accelerated.

Peter glanced at Alex, who gave him a weirdly humorous look, eyebrows raised and face twisted into an odd smile.

"Something, huh?"

"Thank you for this," Peter said.

"Don't mention it," said Alex. "And hey, don't worry, there's a chance they won't connect us."

To Peter this sounded like something to worry about. "Did you cut the cord with Freddy?"

"One way of putting it, yeah," said Alex, studying the road streaking out before them. Elizabeth leaned forward and looked at Alex.

"Why did you send me that e-mail?"

"I tried to lure you here so I could warn you," said Alex, without hesitation.

"Warn me about what?"

"You don't want to know," he said. "She doesn't want to know, right Hans?" He damn near winked when he used the name.

"Right," said Peter, with a look at Elizabeth that was meant to convey that he had no idea what the guy was talking about.

"Just putting a stick in their spokes," said Alex. "Guess we both saw the light about the same time, huh Doc?"

"Right," said Peter

"I mean, the Cold War ends and we keep going. Should've figured it out back then."

"Figured *what* out?" Elizabeth asked, looking back and forth between the two. "What do you want to warn me about?" she asked again, exasperated. Alex rolled his eyes and said nothing. She looked at Peter.

"And if I'm such an apparent threat, why didn't that man just kill me back there? He as much as told me he wasn't allowed to. It looked like he was going to tie me up or something."

"I'm as puzzled as you are," Peter said, and he meant it. He looked at Alex. "That thing I asked you to do? Did you do it?"

Alex frowned, as though unable to remember for a moment, then brightened. "Yeah. Oh yeah. The party in question . . . understands. Knows you had to get out. Is sorry they didn't recognize the danger. Wishes you well."

"Up to a point," offered Peter.

"Yeah, up to a point, that's right," said Alex, with a quick glance at Elizabeth. "Also said to tell you, don't come back."

Peter looked away. Outside the sky was starting to lighten. He thought he smelled jasmine. "The party in question—is that person still with the program?" he asked, lower.

"Hard to tell, dude. On the fence, I would say."

"Goddammit," Elizabeth swore and lunged over the back of the seat, grabbing the ignition keys and switching off the engine before Alex even knew what she was doing.

"Whoa," said Alex in alarm, as the Range Rover rolled to a dead stop. "We seem to have a situation here . . ." Outside, the *coquís* sang. There were no cars coming in either direction but none of them knew how long that would last. Peter looked at Elizabeth pleadingly: she was holding the keys tightly in her fist.

"Listen, we can't just sit out here, we're sitting ducks."

"We'll sit here until I get an explanation," she said.

"So, explain, Hans," said Alex, with careful pronunciation of the name.

"Please, we don't have time for this," Peter begged.

"Before I get on any plane, I want to know what's going on. I thought I was getting to know you," she said to Peter, "but now I don't know if I do at all."

Peter hung his head. "I'm sorry."

"I'm sorry, *Helen*," she spat out.

"I'm sorry, Helen," he repeated, thanking God she had finally given him her name. Then he caught sight of Alex's face.

"Uh-oh . . ." Alex said.

Peter looked back at the woman. "The name's Elizabeth," she said.

"I knew that," he said hopelessly.

"What's my last name?"

He stared at her, then looked away.

"Oh my God in heaven," she said quietly. She looked utterly shattered. "*What happened to you?*"

"We should get gooo-innnggg," Alex said tightly.

"I'm not Hans," Peter said.

"What?"

"I used to be Hans," he said feebly.

"Folks? Can we settle this on the plane, maybe?"

"*Used* to be?" she said in a rage. "What the hell does *that* mean? You *are* him." She gestured vaguely toward his knee. "The scars on your knee—I know them as well as the back of my hand. What did they *do* to you, for God's sake? Fry your brain, or what?"

"No," he said helplessly. "They saved *that*." He wasn't able to say another thing as a car blasted out of the darkness behind them. It was heading straight for them.

"Keys, Elizabeth!" said Alex. Suddenly more frightened than ever, she thrust the keys at him and Alex fumbled them back into the ignition. The engine sprang to life and the Range Rover took off, with a Humvee dangerously close behind. They raced now without heed for anything approaching safety. Ahead, Peter could make out the lights of the Vieques airport, but when he glanced back again, the Humvee was no more than twenty yards behind them. A series of flashes erupted from its frame.

"Don't worry," said Alex. "Just scare tactics. So long as you're with us," he glanced toward Elizabeth, "they won't shoot to kill. Do me a favor, show your face."

"What?" said Elizabeth.

"Look out the back window. Wave."

"Are you crazy? Jesus!" she suddenly said, as the windshield exploded and the Range Rover skidded sideways, flames boiling up from the rear wheel housing. Alex had pitched forward; the vehicle was out of control. Peter dove for the wheel but it was too late. The car was leaving the road airborne, arcing out and down into a stand of mangrove trees. It hit with a huge concussion of water and mud, and then there was darkness. Adrenaline thundered through Peter as he wrenched a door open, allowing Elizabeth to squeeze through. Then he reached for Alex, but the kid had vanished and the driver's door hung open. Peter thought he heard him cry out behind them, urging them to run faster. Then there were other shouts, further off, and the smell of gasoline in the water. In a blind rush, Peter threw himself out of the car and pulled Elizabeth away into the darkness. An instant later the swamp was bright with the white-hot explosion of the Range Rover.

"Holy Mother of God," said Peter, shoving Elizabeth ahead of him. The fireball's gruesome light threw the rest of the swamp into deep and violently dancing shadows.

"Alex!" Peter called.

There was no answer. A silhouette was shaking through the mangroves, but whether it was Alex or one of their pursuers he couldn't tell. To double back would be hopeless. They forged off through the ankle-deep water, the roar of the conflagration veiling their movements. Within minutes they could glimpse the airport through the twisted trees. A light twin-engine turboprop was doing its engine run-up and several people were paused at its boarding stairs, staring back toward the burning swamp. Suddenly Elizabeth was sprinting ahead of Peter, waving frantically—at whom he couldn't see. But as they both broke through the trees into the marsh just below the tarmac, somebody—a flight attendant, it looked like—was running toward them. No, *three* flight attendants in fact.

"Mary?" Elizabeth shouted in amazement as they struggled up the levee elevating the runway from the mangrove swamp. "Mary Blanchard?"

"Lizzer?" the shout came back. Elizabeth was running so fast now that Peter had a sudden terror he was about to lose her forever. She clawed her way to the runway and grabbed the flight attendant, obviously somebody she knew.

"Mary, I need to get out of here now—"

Peter's heart contracted, then he heard her correct herself and he thanked God again: "*We* do, I mean," she said.

Mary stared at them. They were both bleeding, wet and mud-smeared. "Uh, you guys got tickets?"

"No," said Peter, looking over his shoulder at the three vehicles storming along the airport approach road, "but we need to get on board with you." He started to push Elizabeth toward the ramp of the plane, an American Airlines flight, seriously behind schedule due to equipment trouble. But now the pilot, having heard the fuss and in no mood for more delays, stepped in their way.

"Can I help you people?" His tone was flat and without sympathy.

"We want to buy a ticket on your flight," Peter said.

"We're fully booked," the pilot said, looking at their clothes with disdain. "There's a flight tomorrow. Maybe by then you can clean yourselves up a little and—"

Peter swiveled back toward the approach road. The government cars had slowed and fanned out, searching among the planes. But one Humvee seemed to be moving more or less directly toward them.

"I'll pay you a thousand dollars."

"I'll call airport security, how's that sound?" the captain said, stalking to his cockpit and picking up the microphone. Mary Blanchard was taking Elizabeth aside.

"Listen," Peter heard her say, "I don't know what kind of trouble you're in, but we've got to get to Puerto Rico to hook up with the flight we're working, okay? If you can make it there, I'll somehow get you on it. That's a promise. American Flight 99, 6:00 A.M." She cocked her head toward Peter. "I guess he finally showed up, huh?" Without waiting for confirmation, Mary hurried aboard. Beyond, the Humvee had veered and was now heading straight for them. Elizabeth grabbed Peter's hand and pulled him to her.

He followed blindly until he saw where she was running—toward a single-engine Cessna warming up nearby.

"Get the pilot out of there!" she screamed at him.

He looked at her. "You know how to fly?"

"No, you idiot, *you* do!"

Shit, he thought, this Hans is a tough act to follow. Flinging open the door, he pulled out the pilot, a chubby American with a baseball cap that said "I'd Rather Be Flying!" He staggered back in shock as the two mud-encrusted pirates piled into his plane.

"Hey," the man called, but he made no effort to stop them. The look in Peter's eyes was too wild, and besides the damn plane was a rental.

In the cockpit, Peter stared dumbfounded at the bewildering array of instruments and levers.

"Let's go!" Elizabeth screamed. Now two Humvees were bearing down on them at full speed.

"What do I do?"

"Pull that!" she yelled, pointing at the throttle.

Peter pulled it: with an ungodly roar, the aircraft lurched forward, rapidly gaining velocity. Peter tried to steer the control yoke as if he were driving a car—which had absolutely no effect. He had a blinding glimpse of the obvious, realizing airplanes must not steer like that, but he was damned if he knew how they did. In fact, the plane began to veer off the runway. But even as panic raced through his veins, his feet found the rudder pedals and skillfully tapped their individual brakes so that the plane pivoted smartly back onto the runway and was able to speed forward faster and faster, engine whining.

"Are you sure I, um, know how to fly?" he yelled back at her.

"Don't kid around, Hans, or whoever the hell you are. I don't know what's happened to your head, but Hans could fly a plane like this with his eyes closed, so stop thinking and just *do* it!"

He obeyed. Switching off his thoughts, his left hand pulled back gently on the control column and the airplane lifted into the air. He looked down and back in amazement. The runway was already a distant ribbon, the vehicles of their pursuers toy cars.

"Job well done," said Elizabeth.

The blood surged in his skull. Floral patterns swam behind his eyes. He yielded to the madness.

"Good job, Peter," he said to himself.

And thanked God for Hans.

Puerto Rico was less than ten miles from Vieques, that much Peter knew. What he didn't know was what it looked like from the air, at night, among the countless pinpricks of light emanating from boats, stars, houses and businesses on the hundreds of islands and cays dotting the region.

"My understanding of aerodynamics is limited to theory," he said, with an air of lunatic calm, "but I'd say we're gaining altitude."

"We're diving! Pull up!"

He was shocked at her lack of restraint in criticism. Beatrice could be opinionated, but she showed it in more subtle ways. This Elizabeth just said what she thought.

"I'm sure that would be a mistake," he said, trying to calm her. "You see, we're over warm waters so we're almost certainly climbing in thermal updrafts."

"Then why can I see waves!" she shouted.

He looked closer and then he could see them, too, coming up fast. "Damn," he said, wondering how you made an aircraft ascend.

"Pull *up!*"

As combing waves loomed in their windscreen, his mind went blank and his hands immediately hauled back on the steering column. The plane clipped the top of a breaker with its wheels, then sucked itself up into a steep climb. A loud horn sounded in the cabin.

"What's that?" he asked.

"Stall warning, I think. Level off a little!"

"I don't think I—"

"Don't *think*, just *do* it!"

He forced his mind blank, and his arms pushed forward, leveling the plane off smoothly. The horn went silent. His right hand found the throttle and added fuel, then, eerily on its own, trimmed flaps.

"Well, look at that," he marveled. Elizabeth's eyes were wide with terror. He watched his hand reach for the instrument panel, then hesitate.

"I wanted to use the radio," he said, as though observing a bird dog go through field trials.

"Habit," Elizabeth said, through her teeth. "You always set the radios after takeoff. Doesn't your memory tell you any of that?"

"I . . . I'm afraid not."

Without looking at him, she asked, "Why did you say your name was Peter?"

"Because it is," he said.

"That's the name they gave you? Your new identity?"

"Right," he said, hoping that would suffice.

Elizabeth looked out the side window, trying to sort it out. She wondered why she didn't simply hate him. But she didn't. Not yet, anyway.

"I'll tell you what *I* think," she said. "I think you've had some kind of stroke."

"Yes, that's more than possible," he said, wiping the sweat out of his eyes.

"Last night, when you came to see me, you had just been through one."

"From swimming?" In a strange way it made sense. The vessels in his head were throbbing. Maybe . . .

"You were numb, you couldn't speak," she said, trying to convince him of an easier reality. "And I bet that wasn't the first time. You don't remember who you are, who I am, and you've lost part of your higher cognitive skills, too, at least when it comes to flying."

"It's coming back to me, Elizabeth," he said. "Maybe I *have* suffered a few minor strokes." It was true that he felt perilously close to one now. Maybe he *did* have a stroke. But he knew that the fear he was feeling was not because of a stroke. He reminded himself that he damn well never knew how to fly in the first place.

"I remember most of it," he lied, trying to bring some sense of calm and safety into this madness. "Flying, I mean. See how well I'm doing?"

She looked at him, trying to believe he was right. He did fly well when he needed to, it seemed. But the more complex procedures clearly left him baffled.

"What are the coordinates of Puerto Rico?" Elizabeth challenged.

He had no idea whatsoever. "It's right over there," he bluffed. "Experienced pilots don't use coordinates." He straightened up and tried to look like such a pilot.

"Bullshit. Of course they do. *You* do—I've flown with you!"

He felt himself tighten, jealous of his own body. Now his mind was veering in three directions and a fourth was no doubt in the offing. "I'm more of an instinctive pilot now," he said, and out of the corner of his eye he saw her throw up her hands in exasperation. "What I could use at the moment, Elizabeth, is less criticism and more help. Are those lights down there islands or boats?"

She peered down in frustration. "How should I know? They all look the same to me. The more important question is, which of those lights ahead are oncoming airplanes and not stars?"

"Those are all stars. Let's not get paranoid here," he said. "We're going to get through this, and then we're—"

His voice was drowned out by a Piper Seneca howling past so close that from the glow of its instrument panel they could see the startled pilot's face, bathed in horror. Peter's mind froze, but Hans's body executed a superb evasive maneuver. The plane yowled into a steep diving turn and rolled out smooth as silk, wings level, trimmed perfectly. As soon as Peter thought about what had nearly happened, he was piloting the plane terribly again.

"Listen," said Elizabeth, when her voice had returned, "we've got to at least stay in the air lanes."

"Right, okay." He surmised an air lane must be some sort of avian highway. Except how do you see it? This was, he realized, like playing Russian roulette with three or four bullets in the cylinder. He took a deep breath. Better to get some of this out in the open.

"Look," he said. "I'm not a pilot."

She looked at him. Obviously she believed that part rather easily, he thought.

"I'm Peter and I'm not a pilot. I'm a physicist, and no, I'm not Hans's evil twin. Well, maybe I am," he allowed.

Now she was staring at him like she thought he had simply gone mad. "You haven't been involved with physics in twenty years."

"Nothing I'm proud of, that's for sure."

"You were an investment banker, yes or no?"

Something tearful was coming into her voice.

"I've never even balanced a checkbook," he confessed.

"Hans—"

"Peter. Doctor Peter Jance," he added, sickening at the sound of his own name. And then, much lower, "Hans who, incidentally?"

"Brinkman," she said in shaken voice.

He wished he hadn't asked. "I'm Peter Jance and I'm Hans Brinkman."

"Are you telling me you're a multiple personality?"

"It's worse than that. The fact is," he said gravely, relieved to be speaking the truth, "you're considerably safer not knowing."

"Am I? You think I'm safe now, in a plane being flown by a nonpilot schizophrenic?"

"You said they were trying to tie you up. That's not field-manual procedure for assassination. The manual says stick and run. I think they were trying to kidnap you."

She swallowed. She knew this part, at least, made sense. The guy could have killed her and hadn't. "Why? Why would they want to kidnap me?"

"I don't know. Maybe to get me to come back."

"Back where?"

"That's the sixty-four-thousand-dollar question, isn't it?"

She looked at him oddly, and he realized the phrase was alien to her. He also realized that for the last five minutes his mind had been off the controls and his body had been flying the plane flawlessly. Keep talking, he thought. And don't stop to think about flying.

"Hans—Peter—I don't believe you're CIA, if that's what you're still claiming."

"I never claimed to be CIA. That was your assumption. I let you believe it because the alternative, telling you the truth, was too damn risky!" Why was he shouting at her as though she were to blame?

"Risky for whom?" she shouted back. *"Really!"*

"For you," he said, desperately trying to convince himself that this was the truth. "I thought they'd kill you if they knew you knew, not just tie you up and throw you in a cell." It wasn't the whole truth, he thought in disgust. And so he added: "And for me, because I thought you would just walk out the door without even stopping to slap my face."

In shock, she turned and looked at him. There was a terrible vulnerability in his voice and it stopped her anger cold.

"I can't bear to lie to you anymore," he said. "Which puts me in something of a bind, doesn't it? The kind they used to think caused schizophrenia," he went on, aware she might think he was babbling. "I'm hopelessly in love with you, it's beyond insanity and I don't want to die again."

She blinked, thought, softened. *"Again?"*

He closed his eyes against tears. "And the worst of it is, you remind me so much of my wife."

"Oh, God," she groaned.

"I know it's horrible for you to hear. But it's true."

"I remind you of *Yvette?"*

He shook his head. "Beatrice. My wife's name is Beatrice. She's back at the base and I don't know what kind of danger she's in. If she's smart and feels the way I do, she'll play possum, maybe hope I'm making a run for *60 Minutes* or the *New York Times.* In which case, however, you would be useless as bait, and we would both be utterly expendable."

Elizabeth fell silent, her hands shaking.

"On the other hand," Peter went on, wanting to get it over with, "Beatrice may be so angry with me she can't see straight, as angry as you are at this moment. For which I can't blame either of you. She may be of a mind to cooperate with the organization that thinks it owns us both, which makes contacting her potentially suicidal. At least that's how I see it," he said, a note of uncertainty creeping into his voice again. There's something I'm missing here, he thought, something vastly important to both of them.

"Why would you go to the *Times*? What is it you've been working on?"

"I'm working on stopping something," he heard himself say. "Something I started." Then he blurted it out. "A weapon."

He felt her stiffen, but at the same time her gray eyes softened, as though thanking him for his attempt at honesty, no matter how addled she might believe him to be.

"What kind of weapon?" she asked.

"Like any other kind," he said. "It kills. It just happens to do it especially well."

"Like a nuclear device?" she asked, fear creeping into her voice.

"Better than that. Or worse, I should say. It can kill selectively, from a safe distance. Nothing can act as a shield against it. We were making it small and it will get smaller. There's no radiation. You could exterminate a city and move into it the next day. It's just what the doctor ordered, people will say, to put an end to war in the twenty-first century. But it could also vastly expand war, make it cheaper for the aggressors to destroy anyone they don't want in their way. Now," he said, feeling the plane start to roll, "what do you know about air lanes?"

"Not much," she said. Her voice was small and her skin had paled visibly in the last moments of his confession. "Just what you tried to teach me."

"What *Hans* tried to teach you. Go on."

"I know we're supposed to fly a certain direction at a certain altitude."

"Like?"

"Like odd-numbered altitudes for north and south, even-numbered for east and west. Then it's broken down further, like 2,000 feet for east, and 2,200 feet for west."

"Is that it? Odd for north and south, even for east and west, at those altitudes?"

"I just made up those altitudes as an example," she protested. "I'm not sure what they really are—" She broke off as a plane shot by about a thousand feet to their left. It went by like a bullet, sobering both of them.

"What's the lowest you're allowed to fly?" Peter asked quickly.

"Five hundred feet over water, I think, but the air lanes start higher than that."

"Okay, then if we fly at five hundred feet more or less, we shouldn't be meeting anybody else, you think?"

"I think so," she said.

He pushed the control column down and they dropped, lower and lower until they could see the tops of the waves. He leveled off and kept it there. In the back of what he could only think of as his no-mind, he knew it would keep them out of radar view as well, but it was nerve-wracking flying at best. Spray from the breakers bounced off the windscreen; he entertained visions of an errant seagull plowing through the plexiglass like a cannon shell.

"I think it's over there," Peter said, referring to a glow on the horizon that he hoped was Puerto Rico. He angled the airplane toward it, but when they drew nearer, it turned out to be a cruise ship. They flew over it so low they could see some deckhands looking up in alarm. Then they were on into inky blackness, again.

With Elizabeth's help, he found the fuel gauge. It was enough like a car's to read, and it was dangerously close to empty. "Which direction are we going?"

"I think we're heading out to sea," she said, with a glance at the instrument panel. "East is toward Africa. That's five thousand miles away. We want to go west to find Puerto Rico. That's eight miles."

A sense of humor, he thought. That's a hopeful sign. He turned the plane around as best he could—too much cerebration again—and watched the needle on the compass swing around until it pointed at 270 degrees. Then he heard Elizabeth gasp as he looked up to see the lights of Puerto Rico swing into view, a huge panorama of welcome luminescence. He realized that he must have been flying with the island directly behind him for the last five minutes.

"There!" said Elizabeth, pointing at a sweep of green searchlight. Ahead Peter saw the lights of a major runway. He had to fight much harder this time to still his thoughts: he knew instinctively that land-ing was the most dangerous part of flying. He imagined his mind to be a jumbleful of sticks that represented thoughts and bulldozed them into oblivion. The plane banked easily toward Puerto Rico's San Juan International Airport, as if he had suddenly learned how to fly. Perhaps it was just that he was too scared to think about it, and Hans, in fact, had taken over.

He circled three times, each time closer, until he saw a big jetliner abort its descent and climb back up. He gambled that they had been spotted and that traffic was now being diverted. He headed in, letting his hands and feet do the work, trimming rudder, dropping ten de-grees flaps, pulling back on the throttle and letting the plane nose down. He felt the flaps braking the plane and relaxed, confident that his body was doing everything required.

The plane was coming in for a perfect three-point landing when Peter's racing brain broke through the curtain of competence. He was thinking that they needed to get out of the plane before it came to a stop and was wondering how best to land the plane for the maneuver. His hand faltered, the plane came down hard and Peter instantly re-verted to his driver's instincts, trying to steer the aircraft like a car. He turned the control column to the left, which only moved the ailerons, unusable at that speed. Dimly he sensed he should be using his feet on the rudder pedals, but the only foot he was using was his right one, pressing down on the right rudder pedal as though it were a car's brake.

The plane banged down hard on the runway and leapt back into the air at a crabbed angle, engine roaring. Now there was no time for thinking or not thinking: the aircraft was out of airspeed and slammed back hard in an ungainly stall. The right landing gear buckled and the plane's nose went to the runway, its propeller splintering in a shower of sparks. The Cessna skidded right, went up on one wing tip, then collapsed into immobility.

On wobbly legs, they scrambled out.

Sirens and lights were shooting toward them at an alarming speed, perhaps a quarter mile away. They took off in the opposite direction, into the deepest darkness they could find, through sand and grass,

along the cyclone fence surrounding the airport and finally diving behind some brush. Looking back at the runway, they saw emergency
vehicles gathering around the wreck of the Cessna. There was also a
dark Humvee pulling up, its spotlight sweeping the surrounding darkness, darkness already dissipating in the light of dawn cracking from
the east.

Ducking lower, they ran again.

And then Peter fell.

It was as though someone had struck him with an iron bar. He hit
the dirt clutching his head, fiery pain shooting up the back of his neck
and over the crown of his skull, blinding him and driving all thought
and reflex from his brain.

Terrified, Elizabeth shook his shoulders, urging him up. "Peter?
Hans? Oh, God, are you shot?"

He barely heard her voice. All was agony. He tore at his head like
a madman. Then, just as quickly as it had come, it was gone, lifting off
him like some medieval torture device snatched away by a sadistic in-
quisitor.

Breathless and stunned, he sat up.

"Peter?"

"I'm all right." You deserve everything you get, he thought mis-
erably.

"What happened?" She touched his arm.

He struggled to rise, analyzing his own fall. "I think the arteries of
my brain are too brittle. Seventy-six years old. They can't keep up
with the force of this heart."

"Seventy-six—what on *earth* are you talking about?"

"Not my body," he said, too sick to dissemble any longer. "My body
is a hale and hearty thirty-five."

She stared at him as though he were speaking in tongues. He
looked away, her gaze was too intense. Beyond the nearest taxi lane
was the terminal, lots of people and what looked like an empty
shipping container. The odds were that they would at least hesitate to
kill them in public. He grabbed Elizabeth by the hand and they ran
for it.

They made it. Looking back, he didn't see any headlights swerving around, heading for them. He ducked back under cover and looked at the woman next to him. She looked so young and so frightened: it struck him full-force how innocent of all this she was.

"I'm not Hans," he said gently. "I never was. Hans is really dead, Elizabeth. His mind, his brain and all of its memories of you and him—all that's gone. Incinerated on the base at Vieques."

Her hand in his went limp. "What are you saying?" she asked.

"Hans was a clone. My clone, to be specific."

"That's not funny," she said after registering a millisecond of shock. But from the way her lip was trembling, he knew she was beginning to understand the enormity of this insane situation.

"No, you're right, it's not," Peter said, his heart swelling with a drunken mixture of guilt and love. Elizabeth tried to pull her hand away, but he wouldn't let her. "Before you walk out of my life for good, there's one more thing I have to say. We have a plane to catch."

American Flight 99 had been ten minutes away from closing its door and taxiing for takeoff when it was discovered that the crew had been shorted ten meals by the local vendor, Caribbean Food Services. A truck had been sent back to its kitchens, five miles away. Impatient passengers were given free drinks and treated to an NBA highlight tape.

While they waited for the dinners to be brought in, flight attendant Mary Blanchard stood with colleague Heather Zuckerbrod in the open service hatch, enjoying the balmy tropical air. For the first time in months, Mary was taking pleasure in her job, chiefly because she knew she was about to leave it. She was pregnant. Her boyfriend, a first officer for the airline who flew the L.A.–to–New York route, was now willing to marry her. She was getting out and it felt good. No more drunk conventioneers; no more victims of air rage, sneaking cigarettes in the lavatory; no more celebrity parents letting their brats and dogs run wild in first-class. She took a deep, calming breath, trying to picture weekends at home with Charlie instead of being in the air at thirty-five thousand feet.

Out on the runway in the humid dawn, she saw movement. A

ground patrol broadcast had warned them to be on the watch for unauthorized civilians on the taxi lanes, and she had flashed on Elizabeth and her gorgeous friend. If they were the targets of this alert, she was bound and determined to help. What could American do, fire her? Blackball her from the airline industry? She couldn't have cared less.

She looked and she stared, and by God there they were, slipping between two shipping containers. And now a series of moving lights pierced through the lingering darkness, airport police vehicles and Humvees moving down the line of planes waiting for takeoff, training their searchlights on every inch of tarmac.

Mary Blanchard of Waltham, Massachusetts, hurried down the jetway's service stairs, and as swiftly and as inconspicuously as she could, she made her way to the shipping containers. Leaning against one, she took out a cigarette and tried to look like someone catching a quick smoke before departure.

"So," she said casually, shielding her mouth with her cigarette hand, "what have you kids been up to?"

"Mary?" she heard Elizabeth say from between the containers.

"It's me, all right. Just tell me this. If I help you out, do I end up in jail?"

There was a brief pause, not entirely reassuring, and then came the voice of the boyfriend. "She hasn't broken any laws."

"But you have?" Mary asked gamely

"None that those Humvee guys haven't broken, too."

"All right, shut up," said Mary. She turned as the catering truck drew up beside the plane; its driver hopped out. He saw her and stopped, full of apologies.

"Sorry, we got the meals now."

Mary gave him her sternest look. "Tito, you owe me one." The driver looked sheepish. "You forget ten meals and then delay the flight. Now what you have to do for me is just look out there." Baffled but dutiful, Tito stared where she was pointing, toward the runway and away from the containers. Mary gave a wave and Elizabeth and Peter emerged.

"Keep looking," she ordered Tito, and gesturing for them to follow, she led the two into the back of the meal truck. As soon as they were safely out of sight, Mary stuck her head back out.

"What are you waiting for, Tito? Gimme my meals!"

He sprang into action, activating the truck's scissor-lift. Hydraulics whined and the entire cargo section of the truck lifted straight up, stopping level with the plane's open service hatch.

Mary ducked out first, checking her perimeter, then signaled Elizabeth and Peter out of the truck and into the plane's galley. About that time Heather Zuckerbrod rounded the corner and stopped short, gaping at Mary's two companions.

"Special VIPs," Mary said.

"Rr . . . right," Heather said carefully.

Outside the aircraft, a pair of Humvees pulled up. Within seconds, the jetway stairs were clanging with the sound of heavy footsteps.

"Elevator," said Mary to Heather.

Heather, wide-eyed, pulled open a narrow aluminum door. Mary motioned Elizabeth and Peter inside and both of them squeezed in. It was a space designed for one, but somehow they made it in and, somehow, Mary managed to get the door closed. She pressed a button and the elevator started down. Seconds after the stowaways' heads dropped from view, a pair of armed troopers entered the galley from the cabin.

"Did you receive our transmission?" one of them asked. He was young and was looking more than a little annoyed with this exercise.

"Yup, we did," replied Mary. "So, who's supposed to be running around out there?"

"Not for you to know."

"Do you know?"

"No," he admitted. "Man and a woman. Hijackers, maybe, I don't know." He showed her a fax sheet with two photographs, one a driver's license shot of Elizabeth, the other what looked to be a still from a video frame of Peter at a blackboard with an array of numbers and symbols behind him. "You seen 'em?"

"Yeah," Mary said flatly. "Sure, that's them, all right. We gave them an upgrade. As we speak, they're drinking champagne and eating caviar right now in first class."

"Really?"

"Duh," Mary said. The soldier gave her a hurt look and headed down the aisle with another armed man. The first officer came out of the cockpit, empty plastic cup in his hand.

"What's up?"

"Bullshit," said Mary.

"Figures. Once they clear us, we're next out."

"Thank God for small favors," said Mary, filling his cup with fresh coffee. Two minutes later, having checked the faces of the passengers against the photographs they were carrying, the two troopers took a last look in the washrooms and cockpit, then left the aircraft.

Finally shutting the hatches and doors, Mary Blanchard dropped down in her jump seat and grabbed the microphone.

"Ladies and gentlemen, we apologize for the delay, but we are now cleared for takeoff. Please make sure your seat belts are fastened and your trays and seats are in the upright position. Our captain assures us he will make every effort to see that we reach Miami on schedule."

The DC-10 was halfway down the runway when ground control radioed all outgoing flights to hold their positions. In the cockpit, Captain Larry S. Graham knew that if he pulled all power and applied full brakes, he could abort takeoff and perhaps be able to stop by the time he reached the end of the runway. This would cause at least a dozen necks in the cabin to suffer whiplash, trigger half that many lawsuits, ruin $20,000 worth of tires and most certainly screw up his schedule. Specifically, it would keep him two thousand nautical miles away from his weekly poker game in Boston the next night, and he badly needed to make up for last week's losses.

"Fuck those assholes," he said to his second officer, keeping his hand on the throttle.

The DC-10 lifted off.

"Your transmission is breaking up," the second officer grinned and radioed back to ground control. "Please say again. Repeat, please say again."

The plane banked smartly and headed out over open water, heading due north.

The space Elizabeth and Peter found themselves occupying was a low-ceilinged cabin ten feet by six in size. One entire wall was taken up by stowed and locked food carts and a bank of ovens. There were no seats. They sat on the floor, Peter sneaking furtive looks at Elizabeth as he spoke. She sat as far away from him as she could, a space of perhaps four feet. Her arms were wrapped around her knees and her eyes were shut tight. She was, in fact, wishing she could fall asleep, half from fatigue, half from not wanting to finally hear what she was hearing.

"It was done almost as a lark," Peter continued. "Thirty-five years ago. A group of us were working in the same government laboratory complex and one particular scientist took some skin scrapings from the rest of us."

He was talking in a sorrowful whisper, but it was one in which Elizabeth thought she detected an eerie note of pride. It reminded her of something Hans had told her about Robert Oppenheimer and his grand pronouncement after the first A-bomb test. *I have become Shiva, destroyer of worlds.* Some crap like that. Hans had gone on and on about "Oppy," and she remembered it was the night he had confessed that he had abandoned a career in physics. Now here was Peter or whoever he was talking about the same sort of thing. She felt sick at heart, but still she listened. What choice did she have?

"He extracted the DNA and put it into some mothers' eggs, just to see if it would work. This was thirty years ahead of what anybody else was doing. Are you with me?"

"Yes, thirty years, I heard you." *Everything is true for thirty years.* That was one of Hans's favorite sayings.

"The infertile women thought they were getting help from their doctor so they could have children. They became pregnant, that's for sure, but the DNA in their eggs wasn't theirs anymore. In the case of Mrs. Brinkman, the DNA was entirely my own."

"Did you give your permission?" she asked in a hushed voice.

"No," he said.

"Did you know it was happening?"

"No. We were all experimenting on a wide variety of phenomena in physics, biology, mathematics. And we all used each other benignly as guinea pigs. But I'm not making excuses. At a certain point—much, much later—I *did* know. I was told. And I eventually went along with it. I did that."

"Go on," she said, sensing that he was faltering. She was at the center of the known universe and it was hell after all. "So what you're saying is that you're Hans. And that you're Peter. You are Peter's brain in Hans's body."

"That's the simple truth of it, yes. I know you don't think it could be possible, but it is. Now."

"I said go on," she snapped.

"It's appalling. I admit it. I agree."

"You're a murdering asshole," she said, as tears started down her cheeks.

"I told you it was complicated," he said, wanting to take her into his arms. "I'm just human after all."

She looked up at him. "You positive about that?"

"I'm a fool, I know that," he said and believed it with all his heart. "That makes me human."

"And a lying bastard," she added, so loudly he was afraid someone above them might hear. She ignored his alarm. "How could you agree to such a thing?"

He stared at his hands. "I was dying. I refused to do it at first. But at death's door, I broke. And it was something they wanted, it was something they needed so much from me."

"They?"

"My wife. And the man behind it all, Frederick Wolfe. We had been friends and colleagues for many years—the three of us. Beatrice was desperate for me to remain alive and for that I can't blame her. As for myself, I accept full blame, I do. It's unthinkable what I've done."

"They needed you to work on the weapon."

"That was Wolfe's need," he admitted. "I thought it was more out of friendship, but I see now that it was just for his advancement. And for the program's completion. The project, Fountain Society, is everything to him, and to those above him, too. The weapon I was working on, for instance. More than likely it would have died with me. Many other incomplete projects will die unless the lives of their visionaries can be extended."

"And you, you continued to work on this weapon, as before. Never giving it a thought."

"I had my doubts. As time went on more and more."

"Uh-huh."

"Especially after I met you. I promise you that's the truth." He reached out for her.

"Don't."

He took his hand back. There was nothing more he could say.

The crockery on the food carts rattled as the plane hit an air pocket. In miserable silence they sat for a moment, until Elizabeth looked at him.

"And you managed to keep all this secret?" She was dismayed by her own curiosity.

"Wolfe was funded for secrecy," he said. "Then, of course, then the Scots blew everything wide open with that damn sheep, Dolly. And so the government's thinking was, well, the damn Iraqis are going to be putting out cloned armies of Saddams like buns from a baker's oven, why not clone our best and brightest?"

"Don't want to have a clone gap."

He looked at her and grimaced. "Something like that."

"Or have our kids learning Arabic in the first grade." She was seething.

"That's the general idea," he said, looking at her. She saw such regret and frankness and even love in his gaze that she looked sharply away. Don't let this man charm you, she thought. He can do it.

"What did you do in Switzerland?" he asked. "I mean, what *do* you do?"

"I don't care to discuss it."

"You're a writer or an artist?"

"Why the hell would you think that?"

"You just seem so—"

"What?"

"So bright. So intelligent."

"For what? A blonde? Or a model?"

"I see. So you *are* a model."

"You sound disappointed. You're even more of a snob than Hans was."

"Was Hans a snob?"

"You know what? I honest to God don't want to talk about this."

But the next moment she felt her curiosity rise again. She was flashing on the two of them, together, Peter's brain and Hans's body and herself on the beach of Phosphorescent Bay. Or did that make three people? Three's a crowd, she thought, with a giddy sense of horror and black humor, remembering the sound of the *coquís* in the trees. A nameless dread came over her.

"So are you implying that you're not the only one?"

"I am so far. I guess I was the guinea pig."

"Emphasis on the pig," she said. She focused on the engine's whine, trying to drown out the *coquís*, the sounds of which seemed to be mocking her in some horrible fashion from the depths of her memory. "You don't know who else is on the A-list? The other geniuses in this—what do you call it?"

"The code for it is the Fountain Society. And no, I don't know who else might be cloned, I swear to you."

"And the party back at the base—the one whose loyalty you were asking about—that would be your wife?"

"That's right," he said, impressed by her observance and memory. He was gazing at her with admiration and Elizabeth reacted sharply to it.

"I'd appreciate it if you wouldn't look at me like that," she said. "As soon as this plane lands, I'm going back to Switzerland."

"They won't let you," he said, his warning dull and flat. "Not Switzerland, no. That's too obvious. We could try for something else."

"We?" she said in astonishment.

"You might be stuck with me, actually. What you saw back in Vieques was only a fraction of what they're capable of. You haven't even met all the players. You wouldn't know them if they walked up to you in a crowded room. You wouldn't know if they were carrying a knife or a pair of handcuffs or a gun—"

He seemed to be thinking out loud, as though he, too, were learning as well from this litany. And then she saw that his eyes were welling up with tears. "What did your parents do for a living?" he asked.

She gave him one last look of defiance, then shrugged. "My father was in the Navy, my mother was a housewife."

"And where was your dad stationed?"

"I don't remember. For God's sake, why are you crying?"

"Was I? I didn't realize that I was." His voice was filled with exhaustion.

"Were you thinking of your wife?"

He stared at her in gratitude. "Yes, actually, I was."

"You should have stayed with her," she shot back, although not with as much venom as she had intended.

"Yes, I know." He was searching her eyes. No, he was searching her eyebrows. Looking for what?

"And I'm not staying with you, Peter. The minute we land, I'm gone from your life."

His shrug was subtle, which infuriated her. When the elevator motor clanked and whirred sharply, she reflexively reached for Peter's hand. As soon as he squeezed it, she pulled away again, furious again and more confused than ever.

The elevator descended and Mary Blanchard stepped out holding two cups of steaming coffee. Peter and Elizabeth eagerly accepted the gift as Mary scrutinized the couple.

"How are you two doing? Behaving yourselves, I hope not?"

Elizabeth nodded lamely, and Mary, sensing that she had walked in on something serious, began to fuss with the food carts.

"You guys are lucky. The DC-10's the only plane we fly that has a below-decks galley. Most people don't even know it's here."

Peter's eyes were closed. He seemed lost in the steam from his coffee mug. Elizabeth offered a wan smile. Mary sighed.

"Fighting already. Sorry, but maybe all this activity will give you a break. Gotta start breakfast."

She began shoving meals into ovens and twisting dials, ignoring them both. She was right: Her presence helped. Peter's hands unclenched and Elizabeth got up to assist Mary. All the bustle muted the sound of the *coquís* still singing in her ears.

LEARJET N-94838

In the aftermath of the Fountain Society's success with Peter's transplant, Oscar Henderson had assigned the Learjet to Wolfe as a congratulatory plum. Wolfe adored the plane, though its pedigree embarrassed him slightly: it had once been Ollie North's shuttle workhorse for his trips to Central America. That aside, the Learjet had sumptuous leather seats, burl walnut tables and a lavatory with real marble. In his early, underpaid years as a scientist, Wolfe had always expressed disdain for worldly goods. Now he saw his youthful position as just so much posturing. The Learjet had brought out a yearning for the good things in life and it became a symbol of his ever-expanding pride in having achieved the summit he had clawed his way towards through so many years of struggle.

At the controls of the jet this day was Captain Bob Culpepper, a ten-year veteran of NSA, fresh from a flight delivering a sealed package to an agent in Bogotá. Inside that particular package, although Culpepper neither knew nor cared to know, were the head and genitals of a high-level drug operative of the Medellín cartel. The man had killed a Texas DEA agent the day before and a message needed to be sent. For Culpepper, the trip's only significance was that now his digestive tract was disturbed, the result of having eaten two *tapas* he had bought from a vendor at the Bogotá airport.

He cursed himself for his stupidity, turned the controls over to his co-pilot, Second Officer David Anspaugh, and made his way toward the rear of the aircraft.

"Everybody comfortable?" he asked nonchalantly. Since everyone said yes, Culpepper proceeded to the toilet at the tail of the plane.

As soon as he was gone, Henderson and Wolfe put their heads together again.

"I thought this clone sonofabitch was a banker," Henderson fumed.

"He was," said Wolfe quietly, keeping a close eye on Beatrice. She was seated across the cabin, staring out the window at the pink-tinged clouds in apparent absorption but Wolfe still thought she might be listening.

"Well, then," grunted Henderson, "why don't you tell me how your boy managed to cold cock a Navy Seal, not to mention outwit the best civilian muscle money can buy?"

"I can only imagine what the quality of the local muscle is on Vieques," Wolfe said dryly. Henderson said nothing, but inwardly he cursed himself, knowing how pound-foolish he had indeed been.

"As it turns out," said Wolfe, "Hans Brinkman was something of an athlete. I rechecked his dossier: he happened to have been a skilled amateur boxer, quite a skier, and he flew his own jet. He was as accomplished physically as he was intellectually. Not surprising, really, if you consider his provenance. Besides, he was fighting for his life and perhaps even for the girl's. The bottom line is," he concluded in a voice as cold as steel, "if you weren't such a penny-pincher, the team you sent in would all have been Seals."

"It wasn't a matter of money," Henderson shot back. "It was to keep us clean. If there were fingerprints—as indeed there were—we wanted it to look like a robbery."

"And what does it look like now?" Wolfe asked, his anger rising.

"I should have locked him up when I had the chance. Along with your precious grandson."

"Oh, please, both of you just *shut up!*"

Beatrice was turned around in her seat, staring at them with hostility. Wolfe and Henderson fell silent, quarreling children silenced by their mother.

Beatrice moved to the seat directly across from them, surveying them bleakly. "What else do you know about his clone?" she asked.

"Anything you want to hear," Wolfe said gently. Her lovely gray eyes had a pained look he couldn't bear.

"Any other hobbies besides boxing and flying?"

Her crisp tone encouraged him. "Skiing, as I said, tennis, bird-watching, some martial arts. He was an amateur geologist and pale-ontologist."

"Fascinating," she said.

"Yes, isn't it." Wolfe decided to take a risk. "Peter loved paleontol-ogy," he said, assuming a tone of a gentle regret.

Henderson ground out his cigar. "Well, he must have studied tae kwon do with a fucking T. Rex because he certainly kicked serious ass back at the hotel."

Wolfe sighed. "Oscar," he said quietly, "if you made even the fee-blest attempt to display human compassion, this would go much more easily for all of us."

Beatrice waved him off. "That's all right," she said, looking at Hen-derson. "Actually, the most feeling thing you can do right now is to spare me your bankrupt sympathy."

Wolfe fell silent. The pilot was coming back on his way to the cock-pit; the smell from the lavatory was faint but unmistakable.

"Jesus, somebody blow up a fucking dog in here?" Henderson barked. He looked back toward the rear of the plane. "Yo, Lance. Do me a favor."

Lance Russell, the Navy Seal, stood up and closed the lavatory door. He had been listening to the conversation and the look on his face said he wanted very much to meet Peter Jance, Jr. again. Re-turning to his seat and flexing his hands, he imagined Peter's trachea beneath his fingers.

"It's not the first time I've seen this," said Henderson, trying to comply with Wolfe's edict. "A good man brought down by a manipu-lative girl."

Beatrice's nod was noncommittal. "I understand she fought bravely, too." She was staring straight at Wolfe.

"Panicked is what she was," said Henderson, lighting a cigarette. "Anyhow, she's not going far without credit cards. Fact is, she doesn't have an identity anymore."

"Who was she?" asked Beatrice.

Past tense, noted Wolfe. Yes, she won't take much coaxing.

"Elizabeth Parker," said Henderson.

"And how do we know her name?" Beatrice asked.

Wolfe shot Henderson a warning look and refilled Beatrice's wine glass. "That's the name she used when she registered at the hotel."

"She must be special," Beatrice said simply. Wolfe's heart ached for Beatrice. He made a decision to tell her just a bit more, hoping to ease her pain.

"I'm not sure," he said carefully, "but she might have known him before."

Beatrice looked at him. "Peter?"

"No. The clone. She's also from Switzerland. It's possible that she slipped through the cracks in our surveillance of Brinkman. Maybe she was a secret."

"A mistress, you mean?" Beatrice indeed took notice, but Wolfe wasn't sure whether she was reassured or not.

"Possible. So you see, there might be some sort of attraction there, indigenous, if you will, to the body."

Beatrice sat back, speechless for several moments. Then she straightened, her eyes boring into Wolfe's.

"If that were so, what was she doing here? Surely Peter wouldn't have had any conscious knowledge of her existence, let alone her telephone number."

"No," admitted Wolfe uneasily. "Not possible."

Beatrice continued to stare at him.

"Then how would she know to come here?" Beatrice demanded.

Wolfe shifted his weight uneasily. "Alex," he said at last.

Beatrice blinked. "Alex sent for her?"

Wolfe looked away. The intensity of her gaze was downright unsettling. "He was apparently starting to have his doubts."

"About what?"

"About everything. Fountain Project. The Hammer. And certainly Peter's defection didn't help."

Beatrice thought for a moment, stunned by this revelation.

"How did Alex know about her if you didn't?" she asked.

Wolfe shrugged. "He made it his business to know more about the clones than I did. Perhaps he was monitoring this clone's e-mail—I don't really know."

Beatrice mulled this over with great intensity.

"But why call her down here? What did Alex possibly hope to accomplish by that?"

"I suppose," said Wolfe, "he wanted to undermine the project. Maybe this was a monkey wrench in the gears sort of thing."

"Did he meet with her?"

"We don't know, but we think not. Apparently, Alex never knew where to find her. None of us did until Peter did," he added quietly.

"And where is Alex now?"

Wolfe and Henderson exchanged glances. "He's gone AWOL," said Henderson. "Vanished without a trace."

"You don't think he's with them, do you? Peter and, what did you say her name was? Elizabeth?"

"I highly doubt it," said Wolfe. "Third wheel and all that. Understand, I rue the day that I allowed Alex in on the project. He was too damn curious. He must have gotten into the encrypted files somehow. Just like a big kid, really, going through his parents' dresser drawers to see what he can find."

Wolfe took out his pack of Gauloises and offered one to Beatrice.

"And what does this woman do for a living?" said Beatrice, accepting the cigarette.

"Beatrice," said Wolfe, "you don't need to torture yourself." Keep it up, he thought, lighting her Gauloise.

"I just asked you a question."

"She's a photographer's model."

"I see. So she's very beautiful?"

"You don't have to worry, Mrs. Jance," Henderson said. "We'll get her."

"Beatrice. I'm not Mrs. Jance anymore," she said, her voice cold as ice. "And Peter isn't Peter anymore. I think I knew that from the start. If I had been completely honest with myself I could have spared myself a great deal of grief and worry."

"I'm relieved to hear that," said Wolfe. Relieved? Her words thrilled him.

"He fucked us all," Henderson put in gracelessly. "He's a danger we can't ignore."

She nodded, her eyes dead. "I suppose not," she said. "Do you think he's told this model who he really is?"

"Oh," said Wolfe, "I doubt that very much."

"Depends on how much in love he is," said Beatrice. She smiled sadly.

"I don't think he's in love with her," Wolfe said, trying to regain ground. "It's more or less an animal thing under these circumstances."

Beatrice looked away. "Even so, I'd guess Peter's come clean," she said. "I know him."

"In which case she'll probably head for the hills, wouldn't you think?"

Beatrice examined her fingernails. "Or perhaps try to alert the media? In which case, what?" She looked back up at him and there was fire in her eyes now. "You have orders to terminate her?"

"Well," said Wolfe, "no."

"Why not? If Peter's expendable, why isn't she? Or do you intend to use her as bait to lure him back into the fold?"

"No," said Wolfe, "we don't intend to use her as bait."

"So why not just kill her?"

He looked at her full-on. "Because," he said, "she's essential to our future."

Beatrice started back at him. "I don't think I understand."

Wolfe drew on his cigarette and tried to continue casually. "She was born in Vieques. She may have been seen by somebody who knew her. We have to be extremely careful."

Beatrice cocked her head, her mind now racing. "Was her father in the Navy by any chance?"

"Yes," said Wolfe.

"And did she come through your clinic?" she asked.

"Possibly."

"Well," said Beatrice. "*That's* interesting."

She said this last as though it were the understatement of the century, then rose and walked to the rear of the plane, taking a seat near to where Russell sat sharpening a knife on a whetstone. He folded it into his pocket when he saw her, then got up and joined the men at the front of the plane. Beatrice lay her head against the window.

Looking back, Wolfe saw that she was crying. He went and sat beside her, offering his handkerchief.

"I'm sorry," he said. "This is hell for you, I know."

"How long have we known each other, Freddy?"

"I don't know," said Wolfe gently. "I believe it was after the glaciers retreated, but I'm not certain of the exact date."

She laughed mirthlessly and rested her head briefly on his shoulder. Wolfe closed his eyes and smelled her scent, his heart pounding.

"I do trust you," she said quietly. She opened her hand and allowed him to take it in his.

"I hope you do," he said carefully. "Ever since we met, I've wanted you to be happy. In your work, in your marriage. And now that the latter is gone, I feel an impulse to protect you as well. I hope you'll let me do that now. Protect and preserve, you *do* understand what I'm saying, don't you?" He checked back over his shoulder, making sure Henderson and Russell were engaged in their own conversation, then leaned closer to Beatrice. The sparkle in her eyes was emboldening him: "For as long as we're together."

"So where do we go from here?" she asked.

He inhaled deeply. "We've still got risks to assess. The cerebral events Peter experienced, the mini-strokes, they continue to pose a life-threatening problem, though I'm confident the sclerotic changes are reversible if the rest of the organism is healthy. We know a good deal more now."

She traced the veins of his hand with her finger. "You're going to operate again."

"The work must go on. There's still so much to learn. This time it should be easier."

She nodded. "Is he abroad or is he in the U.S.?"

"The subject?"

"The clone," she affirmed.

"New York."

"Is that our eventual destination? New York City?"

"Yes," he answered.

She lifted his hand to her lips. "Thank you for telling me all this."

"You're welcome." He sat beside her for a long moment gathering his courage, then added: "And I don't suppose it's been any secret, either. This most powerful feeling I've had for you all these years . . . I love you, Beatrice. And as right as he might have seemed, I have always felt that Peter was somehow wrong for you."

She gave a small shrug and caressed his hand sadly. "I suppose he proved that, didn't he?"

"Completely," said Wolfe.

"And your intuition is correct. I *have* known all along what you've felt for me," she said quietly. "Thank you for saying it, finally, and thank you, Freddy, for making things easier for me."

"We will be together, Beatrice," he said. "For a long, long time. I have every confidence."

"So do I, Freddy," she said. She kissed his hand. "And now, if you'll excuse me?"

She waited until Wolfe swung his legs out of her way, touched his cheek, then walked down the aisle to the rest room and locked the door.

After the lights flickered on, she stepped close to the mirror and studied her face, running her fingers over her cheeks, her eyes, her hair. She looked at herself for several minutes, with only the faintest tremor, then turned and lifted the commode's seat, kneeled over it and vomited for the first time since she had stopped drinking forty-five years ago. She didn't stop until everything she had shared with those men—every whiff of cigar smoke, every cigarette, every ounce of liquor or wine she had accepted from them—was out of her system and flushed into oblivion.

Beatrice Jance stood up and took out her makeup case. For as long as she remained with this madman and his sycophants, it was important that she look normal. Absolutely normal. And, by God, she would. Even if it killed her.

■ ■ ■

As soon as the Learjet landed in Puerto Rico, Lieutenant Roger Thornton, a stocky U.S. Ranger who ran the security force at Roosevelt Roads, briefed Henderson. Wolfe and Russell listened carefully. Everywhere they looked there were troops and semi-armored vehicles. The airport was under siege.

"We sealed it and searched it, Colonel. There's no way Dr. Jance or anybody with him got through the fence. We have vehicles every hundred yards."

"But you don't have Jance," said Henderson.

"No, sir, we did not find him."

"What about the terminal, the baggage dock?" asked Russell.

"Sir, my troops have searched every building, shed and vehicle on the grounds, as well as every plane."

"Any aircraft take off since the crash?" asked Henderson, whose ears were turning red with fury.

"Only one, sir. American Flight 99. It was midway through its take-off roll when we sealed the airport. But we'd already searched the aircraft thoroughly."

"Where's it headed?"

"Miami International, sir. Should have landed about five minutes ago."

"Then I want a team at every gate five minutes ago!" he screamed, sprinting back toward the Learjet. The others scrambled to catch up, while Beatrice Jance watched intently from the window.

MIAMI, FLORIDA

For twenty minutes after American Flight 99 landed at Miami International, Peter and Elizabeth remained in Mary Blanchard's galley bay. After all the passengers and crew had disembarked, Mary came for them. They emerged from the elevator and slipped down the jetway service stairs. With Mary's card, they entered without incident through a service personnel door, passing through the flight attendants' lounge, down another flight of concrete stairs and through the chaos of baggage handling. Since Mary knew many of the people in these behind-the-scenes areas, they moved quickly and without challenge. If anyone noticed them at all, they were thought to be passengers on an escorted search for lost luggage.

Mary brought them into the public space of the airport near Baggage Carousel 3, which was at the moment tumbling out luggage from an arriving flight from Chicago.

The area was a maelstrom of exhausted passengers, pushing and shoving, grabbing bags and wheeling carts, all eager to be out of the airport and into the southern Florida sunshine.

"This is it for me!" Mary said to Elizabeth and Peter. "You gonna be okay?"

"Thank you, Mary. Thank you so very much," Elizabeth said with tears in her eyes, giving Mary a quick hug. Then they were on their own, weaving through the crowd, heading for the door. Their clothes were still caked with dried mud, causing a few heads to turn.

"Try to smile," Peter said. "And make it look a little like we're together."

She said nothing.

In fact, the entire time they were threading through this massive airport, Elizabeth had ignored all of Peter's attempts to speak to her, pulling away even if their arms accidentally touched. But as they passed at last through the sliding doors into the humid Miami air, they saw three patrol cars pulling up at the curb not more than a hundred feet away. Uniformed officers began pouring out and Peter saw Elizabeth freeze. He eased up beside her, nudging her toward the taxi stand. This time she didn't recoil.

The line for taxis was six deep. Peter fished the last twenty out of his wallet and palmed it into the dispatcher's hand.

"Medical emergency," he explained to the other people waiting for cabs, silencing their instant barks of protest, and hustling Elizabeth inside. He hoped it was no more than a white lie, for during the last five minutes an optical migraine had been causing an ominous pressing in the lower margin of his visual field. As the cab slipped past the squad cars, Peter rolled a thumb and finger into his eyelids, trying to make the lights go away. Then Elizabeth spoke for the first time in a long, long while and her voice was unwittingly tender.

"Peter?" she said. "Are you okay?"

"I've been better," he said, and meant it.

"Are you sure?"

"Yes. But thank you for asking."

Their eyes met for an instant, then she looked away. But in that instant an immense amount of information was conveyed to Peter, although it was all still a jumble. There was hurt, anger, love and terror—all of it transmitted in that one moment. He hadn't felt so protective of anyone since the third year of his marriage when Beatrice had suffered a miscarriage and was thrown into a depression so profound that she didn't know whether she wanted to live or die.

He touched her hand. She didn't respond, but neither did she take it away. And Peter felt overwhelming love for her.

"As I said, Elizabeth, we may be stuck with each other for a while," he said, as their cab, just entering the Dolphin Expressway, passed a string of police cars and Army vehicles going in the opposite direction, roaring into the airport with sirens blaring and lights blazing.

They both fell silent, realizing both how close they had come to being trapped and how ferocious and far-reaching the search for them had become.

"What's that about, man?" the driver wanted to know. He was about forty-five, no taller than five feet, with a keloid scar bulging over his ear like a wad of bubble gum. His head was barely visible above the steering wheel.

"Damned if I know," said Peter.

The driver eyed them in the rearview mirror. "You guys look like you been out in the 'glades. Been hunting 'gators?"

"Just a filthy airplane. Don't every fly Air Guyana."

The driver barked out a laugh. "Hey, I get it. You holding any weed? You bring in a shipment of Marimba?" He was eyeing Elizabeth closely.

"No," she said. "But thanks for asking."

"We were doing some work in Cuba," said Peter, taking a flyer on the cabby's place of origin.

"No shit. What kind of work?"

"Well," said Peter, darting a look at Elizabeth, "let's say something for freedom. They shot down our plane."

"*No shit!* You with the guys who drop leaflets?"

"Something like that," said Peter. They were going to need all the help they could get.

"Right on, man!" the driver erupted, twisting around to shake Peter's hand. Peter took it quickly, eyeing the semi roaring by them six feet away.

"Mind your driving, now," he said.

The driver turned back to the road. "I knew those last guys who got shot down," he said, shaking his head. "Good family guys." He swerved through a tiny opening between two all-terrain vehicles, blasting his horn and shooting them dirty looks. "Bay of Pigs, man. I was just a kid, but I almost got my ass shot off. You know what I say? Good for you. Here, take my card. You ever need anything—a car, a little smoke—you give Ramón Martínez a call."

"How about a nice out-of-the-way hotel? Where we can sort of regroup for a while?"

"*No problema,* man." He rummaged through a tray of business cards and handed one back. To Peter's relief, Elizabeth took it. She was a participant in their flight now, no matter how conflicted about it she might be. He desperately needed her help, and even more desperately wanted her to accept him again, despite every justification for her not doing so. It looked very much like Wolfe and/or Henderson had pulled out all the stops on the hunt. Which meant that some sort of cover story had been concocted to explain the chase's urgency. Most likely it was something that made either him or both of them out to be a threat along the lines of the Unabomber Meets Patty Hearst. The migraine flicked heat lightning inside the lower rims of his eyeballs: he knew he could easily go down with a massive embolism at any moment. But he found he was much more terrified of losing Elizabeth.

By the time they reached the Rosaria Hotel in Coral Gables, Martínez had given them the address of all his favorite restaurants in Havana and the name of his uncle, a one-star general in the Cuban army.

"General Jesús Pinar del Río. He's plotting from the inside to get rid of the old *maricón,* you know what I mean? You need a ticket fixed, any other favor, he's good for it—just pick up the phone and give him a call. Jesús Pinar del Río, don't forget it." He shook both their hands and, refusing payment, drove off.

Peter booked them into adjoining rooms. Elizabeth accepted without comment.

His room was large enough for a bed, a Formica table and a television. The bathroom didn't even have a counter. Clearly the driver and the manager were family, but Peter didn't care. The place felt anonymous, permissive and for the moment—providing his cerebral vessels continued to function—relatively safe. He took a ten-minute shower, letting the hot water warm his skull and, with any luck, expand his blood vessels as well. It seemed to work. Feeling much better, even a little optimistic, he shaved with the Bic razor and lozenge of soap included in the hospitality pack.

He then picked up the phone and from memory dialed Beatrice's lab number. He was so relieved to hear it ring that his teeth began to chatter. Beatrice, I'm still alive, do you care?

There was no answer, and then came the little hiccup in the ring signaling that her voice mail was about to kick in. There was a good chance, he realized, that Henderson had installed a caller ID on the phone, so after listening to her outgoing message, simply to hear the sound of her voice, he put the phone back into its cradle.

Her message had not been altered and that disappointed him. Idiot, he thought, what did you expect? *Hi, if this is Peter calling, all is forgiven.* Even if she were having second thoughts, she wouldn't risk alerting Wolfe—she was too smart and cautious for that.

He sat for a few moments staring at the floor, lost in guilt and conflicted love, then knocked on the door between his room and Elizabeth's. A minute later she let him into her room. She had rinsed out her T-shirt and jeans and dried them with the hair-dryer. "I need to do some shopping," he said. "If you decide to take off, I only ask that you leave a note telling me that it was under your own steam. Not that you owe me such a consideration," he admitted, "but if I thought you might be coming back, I would probably wait for you until—"

"I'll go shopping with you," she said. Her mood was solemn and he sensed there was more she wanted to ask him. He hoped that somehow they would have time together again, but there wasn't that much room to maneuver. He figured they had bought twenty-four hours at most.

They took a cab through Coral Gables, past luxurious Mediterranean houses and manicured lawns. "One of America's first planned communities," the driver told them, mistaking them for tourists.

"We do not speak much English," Elizabeth replied in a preposterously thick Teutonic accent. Peter looked at her. She gave a faint shrug, as if to say "What the hell?"

Then in perfect American English, she turned to Peter. "What's your wife like, Peter?"

He was so taken aback he didn't reply at first.

"I know that's an industrial-size question," she admitted more gently.

His heart skipped a beat. "Beatrice is a force of nature," he said. "A wonderful woman."

"A scientist?"

"Neuroscientist."

"A doctor?"

"She has her M.D." They were passing a freshwater coral lagoon, the Venetian Pool. The driver decided to keep the sightseeing information to himself. He had already concluded that his passengers were having an illicit affair, and he wanted nothing more to do with them. He was a Fundamentalist Baptist and took sin seriously.

"What's she look like?"

Peter looked at her. She wasn't confrontational. She seemed simply curious. He sighed. "What's she look like? She's lovely. Beautiful. A handsome woman, I guess you would say." He was sorry he had added that. Patronizing bastard. The words felt like ashes in his mouth. "We've been married fifty years," he said, as if it mattered.

She took that in. "Fifty."

"Fifty last June."

"Are you still in love with her?" she asked, her voice trying to remain neutral.

He didn't hesitate to answer. "Yes."

"Good. Then do you think it's possible to love two people?" she asked. There was something edgy and accusatory in her tone, but also vaguely playful. Even her having brought up the subject made a certain mad hope spring up in his heart.

"Yes, apparently it's possible."

"You're not sure?"

"No, I am sure. I'm the perfect example. I love her, and I love you, that's all I know."

Elizabeth looked at him for a long time, then the cabby interrupted. They had arrived at their destination.

He had deposited them at the Miracle Mile shopping district. There they each bought enough clothes to last a week, and suitcases in which to carry them. Peter asked Elizabeth's advice on his purchases and she gave it sparingly, usually in a "yes" or "not a good idea" sort of way. Otherwise she went about her business silently. Peter bought shaving supplies, then found an ATM and maxed out his bank card for $300 in twenties. He found a sports store with a survivalist slant and bought a canister of mace and something called a Gerber/Applegate Combat Folder. The latter was a four-and-one-half-inch folding knife that opened with a thumb stud so it could be deployed, the term the clerk used, with one hand. Its handle was made of fiberglass-reinforced nylon, the rear forty percent of its edge was serrated, and it had an overall length, when opened, of ten and one quarter inches. According to the salesman, Ranger and Special Forces personnel, as well as police and game wardens, favored the Combat Folder. Peter bought it, struck by how easy it was to arm yourself in America, but comforted by that dark reality on this day.

His last purchase was made at an electronics store. He had found a set of Motorola citizen-band walkie-talkies. He figured if they were separated, they could keep track of each other. They were small enough to fit in the palm of his hand, and supposedly had a range of up to three miles.

Unfortunately there was, for the first time, a problem with his credit card.

"I've been using it a lot today," he said to the clerk. "It probably raised a flag. Let me talk to them."

The young man handed him the phone.

"Hello, this is Peter Jance."

"This is Peter Jance?" a man asked.

"Yes, I said it was."

"Are you doing an unusual amount of shopping?"

"Yes. We—I'm on vacation. It's quite all right. The card isn't stolen. Do you want to know my mother's maiden name?"

"We noticed that you purchased an item from Coral Gables Wilderness Inc. for ninety-five dollars," the voice said, ignoring Peter's question. "A Gerber/Applegate Combat Folder. Did you make that purchase?"

"Yes," said Peter. The hackles began to rise on his neck. "It's a pocketknife."

"*Combat* Folder, though."

"Yes, well, you know how they like to give fancy names to things these days."

"Do you know how to use it?"

"What?"

"Do you know how to use it?" the voice on the other end of the line repeated the question.

Peter felt a cold shudder shoot up his spine. The man's voice had taken on a harder, more mocking tone.

"Well," the man asked. "Do you?"

"Yes, I do," said Peter as firmly as possible.

"Good. You had better."

There was a pause and then a click. Peter swiveled around.

"Elizabeth!" he shouted. Absurdly, a line from Emily Post, a writer he had devoured at twenty-four when he had begun courting Beatrice, echoed in his mind. A gentleman never calls the name of his lady companion in public.

"*Elizabeth!*" he screamed again.

"Peter?"

He spun around. She was no more than ten yards away.

"Come on," he said. She saw the look on his face and took off with him as he ran out of the store and down the crowded sidewalk to the nearest pedestrian alley. Seconds after they were out of sight, a dark green Ford Bronco with smoked windows pulled to the curb outside Sunshine State Electronics. Five men in civilian dress who looked like military types charged into the shop. Peter and Elizabeth waited until they were out of view, then ran to the other end of the alley, coming out on SW 57th Avenue. Peter started to hail a licensed cab, but Elizabeth steered him toward a gypsy instead.

"No radio," she explained as they fell back onto its torn seats, out of breath. His head was pounding and he had to force himself to remain engaged with her. "Right. They'll call the cab companies."

She nodded. "Be on the lookout for two people wearing clothes that still have the price tags on them."

Peter checked his clothes. On the adjustment strap of his baseball cap, stamped "Gator Hunter," he actually did find a tag; he threw the cap out the window. The taxi was a block away by the time the Marine reinforcements swooped into the shop's perimeter, and completely out of the area before a chopper arrived to get a bigger view. Peter started to give the driver the name of their hotel, but Elizabeth stopped him.

"You paid by credit card," she said.

"You're right again," he said, head throbbing. She was taking charge now. It was as though she could sense his weakened state. In an agonized daze, he considered if that meant that she had decided her best chance for survival lay in sticking with him.

"Vieques," she said softly.

"I'm sorry?"

Her eyes were closed. "Just thinking out loud. The cloning experiments you mentioned. You said they were all conducted on Vieques?"

"I guess I did." He didn't really want to go through this again. "Why?"

"Just sorting through some memories." She looked at him and smiled. But her smile held a touch of acid. "And coincidences. The way we met at Phosphorescent Bay, for instance. Did I mention I dreamed of the place before I saw it? And El Fortín—I knew what it was without looking it up—same for the tree frogs. I didn't mention this?"

He smiled uneasily. "No, I don't think you did."

"And you know, of course, that my father might have been stationed in the Caribbean."

His rising panic was beginning to cloud his brain. "Really, Elizabeth, we should be thinking of how to get out of here. Do you have anyone you can wire for money to buy a couple of plane tickets?"

She looked at him and saw the pain. She got it. "Find a bank," she said to the driver. "And a phone booth."

The driver did both. With her travel bag weighted down with quarters, Elizabeth called Annie in Zurich. Peter stood outside the booth, keeping an eye out for soldiers and cops, but also trying to eavesdrop.

"—in deep shit, Annie," he heard her say. "Am I missing him? Not as much as I'd like to. Sorry to be so cryptic . . . Yeah, I guess it's fair to say I'm feeling awful . . . I hope you can help." He edged closer, but she caught the move and stood there with her eyes on him until he understood and moved well out of earshot.

Peter retreated to a pile of new tires chained to a sign. They were calling from a pay phone at a gas station and he idly watched the business come and go. A metallic taste was creeping into his mouth, either a herald of another mini-stroke or a symptom of his growing confusion. When his stomach growled, he realized that neither of them had eaten in twelve hours.

Finally she hung up. Smiling. They headed back to the mall.

"Mission accomplished?"

"Yes, thanks to Annie."

"Someone who's going to wire money?"

"To Home Savings."

"She must be a very good friend."

"My best in the world." Once inside, Elizabeth scanned the mall restaurants. "From before I had my accident," she added, almost without thinking.

"Your accident?"

"Not worth going into." She swept her hair back from her face. "Listen, do you want anything to eat while we're waiting? I could eat a horse. Or at least a burrito."

She gestured toward a nearby restaurant.

"Of course," he said, taking the rest of the quarters.

"And a Coke, if you would. I need to freshen up. I'll meet you there." She pointed to an empty table.

He bought two burritos, a lemonade and a Coke, swinging his body around as mall security walked past. The uniformed woman, bouncing along to the rap music booming from the mall's PA system, didn't appear to be on any sort of alert. Eventually she vanished into a video store. He bit into his burrito, enjoying the frank uncomplicated goodness of it, finishing it quickly. He also downed the lemonade. He was starting to worry about the pain behind his sternum—wondering whether it was acid reflux or his vagus nerve splices fraying—when he realized that almost twenty minutes had gone by and Elizabeth still hadn't returned. He took her Coke and burrito and went in search of the rest rooms.

The woman's room was open and empty.

For another twenty minutes he refused to face it. Like someone looking for a lost wallet, he kept returning to the same places over and over again, until finally the woman from mall security started to get suspicious.

You knew this had to happen, he told himself, as he turned and walked toward a waiting taxi. But why now? Something was making him stupid, he thought, and then he revised that to conclude that he couldn't blame anything but himself. He *was* stupid. The loss of Elizabeth, the plaque in his cerebral arteries, the accumulation of guilt and suppressed panic washing over him was like the panic of someone coming off hard drugs and suddenly facing years of pain.

What had Beatrice taught him to call this? The rebound effect. Yes, that was it. A sense of black doom descended like a summer storm. He felt like he was six years old again.

He took a cab back to the Rosaria Hotel, and while he was packing, he saw a patrol car pull into the parking lot. Quickly finding the fire stairs, he left by the back entrance. He hailed another cab and asked the driver to take him to the nearest phone booth, which turned out to be out near the Dixie Highway. After instructing the driver to wait, he took what was left of the quarters and dropped one into the pay phone. Again he dialed the number from memory.

A recorded voice came on and announced that it was a long-distance call—$3.35 for the first three minutes and $1.05 for each additional minute. He went back to the driver to break a twenty and ended up taking all the small change the man had for an extra five dollars. Back in the booth, he dialed the cellular number. There were some electronic hems and haws, and then a voice picked up.

"Hello?"

"Hello, Beatrice," he said.

There was a brain-numbing silence on the other end. Sweat sprang out on his forehead. Then her voice came back.

"Peter?"

"Yes, it's me. Are you alone?"

"Yes."

He wondered if it were true. Probably not.

"Where are you?" she asked.

"Where are *you*?"

"Miami. Peter, if you're here in the city, you're in terrible danger."

"Believe me, I know that. Are you all right? I tried to call you at the lab . . ."

"Yes. I'm all right."

"Thank God. Listen," he started to say and then found he couldn't go on. Tears filled his eyes.

"I know why you're calling."

"Then tell me."

"She left you."

"That's not why. I need to see you," he said.

"Does she know now?"

"I had to tell her."

"You had to tell her what?"

Why was she being so obtuse? "Everything," he said.

"Everything? Are you sure?" Her voice carried an odd teasing quality. "And just how did she take it?"

"Not well. How did you expect her to take it?" he said, heartened by the fact that they were at least sparring once more. "I've missed you, Beatrice."

"No, you only think you have."

"Have it your way. I'm sorry. However you want to make me pay—"

"You've had me, Peter. The whole time."

He stopped, took a deep breath.

"Beatrice, you're not making any sense—"

"Just not to you. You were always a beat behind. Like Einstein baffled by his tax returns. Tell me, darling, do you know how to travel through time?"

Darling, was all he could think. Otherwise he was utterly lost.

"Do you think," he heard her say, "you can get back to the summer of '67?"

"Beatrice, my head hurts."

"I know. Just get on the time machine. Someone will meet you, I promise." Her voice went away and came back, this time very loud. "I'm sorry, I don't respond to telephone solicitations," she said into the phone. "How did you get this number, anyway?"

"Beatrice, did someone come in? Freddy? Henderson?"

"And, no," she said, softly again, "I don't forgive you for a minute. Goodbye, darling, and happy landings. Goodbye, goodbye, goodbye."

The summer of '67 had been their first at Vieques. Whenever they wanted to get away from the base or from Freddy or from the burdens of uneasy conscience, Peter and Beatrice would fly to Miami, rent a car and drive the causeway to Key West. It was Key West where they had discovered deep-sea fishing, tantric sex and French cooking. To Peter and Beatrice, Key West was Paradise Regained.

Key West. It hit him like a thunderbolt that that was where she wanted him to go. Key West was where she was waiting for him. Unless, of course, it was a trap.

If it were a trap, then Beatrice had deeper reserves of hatred than he had ever dared guess, more guile than Machiavelli and a real shot at an acting career. What he had heard in her voice was tender condescension and wifely disapproval, not anger. Nor the sound of a woman scorned. She had more the sound of a woman in control. It occurred to him that kind of control could be deadly.

No. She's not going to betray me, he thought. No matter what I deserve.

Still, as the cab rolled down Route 1, he kept turning to look out the back window while he listened for the sound of choppers. And he replayed their phone conversation in his head, over and over. *I told Elizabeth everything.* She might well have passed that along to Wolfe and Henderson. What, after all, did she owe Elizabeth? There Beatrice might prove vindictive, and who could blame her? He had hurt her terribly. He had thrown her over for someone else, someone young like his new self. Fifty years of marriage, and nothing they had built together had withstood the imperatives of newfound youth. That's how she would see it.

But would she want Elizabeth dead?

She had been in collusion when it came to the death of Hans, he reminded himself. She had agonized over it, yes, no question, but in the end, she had approved it. The greatest good for the greatest number. Genius conquers all. Moral piracy, that's what it amounted to, but she had gone for it. Or had she seen that by now? In what he knew any hack psychiatrist would diagnose as obsessive ruminations, he passed through Key Largo, Islamorada, Layton, Key Colony Beach. Somewhere around Marathon or Big Pine he fell into a troubled sleep, dreaming of his wife as a Janus-faced monster, one face young and dismissive, the other smiling and old. Then it was the young face that was tender and the older that of Medusa. The next thing he knew the driver was shaking him and they were at Truman and Duval, in the heart of Key West.

"Where you wanna go, buddy?" the cabby asked.

Peter sat up and rubbed his eyes.

"You know the Café des Artistes?"

"Over on Simonton?"

"That's the one."

He had the driver drop him a block away and approached the place cautiously on foot. Just short of it he stopped. Should he chance it or phone the restaurant from outside? Navy men were going in and out, but they were in uniform and mostly with wives or girlfriends; the people looking for him would be dressed in civilian clothing. Or would they be? He reminded himself that there were several bases here, so the presence of military was no particular cause for concern, in or out of uniform. Besides, the look of the place reeked of intrigue. It was part of an old hotel and was supposedly built in 1934 by Al Capone himself. No wonder Peter was paranoid. He wondered why he and Beatrice had found it so inviting before. More innocent days, perhaps.

He went inside, inquiring at the desk if a Beatrice Jance had arrived.

The desk clerk informed him that she had checked in that morning.

His heart was in full gallop by the time he located the house phones and rang her room. There was no answer. On an impulse, he walked back through the ornate lobby to the restaurant.

The floor tilted under his feet.

He ignored that. Looked around.

And there she was, eating quietly at their favorite table. In that room, sitting amid flowers and paintings by Key West artists and set off by the room's dark woods and linen-covered walls, she was stunning, set like a jewel in his memory. It was as though he had simply returned from one of his solitary walks along the shrimp-boat docks—thirty years ago—to meet her for lunch. Even the Rameau harpsichord suite playing on the stereo, he remembered that too.

"Beatrice?"

She looked up in alarm. "Good Lord, you've lost your mind completely."

Her gray hair was tied in a chignon and she was wearing a loose-fitting beach dress with an orchid print. She looked casually wan and worn and entirely wonderful. "May I sit down?"

She studied his face as though she had forgotten it. "What if I'm being watched? Hasn't that occurred to you?"

"Are you?"

"If they were triangulating my cellular."

"Do they have reason to distrust you?"

"No," she said, and relaxed ever so slightly. "They think I want you six feet under. Jack?"

A waiter scurried over.

"Yes, Mrs. Jance," he said with a Georgia drawl.

"We need to move up to the deck," she said. "It's more private there."

The man glanced at Peter. "I understand."

"Jack, really. This is my son, Peter Junior." She said it so easily that

Peter was caught completely off-guard. He realized she had given more thought to this meeting than he had imagined. Jack, examining Peter through half-closed lids, gave a gasp of delight.

"He looks just like his father!"

"Spitting image, isn't he?" said Beatrice. "He's dead."

"Oh my God. I'm so sorry, Mrs. Jance."

"Don't be. It was a mercy, really."

"I see."

"Senile dementia," she said, shooting a glance at Peter, then gathering her things.

"But thank you so much for your concern, Jack," she said warmly and led the way upstairs and outside.

The deck portion of the restaurant was open to the sky. There was a balmy breeze, the sound of cicadas and few customers this hour. Beatrice chose a table where they could watch the street. Or be watched, thought Peter, despite the emotions that were churning in his heart. Puppy love, it almost felt like, like they were starting all over again. And then he remembered feeling the identical thing for Elizabeth. His head began to swim.

"Well, son," said Beatrice wryly, "you've been a busy boy, haven't you?"

At least, he thought, she isn't smoking. The ashtray on the table downstairs had been empty. No more of Wolfe's damn Gauloises. "It's been interesting," was all he could say. He felt like reaching across the table for her hand, but he knew she would draw it away.

"Don't look at me so moon-eyed," she said, confirming his guess. "The last thing I want is to look like some dowager who's bought a surfer for the weekend."

After his wine arrived, she raised her glass to him slightly and took a thoughtful sip. "So," she said at last. "Now she's left you."

"She disappeared. I suppose you could say she left me," said Peter.

"That's what *I* would call it if *my* lover disappeared." She took out a pack of Gauloises and removed one. His heart sank. "On the other hand, at least it made you call me. You wouldn't have otherwise, I'm sure."

"Beatrice, that isn't true. All the time I was with her—"

"—you were thinking of me? I'm sure you were." She shrugged. "Sorry. It's just that on one level, that's utter nonsense." She looked off, checking the street, then said, "But on another, it's utterly plausible."

She looked at the cigarette, then took the pack of Gauloises and dropped it and the cigarette into the ashtray, moving both to another table. Peter looked at her, but she revealed nothing more.

Jack brought a second menu and a bottle of wine that Beatrice had ordered. It was a cabernet Peter loved. The label had changed slightly over the years, but the memories were still vivid of the times they had gone through a bottle of that wine talking about everything under the stars. When the waiter was gone, Peter leaned across the table.

"Beatrice," he said. "I beg your forgiveness."

"Don't grovel," she said. "Let me think."

He sat back again, this time at a more respectful distance.

When they had ordered, Beatrice fixed her eyes on him. In the glare of her disapproval, he drank his glass of wine down straight and poured himself another.

"You know, sonny boy, that they're planning to kill you on sight?"

"I guessed as much. And ixnay on the onnysay, all right?" The wine was quickly going to his head.

"Alex ran the models and the Hammer looks good to go. They've already started construction back at White Sands."

"Alex is back?" said Peter in disbelief.

"That was the last thing he did before he left. Where he is now, who knows—they're still looking for him, too." She studied him for a moment, then asked: "Tell me, do you love her, Peter?"

"Could we do this down at police headquarters?" he asked defensively. She didn't smile. He shrugged. "Yes, all right, I was infatuated."

"Fickle, aren't you? Frankly, Peter, I'm disappointed. Just infatuated? With her body or her mind?"

"Both," he said angrily. "And it wasn't just infatuation. I loved her. I still do, I think. It's crazy, but it's something much more than infatuation. She knew this body and this body knew her. Do you have any idea of what I'm saying?"

"I'm afraid I do. And thank you for your honesty," she said, and she drank deeply. He refilled her glass.

"You mustn't blame her," he said. "She was in love with Hans Brink-man."

"Spoken like a true man. And what's your excuse?" Since he didn't have one, he said nothing and reached for his glass. Except . . . "Do you remember your research on cellular memory?" he asked.

"Oh, spare me."

"I'm not making excuses. But I think you were on to something."

"You're leaning on a thin reed here."

"I flew a plane. You know I don't know the first thing about flying." He saw she was listening despite herself. "But Hans did. He was a pi-lot, he was skilled at martial arts, he apparently even *liked* to mix it up. You heard about the fight at the hotel, I'm sure."

She nodded, not wanting to give this any credence. But she *had* heard, and every time she had looked at that killer who followed Henderson around, she wondered how Peter could ever have taken him on.

"Answer me this—did you ever in your life see me punch anybody out?"

"At the Nobel dinner. When that little Croatian chemist started needling you."

"I was drunk."

"You're drunk now. Are you saying the devil made you do it?"

"No, I'm not. Unless we've met the devil and he is us. All I'm really saying is that she was blameless. As soon as I told her who I was, she left."

"That's not the only reason why she took off," Beatrice said crypti-cally.

He put his glass down and glared at her. "Beatrice, if you've got some information I should know, tell me, don't torture me!"

"You deserve to be tortured. You're a prick. A superficial, self-justifying, pompous asshole—"

He threw up his hands. Guilty as charged. Peter stared back at the people now staring at them.

"Sorry. Lovers' quarrel."

Everyone looked from Peter to Beatrice, shook their heads and went back to their dinners. Beatrice's face colored.

"Very funny," she said without smiling. She waited while another waiter scurried up and delivered their food, then leaned forward again. "Where do you think she went?"

"I'm not sure, but I'd guess she's making a run for Zurich. Direct flight, I would think, so she won't risk another stop on American soil."

"Which means she'll have to fly out of Miami. We should stop her."

"If she wants to go, it's her decision."

"She doesn't know half the danger she's in," Beatrice said solemnly, "or she wouldn't have taken off on her own."

"I tried to explain," Peter said. "But she's damn near as stubborn as you are."

"Just as, I'd guess," said Beatrice strangely. "They're not going to kill her, you know. Not exactly."

He was starting to feel a deeper terror than usual.

"You're worried about her?"

"We need her help, actually, as much as she needs ours," she said enigmatically, wearing a look that told him nothing except that he knew even less than he thought.

"Why do we need her help?"

"Because we need to find the ninth clone."

Peter let out an audible gasp. "*Ninth?*"

"They're about to harvest him. And I really don't think we want that to happen, do we?"

"So I was what? The eighth?" He could only stare at her, stupefied.

"You were the seventh, Peter," she said, and gave him a haunted look: "Seven was the lucky number."

His head spun. "And the first six?"

She looked away. "They didn't make it. My glue took a long while to get right."

He shuddered. All those years—how naive he had been. Neither his wife of half a century nor his friends nor the true nature of his work had been really known by him.

"The first four died on the table," she went on. "The next one survived the transplant, but suffered brain death. They pulled the plug on that one, which was Barrola's, incidentally."

Peter's eyes grew wider still. He couldn't talk.

"Barrola went into clinical depression. You never noticed, of course. You always wore blinders when it came to other people's moods."

He tried to catch his breath. Some terrible fear was working its way up his gut. "That's five. Number six?"

"He died during transport." Beatrice gathered her sweater around her shoulders. Peter noticed that he felt chilled as well. "Remember," she asked, "that midair collision over Vieques two years ago?"

He remembered. "The two business jets?"

"That's the one. One plane hadn't logged a flight plan, so the other didn't know to look out for it."

"One was bringing in a clone?" he asked, as it all began to dawn on him. "Whose was it, do you know?"

"Moore's."

"The chemist working on the so-called Death Aerosol?"

"That's him. He died of heart failure shortly thereafter. Or maybe a broken heart. Everyone who lost his clone had a hard time with it. Their immortality was almost in their hands and then it ran out through their fingers. And then there was you and yours. Hans Brinkman. And success."

He looked down, ashamed to be part of such a cynical thing. "And the next one?"

"He lives in New York."

"State?"

"City. Where, I don't know."

"New York's a big place, Beatrice. Eight or ten million people. Who told you all this—Wolfe?"

"Correct."

Peter had known. "He's in love with you, isn't he?"

"Grotesquely."

Peter reached across the table again and this time she allowed him to take her hands in his. Her hands were icy. Despite the stares from nearby tables, he continued to hold his wife's hands. "And you were faithful to me," he said.

"And you were faithful to me," said Beatrice matter-of-factly. "In your fashion." Taking her hands from his, she tapped him lightly on the wrist. "Nine clones, Peter." She stared at him until it finally struck him.

He took a deep breath, feeling like a kid tipping over the brim of the highest roller coaster ever built, half-exhilarated, half-terrified.

"Holy Christ," he said under his breath.

"Welcome to the new millennium."

"But it's not . . . possible . . ."

"You of all people should know that anything is possible."

"I would have recognized her—she would have looked exactly like . . ."

"Like me. That's right. She did. Until she was eighteen. Then she had a skiing accident. Destroyed her face. Next came plastic surgery. New cheekbones, new nose, everything. And of course they always do the lips these days, it's practically a default option. I'm a little surprised you didn't recognize the body, but she might have had other things done as well. In for a penny, in for a pound."

"It was her voice, Beatrice. And her eyes. They were yours. Even the love I felt, for godsakes."

"I'd like to think so." She smiled sadly. "Actually, when I look at it from a certain perspective, I almost feel flattered. If I tried, I suppose I could even take some vicarious pleasure in your affair."

"God in heaven," he groaned. The car was over the brink and hurling down a bottomless track. "Do you think she *knows?*"

"She's not stupid," she said proudly. "If she doesn't yet, she'll piece it together soon enough. Did she tell you her father was in the Navy? Caribbean duty?"

"On Vieques?" he asked, reeling.

"For a full two years."

He rubbed his eyes. "So they'll be looking for her for . . ." He looked at Beatrice, not wanting to believe he was thinking what he was thinking.

"For me," Beatrice said simply. "We want to have us both, Peter?"

"Oh, Jesus." He put his head in his hands. "We can't do that, Beatrice."

"You, but not me? Is that it?"

When he looked up there were tears in his eyes.

"Because it's not right."

She stared at him long and hard, and then slipped her hand into his again.

"Thank God," she said. "Now do you see why we have to find her? In a way, she's the child we never had."

She signaled for the check.

"But if you don't go back to Wolfe—"

"He needs us both. His gamble, I'm guessing, is that I'd change my mind once I was young again. There is some precedent to support that theory," she said with only partial irony. "But since I am marginally a better person than you are," she added, her smile warming slightly, "I don't think I'll stay with the program. You wouldn't happen to know Elizabeth's e-mail password?"

"No," said Peter. "That intimate we didn't get."

He cupped her hands in his and kissed them. An enormous burden had been lifted from his heart. For a few precious moments, the fear could wait. And then there was a long and fast drive to make it back to Miami.

The smart thing, Elizabeth reasoned, was not to go to the airport until she absolutely had to. She needed to clear her head big-time, so when the driver cut through Little Havana, she told him to let her off at one of the coffee stands that line Calle Ocho. She ordered the strongest coffee available and the clerk gave her a colada, straight espresso laced with sugar. To his amazement, she downed it straight off and ordered another.

The place was vibrant with pleasant noise, as though her caffeine buzz had gone to everyone's heads. Cigarette smoke floated in the air, along with the sounds of Cuban Spanish and the recitation of baseball scores. For the first time in a very long while, she felt safe.

She looked out the shop window into the morning haze and saw workers and commuters rushing past, most Hispanic or black. How many wars, how many enslavements and horrors had these people or their gene pools survived? And now they were talking and laughing and going on with their lives.

You'll survive this, too, she said, emptying her tray into the trash bin and hurrying outside.

She hailed a taxi for Miami International.

In the cab, she put on sunglasses and a black wig she had bought for $50 at a store called Wig City in a strip mall.

The size of Miami International Airport was another comfort. It was the eighth largest airport in the U.S., Mary Blanchard had told her: 1,500 takeoffs and landings a day, with connections to 2,200 cities on five continents. She remembered those numbers as if Mary had just whispered them in her ear.

Game theory, hadn't Hans given her a lecture about that once? The hugeness of Miami International, plus the likelihood that they wouldn't expect her to exit from the same place she had entered the day before. Thirty million passengers per year equals 82,000 a day; 118 gates in eight concourses, versus say two hundred available surveillance personnel. Hell, the odds were excellent that she wouldn't be spotted.

But she was.

As she took the elevator to the fourth floor and stepped onto the horizontal escalator, she became convinced she was being followed—flurries of footsteps as she passed through the maze of bookstores, bars and boutiques seemed somehow to be matching her own. To reach the Martinair/KLM counter in Concourse B, she had to go halfway around the gigantic horseshoe that constituted the architectural footprint of the airport. She stopped at a sunglass kiosk and tried on a pair of Ray-Bans, examining herself in the rack's tiny mirror. In its reflection, she saw three people behind her who were more or less frozen in position. One was a man about twenty-five, with well-trimmed, sandy hair. He was tying his shoelaces. The second was an airline flight officer or a man dressed as one, who glanced once in Elizabeth's direction and then looked away. The third was a hard-bodied young woman in a track suit, with a bright duffel bag slung over her shoulder. With a weapon in it?

Elizabeth carefully replaced the Ray-Bans and moved to the newsstand where she bought a *Miami Herald*. While waiting for her change she did a quick recheck. The pilot and the muscular young woman were gone, but the man who had been tying his shoelaces was still there, a hundred feet back, pretending to study a departure monitor.

She lost herself by threading through the crowded lobby of the in-terminal hotel, emerging back on the concourse at its opposite end. She hooked a left, took the escalator down a floor, then walked rapidly for a full five minutes without looking back.

At last, near her gate, she stopped in front of a Starbucks window. Carefully scanning the reflections in the glass, she found the man in the crowd. And since her back was turned, he was staring straight at her.

Her throat clenched shut. It was the Navy Seal from the Casa del Francés. And he was now moving toward her. Fighting raw panic, she headed off as fast as she could without drawing attention. Then she heard his running footsteps behind her and broke into a sprint.

He was fast, but she was faster.

In twenty seconds of flat-out running, she had built up a good enough lead to be able to vanish from his sight and into the crowd.

Lieutenant Lance Russell barreled around a corner and braked in alarm.

The bitch wasn't there.

He had spotted her easily enough. Who did she think she was, anyway, thinking she could fool anybody with the black dye-job? But for the moment, she was off the scope.

Worse, an airport security asshole was heading in his direction. Russell ducked into a souvenir shop, trying to control his breathing. Fuck, he thought, the cop had seen him come around that corner at warp speed and had to know something was up.

Russell was more right than he knew: the security guard had, in fact, been told to watch out for a certain Dr. Peter Jance, Jr., age thirty-five. Since this guy with the buzz-cut and pale blue eyes was about that age, the guard popped the thumb strap on his holster and advanced.

"Can I see your ticket, sir?"

I can't catch a break, thought Russell. On an assignment like this, he never carried ID, not even counterfeit ID, and the gate agent who had passed him through the metal detectors was nowhere in sight. His designation was secret and if taken into custody he was expected to remain silent and use his one telephone call to summon help from a properly equipped Naval Security officer. At this badly fucked point in time he couldn't afford to be detained. "I'm meeting someone," he said, and moved away from the shop's entrance.

"I would like to see some kind of ID," the security guard insisted, coming closer, his hand closing around the butt of his 9mm.

Russell smiled broadly as though he were about to comply, but then casually stepped through a door into the men's room. One of the stalls was occupied, but otherwise the place was deserted. As the angered security guard bolted in after him Russell wheeled and struck out with the heel of his hand, driving it upward into the man's chin, dislocating his jaw and knocking him unconscious.

For an instant Russell contemplated killing him, but he decided that the uproar following the discovery of the body would sooner or later come back and bite him on the ass. And so he merely dragged the guard into a stall and slung him upright onto a toilet. He locked the stall from the inside, and then launched himself off the toilet tissue dispenser and vaulted the door, landing an instant before a man in a business suit entered, dragging his wheeled carry-on. Russell walked past him and reentered the concourse. He now had a good idea where the girl had disappeared.

The ladies' room was thirty feet down the corridor. A cleaning lady and her partner were just coming out, pushing their trash cart and a mop bucket on casters. Russell stepped in front of them.

"Miami Health Department. Anybody in there?"

"It's clean," said the lady. "We just clean."

Dumb Guatemalan, she was petrified. "Gotta check it, though. City Code. Anybody in there?"

"One lady."

"She doing important business or just hanging out?"

"Looking in the mirror, washing her hands, looking around. She looked scared."

Good, thought Russell. He liked fear in the eyes of his quarry just before he put them down, and this cunt was owed. His only regret was that he had orders not to kill her. His mandate was to simply keep her from getting on the plane until Wolfe and Henderson arrived. That didn't mean he couldn't hit her. He would just say she put up a fight.

He found a crumpled five in his pocket.

"You keep any ladies from coming in for a few minutes, okay? Just till I do my look-see for the City of Miami."

The cleaning women exchanged glances as the older one took the money.

Russell went inside.

It was larger than the men's room, divided into two sub-areas, one containing stalls, the other sinks, a bench and a baby-changing table. As he entered, he heard one of the stall doors clank shut. He had a clear image of the girl crouched inside, pissing her pants. If she were clever, and he knew she thought she was, she was probably standing on top of the toilet lid, holding her breath, praying he wouldn't do more than look under the stalls from the outside.

She was in for a big surprise.

Slipping his knife from its shoulder sheath, he laid it along his pants leg and eased around the corner into the area where the toilets were.

She wasn't in a stall, though. She was standing before a mirror straightening her skirt. There was something wrong here. As the woman turned around, Russell saw what it was.

"Well," said Beatrice. "Did you take courses in stupidity or were you dumb enough when you enlisted?"

"Ma'am, I'm sorry—"

"Put that knife away before you hurt somebody. Do you understand your assignment or don't you?"

"Yes, ma'am, of course I do."

"She is not to be physically harmed. In any way."

"Yes, well, I've just found the knife to be a good persuader." But he put it away anyway.

"And what if she started screaming?"

"I know how to deal with that, ma'am. We're trained in abduction; otherwise I wouldn't have been assigned to find her. The fact is, ma'am, I made her five minutes ago, and I thought she came in here."

"Hardly. I just saw her walk right down the jetway at Gate 15."

"Beg pardon, ma'am, but why didn't you tell somebody?"

Beatrice's withering look was all the answer Russell needed as he raced out of the ladies' room in a blind fury. Even the cleaning ladies were gone, not watching his back as he had fucking paid them to do. He pulled out his radio and called for backup. Okay, so forget about getting the collar himself; he just wanted to see the bitch in cuffs now.

He careened down the jetway to Gate 15 as more men appeared, running toward the gate. Within sixty seconds, the plane was under siege, with a half-dozen Seals searching it from nose to tail. If necessary, their orders were to go into the baggage and wheel wells.

Meanwhile, María Morales and Elena Contrares—close friends since they had shared a van with fifteen other weeping and terrified illegal immigrants from El Salvador eight years before—stopped at the first-level service bay, just as they had been instructed. During twenty years of having lived in a war zone, they had seen their share of strangeness. They had seen even more the next year while they worked their way north through Guatemala and the mountains of Mexico.

But never had they been asked to do anything so crazy for money, and certainly not by a lady so elegant. A hundred dollars! In America, madness seemed to trickle down from the top. The classy lady was right behind them, having hitched a ride on one of the electric carts reserved for the aged and the handicapped.

"*Hay otras aquí, amigas?*" she asked, as she stepped off the cart, patting a strand of gray hair into place.

"No," they said.

"*Bueno,*" said Beatrice, giving the trash barrel a whack. "All right, end of the line, it's safe."

The paper towels stirred as Elizabeth emerged from the barrel, stunned and grateful, but certainly on guard. "Thank you," she said to Beatrice as María and Elena helped her out.

"Don't mention it," Beatrice replied. "Haven't had so much fun since menopause."

"Who are you?"

"I'm the lady who just saved your life," said Beatrice, regretting the resentment and suspicion in her own voice. Was this kid going to recognize herself or not? She's had her new face for seven years, thought Beatrice. Is it possible she's forgotten the old one or is it so bad she can't recognize herself in such an older version? Maybe she was just plain thick. "Come on, we'll talk in the cab," she said. When Elizabeth hesitated, Beatrice gave her a maternal glare. "Or should we wait until they seal off the airport again?"

Beatrice paid Elena and María another fifty dollars, then made for the taxi stand with Elizabeth following at a wary distance. "Why are you doing this?"

"Because I want you to live," said Beatrice. "Is that a good enough reason? You do have friends in the world."

"Annie? Did she send you?"

"No. Not Annie, whoever that is." Good Lord, she thought, is she faking it or has some of Peter's obtuseness rubbed off on her? She was starting to picture Peter and Elizabeth together and was having trouble not hating her, despite the sympathy she felt for the girl's plight. And the guilt, of course. Would she ever be free of that?

The door to the cab was open, but Elizabeth was still balking. "I think I need to know who you are."

"You'll figure it out. Now get in," said Beatrice sharply, grabbing Elizabeth and shoving her inside. "And if I were you, I'd duck down." This time Elizabeth did as she was told, slumping below window level as the cabby gunned the car out of the airport.

Once they were on the expressway, Elizabeth sat back up and stared at Beatrice. Beatrice did her best not to stare back. I certainly would have known myself, Beatrice thought. In a heartbeat.

"Where are we going?" Elizabeth asked.

"I was thinking of Disney World," Beatrice said.

"Last time I checked," said Elizabeth, "they didn't give discounts anymore for fugitives."

Confident, sardonic—you might even end up liking this woman, Beatrice thought. And wouldn't Narcissus be green with envy? "Yes, well that's true, I suppose. Driver, take the next turnout."

The cabby swung into an emergency pull-off and sounded the horn. "It's all right," Beatrice said as she saw Elizabeth tighten. "We're just picking up another passenger."

The driver peered into the shrubbery ringing the turnout. "*Señora*, are you sure this is where we left him?"

"I'm sure." Elizabeth looked ready to bolt. Beatrice put a steadying hand on her wrist while the cabby got out and stepped over the guardrail.

"*Señor?*" he called.

Since there was no answer, the driver jumped the rail and disappeared into the bushes. Elizabeth was starting to squirm in Beatrice's grip.

"What the hell is this?" Elizabeth demanded.

"Hold steady," said Beatrice. Her heart was starting to sink.

"Who *are* you? You've got to tell me or I'm leaving."

Beatrice kept her eyes on the shrubbery. "My name is Beatrice Jance."

Elizabeth's face turned ashen.

"Your lover's wife—or rather your former lover. You left him, I got him back."

Elizabeth's head sank onto her chest as she covered her face. "Oh my God—"

"—And I suppose I'm also your . . . I don't know quite how to put it—"

Elizabeth peered deep into Beatrice's eyes. And there was the look of terrified, stunned recognition.

"Oh my God," she said.

"Close enough," said Beatrice.

Beatrice started to say something else, then stiffened, letting go of Elizabeth's arm as she threw open the door and stumbled out. Beyond, the driver was carrying somebody out of the bushes, somebody drunk or wounded or worse. Then Elizabeth was out of the cab, too.

Elizabeth could easily have escaped at that moment, but she ran with Beatrice to Peter, whose eyes were closed and whose shirt was stained red. Together they helped support his deadweight. Blood was trickling from his mouth and nose, and his chest was heaving. He seemed barely alive.

"Peter?" Elizabeth said numbly. Only a slurred response. She looked at Beatrice in terror. "It's happening again."

"When did this happen before?"

"Once back in Vieques and then again at the airport in Puerto Rico. But never like this."

"He never bled?" said Beatrice, icy calm.

"Never."

"Was his pulse elevated? Were his pupils dilated?"

Elizabeth took Peter's main weight and eased him into the back of the cab. "I'm not a doctor," she said through clenched teeth.

"Yes, of course you're not," said Beatrice, climbing in.

"And I didn't have anything to do with what made him like this either," Elizabeth said, more pointedly. Beatrice said nothing to that.

"Go on," she said to the driver. "I-95 North."

The car shot forward and Peter's head lolled onto the frayed tweed seat, looking in his delirium as if he were trying to listen to both of them, Beatrice on his left, Elizabeth on his right.

"The first time he kind of glazed over," Elizabeth said more softly, as the cab knifed through traffic. "Then in Puerto Rico, when we were running away from the plane crash, he had a horrendous pain in his head and collapsed. Is it some kind of stroke?"

"Something like that." And then Beatrice's voice softened too. "God knows."

"The blood vessels in his brain, they're still old?"

"Exactly," said Beatrice.

Peter's eyes blinked open. Abruptly he was conscious, though thoroughly dazed. "Very astute," he slurred.

"Thank you," Elizabeth said coldly.

She took a Kleenex and swiped the blood from the corner of his mouth. Peter gave Elizabeth an unreadable look, then swung toward Beatrice.

"You okay?" He reached out awkwardly for his wife's face, nearly poking her in the eye. "Sorry."

"That's all right. I'm fine. How do you feel?"

"With my fingers."

"That's quite frontal-lobish. What's your name?"

"Peter Brinkman."

Beatrice glanced at Elizabeth. "He's all yours," she said. Peter flopped his head over and studied Elizabeth, as if seeing her for the first time.

"Elizabeth?" he said foggily. "You're back?"

Elizabeth jerked her head at Beatrice. "Your wife came and got me."

"Beatrice?" His face twisted in disbelief.

"That's right, Peter," said Beatrice.

"Peter," he repeated.

"And Peter who?" she demanded.

"Peter Jance," he said.

"And you do know who I am?"

"My better half?" he said, looking at Elizabeth for confirmation.

"You're damn right, you old goat," said Beatrice. "How many fingers?" she asked, holding up her hand spread wide.

"Four."

"Try again."

"Four. The other one's a thumb."

He gave a sly, crooked grin. She gave him a shove. "Very funny. Now stop scaring the bejesus out of both of us."

"I scared the shit out of myself," he said solemnly, sitting up and shaking his head. He seemed to be getting more and more lucid. Turning to Elizabeth, he asked if she was okay.

Elizabeth shrugged, holding back tears.

"They almost had her," said Beatrice.

"Is that a fact? See, I said you were better off with us, Elizabeth," Peter said.

"You never said 'us.'"

"I didn't know at the time. So Beatrice saved your life?"

"She has reason to, doesn't she?"

Peter looked at Beatrice. "I told you she would be suspicious."

"She has good reason to be," said Beatrice, echoing Elizabeth's phrase and waving a hand at her. She was actually starting to like this kid. "You can give Hans a hug," Beatrice said. "Just keep your hands off Peter."

"Thank you, I'll pass."

"Up to you," said Beatrice.

The cab swung up the ramp toward I-95. After a moment, Elizabeth turned to Beatrice again, peering right past Peter.

"What did you mean, 'of course I'm not a doctor'?"

"I shouldn't have said that."

"You shouldn't have. You're like those mothers who can bake pies and like it when their daughters can't."

"I couldn't bake a pie to save my life," Beatrice said quietly. "And I bet you would make a crackerjack doctor."

"Did I miss something?" Peter asked.

"Be still," Beatrice said.

She and Elizabeth stared at each other until it seemed silly to continue, and then they all fell silent.

When the cab pulled into Fort Lauderdale/Hollywood International Airport thirty minutes later, they had dressed Peter in a new shirt and had cleaned him up sufficiently so as not to draw attention to themselves. He was weak but alert, and after ditching the Combat Folder and the can of mace Peter had bought in Coral Gables, they all three caught Delta Airlines Flight 406 to New York without incident.

Airborne and eavesdropping on their flight attendants, they learned why their escape had been so easy. A security guard at Miami International had been found half-strangled in a men's room, victim of an apparent terrorist attack, and all extra security at Fort Lauderdale International had been pulled to the site for support.

DELTA FLIGHT 406

The Boeing 767 was only half-full; they were able to find three seats together in the rear, away from the other passengers. For the first thirty minutes, Peter was on edge, half-expecting a tap on his shoulder from a flight attendant.

"He's always been a little jumpy," Beatrice said to Elizabeth. "When we were young and poor, we used to slip into theater lobbies at intermission, then sneak in for the second act. Peter was always sure we'd be hauled off to jail."

"Yes, and one time they did kick us out," Elizabeth said, drawing from an unexpected memory of the usher's hand on her elbow.

Beatrice blinked. "Once," she said carefully. "Some boorish usher who was out to prove something. Once out of ten times." She couldn't go on talking as if it were simple chatter. The girl's memory had profoundly startled her. "Peter, dear, why don't you sit by the window? Elizabeth and I need to have some girl talk."

Peter dutifully got up and exchanged places with his wife. Beatrice sat down next to Elizabeth and leaned closer.

"How many hours do you sleep at night?"

"Is this medical curiosity?" Elizabeth asked.

"Let's call it that, yes."

Elizabeth decided to indulge her. At least Beatrice wasn't treating her like an ordinary person. She actually admired the woman's calm, her sense of irony and resilience. This is me in fifty years, she couldn't help thinking. If I live that long, she corrected herself.

"Never more than six," she answered.

"Early to bed, early to rise?"

"Yes, except when . . . Well, it's my natural pattern."

Elizabeth relaxed a little. Beatrice had a decidedly benign look on her face, just like the physician she had once been. A bedside manner, as people said of doctors. "Oh, and when I get up, I know what time it is, without—"

"—looking at the clock," Beatrice said quietly.

"Plus or minus five minutes."

Beatrice smiled. "So did I. Fascinating. Tell me about your parents."

Her request was said in a monotone, but Elizabeth felt a chill. This was the doctor-scientist talking. "My dad died when I was young."

"Did you worship him?" Beatrice asked bluntly.

"Yes," said Elizabeth, her heart doing somersaults. "You, too?"

"I had a real blind spot. I used to think men were perfect, if you can believe that. Now we both know better, don't we?"

Beatrice's smile grew more tender, not doctorlike at all. Maternal was the word that sprang to Elizabeth's mind.

"Tell me, do you jog?" she asked.

"Not so much since I wrecked my knee."

"It's not good for you anyway. Around fifty, you'll start to see arthritic changes."

"Thanks for the warning," said Elizabeth.

"Do you drink?" Beatrice asked.

"Only my share."

"Tequila, I've found, helps me through a mild depression. Do you like to work on the weekends?"

"Not if I can help it."

"That's good. I admire that. *Dolce far niente*—I've never been able to achieve it. Much too driven. Too excitable. Do you find that?"

"Only where men are concerned."

"That's us, in a nutshell," Beatrice said, and sighed.

Elizabeth had to smile. Whether arrogantly or ignorantly, she realized, this woman had given her her life—flesh from her flesh—and now she had saved it. And the man at the window, shooting occasional glances back at them, was husband and lover to both. That's nothing, she thought; Beatrice is both my mother and my twin. "If I live through this—"

"—you're going to write a book," said Beatrice, anticipating her thoughts.

"Yes."

Beatrice touched her hand. "I can't imagine what you're going through, really, but I do know you will live through this. I promise you."

How can you promise me anything? thought Elizabeth.

"We're going to see to it. Peter and I."

"Not just keeping your options open?"

Beatrice shook her head vehemently. "I swear, no."

"I needed to ask."

"You don't have to take my answer on faith. Think about yourself: are you a devious person?"

Elizabeth smiled faintly. "I haven't had your education."

Beatrice laughed. "You're right—the worst criminals are the educated ones!" Then she grew serious. Her gray eyes bore into Elizabeth's and Elizabeth felt something deep inside herself click. A key into a lock, a modem achieving uplink, a puzzle accepting a last, long-lost piece—that's how it felt to her.

"I don't want your body for my brain, Elizabeth. I think the whole idea is obscene."

"Now you do?"

"I won't insult you with excuses."

Elizabeth moved her hand away, ostensibly to brush her hair from her face, but mostly because she was uncomfortable with such closeness. What fate had these two contrived for them now? What was waiting in New York? She felt the fear creeping back, but oddly, this time it wasn't quite as threatening. Now at least she had someone to talk to.

"How many people is this Wolfe guy planning to clone?" she asked.

"As many as he pleases. If he gets his way," Peter said, this time joining in.

"And who chooses the subjects? Him?"

"Until he's in full control, he'll have to accept advice. Check the guest list at the White House for the past few years."

"*That's* a frightening thought."

Beatrice nodded. "Then there's the matter of spare parts, of course."

"I read something about that. I thought it was science fiction—bodies warehoused just for you."

"It was yesterday's science fiction. Which is today's reality—proprietarily cloned harvest bodies, all higher brain functions removed, just waiting until you need a kidney or a lung or a heart or a bone marrow transplant."

"Or specialty units of killer soldiers," said Peter, really into it now. "Cloned from genetically manipulated eggs that favor extreme aggression. Or how about dulled-down, worker-bee laborers who will happily work for Third World wages? And then, when cryogenic technology catches up, they'll deep-freeze world heroes, hold them for fifty years until history has a chance to evaluate them—discard the ones who don't stand the test and clone the ones that do."

"And once all this looked good to you?" Elizabeth asked.

Beatrice shot her a look. "I was never that kind of visionary."

"That was Wolfe," said Peter. "He never asked 'should we?' It was always just '*can* we?'"

"Well," Beatrice said, "the fact is that I was willing to bend a few moral rules when it came to Peter and me."

Peter nodded. "That's the scary part. What we did, despite misgivings." He got up and went to the rest room. Elizabeth watched him with concern, then looked back to Beatrice, who was looking even more grim now that Peter was gone.

"We have to put a halt to this, Elizabeth. And we need your help."

"Why should I help you?"

"Good question," Beatrice said, without sarcasm. "First of all, if it weren't for our protection, you would now be in a semicoma on your way back to Vieques to have your brain scooped out. Second, because you didn't really want to leave Peter."

Elizabeth began to protest, but Beatrice reached out and touched her hand.

"I know you. I know your feelings. They're mine, too."

"Listen," said Elizabeth, her eyes flashing, "just because our DNA is identical, it doesn't entitle you to read my mind."

"It doesn't take a mind-reader. You can't take your eyes off him."

Elizabeth opened her mouth to say something, then didn't. Or couldn't. Beatrice nodded, as if a pupil had finally understood a mathematical equation. "Now, did Alex Davies ever mention New York?"

"No."

"He didn't hint about other people who might be in danger?"

"We were only in his car for a few minutes before we crashed. We were being chased and shot at. Conversation was pretty much limited."

"And the e-mail?"

"It was just a bogus invitation for a free hotel room in Vieques. Absolutely nothing personal." She glanced up as Peter rejoined them.

"And when you didn't show up at the hotel, did he try to e-mail you again?"

"No," said Elizabeth.

"Are you sure? Have you checked?"

"No, I haven't checked," Elizabeth admitted.

Peter pointed down the aisle. "There's a guy up there with a laptop: 26B. And there's an empty seat next to him."

He looked at them both.

"Worth a try," Beatrice said.

Nothing like being double-teamed, thought Elizabeth.

"This is all we're asking you to do," said Beatrice. "When we get to La Guardia, you're free to go your own way. Not that we're recommending it."

Some people lead normal lives, thought Elizabeth. Thanks to molecular biology, I'm not one of them. She left her seat and went down the aisle to row 26, where a pink-faced man was playing Tetris on his laptop. She went past him, then pretended to double back.

"Is that a Toshiba?" she asked.

"Sure is," he said, not taking his eyes off the screen.

"Happy with it?"

"The best."

"What kind of modem do you have?"

"Fifty-six baud," the man said. He put the game on pause and looked up. Scoped how pretty she was. "Wanna check it out? Sit." He held out his hand. "Darlington—Frank Darlington."

She shook his hand and sat down beside him. "Heidi Boone," she said. "Is it true those things can check e-mail over airplane telephones?"

"Oh, yeah, sure is. Duck soup. Want to check your e-mail?"

She shook her head demurely. "Oh, I couldn't. It would be a long-distance call."

"No, it's just a local."

"To Switzerland?"

"Sure."

"No way."

"Waay," he said, taking out a patch cord. He plugged one end of the cord into the laptop and the other into the telephone on the seat back in front of him, then logged onto AOL and clicked on MAIL. Elizabeth gave him her address, *SwissMs* at the International Access branch of CompuServe.com, and he passed the laptop over.

Her hand shook as she checked her messages.

"Don't be scared, Heidi. It won't bite," Darlington said. To afford her some privacy, he picked up a copy of *Business Week*.

There were a dozen pieces of mail for Elizabeth, including three from the Helvetica Agency. But the last was from IslandMan.

```
Subj:   C8
Date:   99-03-24
From:   IslandMan@AOL.com
To:     SwissMs@Int'lAccessCompuServe.com
Re:     Phillip C. Kenner // 10 West 65th Street
        Apt. 7E // New York, NY 10023
        (212) 724-1386
        d.o.b. Aug. 2, 1966
```

YOU HAVE TO WARN THIS GUY, HE DOESN'T CHECK HIS MES-
SAGES. GOOD LUCK, AD

   PS: IF YOU'RE READING THIS I'M MIA, SO TOO BAD WE
DIDN'T GET TO HANG, I THINK WE WOULD HAVE HIT IT
OFF. YOU'RE THE ONLY ONE WITH BALLS, THEY'RE JUST
BRAINS ON A STALK. FUCK GRAMPA WOLFE AND VIVE LA
REVOLUTION!

   PPS: DELETE THIS MESSAGE AND DON'T GET DELETED
YOURSELF. IF BEATRICE IS WITH YOU SHE'S OK, IF NOT
SHE'S NOT. PETE JR. IS FLAKIER THAN BETTY CROCKER
BUT ANY PIE IN A STORM. DON'T TRY AND FLY SOLO,
YOU'LL END UP IN A SHOEBOX. THUS SPAKE ZARATHUSTRA.

She read the message twice over, memorizing it, then deleted it from the screen and from RECEIVED MAIL.

"Thank you, this was so great of you," she said and returned to her seat. Darlington went back to his game, a little disappointed. Elizabeth turned back halfway up the aisle to make sure that he had.

Rapt, Peter and Beatrice listened as she gave them Phillip Kenner's address, omitting Alex's postscripts.

"So Alex *is* alive. Thank God."

"We're going to warn Kenner, right?" said Elizabeth.

At the "we," Beatrice and Peter exchanged looks. "We have to do more than that," Peter said. "If Wolfe suspects that Kenner's been warned, he'll move on him immediately."

"So what do we do?" said Elizabeth.

"Blow the whistle," said Peter, "on the whole damn operation."

"How? They'll just deny everything."

"Not if we have the clone," Beatrice said.

Elizabeth's eyes grew wider. "Take him to Mike Wallace, if we have to," said Peter. "As soon as we see him, we'll know whose clone he is, and we'll challenge them to do a DNA comparison on both men."

"But Wolfe will claim the clone is that person's identical twin," said Elizabeth, "from a frozen embryo." Then she interrupted herself, even more intrigued. "No, wait, he can't do that. They didn't have freezing technology that advanced when he was born, did they?"

"Bright girl," said Peter, with a nod at Beatrice.

"Don't patronize," said Elizabeth.

Beatrice raised an eyebrow. "Good luck. I've been trying to make him stop that for a lifetime."

"Getting back to what's important here," Elizabeth said. "What if Kenner doesn't believe us?"

"Then we had better stow away on the space shuttle," Peter said. "There certainly won't be anywhere on this planet where we'll be safe. Whoa," he added, as the plane slammed through an air pocket. Elizabeth saw him reach for Beatrice's hand, and then Beatrice grabbed for hers. They all held on to each other while bells chimed and the flight attendants made their way down the aisle, holding on to seat backs for support while they checked seat belts.

"I forgot to ask about phobias," said Beatrice.

"Spiders, yes," said Elizabeth, "flying, no."

"Fascinating," said Beatrice. "So there are differences."

"Maybe nature hates to repeat itself," Elizabeth said gamely. Beatrice nodded.

"It does," she said fervently, as she held Elizabeth's hand in a vise-like grip. "Thank God."

NEW YORK CITY

They got through La Guardia easily enough, but the ride into Manhattan was another story. It was rush hour and the President was making a fund-raising appearance at the St. Regis. And so with half the city shut down and the Long Island Expressway a parking lot, it took the cab two hours to get from the airport to the Upper West Side. Included in the trip was a stop in Queens to buy another Combat Folder and can of mace, which a reluctant clerk in a sporting goods store produced for a fifty dollar bill with a warning that it was illegal. They ended by driving up Eighth Avenue, coming around Columbus Circle to Central Park West and stopping on the Central Park side at 65th

Street. They were about to cross to the residential side when Peter motioned them back behind a parked van.

"Dammit," he said.

On 65th Street, just about where number ten would be, two men bolted from a building and into a shiny black Town Car.

"Wolfe?" said Elizabeth.

They watched the vehicle speed toward Columbus Circle. "And Henderson," said Beatrice.

"Henderson?" said Elizabeth.

"The money and the muscle. Damnation," said Peter.

"Easy," said Beatrice, guessing his pulse rate.

"Maybe Kenner wasn't at home," said Elizabeth.

"Let's hope," said Beatrice. "Peter, you're not having another episode?"

"No," said Peter. "I'm just a little worried, that's all."

"Try to stay calm," said Beatrice. She led them out of hiding and they crossed Central Park West, Peter bringing up the rear, watching the two women. On the plane, he hadn't been able to stare at them without drawing glares. So now he stole a moment to savor them. They had formed a kind of bond, as if he was some sort of unpredictable child who needed looking after and they were increasingly willing to do that. But as they approached the building, his smile disappeared. Now, he thought, it's real time.

The number was ten, all right. The building, a little island of shabbiness in a sea of prosperity, was without a doorman. The inner door was locked, the glass soiled, but Peter could see through enough to know there were no signs of life in the first-floor corridor. Just an umbrella by the stairs, a few muddy footprints and what looked like a single pigeon feather. He scanned the intercom panel. It was etched with graffiti and did not bear the name Kenner. Peter hit the button for 7E.

There was no answer.

"Should we ring the super?" Beatrice wondered aloud.

"And say what?" said Peter. Now Beatrice was turning around and around in a worried little circle.

"Here," said Elizabeth impatiently, starting to push other buttons. She kept on pushing until a voice came over the speaker. "Exterminator," she said.

"About time," the voice rasped. A moment later, the lock buzzed open, allowing the three to enter.

They got into the elevator and Elizabeth pushed seven.

"Uh-oh," she said.

"What?" said Peter, and then saw her upheld finger, red at the tip.

"It may not be blood," he said.

"Sure looks like it," said Elizabeth.

Peter patted his pockets, feeling the hard edges of the Combat Folder in his right and the cylinder of mace in his left. When the elevator door opened he waved the women back, checking behind the fire door and in the stairwell. Nothing there but a three-day-old cooking odor and an echo far below in the thick gray air—someone hurrying down iron stairs, maybe. He couldn't say for sure.

He walked down the corridor, looking as he moved for a blood trail on the threadbare carpeting. He couldn't see one. Turning a corner and finding himself two units from the end, he was in front of Apartment 7E.

The door was ajar.

Beatrice and Elizabeth were coming up quickly behind him. He tried to wave them back, but they wouldn't obey, so he put out his arm, nodding silently toward the partially opened door. Reaching out with his foot, he nudged it open.

It was an academic's apartment, bookshelves on every wall. Stone silent. Peter went in, with Beatrice and Elizabeth following right behind him.

Instinctively, he scanned the shelves. Texts in the fields of math, physics and medicine predominated. He went into the bedroom, even checking under the bed and in the sole closet. No one. Same for the tiny bathroom. As for the kitchen, it was so small that he couldn't have hidden a squirrel in there.

He came back out and joined the women in the living room. On the desk, a computer was turned on, with a cartoon of a DOGZ puppy romping and whining on its screen. Peter nudged the mouse and the screensaver disappeared, revealing a Microsoft Word screen and page 36 of a monograph, "Gauge Theory of Weak Interactions." Peter scrolled through several pages. There was enough there to tell it was good work, a guide to the mathematical tools necessary to understand unified field theory, complete with exercises for the student.

"Peter?" said Beatrice.

"We've lost him, haven't we?" said Elizabeth.

"No sign of struggle. They might have found him gone, like us, and gotten out because someone spooked them. Who knows?"

"Looks like he's a teacher, from the books," Elizabeth said.

"And a good one," Peter agreed.

"Peter . . ." It was Beatrice. She was coming out of the bedroom with a framed photograph in her hand. Sounding and looking shaken, she handed the picture to him.

Peter saw a young man in a mortarboard cap and gown, flanked by proud parents. He had a broad shiny forehead, full lips that turned down at the corners and dark gleaming eyes. "Look like anyone we know?"

"Oh, Jesus," said Peter.

The young man could easily have passed as the son of Frederick Wolfe.

"He waited," said Beatrice.

"Waited? Waited for what?" And then he realized.

"Until it was safe. Six died, and the choice was him or you."

"Christ. I was just the next guinea pig?"

"Exactly. When you survived, it was time for him to make his move. First him—"

"—and then you," Peter realized, with a glance at Beatrice and then at Elizabeth. The blood had drained from both women's faces.

"The clone looks young here, doesn't he?" said Peter. "Nineteen, maybe."

"Younger than we ever knew Freddy."

"We'll need a more recent picture," Peter said, handing the photo back to Beatrice. He went into Phillip Kenner's bedroom.

Here, too, books spilled out of shelves and cartons. Fluffy yellow curtains held back the sun, the only woman's touch in the apartment. Beatrice entered behind him, appearing nervous. "Peter, we should get out of here."

"In a minute," he said, rummaging through drawers of threadbare boxer shorts and mismatched dark socks. Then he felt something crunch beneath his foot. Bending down, he found a broken picture frame and a photograph among the splintered wood and broken glass.

"This is more like it," he said. There was Kenner at age thirty or so, standing with his arm draped over the shoulders of a plump young woman with black corkscrew curls. She was kissing Kenner on the cheek.

"Peter, how did that picture get broken?"

"Good question."

She backed out of the room.

Peter opened the top drawer of the bureau. There he found Kenner's personal effects—a wallet, about twenty dollars in cash, an ancient pocket calculator, a Rubik's Cube and a collection of Yeats's poems.

"Peter?" Beatrice called from the living room. "We're going. It's foolish to hang around here now. Come on."

"Coming." There was a dog-eared copy of Kafka's *The Castle*, and a CD of Haydn's Farewell Symphony. I'd like this guy, Peter thought. Then it occurred to him that he would have probably learned to like Hans, as well. And yet he had stolen his life and his body. And for what? So he could superheat bodily fluids at the cellular level and explode human beings from the inside out? Wonderful. Even if he was no longer that man, he *had* been, so he could hardly pull moral rank on Freddy. In a rush of rediscovered guilt, he leafed through Kenner's wallet—another girl, not the cheek-kisser; an ACLU card; an AAA card noting that he had been a member thirteen years; an ID card for NYU. A life. Kenner, like Hans, had been earning his own scars and rewards, rashly assuming that his life was his own.

Peter put it all back and slammed the drawer shut.

Christ, if only he could put *everything* back. "Jesus, B.," he sighed, hearing her footsteps as she came into the bedroom. As he turned, he found himself staring at the silhouette of a man with a very large knife in his hands.

"Hey, Dr. Jance," said the man.

The shadow stepped into the light, and Peter recognized the Navy Seal from the Casa del Francés.

"Got your pocketknife, Doc?"

Peter froze. He flicked a glance at Russell's blade, terrified that it might already be bloodied. Thank God for the others at least: the knife gleamed clean as a mirror.

"Well, Doc?"

"Don't have it," said Peter, backing toward the doorway.

"You're gonna wish you did," said Russell, advancing. Peter's head spun in dyslexic terror. Instead of reaching for the Combat Folder in his right pocket, he reached for the canister of mace in his left. As Russell lunged toward him, Peter let him have it full in the eyes. Russell reeled away, howling an oath, then started slashing blindly after him, snorting and wheezing and swearing and knocking over everything in his way. Peter heard the women—they came running back from the hall yelling his name as Russell fell headlong over a chair and went down on his face. Peter jumped on the man's wrist with both heels, hearing the wrist splinter, then kicked the knife hard. It spun away and he went for it, fast enough to avoid Russell's agonized fury and quietly enough to leave the man not knowing where he was now.

"Get out!" Peter shouted at Elizabeth and Beatrice.

He ducked to a new position, threw the knife into the living room for Beatrice and Elizabeth to have some kind of weapon, then slammed the bedroom door shut. He turned just in time to take Russell's charge. Acting on full automatic now as Hans Brinkman, Peter twisted away, driving a fist into Russell's solar plexus, sidestepping a second charge and clubbing him with a right that sent Russell crashing to the floor.

He stood staring at his fallen opponent as though waiting for some referee to count him out. Peter realized Hans had always fought by the rules. He was on his own here. His head whirled as he felt warm blood drip from his ear and down his neck. He staggered back, sneezing blood from his nose. Then his vision went red. He realized he was hemorrhaging somewhere inside his brain.

Peter tried to keep his feet under him, even as he saw Russell stir, wheezing like a wounded beast. Fumbling into his cuff with his left hand, the Navy Seal came up with a semiautomatic pistol.

Peter's instincts told him to kick him hard anywhere, but a tide of darkness washed over Peter's eyes and he couldn't move. There was a loud clanging and he thought it might be the devil's gong ushering him into hell. But when he forced his eyelids open, he was still in the bedroom, Russell was motionless on the floor like a sledge-hammered bull, and Beatrice was standing over him with an iron skillet in her hand, breathing in and out in small astonished gasps.

"The pistol," Peter groaned, sinking to the floor and slumping against the wall. Beatrice picked up the semiautomatic gingerly.

"I'll take it. See to Peter!" shouted Elizabeth, snatching up the gun. "I know how to use it!"

She made sure that a round was in the chamber and clicked the gun off safety, leveling it at Russell's bleeding head. Beatrice threw down the skillet and knelt by Peter, peering into his eyes.

"I'm okay. It's stopped. It's exertion that brings it on," he said, surprised at his own calmness. He glanced over at Russell, lying face-down in the doorway. "Is he dead?"

"No. I can see his carotid moving."

"You think you can bring him around?"

"Why?"

"He probably came in with Wolfe, so he knows how Wolfe is getting back to Vieques. Wolfe's got Kenner, no doubt about that."

"On the Learjet?" said Beatrice.

"Maybe, maybe not," said Peter. "Which New York airport do they fly out of?"

"I haven't the faintest—Peter, take it easy."

He waved her away, attempting to rise, but falling instead. Beatrice touched his face and whispered to him. "You rest, Peter. Let us girls have a go."

He watched, blood thumping in his temples, as Beatrice and Elizabeth dragged Russell across the shag rug into the bathroom.

"Ignore any racket," said Beatrice, closing the door behind her.

Peter heard the bolt shoot home, then he heard water splashing: they were reviving Russell, Peter thought, as he tried again to get up but only managed to fall back at an even worse angle. He heard Russell's muffled grunts as he came around; he heard angry female voices. There was a moment's silence and then a string of curses from Russell. Next came a scream of agony, followed by a flurry of whimpered pleas for them to stop.

Then there was a silence again.

The bathroom door opened. Russell was on his feet, yanking up his pants with trembling hands. Elizabeth had the gun aimed at his head and Beatrice was refolding a straight razor and returning it to the edge of the sink.

"Where's the plane?" asked Peter.

"La Guardia," said Beatrice. "Hangar 17 in the General Aviation sector."

"Type?"

"It's a C-20. Twin turbojet," Elizabeth said. "Gray. NX-12 registration numbers on the vertical stabilizer. No other markings."

"Thank you," Peter said to Russell. "That's a very complete description."

"Fuck you," said Russell, and he charged Peter like an enraged bull, sending him sprawling. Almost at the same instant, Peter heard a sharp crack, and then Russell fell headlong on top of him. Peter tried to twist away, but his energy was drained and he was pinned beneath the man.

Fortunately, Russell wasn't moving.

Elizabeth came over and put the smoking gun in the man's ear and gave it a shove. Russell rolled off Peter and onto the floor, blood pooling under his head. There was a ragged exit wound in his forehead and brain matter was on Peter's sleeve.

"Jesus," Peter said wearily, his capacity for astonishment gone with his returning strength. Elizabeth was staring at the gun as though it had just materialized in her hand. "You can give that to me," he said.

She handed it over, looking around at the surrounding wreckage. "Somebody must have heard all this," she said matter-of-factly.

"It's New York," said Beatrice. "People are used to it."

"You've got a point," Peter said.

Even by the time they had left Kenner's apartment—Peter in a fresh shirt and Russell's pistol in his pocket—not a single soul had knocked on the door to ask what was going on. No one had even come into the hallway. Indeed, this was New York. They closed the door behind them, straightened their clothes and went downstairs to hail a cab.

This time, nobody had to talk Elizabeth into anything. She was with them now for the duration.

Between Manhattan and La Guardia, an incident took place in the shiny black Town Car. Clone Nine, thirty-three-year-old physics professor Phillip C. Kenner, had made a desperate bid to get free from his captors. He assumed he was being driven out to be killed anyway, since he owed over $20,000 to his bookie and was unable to pay anything back, despite grim warnings about the Mafia not taking this sort of thing lightly. Between his ex-wife dunning him for every remaining cent he had and the money he had lost investing in Siberian oil stocks, he was flat broke. To complicate matters, he hadn't made tenure and one of his students, a precocious sophomore named Stacy, was threatening to go to the dean if he didn't marry her and legitimize the child she was carrying.

He had very little to lose.

Besides, only one of the men in the car looked like he could handle himself, and Kenner had kicked him hard in the gut before the guy knew what hit him. The other guy must have been the oldest living member of the Mafia and had signaled his reluctance to fight by covering his speckled, bone-white face with his elbows.

Kenner spilled out of the car halfway across the 59th Street Bridge, realizing he could have chosen a better place, but also reckoning that he didn't have much choice. He took off running, and for a while he thought he was home free. Every year since 1982 he had run in the New York Marathon, usually placing in the first five hundred. Loping off at any easy pace, he didn't hear the driver of the Town Car until the guy launched himself over the hood of a Zabar's delivery truck and nailed him with a flying tackle.

In the next instant, Henderson, still purple from the kick to his stomach, arrived in a fury, grabbing Kenner from the driver, dropping him with a kick to the groin and dragging him to the bridge's guardrail. "You want to fly the coop?" he screamed at the terrified professor. "Let's see just how good you can tread air!"

He had the sobbing man halfway over the railing when Wolfe came running up, bright red in the face and sputtering.

"Henderson, what the hell do you think you're doing? That's *me* you're punching around!"

Henderson looked from Wolfe to Wolfe's youthful counterpart. "He fucking sucker-kicked me!"

"Then punch that girder over there! Whatever you do to him, I'll have to live with it for the rest of my life!"

Henderson threw Kenner to the sidewalk.

By now the bridge was at a standstill. Wolfe and Henderson looked back toward Manhattan and saw a sea of gawkers craning for a better look.

"Get him in the car," ordered Wolfe.

Henderson shoved Kenner toward the driver. "Put him in the god-damn car," he echoed.

The driver did as ordered and eased the Town Car through traffic. Kenner sat docile and perplexed between the old man and the thug. The brush with death, if that's what it had been, must have scrambled his brains for the moment, because—liver spots or no—the world's oldest living mafioso now looked, strangely and hideously, like himself as an old and breathless man.

A half-hour later, in Hangar 17 at La Guardia Airport, Henderson es-corted the fucking clone, Dr. Frederick Wolfe and the Vieques medical personnel into the waiting C-20. The plan was either for Henderson to return with the others in the C-20 or to arrive later in the Learjet, depending on how quickly Russell made it back to the airport. Russell was running late, so Henderson watched the medics put Kenner into the same half-coma they had put Jance's clone into the last time they had done this. Once this was accomplished, he gave a curt wave to Wolfe and shut the plane's door from the outside.

Actually, he was relieved not to be traveling with Wolfe. Even though Barrola would be doing the entire procedure, with Wolfe himself on the table, the arrogant old prick was already shifting into his exalted pre-op mode, a state of mind Henderson was glad to be spared.

As he stepped away from the C-20, the co-pilot of the Learjet came over and tapped him on the shoulder.

"Excuse me, sir. I'm afraid our pilot, Captain Culpepper, has come down with a godawful case of the runs."

"Where is he?" asked Henderson. Another screw-up? He had had a bellyful.

"He's in the pilot's lounge claiming he wants to die. Something he ate down in Bogotá, I guess. There's no way he's gonna fly tonight, sir."

"You're kidding, right?"

"No, sir. But we're still a go. This plane practically flies itself. I'll get you there just fine by myself. I just wanted you to know."

Henderson looked him up and down. This guy had cow college written all over him. "What's your name, son?"

"Second Officer David Anspaugh, sir."

"Well, Second Officer David Anspaugh, you damn well better get us back to Vieques without a hitch, because if you don't, I'm going to pull your rectum out through your brainpan, is that perfectly clear?"

Anspaugh's face lost all color, except for two irregular red patches on his cheeks. "Perfectly, sir."

"Excellent," said Henderson, staring the kid down until the co-pilot turned and scurried back to his airplane. Shaking a Camel out of his pack, he watched Wolfe's C-20 taxi away. He would wait for Russell another ten minutes; it would be pretty clear by then something had gone to hell in a handbasket and he would have to go back and check things out at the abduction site. Seals didn't leave their men behind, and neither would he. Besides, Russell already had two strikes against him, and after a series of fuck-ups, men were apt to get loose-lipped. If he had to, he'd wax Russell before he turned up in the *National Enquirer* spilling his guts for a couple grand and a shot at Geraldo.

Henderson walked back toward the Learjet, now realizing that he had better inform this squirrelly pilot that he wouldn't be taking off right away, otherwise the kid might idle for an hour and overheat his engines. All he had to do was sterilize the apartment and come back— an hour and a half, tops, even in this traffic. But what *was* keeping Russell? He tried the walkie-talkie, but got only static. He also tried Russell's cellular and got no answer.

It was starting to eat at him.

He climbed into the Lear and found Anspaugh sitting in the pilot's seat, looking as petrified as a civilian on his first solo.

"You sure you can fly this thing?" Henderson asked.

"Yes, sir!"

He stepped closer. The young man's face looked positively green.

"You sure as hell don't *look* like you can. You getting the runs, too?"

"No, sir."

"Then what the hell's wrong with you?"

Anspaugh's head ratcheted one notch to the right. Henderson turned and found himself looking down the barrel of Russell's 9mm service Beretta.

Jesus, Mary and Joseph, it was Jance.

"You know I've got nothing to lose here, right?" said Peter. "Please sit down."

"Fuck you."

Peter's left hand came around and caught Henderson flush on the jaw. With a snort of surprise, the colonel sank to the floor. Peter took out his Combat Folder, cut a pair of seat belts free and bound Henderson's hands behind his back. He lifted him into a leather seat and locked him in with its seat belts. That accomplished, he gave a whistle. Beatrice and Elizabeth emerged from the lavatory.

"Keep an eye on our friend," he said, passing the Beretta to Elizabeth. Peter went to the co-pilot and stood behind him.

"Let's go. No cute transmissions. If you indicate in any way that things aren't normal," he said in his best Clint Eastwood voice, "I'll cut your head off and put it in your lap." He glanced at Beatrice and Elizabeth, both of whom were wincing at his attempted machismo.

"Please don't do that," said Anspaugh.

"Just follow the flight plan and get us to Vieques."

"No problem."

"There better not be."

19

The Learjet made its way down the East Coast straight as an arrow, past Atlantic City, Philadelphia, Cape May, Chesapeake Bay. Peter watched the co-pilot closely, attempting to anticipate Anspaugh's moves in the cockpit. Though the Learjet was more complicated for him to deal with intellectually, physically he could sense when the plane needed trim or an adjustment of throttle. He was thinking like Peter but flying by the seat of his pants, as a pilot would.

As *Hans* would, he thought.

I've even started to talk like him, he reflected wryly.

Well, all right. Whatever it takes. You borrowed his body for the wrong reasons. Now you're using it for the right reasons.

He looked back at Beatrice and Elizabeth. Their presence gave him strength, even as it filled him with remorse. You wanted them here and you need them here, but what if you start to hemorrhage again? Could they see this through on their own? Would they want to? Beatrice shared his hatred for what they had let themselves become—but Elizabeth? What had she ever done to deserve this? Nothing. But she was here nonetheless, this gritty, determined, beautiful woman.

God help me, he thought, I love them both.

He straightened in his seat, forcing himself to watch the sky. They were coming up on Norfolk, so he kept a weather eye out for air traffic out of the naval base there. Thus far the sky had been clear of anything threatening, but he knew an F-14 could appear in a heartbeat or down them without even being seen. Beatrice approached, offering a mug of coffee.

"Where'd you find that?"

"Big thermos in back. All the pleasures of home."

"How's Elizabeth holding up?"

"She's doing fine."

"Is she having any second thoughts?"

"Plenty, I'm sure. How about you?"

"Oh, I'm feeling fairly addled. It occurs to me that I haven't slept in three days." He took a swallow of coffee and nudged the co-pilot with his foot. "Want some?"

"Yes, please," said Anspaugh. It was the first time he had uttered a word since takeoff.

"You wouldn't try to throw hot coffee at me, would you?"

"No, sir."

Peter looked at Anspaugh for a moment, wondering what he was thinking. Whether he would, if he knew, have an opinion one way or the other about what his government was up to. "You know what they do to people down there on Vieques?"

"No, sir, and I'm not sure I want to."

"Well, it isn't good, and I ought to know—I used to do it. God's work, I used to think it was. Once you tell yourself that, you can get away with anything. B., would you please get this gentleman some coffee?"

"I will," said Beatrice, "if you'll stop annoying him."

"Was I annoying you?" said Peter.

"No, sir."

"It's a dangerous world," said Peter.

"Yes, sir, it certainly is."

"The people who say that generally want to make it more dangerous. At least in my experience. The coffee," he said to Beatrice, who was beginning to trade looks with Elizabeth, still seated across from the unconscious Henderson, beyond the cockpit door.

As Beatrice went back into the cabin, Peter faced front again, feeling shadows move across his mind. Concentrate, he thought. Calculate. They weren't *that* far behind the C-20, so they had a decent chance of getting to Vieques before the operation robbed Kenner of his brain. He was determined not only to save Kenner, but deny Wolfe another fifty years. If he had that much time to continue his mischief, he might actually secure immortality for himself.

But how to get from the Vieques airport and onto the base to do that? Wolfe would certainly have alerted the troops, especially once both Russell and Henderson turned up missing. That would put the entire installation on full alert. Even with an ally on the inside, it would be impossible to get past the gate. And his only ally, Alex Davies, was hiding out God knows where.

"Anspaugh," he said, "you can get a radio transmission from this thing onto a telephone line, can't you?"

"This aircraft has a telephone, yes, sir."

"But that would be monitored, wouldn't it?"

"No, sir. This is a secure telephone."

"Are you trying to trick me?"

"No, sir!"

Of course he was. Peter leaned wearily toward the co-pilot. "If you continue in this vein, I'll amputate your thumbs and big toes so that you'll reel through the rest of your life like a drunken orangutan."

"I would never try to trick you, sir," said the co-pilot, meaning it.

"But there's also a way through the aircraft's radio to make a phone call, isn't there?"

"Yes, sir. I would just call UNICOM and ask for a land line. That's a civilian service. They do it all the time and they have no monitoring policy."

"Good. Do that. Get on the telephone and get me the *New York Times.*"

"I'll call 411, sir," he said as he got on the radio.

Within several minutes, Peter had called the *New York Times,* the *Boston Globe,* the *Washington Post* and the *Wall Street Journal.* Depending on the newspaper, he was either hung up on, met with scornful laughter or, at best, treated with polite curiosity. That is, until the *Post* pulled his name up on their computer and noted that he had been dead for two months. Then on the last call, there was a series of mysterious cracks and sizzles on the line and he hung up.

"Somebody was just listening in. Did you tip them off?"

"No, sir, I swear to God."

He waited for something to happen, some bolt from the sky or a voice to come over the radio, but nothing came. After a while he calmed down and let Beatrice bring the promised coffee. Jittery as he was, he took another one himself. Oddly enough, the second cup seemed to steady him, and he resumed gazing out the window, like a tourist on his first flight to the Caribbean. At Cape Hatteras the coast changed direction, receding southwest. The Learjet struck out over open water, flying a little lower than a commercial jet. The view was much more striking than anything he ever experienced before. Enjoy it while you can, he thought—you may soon be leaving this great blue planet. His scientist's eye noted the subtle differences in the ocean's surface as they passed the edge of the Continental Shelf, saw the waters turn deeper blue and the bottom fall away to the abyss. They were passing over the Blake and Bahama Ridges, great undersea mountain ranges he knew were as high as the Rockies. It was pleasant to know such things, he reflected. Not all his learning had been in the service of destruction. Now he could see all the way across Florida into the Gulf of Mexico and, ahead, the islands of the Bahamas stretching out like the first pearls of some great necklace extending all the way to the end of the Caribbean itself.

They were almost home.

Then he looked out the side window and nearly jumped out of his seat.

He was staring at another human being. It was a pilot, no doubt scrambled from Homestead Air Force Base outside Miami, in a heavily armed F-15C Eagle fighter. The airplane couldn't have been more than fifty feet away; Peter could see the pilot's helmet with a jagged streak of lightning across it. In fact, he could almost read the name on his G-suit. The fighter itself bristled with rockets and guns.

A flat Midwestern voice boomed over the radio.

"Hello Learjet niner-four-eight-three-eight, do you read me?"

Peter turned and put the knife to Anspaugh's ribs.

"Don't make me do it."

"What should I do, sir?"

"Ignore him," said Peter.

Suddenly Anspaugh lost all his previous shyness. "Ignore an F-15? Sir, that's the same as saying you're a marauding aircraft. You know what he's got on that thing? Twenty-millimeter Vulcan cannons, probably four AIM-7 Sparrows, four more Sidewinders. He can take us out in the blink of an eye."

"Can you outrun him?" said Peter, hoping the women were missing what he was seeing and wondering if Henderson had regained consciousness.

"Outrun him? We make 540 knots tops—he does Mach 2.5 plus! He could knock us down just with his sonic boom!"

"Then tell him who you are," Peter ordered, "and say that everything's all right."

Anspaugh gaped at him, convinced now that the man was insane. The radio voice crackled on again.

"Lear niner-four-eight-three-eight, please respond or be considered hostile."

The fighter was drifting closer, the pilot literally peering in their window. Peter waved. "Say hello," he said through his teeth to Anspaugh.

Anspaugh keyed the mike. "Learjet niner-four-eight-three-eight."

"Niner-four-eight-three-eight, say your destination."

"Destination Roosevelt Roads Naval Air Station, Vieques Island."

"Do you have a Dr. Peter Jance aboard?"

Anspaugh looked at Peter for help. "No," Peter told him.

"That is negative," said Anspaugh.

There was some static while the pilot gave them another once-over. "Who is the gentleman sitting to your right in the cockpit?"

Peter felt the sweat beading on his upper lip and hoped it didn't read across forty feet of troposphere. Out of the corner of his eye, he saw Beatrice moving up from the cabin, curious to see what was going on. He waved her back, keeping his hands low.

"Say I'm Colonel Oscar Henderson," Peter said.

"That would be Colonel Oscar Anderson," said the terrified co-pilot.

"Henderson," said Peter.

"Henderson," said Anspaugh.

More static. "I am being asked to speak directly to Colonel Henderson. Could you give him the mike, please?"

The co-pilot looked at Peter, who breathed deeply and took the mike.

"What the hell's the meaning of this?" he demanded in the best Henderson growl he could summon. "You are dangerously close, cowboy! You want to cause a midair? Who's your commanding officer?"

"I am Colonel Howard Price, United States Air Force, and the commanding officer of this wing," said the voice from the fighter. "These men are under my command."

What men? Peter thought. He leaned closer to Anspaugh's window and looked up. His heart missed a beat. There were three more fighters flying in echelon above them.

"Colonel Henderson, I have been instructed to request your mission code. Could you give that to me, please?"

Mission code? Oh Jesus, thought Peter.

"We are Operation Fountain Society," he bluffed.

Static. Then: "And your mission code?"

Now Peter's face was drenched with sweat. "It's in my briefcase. I don't have it with me here."

"I formally request you retrieve that from your briefcase, sir. I need to confirm the code."

His fear was so intense he could barely move without jerking like a marionette. He had once been invited to witness strafing practice on Vieques and he knew what these aircraft and their guns could do. Targets didn't just get shot full of holes, they flew apart into red-hot shrapnel and were unrecognizable afterward.

"Stand by," Peter said. He turned and looked helplessly at his wife.

"What are you going to do?" she asked.

"He doesn't know shit what to do," an all-too-familiar voice boomed from the cabin.

Christ, thought Peter.

It was Henderson, awake and laughing at them.

Peter rose from his seat and started back.

"It's basic fail-safe procedure," Henderson snarled. "You don't have the code, you're Swiss cheese."

Peter grabbed him by the lapels. "Then you're going to give it to me."

"No, I'm not, and you know why?"

"Why?"

"Because you tie a lousy knot," said Henderson matter-of-factly, lunging up, wrists bleeding and chafed, hands free. He threw Peter against the bulkhead with such brute force he was knocked senseless. Behind him, Elizabeth fumbled for the Beretta. "Put that down before you hurt yourself," Henderson sneered, kicking backward without looking, catching Peter in the groin even as he tried to struggle up.

Elizabeth fired.

She missed Henderson, but the window next to him cracked vertically and a jagged hole in its center emitted a horrendous screech of wind and decompression. Beatrice and Elizabeth clutched their ears as the atmospheric pressure plunged, shooting subzero air through the cabin at tremendous velocity. Distracted by the agonizing sound, Elizabeth swung around, too late, as Henderson, bulling forward, twisted the pistol from her hand and knocked her sprawling. He wheeled, intending to level it at Peter, but the tilt of the plane, now climbing at a fearful angle, spilled Peter against the seats and sent Henderson reeling back against the shattered window.

There he stuck, with a look of horror on his face.

In the next instant his abdomen caved in, the window turned red and blew out altogether. Henderson's body was sucked into it with monstrous force. His spine snapped loudly, the body folded double, jamming into the aperture even as his viscera ballooned into his trousers outside the windows. His eyes glistened a moment, then eerily withdrew into his skull. He was slowly imploding, but his body, for the time being at least, had effectively sealed the gap.

"Take us down or we'll blow!" screamed Peter at the co-pilot. He wheeled on Beatrice and Elizabeth. "Strap in!" The stall-warning horn blared as he clawed his way toward Anspaugh, who was struggling to level the plane while the radio crackled, the voice on the other end demanding to know what was going on. Peter flung himself back into his seat. A loud crunch echoed from the cabin.

"He's not going to stay in that window much longer!" Elizabeth yelled.

"Then hang on!" Peter shouted, as Anspaugh shoved the stick forward in a dive.

"Niner-four-eight-three-eight, respond, respond!"

Peter swore and grabbed the mike. "Mayday, Mayday!" he called. "We are experiencing explosive decompression and are diving to lower altitude. Please advise as to nearest base. This is not an evasive action—repeat—this is *not* an evasive action!"

The wind howled past the canopy, screaming through the cabin as the altimeter spun down like a mad, backward clock. Peter could see the fighters diving with them, flaps down.

They leveled off at three thousand feet.

Moments later, the remains of what had once been Oscar Henderson shook loose from the Learjet's window and fell like a spinning husk toward the sea below.

Then the radio crackled again. "Niner-four-eight-three-eight?"

Peter's hands shook convulsively as he picked up the mike. "Niner-four-eight-three-eight."

"Confirm that was a fatality."

"Confirmed."

"Identify?"

". . . Dr. Peter Jance," Peter said.

"Roger that. Did you get that code?"

"Blew out the window with my briefcase," said Peter.

There was a long string of static. "Advise turn west to two hundred sixty degrees, make landing Guantánamo. They are rolling emergency equipment."

"Roger that," said Peter. He keyed the mike twice to say goodbye. As Anspaugh eased the plane into a twenty-degree bank, Peter watched the compass come around.

"Where are we going?" Beatrice asked.

She was just behind him. Elizabeth was back in the cabin, hugging herself to stop the shaking. Anspaugh stared at him, white-faced, mute, waiting for instructions.

"Guantánamo Marine Base, Cuba. Beatrice, you should strap in. Elizabeth, too."

"Why Guantánamo? Isn't the Dominican closer?"

"The Dominican would be civilian. I think they want us down on a military base."

"Better emergency equipment?"

"I hope that's it. Or else it's because there'll be no witnesses who aren't working for the government."

He saw her tighten, then smile, pretending to look far less worried than she felt.

"I think I'm over my fear of turbulence," she said.

"Trauma therapy," said Peter, trying to remain calm by calming her. "So what are we going to do, I wonder?" he said, patting her hand.

She looked at him a long moment. "Peter, I love you very much."

"I love you, too. Always have and always will."

"And Elizabeth?"

He looked out into the deep blue of the sky.

"Yes. She's you and you are her, and I guess I love her a great deal. It's just that she and I haven't gone through what you and I have."

Beatrice nodded. "I always did like your honesty," she said. "And you know what I've realized in talking with her?"

"No, what?"

"If our situations had been reversed? If I had been twenty-four and had met you as you are now? I'd have fallen in love with you, too."

"I see," he said. Did that mean he was a better man today? He hoped so.

"I've always liked your honesty, too."

Beatrice sighed. "I think you should talk to her."

"Elizabeth? Why? Is she coming unglued?"

Beatrice shrugged. "She's got more to lose, but she's not coming apart. In fact, our Elizabeth has an extremely interesting idea."

VIEQUES

The C-20 returning from New York bearing Frederick Wolfe and the semicomatose Phillip C. Kenner was met by considerably more vehicles than had attended Hans Brinkman's arrival from Zurich. In addition to the usual Humvees, there were two APCs, light-armored troop vehicles mounted with 50-caliber machine guns, each carrying ten heavily armed young men assigned to cover the perimeter of the base from both ends of the airstrip.

The plane touched down in the glow of a setting sun, and Kenner was wheeled to the ambulance, Wolfe trotting behind like a mother hen. The medics, he realized, must have miscalculated the anesthesia dosage because Kenner was twisting against the restraints, evidently in the throes of some abduction nightmare.

The soldiers watching from the APCs sat silently, some looking away. God only knew what the old man they called The Reaper was going to do to the poor bastard on the stretcher. They had been ordered never to discuss anything they witnessed on these missions, but after seeing so many Arabs and, more recently, Caucasians arrive in this condition, they all had to wonder. The whole business had gotten so distasteful that the Special Forces troops had taken to drawing straws to determine who would pull the duty.

"Go, go, go!" Wolfe was shouting now, hurriedly scanning the skies as he ran, as though some lightning bolt of judgment was about to strike from the deepening gloom. He had been informed by radio while still in the C-20 that Russell was dead in Kenner's Manhattan apartment, his brains blown out, apparently with his own pistol. He had also been told that their errant Learjet, which had earlier disgorged Henderson's evacuated body from one of its side windows, had—until fifteen minutes ago—been heading straight for Vieques.

As the ambulance sped toward the Fountain Compound, a lieutenant colonel, whose name Wolfe had never bothered to learn, gave him a full briefing.

"The pilot identified himself as Henderson but was unable to give his mission code. The speculation is it's Jance."

"That's impossible," Wolfe asserted.

"Apparently not, sir."

"Where's the Learjet now?"

"It was ordered to Guantánamo, but it deviated. It's over Cuban airspace. NSA monitored a telephone call between an unidentified woman and a General Jesús Pinar del Río."

"A Cuban? A Communist? What the hell do they have to do with this? Who was this woman?"

"As I say, we don't know. The Learjet now appears to be tailgating a Cuban airliner—Cubana de Aviación Flight 1204."

"Shoot them down!"

The lieutenant colonel shook his head.

"Not an option. They're flying too close to the airliner, apparently very skillfully, too. We can't risk an international incident."

"Jesus Christ. It's not Jance, we can be certain of that. He might have managed to kill Russell, but Peter couldn't possibly fly a Learjet. I don't care how much cellular memory he has."

"He's not flying the plane. There's a pilot on board."

"Well, Jesus—what's a few Cubans, for godsakes!"

"Excuse me a second," said the lieutenant colonel, unsnapping his ringing cellular. Furious and shaken, Wolfe eyed Kenner on the gurney. Despite the efforts of the ambulance medics, he was quickly regaining consciousness, twitching and moaning. It put Wolfe in mind of a heart-lung lab in first-year physiology, the poor TAs running around with hypodermics like demented plates-and-sticks jugglers, trying to keep the damn experimental dogs from whimpering. He heard Kenner breathe the word "Mafia," and then he heard the colonel curse.

"What's up?" he demanded, sensing more bad news.

"Now the Learjet's got an escort. Four MiG-23 MLDs, flogger class, armed with Aphid air-to-air missiles."

"Jesus Christ. It's not Jance, it's the bloody Red Cubans."

"We can't be sure of that."

"I'm sure," said Wolfe. "I'm damn sure." Yes, and he should have foreseen it. Black ops security was a famous sieve and Castro had enough dope money to buy any secret he wanted. Well, he thought wildly, this is why we started all this: to keep bastards like him in their place. He knew if *he* were Castro and learned that the U.S. was about to keep its power elite alive for centuries—the very leaders who had squeezed him all these years while he aged and went infirm—then he would sure as hell try to sabotage the effort. It would constitute a grand, heroic last gesture.

Kenner mumbled again, something about hit men and mercy. Wolfe thought he might not want to involve the mob, but otherwise it all made perfect sense. He sighed heavily. The next possibility was far more troubling.

"And what about Mrs. Jance?"

"Mrs. Jance?" said the lieutenant colonel.

"Dr. Beatrice Jance, wife of the fugitive Dr. Peter Jance. Has she returned to the base?"

"No, sir, apparently not."

His heart fluttered darkly. "You're sure?"

"We would know, sir."

"Her last known whereabouts?"

"Miami International."

"She was supposed to be helping us spot the Parker girl."

"Yes, that's right, she was."

"Any idea where *she* is?"

"Elizabeth Parker? Also last seen at Miami International. We think they both might be tied in with Jance at this point."

"In the plane?" he gasped.

"Quite possibly."

No, thought Wolfe, with a shudder. Not possible. The girl, maybe, but Beatrice couldn't be back with Peter. She despised him. And the tenderness she had shown him en route to Miami, that couldn't have been faked. Had she perhaps caught sight of her clone, and started to have second thoughts? No. Beatrice wasn't soft like Peter. Beatrice was steely, like him. Throw away a chance at eternal youth? Never. She would show up eventually, probably with the Parker girl in tow and in handcuffs. He and Beatrice were fated to spend the twenty-first century together: he had all the faith in the world.

Meanwhile, the Communists had to be dealt with.

"I want every incoming flight confirmed by binoculars from the tower," he told the lieutenant colonel. "And all jets forbidden completely until further notice."

"Yes, sir, if that's what you want, we can do that."

"And I want a bulldozer parked at the side of the runway. If a jet ignores our ban, then the driver is to position the bulldozer smack in the middle of the runway, do you understand?"

"We'll do what we can, Dr. Wolfe."

"What you *must*," said Wolfe.

"Yes, sir!"

The ambulance pulled into the compound and Wolfe leaped out. There was much to do. Beatrice or no Beatrice, if this whole dream was going to unravel during the next twenty-four hours, he sure as hell intended to be in his new body by the time it happened.

LEARJET 94838

Elizabeth was thanking God that they were alive and that she still had her wits about her. At first she was sure that the racket in the plane—the wind rattling through the cabin nonstop and the roar of the engines through the broken window—would deafen them all. To say nothing of the fighter out there threatening to shoot them down and then ordering them into Guantánamo Marine Base, where for all she knew they would be terminated by Langley operatives.

And then she had remembered the cab driver in Miami, the little guy with the bubble-gum scar and the uncle who was a general in Castro's army. She still had the business card he gave them. Using her flawless Spanish, Beatrice had called the number and, wonder of wonders, the general himself got on the phone. At least they were fairly sure it was Jesús Pinar del Río—the noise in the cabin had made it nearly impossible to hear.

Then, just as the F-15 had threatened countermeasures, the wide-bodied Cuban airliner had appeared behind them. Anspaugh, goaded on by Peter, executed the maneuver of his career. The Learjet lifted up and over the huge four-turbofan's wing vortexes and slipped into clear air just above and behind it, exactly as Peter told him they could.

Now the Cuban MiG escort, dispatched by the general himself, showed up in a roar and drove the F-15 away.

Yes, she thought, if Peter and Beatrice have offended God, perhaps God has chosen to forgive them.

At least so far.

But maybe not completely.

Even as Elizabeth and Beatrice were marveling at how Peter's body was holding up under the stress, he had begun to suffer double vision and partial paralysis. With Anspaugh staring silently out the windscreen as if no one else were in the cockpit, Beatrice and Elizabeth crouched beside Peter, ministering to him. None of them wanted to be far from each other.

On this Elizabeth was relying heavily. There were things she had wanted to request from the general, but not in front of Beatrice and Peter. She had plans for them both, but she didn't want to risk any premature resistance. Beatrice could be counted upon to be reasonable, but Peter was another story. She watched him, on guard for any sign of a mini-stroke, as he focused on the giant aircraft below them, peering through the windscreen.

"Do they know we're here?" Elizabeth asked, raising her voice above the engine's whine. To their right, the sun was dropping into the sea.

"Hard to say. Let's hope del Río had someone alert them. Wouldn't want them climbing suddenly. Swat us like a fly."

"Does Cuba have an international airport?" Beatrice asked.

"About nine," said Anspaugh, deciding if he couldn't beat them he might as well join them for the time being.

"We're going to Havana," said Beatrice.

"Havana? No," said Peter. "Havana's nine hundred kilometers away. I think this plane we're hitching a ride with is going to Santiago de Cuba. What do you think?" he asked Anspaugh.

Anspaugh pointed below in confirmation. "Yes, sir. It's dropping flaps."

Indeed the airliner was slowing, dropping lower and lower. Anspaugh was hanging back, keeping high, Peter surmised, to avoid the wing-tip turbulence. Then they could see the airport ahead. The MiGs roared overhead and spun off into the sky.

Beatrice was fretful. "They're not going to land and arrest us?" Of the three of them, Elizabeth thought, Beatrice seemed the most worried. As if she knew something that Peter and I don't. But what else could have been left untold at this point? Elizabeth wrote it off to Beatrice's fear of flying.

"If they're going to arrest us, troops will do it at the airport. But you spoke to del Río himself, right? Not an aide, you're sure?"

"I'm not absolutely sure of anything," said Beatrice, "except that I'm not an idiot. It was almost certainly him."

She clenched her fist to keep her fingers from shaking. All they could see as they descended into the dwindling light was a high bluff and a bay pouching darkly below. The lights of the city and mountains lay beyond. In the next minute, the airport lights were streaking below them. Then there were the exhaust-spouting Russian jeeps racing to keep up with the Learjet, and beyond, silhouetted against the glare, enough soldiers, trucks and armored vehicles to start a small revolution.

The Learjet touched down, braked and came to a noisy stop. They were all amazed by how loud a jet was if a window was missing.

"Leave the engines running," Peter yelled at Anspaugh, who nodded, as if in this surreal environment he were ready to accept anything. "Let's expect the worst," Peter said to Beatrice and Elizabeth, "then we'll almost certainly be pleasantly surprised." He hobbled off toward the door, opened it and popped the stairs, then stepped down into the glare of countless lights.

From the open doorway, Elizabeth could see soldiers running and vehicles shooting past. And then a white-haired, leonine man in fatigue uniform strode toward Peter, hand outstretched.

"Welcome to Santiago de Cuba!" he shouted over the whine of jets. "I am General Jesús Pinar del Río. I welcome you in the name of the three Fs—freedom, friendship—" he eyed Elizabeth, "—and felicity. Are you the woman I spoke to on the phone?" he asked Elizabeth.

"That was me," said Beatrice, appearing in the doorway behind Elizabeth.

"Beautiful Spanish, *señora!*"

"*Gracias.*"

He grinned at them all. "I'm completely at your service. Whatever you require," he said, climbing the stairs to kiss the women's hands. He had large, animated eyes and a wide mouth enclosed by two deep parentheses. "How's my nephew Ramón? Is he still driving a taxi?"

"Yes," said Elizabeth. "And thank God for that."

"My sister's boy. Has he grown any taller?"

"Absolutely," said Beatrice. "He must be at least six feet tall now."

The general threw back his head and laughed. "Poor niño—he was doing good growth until eleven, and then no taller."

"He is an excellent driver nonetheless," said Peter, introducing himself, not forgetting to include his doctor's title. The general shook his hand solemnly.

"He spoke so highly of you." The creases deepened around his mouth as the women approached. The plane was surrounded and wasn't going anywhere. "And these ladies?"

Peter put his arm around Beatrice. "This is my wife, Dr. Beatrice Jance." The general shrugged happily, as if to say "Good for you both!" Then he looked at Elizabeth.

Peter put his other arm around her. "And this is our very dear and loyal friend Elizabeth."

"Yes? I would have guessed your daughter."

"Many would," said Peter. He took a breath. "We are all three of us on the run from people who are enemies of freedom, friendship and felicity, and we need your help."

"So I gathered," said the general with a sudden frown as the engines of the Learjet gave a cough. There was a long wind-down and then an ominous silence. One of the soldiers who had strolled to the other side of the plane called out something to the general, pointing. The general ducked under the plane, then let out a low whistle in the dark.

"Looks like you landed just in time, my friends," he said, darting a look at Anspaugh, who was descending from the aircraft in a daze. "You have a hole in your gas tank."

He ran his finger along the edge of a ragged tear where Elizabeth's wild shot had torn into the wing after penetrating the window. Then he looked up at the blown-out window and at the long smear of red along the fuselage from window to tail.

"You have had some trouble, yes?"

"*Un pocito,*" said Beatrice quietly. She smiled demurely. "What exactly did your nephew tell you about us?" Peter asked.

"He told me you were a good man," said the general. "Are you?"

"I am now," said Peter, with a glance at Elizabeth. This is not exactly the time to split hairs, she thought, but she noticed that the general nodded sympathetically.

"You were not always fighting for freedom?"

"I thought I was."

"I completely understand," del Río said openly. "I have traveled a similar road and I also wish freedom for my country. But at some point there will arrive tonight others who may have less understanding. What can I do to help you before that time comes, my friend?"

Elizabeth watched as Peter drew the general aside. She chafed at being excluded, as did Beatrice. They were both about to go over and insist on being part of the discussion when the two men shook hands. Del Río shouted orders and several soldiers ran into the airplane.

"What was that all about?" said Beatrice. "Guy talk?"

Peter gave her a look. "I asked if he could recommend a place where we could regroup."

"And?"

"He's asked us to his house for dinner."

"And the pilot?"

"They'll find a room for him near the airport. Come morning, there's a flight off the island."

As she watched the general's men lead Anspaugh toward the terminal, Elizabeth began to breathe more easily. The three travelers bundled into the general's vintage Bonneville, del Río waving off his aide and declaring that he would drive himself. On the way into the dark green hills, he kept up a stream of chatter, pointing out the textile mill, the oil refinery and the road to Sierra Maestra, where Castro had holed up with his followers. As he spoke of the man he had once loved and had subsequently turned against, his deep baritone voice thickened with sadness.

The general's hacienda was at the end of a dusty moonlit road that from time to time was crossed by the blur of feline forms. He was a breeder of cats, he explained, a hobby that supplied his animal-loving wife with house pets and his troops with adequate protein during hard winters. The house had an American feel to it, turning out to be a rough copy of a Palm Springs mansion its former owner, an American professional gambler, had built for his Cuban mistress. It was nestled in the middle of a fifty-hectare coffee plantation.

As she took her place at the dinner table, next to del Río's delighted wife, Elizabeth felt herself relax for the first time in days. The woman wanted to know everything there was to know about fashion, makeup and Tom Cruise. Elizabeth was delighted to turn her attention to such trivia for a change. The worry left Beatrice's face as well, and Peter was positively lighthearted, engaging the general in spirited argument over the relative merits of Haydn's string quartets and Mozart's. Then the talk turned to Castro again, and both men sobered.

Cigars came out and the room was soon wreathed in wonderfully fragrant smoke.

"Reforms have a way of becoming problems," the general observed. "And despotism is despotism. In America, you have always freedom of choice."

Peter said nothing. He didn't have the heart and, besides, he didn't want to spoil the euphoria of at last being safe and sheltered on solid ground. It seemed for the moment as if the worst was behind them. The general made it clear they were to spend the night, and left to make arrangements with the help. Beatrice was about to say how safe she felt, when she caught Peter looking at his watch, his expression suddenly grave.

"What is it?"

"I was just thinking."

"You weren't just thinking. Tell me, Peter, and don't lie to me."

He looked at her for a long moment, then shrugged. "They probably won't be starting the transplant operation for several hours," he mused. "Barrola's on his own this time, and Wolfe will want to go over everything with him before he goes under the knife."

She looked at him, her face tightening. "Peter, you need to put this out of your mind," she said.

He smiled and put his arm around her shoulders. "You're right. There's nothing to be done about it now. By the time we chartered a boat and covered the six hundred miles to Vieques, Wolfe would be out of recovery—"

"Peter," said Beatrice.

"—and who knows if Hans ever handled a boat? I know I never have—"

"He didn't," said Elizabeth. They turned. She was just ten feet away and had obviously been listening. "That's why you wanted me to hire a boat, remember?"

Peter nodded, contrite. "I'm not much of a swimmer now, I noticed that. And besides, what would I do once I got there?"

Beatrice was eyeing him like a hawk now, not liking this ass-backward way of suggesting some hare-brained scheme. "The base is armed to the teeth," she said. "I hope you're not feeling heroic at this point. We're all lucky to be alive."

"I could chain myself to the gate," he said a little dreamily.

"Right. And Elizabeth and I could bring you food."

"A cheeseburger, please. Everything on it."

"You'd *be* cheeseburger. National security hash—and it wouldn't save Kenner—so just forget whatever nonsense you're thinking, Peter. You've done all you can. You didn't even *know* Kenner."

"That makes it all right?"

She stood glaring at him, and he at her, until Beatrice broke eye contact.

"I'll ask the general which room he wants us in," said Beatrice.

"I see a nice big hammock out back. Lucky to fall asleep under the stars. Remember, B., that first summer in Bar Harbor? That wonderful double hammock?"

"Yes, I do. You go if you want to. My old bones could use a bed, and the softer the better."

He kissed her and walked off onto the terrace.

Beatrice and Elizabeth kept an eye on him as they spoke.

"I don't want to sound like an alarmist," Beatrice remarked, "but we do have to think about what's next. We can't stay here. The general made it pretty clear that he is an exception. We don't want to end up in a Havana jail or at the center of a big trial."

"Del Río said he'll help us," Elizabeth said.

"Yes? How?"

"He says he knows of a place in the Caymans. A tiny island and a cabin invisible from the air, with all the amenities. You could hide out there for a while until things blow over."

"It's a lovely thought."

"It's not just a thought," Elizabeth insisted. "It's doable."

Beatrice squeezed her arm. "You're very sweet. But this isn't going to blow over for Peter and me, Elizabeth. We're in too deep and too much is at stake for very powerful people." She kissed her, and then the two embraced. There were tears in Elizabeth's eyes, as there were in Beatrice's.

"I couldn't have asked for a better gift than you," Beatrice said. "Now go say good night to Peter. I know he would want you to."

She gave Elizabeth another hug, then went off to find her bedroom.

Elizabeth looked to the terrace.

Peter was still swinging in the hammock, rapt as a child beneath the stars.

She walked out to him and stood by the hammock. The grass was white with moonlight. "Those huge stars, remember? Above the bay?" he asked.

"Of course I remember," she said.

She sat beside him and they readjusted their weight until they were balanced. "Are those *coquís?*" she asked, listening to the trees.

"You tell me. You're a child of the Caribbean."

She winced. "Don't remind me."

He put out his hand, grazing her cheek with his knuckle. "I'm sorry," he said.

"About what?"

"Things. Everything."

"Don't be. I made a whole bunch of choices, in case you've forgotten."

"You're a danger junkie, I forgot."

"Only up to a point. But actually," she said gently, "I wouldn't have missed it for the world."

"I feel better then. Not that I believe you."

"But you should," she said.

"Would you do it all over again?"

"I wouldn't go *that* far."

"Ah, see, you've failed Nietzsche's test. If you wouldn't live your life over, why bother to live at all?"

"Because once is funny," said Elizabeth. "Twice isn't."

He laughed, and when she bent to kiss his cheek he turned his head and their lips met softly for a long moment. Then she walked back into the house.

She found her bedroom and lay facedown on the bed, exhausted. Peter had abandoned the hammock, and she could hear him talking with Beatrice on the other side of the wall. She fell asleep, dreaming of Switzerland and woke to the sound of ravens in the cedar grove.

Breakfast was on the veranda, set for three.

She came out and the servant girl nodded shyly.

"Where's General del Río?"

The girl only spoke a little English, but she managed to tell Elizabeth that the general was away for a while, but that he had left her something in the library. She went in and found a nautical atlas, one of its pages held down by a magnifying glass. In the center of the magnification was a beautiful little circle of emerald: Isla Traquillo.

Carrying the atlas to Peter and Beatrice's room, she found the door open and the room empty. The bed had been slept in on both sides. On one of the pillows was a bloodstain the size of a thumbnail.

She ran frantically through the house, calling Peter and Beatrice's names. Nobody responded. On the veranda, the housekeeper was removing two of the three breakfast settings. "Where is the young man who was staying here?" Elizabeth demanded.

"He take breakfast. He go."

"Where?"

"Con el general."

Her heart sank. "What about his wife? The lady with the gray hair?"

"She go later. Take taxi to the airport."

Elizabeth's whole body began to tremble.

It took forever for the housekeeper to find her another taxi service willing to go that far. By the time she reached the airport in Santiago, Peter was already airborne.

SANTIAGO DE CUBA AIRPORT

The ancient DC-3 was General del Río's half of the bargain Peter had struck immediately upon landing. The airplane was new when it had been flown in the Berlin Airlift, still sturdy when it had dropped paratroopers in Korea, and fairly reliable when it had transported parcel post for the U.S. Post Office. Bought at auction by counterculture entrepreneurs, it continued to hold up during marijuana runs from Cartagena until it suffered engine problems and was forced to land in Port-au-Prince, Haiti. There it was confiscated by the Tonton Macoutes.

For a cache of Russian arms and Cuban cigars, Papa Doc traded the plane to Fidel Castro, who flew it another five thousand hours and then gave it outright to General Jesús Pinar del Río. To the general, this trade made eminent sense: one old DC-3 in return for one slightly damaged but brand-new Learjet 60 with marble in the bathroom and seats made of leather.

The general gave Peter the gasoline for nothing.

Ten minutes after arriving at the airport, Peter was taxiing the taildragger down the runway. The controls were in many ways easier than those of the single-engine Cessna he had flown—or rather *Hans* had flown—because they were simpler. This was, after all, a plane built more than half a century ago; it actually had caned cockpit seats. But taxiing with the tail dragging on a six-inch wheel was something else. The plane veered and slewed badly until he let his mind go slack and just gunned it. Once it gained sufficient speed, the old plane straightened out. But would it lift off?

Peter kept the throttle full out and his own thoughts out of his head. At the very end of the runway the plane rose gently and cleared the palm trees by six feet.

I'm getting pretty good at this, Peter thought. One of these days, I might even take flying lessons.

He sank back and let his hands trim flaps and ailerons, clearing up the drag coefficient until the plane was flying smoothly and lifting well. Then he banked and headed east parallel to the runway, looked down in time to see a dozen cars and armored vehicles moving rapidly into the airport area from the approach road. On the way to the airport, the general had been obliged several times to duck down side roads in order to allow suspicious military traffic to pass. He explained it was altogether possible that Peter had been spotted last evening in the Bonneville and had aroused suspicions. So even though he had done his best to keep outside authority away, they had apparently arrived at the house to ask questions. Peter prayed that they had been decent to Beatrice and Elizabeth, although he suspected one of the house workers had blurted out that the general and the gringo had gone to the airport.

Then he saw the fighters—tiny dots moving swiftly toward him from above. They disappeared as quickly as they came, but moments later there was a surging roar and they reemerged on both sides of him, flaps fully deployed, air brakes vertical in order to fly slowly enough to stay with him. They were Cuban, but if they were under the command of the newcomers below at the airport, it would be all over for him.

He prepared himself to be blown to smithereens, but when he looked across to the lead plane, its pilot waved and gave him a thumbs-up.

"I'll be damned," he said aloud. "Del Río's really a man of power."

"Good thing, or we would be fish food," said a voice coming directly from behind him.

For a moment he thought he was hallucinating. His ear had leaked blood all night.

"Beatrice?" he whispered, not daring to look around, for fear he would see nothing. Then he jumped involuntarily as she twisted into the co-pilot's seat beside him. He couldn't believe his eyes. "Beatrice, what are you doing here?"

"Please don't ask me that," she said. She gave him a cool glance and then patted his arm. "Standing by my man, I suppose."

"How did you get in here?"

"My taxi beat you. The general must have been delayed. Apparently your trade was the talk of the airport."

"You knew all along I was up to something?"

"Peter, do you have any idea how transparent you are?"

"If I'd simply agreed to lay low, you wouldn't have believed me."

"I didn't believe you anyway."

He sank back in his seat and shook his head. Women were indeed a superior species, he decided.

"Don't feel too badly, darling," Beatrice said. "Elizabeth bought it."

"She hasn't known me as long as you have." He looked at her. "You left without telling her?"

"Yup," said Beatrice.

"Good. We've put her through enough. I do have to finish this, you know."

"I know," she said with a sigh.

"After all, I started it."

"*We* started it. And if you had known I had stowed away, you would have never taken off."

"Of course I would have," he lied. She was asking him to tell her what they were doing was rational. "I love you, B."

"I love you, too, you old coot." She nodded out the window at the Cuban fighters. "I assume those planes are all friendly or we would be a hole in the ground?"

"Seems so."

"Will they escort us all the way to Vieques?"

"That's a little too much to hope for. Maybe to the edge of their airspace. After that, we're on our own. Anyway, what's that line from Dickens?"

"'It is a far, far better thing that I do—'" she said, and smiled.

"'—than I have ever done—before'? Or just 'done.'?"

"Just 'done,' I think."

"You were always better at *Bartlett's*."

"My favorite right now is that one from Voltaire. 'God is a comedian playing to an audience who's afraid to laugh.'"

Peter laughed, realizing he was unafraid at last. "My favorite is 'A man's trouble stems from his inability to sit quietly in his room,'" he said.

"Pascal, right?"

"*Very* good." He looked at her tenderly. "But we've spent most of our lives in quiet rooms, haven't we? Maybe I should switch to 'Live by the sword, die by the sword,' or something like that."

"The New Testament is always good," she said.

"Or maybe 'Woe unto you when all men speak well of you.' Do you suppose they'll speak well of us, Beatrice?"

"I wouldn't count on it, at this point."

"Then we must be doing the right thing," he said. They smiled and fell silent.

For more than a hundred miles the Cuban jets stayed with them, then peeled off over Haiti, shooting off like rockets into the cloud formations above.

"Must be interesting to fly like that," Beatrice remarked.

"They say it smells of kerosene in the cockpits," Peter said thoughtfully. "Can't spit out the windows the way you can in these babies."

"True," she said, reaching out and touching his hand. "And you can't take the wife along with you."

He squeezed her hand as hard as she was squeezing his. Their thoughts flowed together. She knew what he had to do. His heart soared with love for her and for the whole godforsaken world.

"That's exactly right," he said.

VIEQUES

In Wolfe's operating theater, things had moved rapidly that morning, far too rapidly for Dr. Emilio Barrola's taste.

He was under the strictest orders from Wolfe to make the transfer no matter what happened. Wolfe had sweetened the deal by promising Barrola to clone him again as soon as he was back on his feet in his new body. But no one had bothered to tell Barrola what the damn rush was all about, and the rumors about Cuban terrorists or some such nonsense flying around the OR simply made his head hurt. Politics had always bored him silly, and that was not the state of mind he wished to be in. I should have learned to meditate, he reflected, watching his assistants transfer the subject, a man apparently named Phillip C. Kenner, from the gurney to the operating table. The name meant nothing to Barrola. As far as he was concerned, and certainly to all appearances, it was simply Wolfe's body set back in time forty years or so.

The young man's eyes opened. He looked around groggily, scanning the lights, the gleaming equipment, the figures surrounding him in surgical gowns and masks.

"Oh, shit," said Kenner in a slurred voice. "This isn't a Mafia thing at all, *is* it?"

"Just relax, now," said Barrola. "This will be over in a minute." He gave a nod and a male nurse plunged a hypodermic needle into Kenner's upper arm.

Kenner felt himself go numb. He twisted around, and in one horrific moment thought he saw himself as an old man on a parallel gurney, staring back at himself with the most terrifying look of hunger imaginable. Then everything went black.

Wolfe, who had insisted not only on being briefed about the situation outside the OR but on observing the procedure until the last possible moment, now began to mumble unwanted instructions, even as the Valium dripped into his veins. Barrola was reminded of his father, who had stood over his shoulder every time the family car had a flat, telling him to look out or the jack would crush his hand. It's a wonder I'm able to dress myself, Barrola thought.

In a matter of a few hours he had opened Kenner's cranium and cut the nerve bundles behind the man's throat. And with those moves— brilliantly done, in Barrola's estimation, despite Wolfe's constant carping—Phillip C. Kenner, thirty-three years from his birth and with a once promising career as a physics professor or professional gambler, ceased to exist. Shortly thereafter, to Barrola's further annoyance, a uniformed aide of the lieutenant colonel now in charge of the project's security entered the OR and relayed a message to Wolfe on the table. Barrola stood biting his tongue, eavesdropping. Apparently an unmarked DC-3 was being tracked moving toward them from Cuba. It had been escorted out of Cuban airspace by communist fighters and was thought to be piloted by Jance.

The situation was politically tricky. If they knew for sure that Jance and only Jance was on board, they could simply shoot the plane down with impunity. But if he was with Cubans, who had every right to fly around the Caribbean legally, such action would be sticky indeed. And if Jance wasn't on board at all, for all they knew they would be shooting a planeload of schoolchildren out of the sky, earning the wrath of the world and gaining nothing in the pursuit of Dr. Peter Jance.

Wolfe muttered something fearful about Dr. *Beatrice* Jance when he heard orders had been given to harass and challenge the plane. He further mumbled that there was a good chance that if it failed to respond to radio transmissions, the U.S. would shoot it down.

How I'm expected to work under these conditions is anybody's guess, thought Barrola. He discreetly signaled for Wolfe's anesthetic to be increased: soon the old man's eyelids fluttered shut. Thank God.

But then, to Barrola's audible frustration, Wolfe's eyes reopened one last time. They shone darkly, revealing what could be construed as wisdom.

"It's not the Communists," he said, in a thick voice, whatever that meant. Then his eyes closed once again as Barrola bent to his task, and Frederick Wolfe dropped into a dreamless sleep.

DC-3

The plane swooped low over Haiti's green hills, bridged the mountains mid-island and passed over the Dominican Republic, dipping so low that they could see workers in the cane fields and bathers on the beaches, everything gilded in gold by the afternoon sun. They flew over open ocean for a while, marveling at the different shades of blue.

"Nassau," they said, nearly in unison.

"God," said Beatrice, "remember how glad we were to get there?"

"What was the name of the ship?"

"The *Homeric*?"

"Did your father pay for the entire honeymoon? Or just the cruise?" Peter asked.

"I think we bought the sherry."

"That's right, we drank sherry in the stateroom," Peter said. "It had bunk beds."

"Like being in jail, with a chance of drowning."

"Samuel Johnson. And a bathroom in the hall. Like our apartment on 31st Street, with the bathtub in the kitchen? That door that went over it, to form a counter?"

"And that lady who used to bang on the ceiling with her broom?" Beatrice laughed.

"Right. Every time we made love. She looked like her picture belonged on the one-dollar bill."

They laughed at their memories until the coast of Puerto Rico passed below them, and then they grew quiet: the island of Vieques was coming up. For a long while they remained silent. Then, as though no time at all had passed, they picked up where they had left off.

"Which was the apartment we got evicted from?" she asked.

"The one on Fourth Street. You were in your third year of med school."

"No, wasn't I still preclinical?"

"I'm positive. Remember, we wore out the bed and the springs broke so we put the mattress on the floor."

"That was so hideous."

"The fleas from our terrier!" he shouted.

"Buntle. Who used to lick the toilet seat."

"I used to sleep in my socks and in the morning I'd have anklets of fleabites."

"You kept saying the roaches were going to carry the mattress away," she said, roaring with laughter.

"Those were huge roaches! It could've been like the Lilliputians carrying Gulliver." He patted her hand.

"What's the matter?" she asked.

"Nothing."

"No, tell me what just crossed your mind."

"A conversation I once had. Talking about Swift reminded me."

"With who?"

"You weren't there. With Freddy. About why it's no picnic to live forever—"

He broke off. From straight ahead an F-14 drew up on them, a speck, then a blur, then an enormous shape strobing by their cockpit windows at astonishing speed and without the slightest sound. Then the sonic boom struck like Thor's hammer, bowing in their windscreen with a thousand spiders of fractured glass. It left them both clutching their ears. The DC-3 bucked hard in the violent surge of wind, and Peter felt the warm rush of blood from his nose even as he fought to bring the plane under control.

"Good God," he said.

"Can we get them on the radio?"

"Yes, I'm trying." The ancient device wasn't responding. "The sonic shock—"

"Jarred the tubes, you think?"

"Possibly." He slid open the side window and waved into the sky.

"I don't think they can see you," said Beatrice. She peered out the window. "Is that the airstrip at Vieques?"

"That's it. We're all right," he said. "Might get a little turbulent. There's some blood on your cheek."

She dabbed at it. "I think my left ear may have checked out."

"Yes. It's temporary, though. We're fine," he said.

Something exploded off their starboard side.

"Sidewinder missile," said Peter. He surrendered to being a scientist and nothing else. "Does Mach 4. Homed in on our exhaust. That was lucky. If we had been in a modern jet, it would have read us correctly. These old engines give off a lot less heat."

"Makes sense," Beatrice said, just as nonchalantly. "But I do think something's happened to the plane."

It was yawing wildly. "A piece of shrapnel must have gone through the fuselage. Maybe cut a control cable. Or maybe it dinged the vertical stabilizer. Are you all right?"

She nodded tightly. "You?"

"I'm fine. I can see the runway. They won't shoot again, not while we're this close to other people."

"Okay," she said. She did not sound convinced.

"Okay? Try and hang on. You know, I think I'm wrong. I think it was your second year of med school. All those mnemonics you made up for pathology class because you cut classes so many times that year. They applauded when you showed up for your final. You're right, that was definitely Fourth Street. We were happy there."

"We were happy everywhere," said Beatrice.

"We were," said Peter. "Even when we were doing the devil's work. Would you do it all over again?"

"The same life exactly?"

"Not just the good moments. The good, the bad, the mistakes, the misjudgments, the compromises, all the lies we told ourselves?"

"If we could make it right," said Beatrice as a second Sidewinder exploded a hundred yards nearer than the first. "Peter?" she said faintly.

"I'm here. I've got it," he said, wrestling with the control column. Beatrice was clutching her ribs. There was a hole in the cockpit wall next to her, and beyond, the starboard engine was burning fiercely. Not even thinking about it, Peter cut the fuel and feathered the prop before the plane swung around entirely. Then he grabbed his wife.

"Beatrice?"

Her head came up. She reached up and touched his face. Then her hand fell away. Blood was oozing from her side.

"Beatrice!"

"I'm here, Peter."

"Oh, Jesus, Beatrice."

"Yes. I'm all right. Don't worry about me. You're doing fine. We're doing fine."

"I know. Just hold on. We're going to make it," he said, feeling his head swim uncontrollably. The DC-3 rolled sharply and began a shallow dive. He fought it the best he could, but his vision was clouding with tears, his heart was racing out of control, and the single remaining engine could no longer carry the plane by itself. Five thousand feet below he could see the Vieques runway stretching out before him. But now there were armored vehicles on either side and a bulldozer dead in the middle of the runway.

Peter looked beyond to the secret structures of the Fountain Society, encased in the base's center and surrounded by fence-lines of concertina razor wire. He would never get in there, he realized. Never on foot. With his last nerve he located the structure he was looking for, pushed the stick forward and dived the plane right for it.

"Beatrice? Brace yourself, my darling."

She didn't answer. Her eyes were closed and her fingers were entwined with his as her blood streamed down her dress and onto the deck of the cockpit. Peter felt her hand go limp and let out a howl of grief. He kept on howling as the oblong shape of Wolfe's operating theater loomed up before his windscreen.

Just before impact, Dr. Peter Jance closed his eyes and gripped his dead wife's hand for all he was worth.

∎ ∎ ∎

The people in the OR heard only a split second of an engine's roar before the ceiling exploded as the fuel in the DC-3's tanks detonated.
The impact and the explosion, doubled by dozens of atomizing oxygen bottles, ripped through the room, blowing the operating theater
and everything in it to smithereens.

An orange and black thunderhead of burning fuel and debris roiled
into the sky. Five miles away in Esperanza, in beachfront cafés, it
could be seen by people cradling drinks festooned with tiny umbrel-
las. Some tourists, twenty miles away at the far end of the island,
thought it was thunder and looked with puzzlement to the clear blue
skies. The native population chalked it up to another day of bombing
practice.

Most everyone cursed the Navy.

COPACABANA HOTEL, HAVANA, CUBA

Elizabeth sat finishing her second cup of coffee, watching the young reporter fiddle with his laptop. He removed the floppy disk and stuffed it into his shirt pocket.

"I don't know if anyone will believe this," he said. "They sent me here to do a story on the long-range aftermath of the Pope's visit, not to write about Brave New World."

She lit a cigarette. In the last few days, she had gone back to smoking again. Beatrice, she recalled, had smoked off and on and Peter had disapproved. Now whenever she lit up, she felt closer to them both. It was not a particularly rational feeling, but she didn't expect to feel rational for a good long while.

"Then just hang on to it," she told the reporter. He was supposed to be a stringer for the *New York Times* and had the ID to prove it, but her reservoir of trust was running low these days. With his baby fat and watery blue eyes, he seemed too young to be employed by anyone but McDonald's. But people were looking younger and younger to her of late, and their voices were getting higher and more alike. Peter had pointed that out to her, or had it been Hans? "Apparently," she said, "the explosion at Vieques was a nonevent so far as the U.S. is concerned. They even bought me a ticket to Zurich."

"See, *that* would worry me," the reporter said.

She looked off toward the street and the blazing white facades of the apartment houses across from the hotel. "If anything happens to me, though, you've got that floppy. And my tissue sample. And if I do succeed in getting Mrs. Jance's remains—"

"I wouldn't count on that, either. What you're telling me, they'll probably say she was vaporized."

Elizabeth exhaled. "That doesn't make it true, does it?"

He looked at her, and for a moment he didn't look so young. He looked sober and real. "You're taking quite a chance you know, pursuing this."

"I loved them both very much."

"Did you? Excuse me for saying this, but they sound like monsters to me."

"Monsters?"

"Intellectual giants, moral cretins."

He hadn't understood at all. Or he didn't believe a single word and thought she needed a rewrite. "They could have gone into hiding," she pointed out. "I tried to get them to do that. To live out the rest of their lives together."

"Maybe they thought they owed God a death or two."

"She didn't want him to die, I know that. She adored him."

"Oh, right, and the rest was secondary. Everything she was involved in?"

She pulled hard on her cigarette. "Have you ever been in love?"

"Not really," he said with a casual shrug, as though she had just asked him if he had ever been to Afghanistan or had ever eaten tiramisu.

"The thing is, you want it to last. And if you have the means to achieve that—"

"—Ethics be damned," the reporter finished. He watched her crush out her cigarette and finally seemed to be aware of her irritation. "I'm sorry. I didn't know them. I wasn't there. I'm sure they were both good people, who just made some bad choices along the way, like the rest of us, only more so." He looked at his watch. "You gonna be okay?"

"Bet on it," she said, signaling the waiter.

"What are you going to do now?"

"Weigh my options."

"You know," he said helpfully, "Cindy Crawford majored in chemical engineering at Northwestern."

"Is that a fact?"

"Yep. And Brooke Shields was magna cum laude at Princeton."

"I'm sure you're driving at something," she said.

"You just seem so . . . knowledgeable. So intelligent."

"Compared to what?" she said.

"Nothing. Never mind. I guess I'm just being . . . what?"

"Geno-centric?" she suggested.

"Yeah, okay. Actually, stupid is the word I was looking for. Listen, is there anything else I can do for you?"

She considered. "Does your computer have a modem?"

"It sure does."

Within minutes she was online to her own computer in St. Maurice. To her great joy, there was another message from Alex.

She read it once, and then erased it.

"Thank you," she said, standing and shaking the reporter's hand. Then she went through the lobby to catch a cab to José Martí International Airport.

The message, which she had memorized without effort, went around and around in her head.

```
Subj:   Endgame
Date:   99-03-30
From:   IslandMan@AOL.com
To:     SwissMs@Int'lAccessCompuServe.com
  JUST THOUGHT YOU'D LIKE TO KNOW, THE WEAPON IS
WAY OVERAMPED. I FAKED ALL THE COMPUTER MODELS.
HOPE THAT HELPS. HAVE A GOOD LIFE, YOU EARNED IT.
MAYBE WE'LL MEET AGAIN SOME DAY.
```

WHITE SANDS: SIX MONTHS LATER

The weapon had been finished in record time. With the Fountain Project closed down, extra funding for the Hammer had poured in. And Peter Jance's notes and computer files had all survived the explosion at Vieques, having been carefully archived by Alex Davies before his defection and then recovered upon his return. There were more than two hundred animals on the hillside, tethered and monitored, as well as Russian tanks captured during the Gulf War and other weapons being tested for resistance to assault. And more cameras than had witnessed the launching of Apollo 13.

The weapon itself was small enough to fit on a modified Abrams assault tank, an astonishing reduction in bulk that delighted the development team in the cramped bunker. In addition to Alex, whose attendance was deemed essential by Henderson's successors, all of Peter's eager young acolytes—Hank Flannagan, Cap Chu and Rosemarie Wiener—were present. None had been near enough the medical facilities to suffer so much as a nosebleed from the explosion, although Flannagan, a born-again Christian, had been jolted out of bed and thought for a moment that the Second Coming was at hand. The wrangler, Perkins, was there as well, although he had come to hate the entire project with a passion. He could only bear it because in two weeks he was leaving to begin studying veterinary science at Utah State University. He was looking forward to the many years he would spend saving animals rather than setting them up for incineration, but right now he needed these last two weeks to pay for tuition.

Everyone braced for the countdown.

On zero, the weapon fired and disappeared from the face of the earth. It self-destructed with such force that the blast doors of the bunker were blown ajar as $2.5 billion dollars worth of research and development was reduced to atoms. The cloud of hot gases was so intense that it shot heavenward, sucking an acre of dust and scrub brush along with it.

Everyone in the bunker was blown off his or her feet by the impact, but the three-foot-thick walls managed to spare them their lives.

Nobody could remember exactly how long it took to regain their senses, but eventually they all staggered out into the desert glare.

One entire side of the sky was blackened by the soaring cloud, which was now taking on the familiar mushroom shape of a nuclear detonation. Charred sagebrush, rocks and glassy chunks of fused sand poured down as the survivors huddled for protection under the overhang of the bunker.

"Well I'll be dead and rained on," Perkins finally said.

"Can't win 'em all," agreed Alex, nodding solemnly.

He pointed off in the opposite direction from the smoking crater where the weapon had once been. There on the hillside were the animals' overturned cages, with snapped chains and pulled-up stakes. The creatures themselves were nothing more than a series of dots racing over the hill beyond. And to judge by their speed and their determination, these animals weren't going to be looking back to their human caretakers anytime soon.

Alex thought that Elizabeth, Peter and Beatrice would have been pleased.